THE SNOW
LIES DEEP

ALSO BY PAULA MUNIER

THE NIGHT WOODS

HOME AT NIGHT

THE WEDDING PLOT

THE HIDING PLACE

BLIND SEARCH

A BORROWING OF BONES

THE SNOW LIES DEEP

A MERCY CARR MYSTERY

PAULA MUNIER

MINOTAUR BOOKS
NEW YORK

This is a work of fiction. All of the characters, organizations, and events portrayed in this novel are either products of the author's imagination or are used fictitiously.

First published in the United States by Minotaur Books,
an imprint of St. Martin's Publishing Group

EU Representative: Macmillan Publishers Ireland Ltd, 1st Floor, The Liffey Trust Centre, 117–126 Sheriff Street Upper, Dublin 1, DO1 YC43

THE SNOW LIES DEEP. Copyright © 2025 by Paula Munier. All rights reserved. Printed in the United States of America. For information, address St. Martin's Publishing Group, 120 Broadway, New York, NY 10271.

www.minotaurbooks.com

The Library of Congress Cataloging-in-Publication Data is available upon request.

ISBN 978-1-250-38998-5 (hardcover)
ISBN 978-1-250-38999-2 (ebook)

The publisher of this book does not authorize the use or reproduction of any part of this book in any manner for the purpose of training artificial intelligence technologies or systems. The publisher of this book expressly reserves this book from the Text and Data Mining exception in accordance with Article 4(3) of the European Union Digital Single Market Directive 2019/790.

Our books may be purchased in bulk for specialty retail/wholesale, literacy, corporate/premium, educational, and subscription box use. Please contact MacmillanSpecialMarkets@macmillan.com.

First Edition: 2025

10 9 8 7 6 5 4 3 2 1

For Pete
who loves a Christmas miracle

The snow lies deep upon the ground,
And winter's brightness all around
Decks bravely out the forest sere,
With jewels of the brave old year. . . .

—PAUL LAWRENCE DUNBAR,
"Christmas in the Heart"

Over the heights the snow lies deep,
Sunk is the land in peaceful sleep;
Here by the house of God we pray,
Lead, Lord, our souls today. . . .

—CAROLINE ALICE ELGAR,
"Aspiration"

SOMEWHERE IN THE GREEN MOUNTAINS, WINTER 2010

The snow lies deep as a grave upon the ground. A howling blizzard has come and gone, burying the forest in a shroud that clings to my legs as I plow through the knee-deep drifts. At this rate, I will never make it in time. He will catch up with me, and I will die. I will die here in the snow, long before spring. Like the Snow Maiden in the old fairy tale.

I shoulder my long gun. It's a good hunting rifle if you're after white-tailed deer, but the old Winchester Model 70 is probably no match for whatever the guy who is after me is carrying. Probably some fancy sniper rifle, like the Accuracy International AT308, with which he could take me down at a thousand yards. Depending on how good he is. And I suspect that he is very, very good.

He is quiet, I'll give him that. Well-schooled in the art of silent tracking. Every once in a while, I hear the crunch of snow or the snap of a twig. But other than that, apart from the hooting of an owl or the drumming of a woodpecker, I hear nothing.

My only chance is to make it to the old deer stand in time to climb out of sight. In time to see him coming. In time to take my best shot.

And pray my best shot will prove good enough to save me.

I push my way through a thicket of winterberry into a small clearing cluttered by deadfall. Emerging from the snow like an island from a stormy sea is a hulking, ragged stump of a massive oak. Most likely felled by lightning, by the looks of it. The scarred, split trunk dominates the litter of snags, serving as my landmark.

I am close now. The deer stand should be nearby, on one of the tall trees that tower above me. I look around and spot the metal ladder on a sturdy maple tree to my right. Some kind of antlered headgear dangles from the bottom rung, perhaps another hunter's way of marking the spot. No business of mine.

I tramp over to the copse of pine trees that flank the other end of the clearing. I stand inside the copse under the canopy of evergreen, breathing heavily, my breath clouds dissolving into the crisp winter air.

Grabbing a downed pine limb, I circle back to the maple with the deer stand, brushing my tracks away behind me. Given the amount of snow and the depth of my boot prints, this attempt to erase my trail won't fool a trained eye for long. But as the sun begins to set, the gathering gloom might obfuscate my wandering just long enough for me to scale the stand and take aim.

I toss the branch behind the maple and climb the rickety rungs to the top of the deer stand. The rusty perch hangs high on the tree, some thirty feet in the air. The better to hide. The better to shift from prey to predator.

Shrugging off my rifle, I settle onto the cold seat. I lift the rifle to my shoulder and take aim. I listen, hard. I hear the crack of splintered wood under a heavy boot.

There he is. A wiry man in full winter camouflage. Father Frost with a gun. I watch as he follows my tracks to the pine copse. I steady my aim.

He peers inside the small grove of evergreen trees, then turns abruptly, pulling his sniper's rifle off his shoulder so quickly I would have missed it had I blinked.

One blink from death.

I fire.

DECEMBER 21

WINTER SOLSTICE

In December ring
Every day the chimes;
Loud the gleemen sing
In the streets their merry rhymes.
Let us by the fire
Ever higher
Sing them till the night expire . . .

—HENRY WADSWORTH LONGFELLOW

CHAPTER ONE

December, being the last month of the year, cannot help but make us think of what is to come.

—FENNEL HUDSON

WHAT THEY DON'T TELL YOU ABOUT BECOMING A MOTHER IS how hard you fall. And you do fall *hard*. Of course, Mercy Carr knew she'd love her baby—everybody loves their baby—but the depth and fierceness of the love she felt for little Felicity surprised her. All-encompassing, completely consuming, entirely irrevocable.

For the first time, she understood how those mothers you heard about—you know, the ones who lifted two-ton automobiles to save their children pinned underneath—summoned the inhuman strength to do what needed to be done. These were mothers who would do anything for their children. Just as she would do anything for hers.

Which is why on the longest night of the year Mercy found herself standing in front of the Northshire Town Hall in a long line of moms and kids waiting for Santa Claus, her nine-month-old baby, Felicity, balanced on her hip, her steadfast dog, Elvis, at her side.

They stood about ten feet from the steps of the magnificent Greek Revival building, Felicity's bright blue eyes on St. Nick, Mercy and Elvis surveying the crowd. It seemed like the whole county was here on the common tonight, along with legions of out-of-towners in for a picture-perfect Christmas market on a picture-perfect holiday in a picture-perfect New England village.

Felicity wanted to see Santa Claus. Giggling, she pointed her pudgy little mittened hand toward the man in the long white beard, someone else's child on his lap. This baby boy looked to be about Felicity's age, but he was not happy. He shrieked like only a baby can shriek while his poor mother tried to snap the obligatory photograph, capturing the big moment for posterity: *Baby Screams While Santa Smiles*.

Elvis pricked his ears at the wailing. The Belgian Shepherd stood alert, his triangular ears perked, his eyes scanning the throng, his nose touching Mercy's hand under her baby's bottom. He'd always been protective of Mercy, but now that protectiveness included her daughter as well.

"This is supposed to be fun, you know." Amy turned toward Mercy, her four-year-old mini-me daughter, Helena, pulling at her parka. Two gray-eyed blond peas in a pod.

"Right." Mercy's idea of fun was being home at Grackle Tree Farm, caring for Felicity. She was endlessly fascinated with every moment of her baby's every move. Every day brought a bright new discovery: first smile, first tooth, first *Mama*. She was still waiting for that first *Mama*.

"Come on, Mommy!" Helena bounced up and down on her toes in excitement. "We're almost there!"

Amy and Helena, who lived in the guesthouse on Mercy and Troy's property, were like family. Amy, who'd had Helena when she was only a kid herself, had taught Mercy a lot about what it means to be a good mom—and apparently dragging your kid out in the cold to see a man in a faux beard and belly was part of that.

"*Not*," said Mercy.

Amy laughed. "Being a mom is all about lines. You'll get used to it."

"I know all about lines. In the army, you line up for everything. Drill, chow, latrine. I never got used to it." She'd thought she was done with lines when she left the service. One more way in which motherhood was proving to be more like the military than she'd ever imagined.

"You have to admit it's festive," said Amy, her gray eyes taking in the merriment all around them. "Pretty."

"Pretty," conceded Mercy.

And it *was* pretty. Northshire did December right: candles gleaming in the windows of its lovely Colonial and Federal-era houses, fir wreaths tied with red bows bedecking every door, pine boughs trimmed in red ribbon wrapping every streetlamp as prettily as presents under a Christmas tree.

And the lights! Miles and miles and miles of white lights crisscrossed the streets, twinkled in the branches of bare trees and evergreens alike, and brightened the shops and restaurants along Main Street. The starry effect was especially dazzling here at the Christmas market on the common, where shining paths led from one little chalet-style booth to the next, all strung with lights, lights, and more lights.

When it came to illumination, their little village did the wonder of winter lights proud. Mother Nature appeared to agree, dusting the village earlier that day with a new blanket of fresh snow that reflected the glow of all that radiance. Now the sky was clear and the crisp winter air was rich with the scent of roasting chestnuts and hot chocolate and fried dough. It was cold, below freezing, but the freestanding heaters placed at intervals along the pathways gave visitors a place to huddle and warm up when they grew too chilled.

"I think Northshire is the best place in the world to be this time of year." Amy smiled, leaning in toward Mercy. "Come on, you have to love the Solstice Soirée."

The Solstice Soirée was the village's official holiday countdown, twelve days of eating, drinking, and making merry, beginning on the winter solstice and continuing through Hanukkah and Kwanzaa and Christmas right on to New Year's Day. An ecumenical approach to the holy season, encompassing all manner of traditions. Starting with tonight and the Druids' bonfire.

"I do like a good bonfire," said Mercy, even though in truth what she liked most about this Solstice Soirée so far was the snow. She gazed up at the town hall's grand Palladiun windows glowing in light and greenery, wishing that she were back at Grackle Tree Farm with her husband, Troy, and Felicity. But it was trapping season, and game wardens like Troy were out patrolling the woods, making sure hunters and trappers followed the rules—and on the lookout for poachers. Her husband wasn't home anyway, so she might as well be here, giving her infant daughter the childish pleasure of a visit with Santa.

Felicity giggled again, and Mercy giggled along with her. Her baby was loving this, and so she was loving it, too. Lines and crowds and all.

A big gap formed in the line as one tired mother with several restless kids in tow gave up on the long wait and ushered her brood toward the gingerbread chalet. Mercy would have loved to go with them, but instead she said a quiet prayer of thanks.

Helena raced ahead and the rest of them followed, tightening up the line.

"We're up next," said Amy, stepping onto the low stairs of the narrow stone porch that fronted the town hall.

In the middle of the porch, framed by massive stone columns, Santa Claus held court in a tall red velvet chair flanked by two elves. One of the elves looked very familiar.

"Tell me that's not Tandie."

Tandie was Mercy's sixteen-year-old cousin; she'd come to live with them before the baby was born after getting kicked out of yet another boarding school. As far as Mercy was concerned, it was the school's loss and their gain.

"Yes, doesn't she look cute?" Amy and Helena waved at Tandie and she waved back, far less enthusiastically.

The elves were wearing the quintessential green-and-red costume with the pointy shoes and hat. With her pink hair and piercings, Tandie lent the ensemble a decidedly punk look.

"Tandie is the Number One Elf," said little Helena proudly.

Mercy laughed. "I can't believe she'd be seen in public in that outfit." She kissed the top of her baby's head.

"I think 'Over my dead body' is what she said." Amy laughed, too. "But when one of the elves called in sick, your mother asked her to sub for her."

That explained it. Mercy's mother, Grace, was the Solstice Soirée's committee chair this year, and no one said no to Grace. Except for Mercy, and now that she was a mother herself, she found herself far less likely to refuse her own mother—and even agreeing with her more often than not. A sobering phenomenon.

She smiled at Tandie, then frowned as she got a closer look at St. Nick himself. "That's not the real Santa." This Santa was too tall and too skinny and too timid. His smile was forced and his laugh was more of a whine and his belly did not shake like a bowlful of jelly. "Where's Pizza Bob?"

"They had to get a new Santa," said Amy.

"What? Why?" Pizza Bob, beloved owner and proprietor of Northshire's premier pizza joint, had been the town's Santa Claus for as long as Mercy could remember.

"Family emergency. Pizza Bob's grandmother is sick."

"Oh no. Poor Pizza Bob." Mercy frowned. "So who is this guy?"

"Look closer," teased Amy.

Mercy studied the interloper in the fur-trimmed red suit. Under the heavily blushed red cheeks and the phony white mustache and beard, she recognized Lazlo Ford, an old family friend who became the acting mayor when the town's longtime mayor died during last month's nor'easter. "Uncle Laz? Seriously?"

"I know." Amy lowered her voice. "Not exactly typecasting."

Uncle Laz was a shy CPA who'd served his community well as the town's treasurer for many years. He'd helped Mercy sort out her finances when she got home from Afghanistan, allowing her to buy her little cottage on her own, without her family's help. She'd always be grateful to him for that. But Santa Claus he wasn't.

Uncle Laz kept himself to himself, apart from his Maine Coon cat, Boris; as far as Mercy knew his only social activity outside work was playing the organ at church. He was a sweet, self-contained man, far more comfortable with the quiet reliability of numbers and notes than the noisy reality of people. And children truly rattled him.

The longtime bachelor had been a frequent guest at her grandmother's house. Patience made sure he wasn't alone on special occasions, inviting him to holiday dinners and summer barbecues and birthday parties year-round. When Mercy and her brother Nick were young, they'd tortured the poor man with their silly tricks. Like putting a whoopee cushion under his seat at the table and popping balloons behind his back and dabbing his nose with red paint while he snored during his after-dinner nap.

But once they'd outgrown such pranks, Mercy and Nick warmed to Uncle Laz, and he to them. He taught them to play poker. The clever man was a card shark of sorts; her grandmother said that once upon a time he'd been ejected from Caesars Palace for counting cards. The one big adventure of his life.

Until now.

"This is wrong on so many levels." Mercy wondered how desperate the town must have been to appoint him acting mayor and how desperate her mother must have been to ask him to sit on that red velvet throne. Everyone else must have been busy. She was tempted to leave; as much as she loved Uncle Laz, she did not want her daughter's first encounter with jolly old St. Nick to be this nervous Nellie.

"Time to meet Santa Claus!" welcomed Tandie in a bored, singsong voice. "Come on up, Helena!"

Too late, thought Mercy, as Helena skipped forward into the teenage elf's arms, squealing with delight.

Tandie lifted the little girl onto Santa's knee.

"Ho ho ho!" said Laz with an uneasy chuckle.

"I've been a very good girl," said Helena primly, hands folded on her lap. "I'd like a Bitty Baby, please."

"Well, now—" The calming tones of Debussy's *Clair de Lune* interrupted him, and he stopped short. Santa fished his mobile phone from his pocket and looked down at it. Paling under his makeup, he tucked his cell under his bearded chin. He grabbed little Helena by the waist and thrust her back at Tandie. "Excuse me, I've got to take this. I'll be right back."

"What are you doing?" Mercy moved forward. "Uncle Laz, uh, Santa, what's wrong?"

"I have to go, Mercy. Sorry." Lazlo stumbled down the stone steps, bumping a little boy and bouncing him into the arms of his alarmed mother. "Sorry, sorry."

Helena started to cry. Felicity started to cry. All the kids in the long line started to cry. And their parents started to yell. "Slow down, Santa. Get back here. Where do you think you're going?"

Elvis pulled at his leash.

Still, the wayward Santa Claus ran on.

The crowd parted as he sprinted across the common toward the First Congregational Church. Tandie and Amy comforted Helena while Mercy rocked Felicity back to sleep. Elvis pulled at his leash again.

"Worst. Santa. Ever." Tandie plucked the pointy cap from her pink-haired head. "Grace is not going be happy."

"Poor Uncle Laz." Mercy wondered what had panicked him so badly.

"Is Santa Claus coming back, Mommy?" asked Helena, eyes full of tears.

"Yes, baby. He said he was coming right back." Amy looked at Mercy for confirmation.

"Sure, sweetheart." Mercy handed Felicity to Tandie. "Hold her for a minute."

"What are you doing?" asked Amy.

"Elvis and I are going after him." She hated to leave the baby, even for a minute, but she knew Elvis wouldn't take long to find Uncle Laz. The shepherd was very quick on his feet—and the middle-aged man was, well, not.

"But he's a terrible Santa," said Tandie.

"Bad Santa," said Helena through her tears.

"It's the principle of the thing." Mercy grinned. "No one cheats our kids out of a visit to Santa. Not even Uncle Laz."

"Doesn't look like he's coming back," said Tandie, hugging Felicity to her with one hand and pointing out across the common with the other. "He's headed into the woods."

Mercy spotted the man in the red suit slip into a patch of trees flanking the church that led to the forest beyond.

"This just gets weirder and weirder," said Amy.

"We shouldn't be gone long." Mercy shrugged her backpack off her shoulders, pulled out a zippered diaper bag, and dropped it at Tandie's feet. "Everything you need should be in there. A sling, too, if she gets too heavy to hold."

"What do we do in the meantime?" The teenage elf nodded her head at the increasingly unruly children and their disgruntled parents.

"Tell them a new, improved Santa is on the way. Text my mother and tell her that Uncle Laz has gone AWOL and we need another St. Nick up here, pronto."

"Right."

Mercy smiled at Felicity. "I'll be right back, sweetheart." She tugged the pack back on and unclipped Elvis's leash. The Belgian Shepherd looked up at her, and she gave the command she knew he was waiting to hear. "Search."

CHAPTER TWO

*December's immaculate coldness feels warm.
December feels like blood.*

—ZINAIDA GIPPIUS

Elvis leapt down the steps of the town hall and barreled into the crush of solstice revelers and Christmas shoppers. Mercy jogged toward the woods where Helena's bad Santa had disappeared, knowing Elvis was undoubtedly headed that way, intent on finding his quarry.

What was she running for anyway? All this weaving through the holiday jumble of parents with kids and dogs in tow, carolers making the rounds, teenage girls giggling at teenage boys, couples holding hands and strolling the paths, vendors selling all manner of food and drink and Christmas trinkets—just to dress down a Kris Kringle gone astray?

Now that she thought about it, Uncle Laz—loyal to the village of Northshire through and through—must have had a good reason for abandoning his post. Mercy laughed at herself. She was already learning the insane lengths to which a mother would go not only to protect her child, but to please that child as well. She slowed down, now regretting sending Elvis after Lazlo Ford. Even though Uncle Laz knew Elvis, the Malinois could alarm even those who knew him best when he was in full-on mission mode. The dog might scare the man silly.

As she approached the edge of the common and the patch of woodland near the First Congregational Church, she considered calling Elvis back with a whistle. But before she could purse her lips, the shepherd bounded into view, startling several people queued up at the nearby hot dog chalet and scattering swirls of snow as he skidded to a tight halt at her feet.

Elvis barked once, pivoted swiftly, and darted back into the woods again. No point in whistling now. The shepherd had found something, and there was no stopping him.

Mercy hustled after him, moving around the two-hundred-year-old church and through a break in the eastern cedar hedge that separated the sanctuary from the forest. Towering overhead were sugar maples and oaks, hemlock and white pine, birch and beech. It was colder here than on the common. And darker. The starry lights of the Solstice Soirée were behind her now, and the growing gloom of the forest in winter was settling in all around her.

Mercy pulled out a flashlight from her pack, and trained the light on the forest floor. She followed Elvis's prints, faint but visible in the shallow sweep of soft snow that covered the ground. His were not the only tracks she spotted—there were also turkey, deer, fox, raccoon, and moose tracks, for a start.

But there were no sets of human footprints, at least not yet. Ford had been wearing black boots, as befitted his role as old St. Nick, but he had not come this way. Elvis may have picked up his scent on another trail, but then chosen a faster, more direct, as-the-crow-flies route back-and-forth to Mercy. Assuming that signal bark was all about locating Uncle Laz, and not some other discovery the shepherd had made in the deep woods.

And they were deep in the woods. Here in Vermont, where 80 percent of the land was forested, the deep woods were always much closer than you might think. One wrong turn, and you could lose your bearings—and the wilderness wins.

The dog's tracks veered into a copse of standing dead trees, a snarl of snags and downed branches and rotting stumps. Here the tracks dissolved into a trampled crumple of leaves and bark and twigs and snow and scat and indecipherable markings left by all the beasts, wild and otherwise, who'd passed through the old grove.

Mercy stood in the middle of the debris, listening. She heard the shrill whinny of screech owls and the distant wail of coyotes. And a high-pitched yelp descending into a thundering bellow.

Elvis.

ORLOV TRAINED HIS STEINER binoculars on the howling Malinois in the clearing. They were smart, tough dogs, these Belgian Shepherds. He'd encountered a few in the FSB. He thought about shooting the dog, a relatively easy shot at this distance, but he didn't like killing anything he wasn't paid to kill. It was bad business practice.

He'd done what he'd come to do, and now he would fly away. Just like his namesake, Orlov. The eagle. He liked his new name. It suited him. Swoop in, kill, swoop out. Just like the eagle. But unlike the eagle, he didn't have to fly off with his prey in his talons. He could simply fly off.

MERCY WHISTLED, AND ELVIS yowled in return. Chasing the sound, she picked her way across the messy forest floor with the help of the flashlight's bouncing beam. The fact that the dog was staying put rather than coming to fetch her meant that he'd found something worthy of his vigil.

She came upon a thicket of scarlet winterberry lit from behind by an orange glow. *Fire?*

"Elvis!" she called, advancing more quickly now toward the strange light in the forest, praying to hear the crash of the shepherd hurtling back to her. But he only barked his response, an insistent baying that demanded she go to him.

A curving of massive oaks loomed ahead. She stepped through the trees and as if she were tumbling into a fairy tale, she stumbled over thick roots into a small clearing. The oaks towered over the open space that seemed too precisely drawn, too cleanly swept, too meanly occupied to be the work of Mother Nature. Or maybe it was just the shelf of granite slabs that anchored the far edge of the clearing that gave her that impression, a sloped piling of rock vaguely resembling a beehive.

The beehive was the backdrop to a macabre scene. A scene that staggered the imagination, staged in such a disquieting manner that it, too, could only be the work of humans. Disturbed humans.

There lay Santa Claus on the bare forest floor, his white beard flowing over his chest, his gloved hands at his sides, his legs set out straight as sticks. And where the bowlful of jelly he lacked should have been burned the bright fire of a Yule log.

Uncle Laz.

Elvis had settled into his Sphinx position, his nose inches from the jolly old elf's black boots. He perked up his ears at her, awaiting instruction.

But Mercy said nothing. For one long, terrible moment, she did not move. She couldn't move, somehow stricken by the strange, surreal, medieval phantasm of it all.

Elvis trotted over to her, nuzzling her hand with his long nose, breaking the solstice spell. She thought the man might be dead, but she couldn't be sure. She reeled toward the fiery Santa, pulling her water bottle from her pack, praying that she wasn't too late. Praying that she could save him.

The two-foot rough-cut oak log was typical of the ones that graced many a fireplace this time of year, at least at first glance. The hollow in the center had been filled with kindling to get the fire started, but the flames had spread to the surrounding bark. Flares licking toward the prone Santa's red suit, sparks threatening to set him fully ablaze.

Mercy doused the fire with the water, and it sizzled and sputtered. Smoke snaked into her mouth and nose and hair. But still the fire burned on.

She yanked off her backpack, tossing it to the ground. Pulling off her leather jacket, she slapped it at the smoldering blaze. She considered pushing the Yule log away, but thought better of it. She had no way of knowing how much of the poor man's skin the log might take with it.

Elvis skittered around her, whining.

Mercy knew that the retired bomb-sniffing dog was not a fan of fire. Neither was she. They'd seen too much of its deadly force at work in Afghanistan. As lethal as any bullet or bomb. "It's okay, boy."

Santa remained still and silent. Mercy figured that poor Uncle Laz must already be dead. But she fought on, grateful she was wearing gloves as she continued to beat down the conflagration with her coat. If she couldn't save him, at least she could prevent a wildfire here in the forest. Not as likely in winter, but it was known to happen.

Not on her watch. As she whacked what was left of the fire with her jacket, she wondered who could do such a thing—Santas did not light themselves on fire with Yule logs—and where whoever had done this terrible thing was now. Long gone, apparently.

She tossed her jacket on the embers in a final act of smothering. Another one of her mother's chic gifts ruined. At least she'd worn this one, for a while anyway.

She felt for a pulse on Uncle Laz's neck. *Nothing.* She stared at the quiet man she'd known much of her life. Whose life had come to an end in a way he could never have imagined. A way no one could ever have imagined.

Except his killer.

She forced herself to study the corpse, focusing on the man's face, his fake beard, his fur-trimmed red cap. She looked again at the cap. At the pointed end of the funnel-shaped hat. Something seemed off. Although this entire crime scene was off, truth be told.

The pompom.

Every Santa's cap she'd ever seen sported a white fur pompom at its pointed end. But not this one. She leaned in closer, the better to see. There was a thread there, and a rip where the pompom should be.

Elvis nudged her knee with his nose. Pressing her to get on with it.

"You're right. Time to call this in. Get back to Felicity." She fished her cell out of her cargo pants pocket. *No signal.* She cursed. Only in northern New England could somewhere so close to town still be off the grid. She turned to Elvis. "Stay. Guard."

Mercy huffed through the woods, flashlight bouncing in front of her in time to her gait, retracing her steps and trying her cell every few minutes until she spotted the church beyond the cedar hedge. Now she could get a signal.

She called 911 and texted Troy, Thrasher, and Tandie, in that order. Telling them all about Uncle Laz and ordering Tandie to stay right where she was with Felicity at the town hall and keep Amy and Helena with her.

Mercy ran back through woods to join Elvis at the crime scene. She snapped photos on her cell, then used the duct tape in her pack to rope off the area. Nothing to do now but wait. She hoped the authorities wouldn't be long. She was desperate to get back to Felicity.

She settled onto a stump not far from the body. Elvis stretched out at her feet. She kept the flashlight trained on the corpse, the better to protect a crime scene in the deep woods, a deep woods alive with predators and scavengers and a killer on the loose. And the better to study the details of what had to be the most bizarre murder she'd ever seen.

For certainly this was murder. An ominous beginning to the Solstice Soirée. The shortest day of the year. And the longest night.

"*. . . it hath been the longest night,*" she whispered to her poor departed Uncle Laz, in a kind of prayer. "*That e'er I watch'd and the most heaviest.*"

CHAPTER THREE

*We're taking home the big Yule log,
it's hard enough to do, but Santa brings
so many things he couldn't bring that too.*

—VINTAGE CHRISTMAS CARD, FROM
OLD MOORE'S ALMANAC

"DEATH BY YULE LOG," SAID DR. DARLING. "THAT'S A FIRST FOR ME." Mercy smiled at the medical examiner. She and Elvis had stood sentinel over Lazlo Ford's body until local law enforcement arrived to secure the scene. Dr. Darling and the Crime Scene Search Team came shortly thereafter, just as a light snow began to fall.

So far, the press and the public were absent, but it was only a matter of time before they showed up. Even her mother Grace wouldn't be able to keep them away forever.

"We need to get a move on," yelled a tall, skinny man in a Tyvek suit from across the glade.

"Hi, Bob," Mercy yelled back.

He grunted in response and went back to work. Bob Cato was the leader of the Crime Scene Search Team, known as The Turtle to all who knew and loved him. His slow and steady thoroughness drove local law enforcement mad, but the always patient and unflappable Dr. Darling loved him.

"Seems like The Turtle's in a hurry." Dr. Darling winked at Mercy.

"Uh-oh," said Mercy. The fact that Bob was pushing for promptness meant that the entire CSST team was expecting the press to show up any minute.

"I'm on it," Dr. Darling called over to Bob, then addressed Mercy. "You know how he hates the spotlight."

"He makes a good point this time. The press will have a field day with this one."

As Bob and his crime scene techs erected a forensics tent around the victim, Dr. Darling donned her white suit. She grinned at Mercy. "It'll be their first Yule log murder, too. Everyone loves a first."

"You don't really think that the log is the murder weapon."

"Probably not. We'll find out soon enough." Dr. Darling sighed, and waved her arm at the crime scene behind her. "I suspect this is all window dressing. To showcase what exactly, I'm not sure."

Mercy looked past the medical examiner and studied the Yule log once more. A longer look prompted her to rethink her original conclusion that the log itself was the usual New Englander's do-it-yourself solstice project. "It looks like the ones Rory Craig sells at the Christmas market. The log's got that rough artistry he's known for." She looked back at Dr. Darling. "You might check out those carvings of holly that bookend the ends of the log."

"Seen and noted."

"I think that's your Holly King, dying as the Oak King is reborn."

"You know your solstice lore." Dr. Darling grinned.

"Don't we all."

Anyone who'd spent any time in Northshire at Christmastime knew the story. The neo-pagan legend recounted the story of two brothers, the Holly King and the Oak King, and their endless battle of the seasons. The Holly King ruled winter, personifying darkness and death. As the longest night of the year, the winter solstice marked the victory of the Oak King, ushering in the shorter nights, brighter days, and rebirth to come as winter waned. Until the summer solstice, when the Holly King won the crown, and the days thereafter grew shorter and the nights grew longer as winter waxed.

"Can't escape it during the Solstice Soirée," agreed Dr. Darling.

The never-ending drama between light and dark was enacted by puppeteers in booths at the Christmas market, local schoolchildren on the stage at the town hall, and solstice revelers themselves dressed in holly and oak costumes and wielding fake swords in impromptu fights on the common. All in good fun. Until now.

"What do you think of the carvings?"

"Could be Rory's handiwork. Although seems like every woodworker in New England is selling Yule logs these days." The medical examiner shrugged. "When we turn over the Yule log, I'll look for a carver's mark. I know Rory always marks his pieces."

Rory Craig was a beloved Northshire artisan who hewed popular sculptures and furniture from native woods with a chain saw. His signature mark was a stylized ox head branded into the wood, usually on the bottom of the piece. Tourists and locals alike loved his carvings of bears, eagles, fish, and other wild creatures. Her grandmother Patience had one of a standing black bear on her back porch; Mercy liked it so much, she'd commissioned a similar one for Troy's shop. This time of year, though, Rory sold a lot of Yule logs. Bread-and-butter money for his small business.

"And there's something else," said Mercy.

The medical examiner raised an eyebrow. "With you there always is."

"Santa's hat."

"What about it?" Dr. Darling waited.

"No tassel."

"What?"

"The pompom at the tail of his red stocking cap is missing." Mercy paused. "I suppose it could have fallen off in the struggle. But—"

Dr. Darling interrupted her. "The crime scene techs say there's no sign of a struggle so far."

"Right."

"I'll check that, too."

"Weird," said Mercy.

The medical examiner tapped the side of her nose as if she were Santa herself. "'Weird' doesn't even begin to cover it."

"I'm sorry about putting the fire out," said Mercy. "Destroying potential evidence."

"You had to do it—our victim may still have been alive. Besides, you couldn't risk a fire." Dr. Darling snapped on her plastic gloves. "That's one bonfire we don't want burning tonight." She leaned toward Mercy. "I'm so sorry. I know he was a friend of the family."

"Uncle Laz."

"Your mother will be very upset." The medical examiner regarded her with sympathy. "I can't imagine Lazlo Ford wanted to be Santa Claus any more than he wanted to be the acting mayor."

"No, poor Uncle Laz did it for her. And for the town."

"And now he's dead." Dr. Darling's normally sunny expression dimmed. "A dead mayor is bad enough. But a dead Santa is a bad omen."

"I haven't seen my mother yet."

"But she knows."

"She knows."

"Don't let Grace go blaming herself."

Mercy sighed. Dr. Darling was right. Her mother would blame herself for Lazlo's death, even though it wasn't her fault.

"Who'll be Santa now?"

"I don't know. But you know she'll find one." Mercy felt bad for her mother, who'd be obligated to carry on with the Solstice Soirée regardless. Grace was very good at carrying on.

"Pizza Bob?"

"I hope so. If he's back from visiting his grandmother."

"I love Pizza Bob. He makes a great pizza and a great Santa." The medical examiner looked over at the corpse. "Lazlo Ford was a good town treasurer."

"And a good friend." Mercy paused. "And a good organist."

"Of course." Dr. Darling clucked like the mother hen she was. "No wonder The Turtle is in such a state."

"What do you mean?"

"Bob's the new choirmaster at the First Congregational Church. And he's in charge of Northshire's first Singing Christmas Tree."

Mercy would never have guessed that that the dour, painstakingly diligent head of the crime scene techs was a music lover, or a churchgoer for that matter. That was the beauty of human beings—all those inconsistencies, all those incongruities, all those inconstancies. Light and dark, good and bad, seen and unseen. *And one man in his time plays many parts. . . .*

"Poor Bob. Uncle Laz won't be playing the organ for them now." *Another problem for my mother to solve,* thought Mercy.

"Ford as St. Nick is easily replaced," mused Dr. Darling, moving on. "But who'll replace him as mayor?"

"Uncle Laz was just the acting mayor. He was desperate for the town council to set a date for a special election so he could pass the torch and go back to keeping the village books." With his untimely death, the introverted man was leaving a hole far bigger than he might have imagined, thought Mercy. She wondered how he would have felt about that.

"To whom?"

"I don't know. That's a question for my mother."

"She should run for office herself."

"Don't even say that out loud." As fine a mayor as her mother might be, and as much as it might benefit the village, Mercy hated the idea of being a part of a political family. Not that she'd ever say as much to Grace.

Dr. Darling wrinkled her small nose, the one that was so good at sniffing out a victim's secrets. "Grace knows where all the bodies are buried."

True enough, thought Mercy. But she said nothing.

"She'd be great," insisted the medical examiner. "And you know that's what Jim Drake would have wanted."

Mercy thought about that. Drake had been mayor as long as she could remember—one of the most popular and beloved politicians in the state.

"Your mother is one of the few Vermonters worthy to be his successor."

"She doesn't want the job."

"Doesn't she?"

Mercy changed the subject. "We've lost two mayors in two months. Jim Drake and now Uncle Laz."

"I share your skepticism about coincidences," said Dr. Darling. "But Mayor Drake's death was ruled natural causes. The man had a heart attack brought on by overexertion during a nor'easter. Typical tie-down."

"Meaning?"

"The foolish man was trying to tie down his deck furniture when the high winds hit. Like shoveling snow in the cold, tie-downs can bring on a heart attack. There was nothing to suggest foul play."

"Right." Mercy stared at the remains of the Yule log. "And it looked nothing like this."

"No crime scene in Vermont ever looked like this." The medical examiner lifted a gloved finger and spun it around in a circle over her head. "It means something, this lethal little stage set."

They stood quietly for a moment, studying the scene. Mercy took in the Yule log, the oak trees, the slabs of stone. "Could that be one of those old stone chambers?"

The stone chambers were strange man-made structures found all over New England. Some said they were cairns built by Vikings or Celts or Native Americans. Others said they were built by colonists as root cellars. No one really knew where they came from.

"You mean like Mystery Hill in New Hampshire?"

"Yes. My dad took me there when I was a kid." The mysterious stone maze of chambers was known as America's Stonehenge. Some claimed it was built more than four thousand years ago by an ancient people who knew their astronomy and their construction techniques.

"Where?"

Mercy pointed at the ruin of rocks at the other side of the clearing.

"Maybe." Dr. Darling leaned forward, peering across the clearing. "If so, it's seen better days. Looks more a fallen Jenga game than a sacred cairn." She looked at Mercy. "If you're right, that adds yet another element of weirdness to this crime scene." She straightened up, placed her hands on her hips, and arched her back.

"Are you all right?"

"Just needed a good stretch." She smiled at Mercy. "You could be right about those stones. I'd never bet against Mercy Carr."

"Maybe I'm just seeing things. Mysteries where there are none. Clues where there are none."

"Don't worry, I'm sure you'll figure it out."

"Not my job." Mercy smiled back. "My job is all mom, all the time."

"Understood." Dr. Darling's smile grew even wider at the thought of the baby. "She's a lovely girlie, your Felicity."

"Thank you. She's our little treasure."

"That she is. And I know what a wonderful time this is for you and Troy. The years go by so fast." She closed her eyes, seemingly lost in memory. A moment later she blinked, focusing once again on Mercy. "I stayed home with my children, too, as much as I could when they were small. Only worked part-time for years. Loved every minute of it."

"But?" Mercy waited for the "but" she knew was coming.

"But I still worked part-time. Kept me sharp." The medical examiner paused. "And sane."

"You were always sharp," said Mercy. "And sane."

Dr. Darling laughed. "If you really think you're going to be able to stay out of this investigation, you're dreaming."

"Not my investigation."

"Maybe it should be."

"I really don't have the time." Mercy shrugged.

"You won't be able to resist the call of this conundrum."

"I've got my baby and I've got my wildlife studies. That's enough to keep me occupied."

"I don't have to tell you that *man* is the wildest beast," said Dr. Darling as she slipped under the crime scene tape and headed for the corpse. "The wildest beast in the forest."

CHAPTER FOUR

Whether we wake or we sleep, Whether we carol or weep, The Sun with his Planets in chime, Marketh the going of Time.

—EDWARD FITZGERALD

"Where's that adorable baby?" Officer Alma Goodlove stepped forward as the medical examiner disappeared under the tent.

"She's back at the common with my family." Mercy smiled at the police officer she was proud to call her friend. "I need to get back there."

"I'm sure." Alma smiled back. "But we'll need to take your statement first."

"Can't it wait? Felicity is visiting Santa Claus for the first time and I don't want to miss it." Not to mention that she'd had enough of bad omens and dead Santas, and she knew that a high-profile case like this one meant that Alma's boss, Detective Kai Harrington, would be showing up any minute. She'd like to return to Felicity and the Solstice Soirée before that happened. A quick how-d'you-do with St. Nick and then home to Grackle Tree Farm, the sooner, the better.

"You know how important the first twenty-four hours are," said Alma. After only a few years on the force, the young woman had proved to be a good cop, walking the fine line between friendship and duty as gracefully as possible.

Not always easy, given her boss's mercurial attitude toward Mercy. She and the detective had had their differences, but they'd finally come to a kind of respectful détente. A détente that could very well be tested by a murdered mayor in a Santa suit.

Mercy sighed. "Make it quick."

"Understood," said Alma, petting Elvis before reaching for her notebook. "Let me take your statement, and you can go."

Mercy quickly related her activities over the past couple of hours, from the time she arrived at Santa's red velvet throne to when she secured the crime scene. She answered the officer's questions and promised to make herself available should they need to contact her again.

"That should do it." Alma closed her notebook, slipping it into the breast pocket of her uniform coat.

"Great, thank you." Mercy turned to Elvis. "Let's go, boy."

"Hold on." Dr. Darling exited the tent and waved a gloved hand at her. "I don't think you'll want to miss this."

Alma sighed. "I'm not hearing this."

Mercy smiled. Cops preferred not to share information with civilians—and despite Mercy's years in the Military Police and her unofficial involvement in criminal investigations here in Northshire over the past couple of years, she was still a civilian.

Dr. Darling made no such distinctions. To the dismay of local law enforcement, she was always forthright with Mercy. The medical examiner loved to talk shop, and she loved talking shop with Mercy, despite her lack of official status. They had a history of working well together, and a similarly unique—some would say off-kilter—way of looking at a crime scene.

But not this time.

"Tell Officer Goodlove here." Mercy moved away with Elvis, toward the trail. "I'm going back to my baby now."

"Your mother is going to want to know everything," called Dr. Darling after her.

Mercy turned back. As much as she hated to admit it, she knew the medical examiner was right. "Two minutes."

"It appears that our victim was already dead when the Yule log was placed on his stomach and set on fire," said Dr. Darling.

"Cause of death?" asked Alma.

"He was shot. Two entry wounds were revealed when we removed the log."

"Poor man," said Mercy. "Caliber?"

"I'm guessing something smallish, like a thirty-two. But that's just a guess."

"Close range?" asked Alma.

"Yes."

"So he probably knew his killer." Mercy thought about it. "Or not." She pictured Uncle Laz decked out like St. Nick. "When you're Santa, everyone approaches you as Santa."

"Interesting point. Even if you were a stranger to him, Santa may have assumed you were a fan, not a killer."

"Looking to wish him a Merry Christmas, not to kill him." Mercy tried to imagine shooting Santa Claus—and could not.

"Premediated then," said Alma.

"No defensive wounds on his hands," said the medical examiner.

"And still no signs of a struggle?" asked Mercy.

"Nope."

"So he was taken by surprise," said Alma. "They shot him and planted a Yule log on him and left him to die."

"They might not have had too long to wait," said Dr. Darling. "Even if the bullets did not ricochet inside, he probably would have bled out quickly. I'll know more when I've done the postmortem."

"Poor Uncle Laz."

"Yes." Dr. Darling nodded in agreement, a fleeting crease ruffling across her brow. Then she smiled like the cat who's caught the canary. "Now to the most interesting part."

"There's a more interesting part?" Mercy wondered how you could possibly top a murdered man dressed as Santa laid out in the woods with a Yule log ablaze on his belly in front of a peculiar pile of rocks.

"Seems unlikely," said Alma.

"I know, right?" The medical examiner grinned. "I found this stuffed in the victim's glove." She dangled a plastic bag in front of them with gloved fingers, looking positively gleeful.

"What is it?" asked Alma.

The medical examiner held out her hand, the clear bag splayed across her open palm. "See for yourself."

Mercy held back, waiting for the policewoman to take the first look.

Alma exhaled heavily in resignation. "Go ahead."

Mercy stepped forward and leaned down to view the evidence up close.

Through the clear plastic she saw a piece of lined paper. "Looks like a bit of torn sheet music."

"That's right."

Mercy peered at the notes on the slip of paper, and tried to remember what little she'd learned from the piano lessons she'd taken as a child. Maybe C sharp, C, D sharp . . . There was no point in going on. She wasn't sure about the musical notation. But the lyrics that ran beneath the notes she could read. Well, at least she could read three of the words. "Dark. Night. Wakes."

"Correct."

"It's a Christmas carol." Mercy moved back and let Alma take her turn examining the evidence.

Dr. Darling smiled. "And?"

"Give me a minute." Mercy closed her eyes and hummed the tune to herself. She smiled when she got to the fourth verse, and sung it under her breath.

> *Where children pure and happy pray to the blessed Child,*
> *Where misery cries out to Thee, Son of the mother mild;*
> *Where charity stands watching and faith holds wide the door,*
> *The dark night wakes, the glory breaks, and Christmas comes once more.*

She opened her eyes. "'O Little Town of Bethlehem.' This is the fourth verse."

"Well done." Dr. Darling clapped. "I had to ask Bob."

"Bob?"

"I told you, he's the new choirmaster. A walking, talking encyclopedia of hymns, Christmas and otherwise."

"Impressive."

"You should come to the Christmas Eve service at the First Congregational Church. Bob's church choir is the best in Vermont. It's lovely."

"I'm sure."

"At least bring little Felicity to the Singing Christmas Tree. Premier performance tomorrow night."

Alma turned to Mercy. "How did you know that? About the Christmas carol?" The officer had finished her examination of the sheet music and was regarding her with interest.

"Mercy has a very good memory," said Dr. Darling.

"True." Mercy thought about her mother and her grandmother, neither of whom ever missed a trick and both of whom never forgot one, either. "A good memory runs in the family."

"Still," said Alma. "Who knows all the verses to every Christmas carol?" She looked from the medical examiner to Mercy. "Besides Bob."

"When I was ten," Mercy admitted, "I was in the children's chorus at church. My one and only solo was 'O Little Town of Bethlehem.'"

"That was a long time ago," said Alma.

"Not that long ago." Mercy smiled at Alma, who was not much younger than she was.

"Music is good for our brain," said Dr. Darling. "It can improve our memory and help us concentrate and focus—especially when we're exposed to music at a young age. The fact that Mercy forged this music memory in her youth is one of the reasons she remembers these lyrics so well—and odds are she'll never forget them."

"Got it." Alma nodded. "My grandmother has dementia, and music is part of her therapy. When she gets agitated, we put on Frank Sinatra. Works every time." The officer paused. "What does this sheet music mean?"

"I imagine it's a message of some sort," said Dr. Darling. "Another puzzle for you to solve, Mercy."

"Someone who hates Christmas or Lazlo Ford or both." Alma turned to Mercy. "That's some puzzle. Better you than me."

"I really have to go now." Mercy slapped her thigh for Elvis. The shepherd joined her, at the ready.

The crime scene techs appeared at the opening to the tent. Mercy and Elvis stepped back, waiting with Alma and Dr. Darling in silence as the techs transported the body bag holding Lazlo Ford out of the tent.

"Later," called Bob over his shoulder as he led his team off through the woods toward the common.

No one said anything for a moment, each mulling over the odd particulars of the strange killing. Dr. Darling broke their pregnant silence. "And why the log?" She lifted her hand in the sign of the horns, a pagan gesture said to protect against evil spirits. "Maybe one of your Druid friends can shed some light on this."

Mercy smiled. Alma frowned.

"No pun intended," said Dr. Darling, lowering her arm.

"Of course not." Mercy bit back a laugh. The cheerful medical examiner never could resist a gallows humor pun.

"You don't think the Druids had something to do with this," said Alma.

"No, I don't," said Dr. Darling. "I know our Northshire Druids do take the solstice very seriously."

"To my mind, Oisin has always been an honorable man," said Alma. "He and his Druids have been on-site preparing for the bonfire. They've got a special permit to stay on the common all night in preparation for their sunrise celebration. Maybe they saw something."

The medical examiner nodded. "I can't imagine they'd desecrate their solstice ritual with something like this. But they may know someone who would."

Mercy considered this. She'd befriended Oisin, the local high priest, during a previous case. She knew him and many of his acolytes. "Even if I believed that Oisin was capable of this, which I don't, it's not really his style. Too on the nose. He's always struck me as a discerning man of the spirit, who wields his staff with a subtle wisdom. Someone else did this."

"True," said Dr. Darling. "This crime scene is nothing if not obvious. More campy than mystical."

"Like an *SNL* skit," said Alma.

"Maybe our killer thinks he's funny," said Mercy. "Certainly, he wanted his victim to be found. And he wanted people to notice, to talk about it."

"And talk they will," said the good doctor.

"Maybe he's a comedian," said Alma. "A psychotic comedian."

"A murderer with a sense of humor," said the medical examiner. "Now there's a jolly thought."

"Ho ho ho," said Mercy quietly, remembering Uncle Laz's lame chuckle. He may have made a terrible Santa Claus and a terrible mayor, but he was a man of God. Or at least God's music. He didn't deserve to die like this. Like something out of a *New Yorker* cartoon. "I've got to get back to Felicity."

"I'll leave the strange business of the Yule log to you, Mercy," said Dr. Darling with a grin. "I look forward to hearing whatever theories you come up with."

"Detective," interrupted Alma, whether by way of greeting or warning or both, Mercy couldn't say.

Kai Harrington, the handsome head of the Criminal Division's Major Crime Unit, part of the Department of Public Safety's Vermont State Police, appeared at the edge of the clearing. He looked as sharp as ever in his bespoke dark suit and wool overcoat and shearling-lined Italian leather boots. He approached the group with a swagger that made it clear he was the boss.

"Mercy Carr." He crossed his arms. "I hear you've outdone yourself this time."

CHAPTER FIVE

To go in the dark with a light is to know the light.

—WENDELL BERRY

"WE WERE JUST LEAVING," SAID MERCY, ELVIS AT HER HIP. "A dead Santa in the woods on the first night of the Solstice Soirée." Harrington shook his head, and his straight black hair swayed with the movement but then fell perfectly back into place, as he undoubtedly knew it would.

"It was all Elvis," Mercy said. "He found the body."

"Of course he did." Harrington sighed. "Very bad timing."

"Is there ever a good time for a dead Santa?" she asked. She wondered how many children in Northshire would hear about the murdered Saint Nicholas and suffer nightmares as a result.

"I was referring to the deceased's role as mayor."

"That too." She suspected that the detective's ambitions ran all the way to the governor's mansion, if not beyond. He was undeniably a good cop, but that would never be enough for him. That made him very sensitive to the winds of political change; you'd never catch him on the wrong side of the optics. "It's a terrible thing."

"Indeed." Harrington frowned. "I understand that Goodlove has taken your statement."

"Yes, sir," said Alma.

"So, you can be on your way."

"Amen to that." Mercy snapped her fingers, and Elvis leapt to his feet.

"Let's hear it, Doc," Harrington said, switching his focus to Dr. Darling. Which was fine by Mercy. She was eager to put the awful image of Uncle Laz on fire in the woods out of her mind and get back to her baby and the happier manifestations of the holiday season. She and Elvis took the shortcut the shepherd had blazed earlier instead of the more well-traveled trail the CSST team and local law enforcement were using.

A harried-looking young woman in hiking clothes and a backpack approached them, phone to her ear, heading toward the crime scene. A reporter, if the lanyard around her neck was any indication. Mercy knew a few of the local reporters, but she didn't recognize this one. No surprise: The Solstice Soirée drew journalists from around the state. And once word got out about Laz's murder, they'd come from all over New England.

"Hey." The small woman slipped the cell into her pants pocket. She held up her press pass. "Cat Torano. *Northshire Herald*. I'd like to ask you a few questions."

With her thick black bangs nearly obscuring her dark eyes and her determined manner, she reminded Mercy of a Tibetan terrier. The holy dogs of Tibet were holy terrors, known for their sure-footed ability to find and retrieve things that had fallen down the slopes of steep mountains. She suspected Cat was a holy terror, too, who'd brave any chasm to get her story.

Elvis skidded to a stop, lifting his nose in the air and pointing it toward the stranger. His way of sniffing out the good guys from the bad guys. When it came to the press, it could go either way.

"Hey, pretty dog," the woman cooed. "Come here."

He tilted his head at Mercy. She laughed. Elvis would never come when a stranger called. He distrusted everyone he didn't know, and many he did know.

Cat stared at Elvis. "I know you, dog." She looked at Mercy. "This dog is famous."

Mercy smiled at that. People might forget her, but they never forgot Elvis. She switched course, zigzagging away from the young woman. "Come on, boy."

The Malinois raced ahead. Mercy huffed along behind him. The more ground they could put between that reporter and themselves, the better off they would be.

Cat jogged after them. "What's happened in the woods?"

Mercy ignored her. When Cat Torano realized that they were drawing her away from the crime scene, she'd stop chasing them. She'd turn around and chase the story instead.

The word was out.

Cat dropped back, as Mercy knew she would, when they were within fifty yards of the common. It was more crowded than ever now. News traveled fast in a small town, where listening to the police scanner passed as prime entertainment. And news spread even faster when half the town was already gathered on the town green for the solstice festivities.

Police had roped off the opening in the cedar hedge behind the church on the green. Uniforms were positioned all along that side of the common's perimeter. They were outnumbered, and it was only a matter of time before more journalists like Cat slipped past law enforcement and on to the crime scene. There were many ways into the woods.

Everyone here was clamoring for a look. Tourists, locals, grandparents and kids and grandkids thronged the churchyard. Several members of the local press were yelling at Officer Becker, who was manning the thicket that separated the church from the woods. They knew there was a good story beyond those trees.

Mercy gave Becker a sympathetic nod. Crowd control was never easy—and the transition from crowd to mob was just one volatile impulse away. The sooner she got Felicity and the others back home, the better.

She clipped the lead back onto Elvis and together they navigated the sea of solstice partiers and crime scene gawkers. They passed Oisin, Arch-Druid of the Cosmic Ash Grove, Order of the Bards, Ovates, and Druids. He and his fellow Druids had congregated around the Fountain of the Muses in the center of the common in advance of the lighting of the bonfire.

She wondered what the Arch-Druid would make of the murdered mayor and the Yule log, but she couldn't stop to ask. Not right now. Oisin raised his carved maple staff at Mercy, and she waved back, but kept on toward the town hall.

She and Elvis found her daughter safe with the regular Santa—Pizza Bob. Felicity giggled wildly as he bounced her on his knee and her grandmother Patience snapped photos on her cell to memorialize the moment.

Now there's a real Santa, Mercy thought, lamenting the death of Uncle Laz and yet still admiring the easy way this big man with the naturally ruddy cheeks had with children. This Santa's smile was confident; his happy grin seemed to light up his entire being, as if he himself were strung with lights, just like the town he loved so much. The contrast between his Santa and Uncle Laz's was heartbreaking in more ways than one.

Tandie had resumed her post as the Number One Elf, looking as profoundly bored as only an adolescent could. She brightened when she saw Mercy. "Tell us everything."

"Give it a minute," said Patience as she greeted Elvis with a welcome scratch between his ears. His cosine-curved tail wagged hard in appreciation. Northshire's favorite vet was one of the shepherd's favorite people, and the feeling was mutual.

"Pizza Bob is back," Mercy said.

"His grandmother is on the mend, so he's free to resume his post," said Patience.

"Good on both counts." Mercy watched her baby play with Pizza Bob Santa. "Felicity is loving this."

Inwardly she kicked herself for missing most of this first: Felicity's first visit with Santa. This must be how Troy felt whenever he was away at work, she thought. She was lucky; she could just go off into the woods with Elvis as her wingman and do her wildlife thing with Felicity right there in the carrier on her back. Which is exactly what she'd been doing.

Until today.

"We didn't know how long you'd be, and the lines were so long, we didn't want to lose our place and have to wait all over again. So we went ahead without you." Patience gave the shepherd's sleek head a final pat and reached for Felicity, scooping her off Santa's lap and handing her to Mercy. "I hope you don't mind."

"No problem." Mercy smiled at her grandmother as she took her happy daughter into her arms and balanced her on one hip. Babies adored Patience, just like puppies and kittens and foals did. The youngest and most vulnerable creatures understood when they were in good hands. And Patience had the surest and gentlest of hands.

Mercy felt Elvis nuzzle Felicity's bottom with his cold nose. "Did you have a good time with Santa, sweetheart?"

"She had a wonderful time," said Patience.

Mercy turned to Pizza Bob, who even outfitted as St. Nick smelled of garlic and oregano and olive oil, tomato sauce and baked bread. Her stomach growled at the mere scent of him. "I'm glad to hear your grandmother is doing better, Santa."

Santa smiled at her. "Thank you, Mercy."

"Thank *you*. For everything. Merry Christmas."

"Merry Christmas!" he bellowed back before beckoning to the next child in line waiting to see him.

"Are you okay?" asked Patience, leading Mercy past the red velvet throne to the other side of the porch, where Amy held a sleepy Helena in her arms.

"I'm fine, just a little hungry." Mercy slung Felicity into the carrier and slipped it onto her shoulders. Right where her baby belonged. She knew she would have to get used to sharing Felicity with the rest of the world, but not right now. Enough sharing for one day.

"We can fix that. There's food everywhere here." Patience laughed. "Having Pizza Bob back as Santa Claus must be good for business. One sniff and you head to the food booths."

"Let's talk to Mom first."

"Of course. She's worried, as you might imagine."

Grace leaned against one of the town hall's massive columns, chic as a *Vogue* cover in her designer burgundy wool pants and matching fur-trimmed coat. The only hint that the director of this year's Northshire's Solstice Soirée was concerned about the dark events threatening the longest night on her watch was the slight tightening around her lips.

Tandie abandoned her post without so much as a jinglejangle and joined their tight little circle. "Tell us everything," the teenager demanded again.

Mercy glanced at her mother.

Grace sighed dramatically before waving her elegantly gloved hand as if in defeat. "Go ahead. We may as well hear the worst of it."

Mercy filled them in on what she and Elvis had found in the woods. They all blanched at her description of the Yule log illuminating Uncle Laz.

"Creepy," said Amy.

"This is way worse than just creepy." Tandie looked around before continuing in a whisper. "This is serial killer creepy."

"Let's not get carried away," said Patience.

"There is no evidence of that," said Mercy.

"We should get out of here," said Tandie. "Go home to the farm. While we still can. Seriously."

"I think you're overreacting." Grace gave the teenager one of her death glares.

"Tell me you're not worried, Mercy." Tandie looked at her, her eyes dark with worry. "Tell me this isn't, like, Hannibal Lecter time."

"Minus a few victims," Patience said dryly.

"Patience is right. One murder does not a serial killer make." Even as she said it, Mercy remembered the strange scene in the woods. The dead Santa glowing with Yuletide fire in the glade. The Yule log. The stone cairn. The missing pompom. The sheet music of "O Little Town of Bethlehem" clutched in his hand. "Listen, you're right that it's a pretty weird crime scene. But it's too early to come to any such conclusions."

"Right." Tandie nodded. "We need to stick to the facts: means, motive, opportunity." The clever teenager had tagged along with Mercy on a case several months ago and had proved a very worthy Watson to her Sherlock. Now she was obsessed with all things criminal.

"I liked Mr. Lazlo." Amy shook her head and wrapped her free arm around Helena's ears as if to make sure her little girl didn't hear anything about serial killers. "He was a nice man."

"Yes, he was." Grace turned to Mercy. "This is all simply unacceptable."

"What's going to happen now?" asked Amy. "Are you going to have to cancel the Solstice Soirée?"

"Absolutely not." Her mother leaned toward Mercy, frowning. "I loved Lazlo, but we cannot cancel. This is our biggest fundraiser of the year. And this is only the first day of the festival."

Mercy hated to mention it and add to her mother's growing to-do list, but it needed to be done. "What about the Singing Christmas Tree?"

"Oh no," said Grace, falling back against the column. "The Singing Christmas Tree."

"What about it?" asked Tandie.

"Uncle Laz was the organist," explained Mercy. She thought about Bob Cato, who back at the crime scene had not mentioned that with Uncle Laz's death, he was now short one organist. Always the professional, The

Turtle had been focused on the job at hand. Or maybe he just trusted Grace to come up with a solution. Or both.

"They could sing a cappella," offered Amy. "Or sing along to a tape."

"With accompaniment is always better than without," said Tandie firmly. "And live is always better than tape. Besides, the organ is a cool instrument."

"Do you play?" asked Amy.

"No," admitted Tandie.

Mercy looked at her grandmother Patience. "But you do."

"Of course!" Grace straightened, her elegant face shining as she regarded her mother with relief. "You can take Laz's place at the organ."

"I don't think so." Patience frowned. "It's been a long time."

"You still play," said Grace. "You still play *well*."

"But not in *public*."

"Patience was the organist when I was a kid in the church choir," Mercy told Amy and Tandie. "She was great. She taught us to sing *Christmas Is Coming* in rounds." She bounced Felicity up and down, singing "Christmas is coming, the goose is getting fat."

"You are not helping," Patience said to Mercy.

"Perfect." Grace whipped out her phone and sent a text. "I've alerted the choirmaster that you'll be replacing Uncle Laz at the organ," she told Patience. "Bob Cato will be in touch shortly."

"But—"

"No time for buts, Mother."

Mercy bit back a smile. She knew how much Patience hated being called *Mother*.

"Organ problem solved. Let's move on to the other problem."

"You mean the serial killer?" asked Tandie.

Grace ignored that. She placed her gloved hands on Mercy's shoulders. "We have eleven days to go. I cannot permit this tragedy, however terrible, to ruin the rest of our soirée." She moved her hands from Mercy's shoulders and cupped her granddaughter's little face. Her frown disappeared as she smiled brightly at the baby. "Or our precious Felicity's first Christmas."

"Lazlo would agree with you," said Patience. "He loved this family and he loved this town. I'll do my part as best I can. Because Laz would want us to go on."

Grace tapped the baby's cheek lightly and rose up to her full imperious height. "He'd also want us to solve his murder."

In unison, everyone looked at Mercy. Elvis barked.

"Oh no you don't." Mercy stepped back. "I'm staying well out of it."

"Lazlo was a lovely man, really," said Patience. "We can't let this dreadful ending of his life be what people remember about him. He deserves better than that."

Her grandmother had a point. Poor Uncle Laz had been a very private person, and now, given the sensational manner of his death, they'd be digging into every aspect of his life. There'd be memes of the dead Santa and the blazing Yule log in no time. He would have hated that. Well, who wouldn't.

"May he rest in peace," said Tandie.

"We can't let his killer get away with it," said Amy.

"We owe him that much," said Patience. "We were the only family he had."

"Harrington has already warned me off," said Mercy.

"I bet he has." Grace crossed her arms across her chest, fur cuffs setting off her trim waistline. "But he's going to need your help."

"He always ends up needing your help, Mercy," said Amy, repositioning the dozing Helena on her hip.

"Always," echoed Tandie.

"Harrington will make sure that law enforcement is all over this. Look around. He's already doubled the police presence here."

Amy and Tandie looked around. Grace and Patience did not.

"You're right," said Tandie. "There are cops everywhere."

"Harrington and his team don't need me." Mercy rubbed her nose lightly against Felicity's own little button nose, breathing in the sweet smell of baby. "I'm going to be busy Hallmarking the heck out of Christmas."

Grace and Patience exchanged skeptical glances with Amy and Tandie.

"Famous last words," said Grace.

CHAPTER SIX

And once, says Ernest Thompson Seton—once, a man shot an eagle out of the sky. He examined the eagle and found the dry skull of a weasel fixed by the jaws to his throat. The supposition is that the eagle had pounced on the weasel and the weasel swiveled and bit as instinct taught him, tooth to neck, and nearly won.

—ANNIE DILLARD

TROY WARNER CROUCHED BEHIND A COUPLE OF HUGE OAK SNAGS fronting a stand of aspens in a remote area of the southern Green Mountains. Susie Bear, his Newfie mix search-and-rescue dog, was stretched out asleep by his side, in her usual "Wake me when something happens" approach to surveillance.

Troy could hardly blame the dog for dozing. They'd been out here for nearly twenty-four hours now, waiting for a poacher who'd been trapping on this posted private land illegally. Waiting for the rogue trapper to return to the scene of his crime. Nothing to surveil unless or until the man showed up.

He'd show up. Troy would bet his truck that he'd show up.

The latter half of December was fur trapping season for fisher, mink, skunk, fox, raccoon, coyote, opossum, and weasel. The going market price for fisher and mink fur—two of the most prized pelts in the weasel family—was higher than ever. The two closely related mammals could be hard to tell apart, but the fisher was bigger, with a longer, bushier tail. Both were promising targets for poachers.

Troy hated fur trapping season, arguably his least favorite time on the job. He'd grown up hunting and fishing with his grandfather, who believed that being a good hunter meant that you eat what you kill. Which meant venison was the meat of choice at the family table all year long.

Troy had given up hunting after his tours in Afghanistan, but he respected those hunters who followed the rules and regulations. As a game warden for the Vermont Fish & Wildlife Department, it was his duty and his mission to apprehend those who did not.

Trappers were another story. When it came to fur trapping, it was all about the fur, not the meat. And despite all the talk about humane ways to trap animals, Troy remained unconvinced. To his mind, a well-placed shot seemed a far more efficient and far less cruel a way to harvest an animal.

Traps were unpredictable; there was no guarantee that you'd catch what you were looking for. Every year, traps ensnared endangered species like lynx and marten, as well as deer, reptiles, birds, and even pets. Anything caught in a live trap could suffer a lingering and painful death, which is why trappers were required by law to check their traps every day, rain or shine or snowstorm.

This poacher regularly failed to check his traps every day. Worse, he used body-grip traps that were too big to set on the ground; they were only legal here in the state of Vermont if suspended at least five feet aboveground or placed under water or ice. This guy had taken a downed branch and positioned it in a low crook of an old oak, creating the kind of leaning pole fishers loved to climb—that's why fishers were sometimes called pole cats—and then he secured the trap to the branch only about four feet from the ground.

The landowner had filed several trespassing complaints against the guy to no avail—and that, along with all the poacher's other violations, infuriated Troy. He hated poachers, and since the department figured that for every poacher caught in the act ten got away clean, Troy was determined to catch as many of them as he could.

He was particularly determined to catch this sneaky perp. He'd placed a trail camera in the lower branch of a sugar maple not far from the trap site—and two days ago, the trail camera had recorded a large black male fisher falling victim to the trap.

Twenty-four hours passed. Troy and Susie Bear came to check the site. The dead fisher was still there, although there was less of him thanks to hungry creatures all around. No evidence on the trail camera, either, that the poacher had come to check the trap as required by law. Troy was *this* close to nailing him.

Fisher pelts were in high demand these days—and poaching was on the rise. Troy had contacted his pal Gil Guerrette, who wanted this same guy on similar charges of crimes committed in the Green Mountain National Forest. The park ranger would be joining them when he could. Like game wardens, park rangers were working overtime this time of year, given their small numbers and their large territories. Troy and his colleagues covered around three hundred square miles each all on their own, and he knew that the rangers were spread just as thin.

Gil would show up eventually. Meanwhile, Troy and Susie Bear had settled in to wait.

And they'd been waiting all day.

Usually trappers came to check their traps in the morning, since their prey were nocturnal creatures most likely to be caught between sunset and sunrise. Coming after dawn allowed the trappers to retrieve their catch before any other animal—human or otherwise—discovered it. This guy was late.

Troy cursed the man for keeping him away from his family. He loved the woods, and until Mercy and Felicity came into his life he'd preferred the forest over any other place on earth. But now his favorite place was the sofa in their living room in their old Victorian house on their old New England property.

It occurred to Troy that the poacher may have eluded arrest so far simply by not coming to the site during the day. "We'll stay a little longer, girl," he told the chillin' Newfoundland. "But if he doesn't show soon, we're going home."

Susie Bear ignored him. Troy kept his eyes on the trap. As dusk began to fall, the forest came alive again as the creatures of the night appeared. A deer skittered by them, intent on a bedtime snack of the bright red fruit of the winterberry clustered on the other side of the blowdown. A couple of bats squeaked overhead, and a porcupine lumbered toward a copse of eastern white pine for supper.

Porcupine. Where you find porcupine, you find fisher. Fisher being one of the primary predators of the porcupine. Unlike many other species, they were undeterred by those nasty quills. The clever pole cats circled their prickly prey, biting their quill-free faces and then flipping them onto their backs to feast on their quill-free underbellies.

Susie Bear opened her eyes and raised her shaggy black head, no doubt roused by the sticky cheese scent of the prickly creature.

"Stay, girl. You know you're no fisher." It was a rare dog that could resist a porcupine, despite the consequences. Canine curiosity often ended in impalement; Troy had dragged a very unhappy Susie Bear to the vet to have the painful spikes removed more than once.

The porcupine lumbered on, disappearing into the pine grove. Susie Bear stayed put, even as she regarded Troy with those big baleful brown eyes.

"Good girl," said Troy.

Susie Bear lowered her head, then raised it again, her attention now directed elsewhere.

Her plumed tail pounded the forest floor in a slow *whomp*. Her way of saying they had company.

Friend, not foe.

Troy heard a slight rustling behind him, and Gil Guerrette stepped forward.

"*Bonjour, mon ami.*" The ranger slapped him on the shoulder as he squatted himself down between Troy and Susie Bear. He scratched the sweet spot between the dog's fuzzy ears. "Why are you out here in the woods? You should be at home playing Santa Claus with *la belle* Mercy and *la petite cherie* Felicity."

"I'm doing double shifts so I can have Christmas Day off."

"Good plan. Your baby girl's first Christmas is very important." Gil had three daughters of his own, so he knew what he was talking about. Troy had grown up with brothers, so women sometimes confounded him. His full-of-advice friend was always quick to set him straight, whether Troy wanted him to or not.

"Agreed. Let's get this guy and then we can all go home."

Gil pushed aside a snowy bare bough of an aspen for a better view of the trap in the blowdown. "Looked like he uses squirrel carcasses for bait instead of beaver carrion. Probably poaching beaver, too."

"Probably. Beaver's getting top dollar for felt. Cowboy hats."

"Not just cowboys, *mon ami*." Gil laughed. "The viral mob wife aesthetic is also hot now."

"I don't even know what that means."

"Everything eighties is new again. Animal prints. Leather. Furs."

"And you know this because . . ."

"Because I have three girls. The ultimate authority on all things fashion. And all things viral." Gil leaned toward him. "Just wait until little Felicity is old enough for a smartphone."

"Don't even say that out loud." Troy dreaded the day. He shook off the terrible thought of his lovely baby girl Felicity as a tween and turned his attention back to the job at hand. "Bad news for the fisher. And all the other fur-bearing mammals."

"Bad news for us, too," said Gil. "We'll be spending even more time out here tracking down poachers."

"Right. Starting with this one."

"So what have we got here?" Gil held up his right hand, and began to tick off the man's offenses. "Trespassing, failure to check the trap daily, failure to tag the trap with name and address, and illegal use of a body-gripping trap." The park ranger looked at Troy with his dark eyes. "Did I miss anything?"

Troy checked his watch. "Ten more minutes, and we can add failure to report the taking of a fisher to a game warden within forty-eight hours."

"Let's sit tight then." Gil grinned at him.

The three of them—warden, ranger, dog—waited.

As if on cue, ten minutes later Susie Bear shuffled to her feet. Meaning someone or something was out there. Moments later the sound of a human tramping through the forest reached Troy and Gil's lesser human ears as well.

"*Allons y!*" whispered Gil.

"Down," Troy ordered Susie Bear quietly, and they all moved behind a ragged hedge of hemlock to hide.

The all-too-human noise of a careless hunter echoed through the silent forest. The crunch of boots on the frosty ground. The snap of twigs and branches underfoot. The swoosh of snow as it fell from swaying limbs. And the skittering of crepuscular creatures in advance of the coming stumblebum.

A clumsy behemoth of a man careened into the small clearing. He stood at least six-five—not counting the formidable crown of antlers he wore upon his basketball-sized head. Standing there in the snow in the long, dark shadows of the night woods, the antlered man reminded Troy of the monsters in the horror movies he and his brothers had dared each other to watch as kids.

"*Wendigo,*" said Gil, laughing.

Together they watched the horned man lurch toward the trap with the dead fisher, his rifle flung over his shoulder, flopping against his great girth.

"An *intoxicated* wendigo." Gil laughed again.

Troy sighed. At times like these he despaired for the human race—and all the species at its mercy. "Just another drunken wannabe Druid on the eve of the winter solstice poaching fisher cats for—what did you call them?—mob wife fashionistas?"

"Close enough." Gil slid his dark eyes toward the man in the antlers, who was nearly within reach of the dead fisher. "You think too much, *mon ami.*"

"Maybe."

Troy counted down the seconds as they waited to catch the poacher red-handed with his prey. The guy leaned his rifle against a nearby tree, preparing to release the unfortunate fisher from the trap.

Troy and Gil crouch-walked in different directions until they were on opposite sides of the deadfall, flanking their perp. Troy nodded at Gil, then rose to his feet and stepped through the hemlocks. "Vermont Fish and Wildlife."

The antlers bounced as the man jerked up his head. He dropped the fisher at his feet and moved toward his rifle.

"Don't even think about it," warned Troy.

CHAPTER SEVEN

Though my soul may set in darkness, it will rise in perfect light;
I have loved the stars too fondly to be fearful of the night.

—SARAH WILLIAMS

FELICITY WRIGGLED IN MERCY'S ARMS, AND STARTED TO FUSS. The cute kind of tiny cries that always reminded Mercy of baby wrens chirping in their mama's nest. "She must be hungry by now."

"We gave her a bottle, but that was a while ago," said Patience.

"Now that she's eating some solid foods, she's hungrier than ever," said Mercy.

"Such a little chowhound," said Grace with a smile. "Just like you were. *Are.*" She looked at Mercy. "Let's just hope she's inherited your metabolism to go along with your appetite."

"Maybe we should take her home for you." Amy glanced at Grace out of the corner of her eye. "So you can get on with it."

"On with what?"

"Finding the serial killer before he strikes again," said Tandie.

"Lower your voice," said Grace firmly. "And unless you want to do elf duty for the rest of the season, do not utter the words 'serial killer' ever again."

"No way." Tandie blanched at the thought of putting in any more time as Santa's little helper.

"Let me rephrase that for you, Tandie." Patience turned to Mercy. "We'll take Felicity home. You stay here and do your investigative thing."

"That should work," said Grace, as her phone pinged and she checked the message. "But Patience, you'll need to come right back after you drop them off. You're needed at the rehearsal for the Singing Christmas Tree. Bob Cato will text you the details."

"I can't ask you to do that," said Mercy.

"Of course you can." Patience reached for her great-granddaughter.

"Not so fast," Mercy hesitated. "I rely on you all too much as it is."

"It takes a village," said her grandmother.

"We're *your* village," seconded Amy.

"You can't fight a village," added her mother.

Mercy smiled in spite of herself. As much as she'd have liked to keep Felicity all to herself, she could not. If she didn't have a village, nobody did. Neither she nor Troy ever needed to ask for help with the baby; they were surrounded—you might say *bombarded*—by eager sitters. Felicity had so many people who loved her—Mercy's family, Troy's family, friends, colleagues—an entire community, all devoted to her health and happiness. She knew that her daughter was a very lucky little girl, with two very lucky parents. When it came to villages, you couldn't beat Northshire. Even if she resented the crowd of villagers from time to time.

"A village," she repeated. Felicity squeaked again, the kind of gathering trill that often preceded an all-out bawling. Mercy rocked her baby back to a temporary calm. "Felicity is hungry and she needs a bath. So do I."

"You can wait," said her mother.

"Bath, book, bed," said Amy, referring to the fail-safe bedtime ritual all smart mothers had used for generations to soothe their fussy children into sweet dreamland. "Don't worry, we've got this."

"I'm starving," Mercy said. The last thing she wanted to do was stay here on the common to look into this bizarre killing. She just wanted to go home. She was battling hunger and fatigue, too, just like Felicity. It had been a long day, as all days were with a nine-month-old infant. Throw in the Solstice Soirée and a murder, and she was ready for supper and sleep. Not to mention a long, hot bath to scrub away the dead Santa vibe.

"You can sleep when your daughter goes off to college or joins the army." Her mother gave her a look saying that while she may have forgiven her only daughter for choosing the military over law school and the family law firm, she had not forgotten it. "Then there'll be nothing you can do about anything Felicity does anyway, so you might as well sleep.

But until then"—now her mother's confident convince-the-jury voice wavered a bit—"we could really use your assistance here."

There was no denying Grace when she asked for help, if only because she so rarely stooped to ask for it. It humbled her to do so. And Mercy couldn't bear to see her proud mother humbled.

If Mercy did have to investigate this crime, for her mother's sake and the town's sake and poor Uncle Laz's sake, she really should attend the lighting of the bonfire. Hosted by the Druids of the Cosmic Ash Grove, the ceremony was the highlight of the first day of the twelve-day festival, drawing visitors from all over the state and beyond.

And it was all about burning Yule logs.

Oisin—Arch-Druid of Order of the Bards, Ovates, and Druids—would lead the ritual, accompanied by the local Druids, Wiccans, and Celtic Christians. She'd love to talk to Oisin; maybe she could take him aside after the ceremony and ask him what he thought about the murder and its apparent solstice connection.

The killer could very well be at the bonfire, drawn by the irresistible pull of the Druidic observance of the winter solstice, Yule log and all. She could surveil the crowd, see if she could spot anything—or anyone—suspicious.

"Felicity does need to get home," Mercy said.

"Your father and I must stay through the official lighting of the bonfire," said Grace. "We're obligated to be there."

"No problem," said Patience. "I can drive all the girls back to Grackle Tree Farm." She looked at Grace. "And then go to the rehearsal."

"Duncan and I will meet you there as soon as the lighting of the bonfire is over." Grace smoothed her fur cuffs and glanced around their tight little circle to make sure everyone was on board. No one objected. "Well now, that's settled."

"Right." Mercy fought a yawn even as her stomach growled.

"I heard that," said her mother. "Let's get you a fried dough. You know you love fried dough. Maybe a grilled sausage sandwich, too, with caramelized onions and peppers."

"And a hot chocolate to wake you up," said Amy.

"Excellent idea." Mercy kissed her baby girl's sweet forehead. The baby's cheeks were flushed from the night air but she was snug and warm in her little designer snowsuit. She looked like a chic strawberry in her pink down-filled suit, with her red curls peeking out from her cap. Thanks to her grandmother Grace, Felicity really was the best dressed baby in Vermont, if not the world.

Helena opened her eyes and slid off her mother's hip, suddenly as awake and alert as a puppy at play. "I want hot chocolate, too."

"We're going home," said Amy, "but we'll make some there."

Helena considered that, frowning.

"With marshmallows," her mother said.

"With marshmallows," repeated the little girl emphatically.

"Deal," said Amy.

"And I've got a cake in the car," said Patience.

"I hope it's your Bûche De Noël," said Grace.

Patience smiled. "You know it is."

The Bûche De Noël was the traditional Yule log dessert—and nobody made a prettier, tastier one than Patience. She layered homemade chocolate sponge cake with cocoa hazelnut whipped cream and rolled it into a log. She iced the log with chocolate ganache, garnishing the top with fresh sprigs of rosemary and sugared cranberries.

Helena clapped her hands. "Cake!"

"Save some for me," said Mercy.

Helena looked up at her with her big gray eyes. "We will," she said earnestly.

"Thank you," said Mercy.

Grace checked her watch. "It's nearly time for the lighting of the bonfire."

"That's our cue," said Patience. "Come on, girls."

"I'm staying with Mercy," announced Tandie.

No surprise there, thought Mercy. The game was afoot, and all that.

Her grandmother looked at Mercy.

"Sure," she said.

Tandie pulled her green peaked elf's hat from her head, revealing a red wool beanie covering most of her choppy pink hair. She pulled it down lower on her forehead and ears. "That's better." She stuffed the green elf's hat in the pocket of her green elf's jacket. She looked down at the rest of her green elf's costume. "I guess this will have to do. Sorry, Mercy. Not exactly incognito."

"You'll blend right in," said Grace. "Many of our solstice guests dress up for the bonfire."

"Dress up?"

"They dress up as their favorite holiday. You'll see King Arthur and Merlin for the winter solstice, Hanukkah gelt and dreidels for Hanukkah, Christmas trees and candy canes and Rudolph the Red-Nosed Reindeer, along with your usual Santa Clauses, snowmen, and Disney princesses," said Grace. "Believe me, you won't be the only elf out there."

Tandie looked unconvinced.

"You look fine," said Mercy. "As long as you're warm enough."

"I'm good. Got my long johns on underneath."

Patience reached for Felicity once more, and this time Mercy passed her baby on with one last kiss. "Good night, sweetheart. I'll be home soon."

"Go on, save our town from the Yuletide Killer," said Amy, as she scrolled through her cell with one hand and took hold of Helena's little fingers with the other.

"The Yuletide killer," repeated Tandie, checking her own phone. "Awesome."

"What did you say?" asked Grace icily.

"Don't blame me." Tandie raised her arms in surrender. "That's what they're calling the serial killer on social media."

"Oh no." Grace pulled out her cell and started to scroll. "'Yuletide Killer slays Santa on the winter solstice,'" she read aloud. She looked at Mercy. "It goes on to mention 'the body's proximity to Northshire's Solstice Soirée on the common.'" She tucked her phone back into the pocket of her coat. "This is going to be a PR nightmare."

"Good grief," said Patience. "Definitely time to go. Come on, kids." She blew Mercy a kiss and, holding Felicity in the crook of her arm, ushered Amy and Helena down the gravel path that led out of the town green.

A deep haunting call sounded through the common, eerie strains that seemed to go on and on and on. The fugue of fierce wails pierced the air, capturing the crowd and holding them hostage. The otherworldly trumpeting moved the Solstice Soirée revelers to a silent stillness—and silently still they stayed.

"What is that?" whispered Tandie, her eyes wide.

"The call of the carnyx." At the teenager's blank look, Mercy elaborated. "It's the horn used by the ancient Celts to frighten their enemies on the eve of battle. And to welcome the sun back at the winter solstice."

"It's starting," said Grace. "Your father and I better get over to the Ogham Standing Stones. You two get something to eat and meet us there."

CHAPTER EIGHT

It was a stag, a stag of ten, Bearing its branches sturdily;
He came silently down the glen, Ever sing hardily, hardily.

—SIR WALTER SCOTT

THE GUY WITH THE ANTLERS STARED AT TROY AND GIL. HE DIDN'T move. Just stood there holding his illegally harvested fisher cat, gawking at them. Maybe he was drunk, maybe he was high, maybe he was just dim. Troy didn't know and didn't much care.

"We've got you, Antler Man," said Gil. "Drop the fisher and raise your hands."

The man's eyes shifted from Gil to Troy and back again.

Susie Bear barked—her *Don't mess with my game warden* bark—and Antler Man switched his focus to the big dog.

"What kind of monster dog is that, man?"

The large Newfie lumbered toward him, and he stumbled backward. Before you could say "wendigo," he fell to the ground, cursing and screaming. The headband holding the horns slipped off his skull. The antlers splintered on the forest floor.

Gil retrieved the poacher's rifle, and Troy stepped forward. But Susie Bear beat Troy to the Antler Man, leaping toward him with an elephantine grace and landing heavily on his chest. The thud sounded like broken ribs.

"Get off me!" The guy reached with his uninjured hand into his back pocket, pulling out his hunter's knife.

"Don't make me shoot you." Troy stood over him, to Susie Bear's right; Gil flanked him, to Susie Bear's left. A law enforcement sandwich with an eighty-five-pound furry filling of dog. When the guy hesitated, Troy clomped on his forearm with his hefty field boot. Antler Man squealed and the knife slipped from his fingers. Gil snatched up the blade.

"Good girl," Troy told Susie Bear. He snapped his fingers, and she shambled off the man's barrel chest, plumed tail wagging. She slumped down into a splayed sit to watch the rest of the proceedings at her leisure. Her job was done.

Troy and Gil dragged the man to his feet. Gil handcuffed him, and searched him for additional weapons.

"Nothing but a wallet, a cell phone, and a key fob," Gil told Troy.

"What, no hunting license?"

"It's in the glove box in my truck," said the big guy.

"Sure it is," said Gil.

"And where is your truck?" asked Troy.

"Parked by the trailhead." Antler Man winced, his massive shoulders heaving. Probably from the pain of the broken ribs. Not to mention his injured hand. "I done nothing wrong."

"What's your name?" ask Gil.

"Not saying nothing without my lawyer."

"You have a lawyer, do you?"

"On retainer, no doubt." Gil consulted the driver's license in the wallet he'd found in the poacher's back pocket when patting him down. "Leland Hallett from Biddeford, Maine."

"You're a long way from home." Troy smiled at him.

Hallett said nothing. He looked pale. As if he were about to faint or have a heart attack.

Troy pointed to a large downed log next to Hallett, hoping it was still intact enough to hold the man's weight. "Sit."

"You've got good hunting in Maine," said Gil. "I don't know why you needed to come here. You could have stayed home and gotten arrested."

"And the trapping season is longer there," added Troy.

Hallett stared at his crown of antlers, lying broken on the snowy ground. He looked *sad*, thought Troy.

"I think our friend was here in Northshire for the Solstice Soirée. The poaching was just a bonus."

"I'm afraid you're going to miss the lighting of the bonfire tonight."

Troy listed the charges against him and read him his rights while Gil clicked the handcuffs around the man's huge wrists behind his back.

Hallett hung his head, whether in shame or in exhaustion Troy couldn't say. The man's trunk-like legs were crossed in front of the stump at the ankles. His breath was ragged.

"Take it easy," said Troy. "Sit tight. We'll give you a couple of minutes to catch your breath. And then we'll go back to the trailhead. The good news is we'll get someone to look at those ribs."

"The bad news is you're going to jail," said Gil.

Hallett closed his eyes, and kept on breathing. He shifted his considerable weight on the tree stump, in an apparent effort to get comfortable. Slowly he straightened out his right leg, propping up his field boot on a downed limb. As he leaned on his haunches to stretch out his other leg, a terrible crack sounded from below his hips. The rotting stump gave way and collapsed, dropping Hallett unceremoniously onto the splintered wood.

He roared as the shards pierced his buttocks, lurching to his feet, his wrists still handcuffed behind him. His face was flushed and shining with sweat. Even without his antlers, Hallett looked like a very angry wendigo now.

Susie Bear growled, a deep rough rumbling that surprised even Troy with its fierceness.

Gil pulled his weapon, aiming it at the irate man.

"I know that must hurt." Troy tried a more conciliatory approach. "If you can walk, let's get you to the hospital."

Hallett stopped ranting as suddenly as he began. For a moment he simply stood there, as if rooted into the ground as securely as an oak, his bloodshot eyes trained on something Troy could not see.

"Hallett," said Troy.

He didn't answer.

"What's he looking at?" asked Gil, his voice thick with irritation.

"Hallett," repeated Troy. "Look at me."

The big man swiveled in slow motion, tipping his huge head down toward the snag where he'd fallen so hard on his butt. "It's, it's," he stammered. And fell silent again as he stared down at the stump as if staring into the abyss.

"It's *what*?"

Hallett's heavy shoulders began to shake, and he began to sway.

"He's going down," said Troy, motioning to Gil to lower his gun and moving quickly for Hallett.

But not quickly enough.

Antler Man toppled toward the forest floor like an old-growth tree felled by a chain saw. Troy dove to the ground, breaking the man's fall with his arms, softening the blows to his massive skull. He cradled Hallett's head in his arms.

The man's eyes were closed.

"Is he all right?" Gil squatted next to Troy, Susie Bear at his side.

"I don't know. Get some water."

"Roger that." Gil holstered his gun and grabbed his water bottle from his backpack. Before he could untwist the cap, Susie Bear pushed her muzzle up to Hallett's chin, and began to lick his face with her thick, long tongue.

The disoriented poacher opened his eyes.

"And he's back." Troy smiled at Susie Bear. "That's enough, girl." The Newfie snorted and snuffled and slowly backed up.

"Stay with us, Hallett," said Gil.

"My arms are falling asleep," said Troy. "Let's swap them out for your pack."

"Sure."

Gil pulled the man up by his jacket, while Troy tugged his arms out, slipping the park ranger's pack under the guy's head instead.

"Drink," Gil ordered, dribbling water into the man's mouth.

Troy didn't know whether it was the slobber or the water, but either way Hallett seemed to be improving. His color was better and his breathing more regular. "He's looking better."

As if to prove Troy's point, the man roused. He raised his head, his eyes darting from Gil to Troy to the trees beyond. "Is it gone?"

"Is what gone?" asked Gil.

The effort cost Hallett. His head dropped back onto the pack. He closed his eyes again, and moaned.

Susie Bear barked—an excited yelp that signaled she'd found something of importance. Troy looked over at the exuberant Newfie. She'd settled into an alert position, her tail thumping steadily, a canine metronome of accomplishment. Her nose was poised at the very edge of the broken stump. The very same place that had so disturbed their poacher.

"What's she doing?" asked Gil.

"She's found something. Let me check it out." Troy drew himself up to his feet and jogged over to Susie Bear. He knelt by the shaggy dog and examined what was left of the old stump.

There, nestled in fallen leaves and jagged bark and deadwood, rested a bowl-sized object dusted with decades of dirt. Still, the shape was unmistakable.

It was a human skull.

A human skull crowned in antlers.

Troy gazed at the weathered old leather headband that held the six-pointer rack. The design was very similar to the helmet that Hallett had been wearing. Only this one had bigger horns.

And what looked like a bullet hole right between the eyes.

Susie Bear whined, reminding him that she deserved a reward for her find. Without taking his eyes off the skull, he pulled a doggy biscuit from his pocket and tossed it to the Newfie. She caught it in midair.

"Good girl," he said. Raising his voice, he called to Gil. "You're not going to believe this."

"Coming."

Troy heard Gil promise Hallett that he'd be right back. The poacher moaned in response, and muttered something about not leaving him alone.

"What's up?" asked the ranger, one eye on Hallett and the other on Troy.

"See for yourself." Troy retreated so Gil could get a good look inside the stump.

"Mon dieu." The ranger crossed himself. "This is a very bad omen."

"You aren't worried, are you?" Troy smiled at him, knowing full well that his friend was a little too well-versed in legend and lore for his own good.

"Pas moi. Not me. But many people believe in these pagan gods," said Gil. "They say they go by many names. *Wendigo. Cernunnos. Oak King.* They say that they walk among us. Especially at the solstice."

"Superstition," said Troy.

"Tell that to the Druids."

"This is another Antler Man," said Troy. "Like our friend Hallett over there. Another drunken wannabe Druid. Only this one's dead. Looks like he's been that way for quite a while."

Gil took off his ranger cap, raked his fingers through his dark brown hair, and put his cap back on again. "You see but you do not see, *mon ami*."

"What I see is not bad omens or pagan gods or solstice sacrifices. What I see is man's inhumanity to man. Murder, plain and simple."

CHAPTER NINE

The fire itself can put it out, and that
By burning out, and before it burns out
It will have roared first and mixed sparks with stars,
And sweeping round it with a flaming sword,
Made the dim trees stand back in wider circle—

—ROBERT FROST

Two hot chocolates, a six-inch loaded sausage sandwich, and a fried dough with extra powdered sugar later, Mercy was feeling much better. Elvis had been well-fortified too, with a burger *sans* bun and a bowlful of water—and Tandie had scarfed down three slices of veggie pizza, a soda, and a warm chocolate chip cookie the size of a small sun.

"Let's do this." With Elvis at her hip and Tandie trailing behind snapping photos of the most outrageously costumed revelers, Mercy snaked through the crowd.

"It's like, Halloween, only better," said Tandie. "Dungeons and Dragons and Christmas and Disney World all together."

Mercy laughed. The teenager had a point. There were Oisin's real-life Druids in long white robes and wannabe Druids in long white robes. Viking warriors in horned helmets and Norse princesses in horned crowns, Holly Kings and Oak Kings. Couples dressed in Santa Claus and Mrs. Claus suits, his and hers ugly holiday sweaters, the Grinch and Cindy Lou Who—not to mention entire extended families in matching Christmas pajamas. And just like her mother Grace had promised Tandie, lots and lots of elves.

There were even some random unicorns, baby sharks, and superheroes. Many of the people in attendance had dressed up their pets as well. Elvis held his muzzle high as he passed a pair of dachshunds wearing antlers. It was clear he did not approve.

They passed the Fountain of the Muses in the center of the common, where Mercy had spotted Oisin and his fellow Druids earlier that day. By now they were headed over to the Ogham Standing Stones, gathering in the circular garden that served as the setting for the annual lighting of the bonfire.

Mercy could see the twenty-foot towers of granite that anchored the solstice garden. The pillars loomed above the growing number of people heading over to watch the proceedings. Cutting imposing figures in their heavy white wool robes and matching capes, the Druids streamed into the garden, sprigs of mistletoe pinned to their chests. Spectators pooled outside the garden, settling in on lawn chairs and blankets and camping stools to enjoy the bonfire and watch the festivities.

Originally, the ceremony had been a simple affair. Oisin and the members of his grove had petitioned the town council to allow them to build their bonfire on the common, in concert with the community's Solstice Soirée.

Over the years, the burning of the Yule logs and the Druids' ceremonial ritual to welcome back the light on the longest night of the year grew very popular with tourists and locals alike. So much so that the lighting of the bonfire became an annual event—and one of the biggest draws of the Solstice Soirée.

As people swarmed the perimeter of the garden, hoping for a better view of the proceedings, Mercy took Tandie by the hand and allowed Elvis to nose his way through the throng. His fierce focus radiated a steer-clear energy, and the revelers parted as cleanly as the Red Sea to let them pass.

The shepherd led them to the two-foot-high rock wall that enclosed the labyrinthine space. On top of the low wall stood stanchions with velvet ropes, cordoning off the entire garden. Only the Druids of the Cosmic Ash Grove were allowed inside the actual sacred circle.

Elvis veered to the left and headed toward the entrance, where Mercy's parents Grace and Duncan were standing with Daniel Feinberg and Lillian Jenkins. Feinberg was Vermont's only billionaire, and Mercy's friend and occasional employer. Lillian was her grandmother's best friend and the grande dame of Northshire. When Grace was named director of the Solstice Soirée, she'd made sure that the town's two most influential citizens were on her board.

And here they were, standing right next to the garden entrance, flanked by two uniforms. Harrington wasn't taking any chances, thought Mercy. The police presence was strong here, nearly as strong as it had been at the churchyard.

She and Tandie followed Elvis as he trotted up to her father, who always had a doggy biscuit in his pocket for his favorite Malinois.

"Mercy." Lillian stepped up to give her a hug. "Thank you for coming. Your mother's been telling us all about your finding poor dear Lazlo. Who would do such a thing?"

"I'm so sorry."

Lillian sighed, and squeezed Mercy's shoulders. "You will find whoever killed him, won't you?" She paused. "Quickly?"

"She promised," said her mother, nodding.

"Mercy will do her best, as she always does," said Duncan.

"Thanks, Dad." She could always count on her father to try to help manage her mother's overly high expectations.

"You've had quite the day, Mercy." Feinberg smiled at her, but she could almost see the wheels spinning in his billionaire brain.

She wondered exactly what he was thinking, but before she could ask, Tandie launched into an animated dramatization of the Santa Claus in the woods with the blazing Yule log on his stomach. Mercy had to give the teenager credit; she wasn't even there, but her overactive imagination and her enthusiasm lent her rather lurid telling a certain authenticity.

"Quite the day," repeated Feinberg when Tandie finished her tale with an alliterative "slain Santa shot to smithereens" flourish.

"Poor Lazlo." Lillian looked pale. "What a terrible way to die."

"Isn't it about time for the ceremony to begin?" asked Mercy in a lame attempt to change the subject.

Her mother glanced at her watch. "Soon."

As if the Arch-Druid himself had heard her, the carnyx sounded again. From their vantage point, Mercy had a clear view of the garden. She couldn't help but admire the transformation that had taken place here, thanks to her mother and Feinberg.

At Grace's urging, Feinberg had gifted the town with the Ogham Standing Stones, a spectacular installation by up-and-coming local artist Jalen Campbell. The dirt pit that had once housed the bonfire was now a football field–sized labyrinth of flower beds and gravel paths. At its center was a large granite slab upon which stood Campbell's imposing sculpture.

The modern work was a stylized reimagining of the ancient Ogham stones built by the Druids. It was believed that the stones were mainly meant to identify and mark sacred trees in the forest. They also served as memorials and gravestones.

Carved into the edges of these ancient stones were a series of notches, forming Ogham letters from the Celtic Tree Alphabet used by the secretive Druids. The notches were placed along the natural "stem line" of the stone, like twigs growing from the trunk of a tree. You read them from the bottom of the left-hand edge of the stone and up and around and down the right-hand edge of the stone.

Campbell had cut similar grooves along the two standing stones of his sculpture. On the taller granite pillar, he spelled out "The Druids helped" in the Celtic Tree Alphabet. Those very words had been found on an ancient standing stone that had survived for centuries—a long-lost legacy of Celtic Europe—and the sculptor had repeated it here.

The notches on the other stone marked the celebration of the winter solstice itself. On this pillar, Campbell had cut the Ogham letter T—for *Teine,* meaning holly—and the Ogham letter D—for *Dair,* meaning oak. A not-so-subtle reference to the never-ending battle between the Holly King and the Oak King.

But to Mercy, the most beautiful carvings on Campbell's stones were not the Ogham letters, but the old Celtic symbols the sculptor had also cut into the rock, inspired curlicues of sun wheels and spirals. The sun wheels honored the sun, especially appropriate for the solstice. The spirals, one of the oldest of the Celtic patterns, represented eternal life, which Mercy figured was appropriate anytime. She loved that the whorls echoed the shape of the labyrinth itself.

"It's so beautiful, Daniel." Every time she saw the sculpture, Mercy was struck by its stark, otherworldly beauty.

"You know everyone hated it at first," he said.

What Daniel said was true. When they'd first unveiled the installation, many locals complained. Too tall, they said, though in truth the stones stood only around two stories high on a village green where many of the hundred-year-old maples reached six or seven stories.

"They hated the Eiffel Tower, too," said Tandie.

Feinberg smiled at the teenager. "That they did."

"That was then," said Lillian, opening her arms wide to encompass the sculpture, the labyrinth, the Druids, and the crowd. "This is now."

Grace raised her chin. "Together Daniel and the Druids transformed this space. Attendance at the winter solstice has doubled because of it. This year we're expecting a record turnout, with people coming from all over the world."

"It was all your idea," said Feinberg. "You found Campbell."

"And you found the money."

Grace and Feinberg exchanged nods. Between the two of them, thought Mercy, any naysayers wouldn't stand a chance.

"And they don't only come during the holidays. Tourists love to walk the labyrinth all year long," said Lillian. "The garden is lovely in the summer, and full of magical plants."

"Magical?" asked Tandie. "Really?"

"So say the Druids." Mercy explained that during the warmer months of the year, the curved beds of the labyrinth that led to the centerpiece of standing stones were bright with flowers and herbs once cultivated by the mystical priests.

"All planted and maintained by members of the Northshire Garden Club and Oisin and his grove members working together," said Grace.

"Which makes them magical, like how?"

"Oh, ye of little faith," interrupted Adah Beecher.

Mercy's neighbor joined their little group. Adah was an herbalist who'd parlayed her extraordinary knowledge of the natural world into a very profitable line of organic beauty products. She also had a remarkable gift for knowing what you were thinking; some people called her a witch, but Mercy just called her wise.

Even in the midst of this throng of costumed revelers, the woman stood out. She wore a sweeping black velvet cape embroidered with suns and spirals in golden thread over a matching midi velvet skirt and a quilted velvet jacket with knee-high, black suede snow boots with buckles. Under the velvet hood, her thick, gray-streaked brown hair was braided and curled around her ears Princess Leia style. For a woman usually found in peasant dresses and ponchos, this was the equivalent of dressing up for church on Sunday.

"You look lovely," said Mercy.

Adah smiled in acknowledgment of the compliment, but she addressed Tandie. "The flowers and herbs we choose for the solstice garden are those deemed sacred by the Druidic tradition."

"Like what?"

She ticked them off on her black fingerless gloves. "Chamomile for calm and starflower for courage, primrose for love and heather for luck, lady's mantle for magic and mint for clarity, meadowsweet for transition and fern for fertility, vervain and yarrow for divination."

"Divination," said Tandie. "You mean, like, fortune-telling."

"We don't call it that. But you may if you like." Adah smiled at them all. "Perfect evening for a bonfire." She looked up and they all followed suit.

Mercy, too. It had stopped snowing; the thick clouds obscuring the sky had finally scudded off.

Nightfall was quickly approaching, and as Adah said, it promised to be a clear and lovely night.

"That it is," said Feinberg.

"At least the weather is cooperating," said Grace.

Adah reached over and patted her hand. "I know it's been a difficult day, but everything will be fine come the New Year. Mercy and Troy and their clever canine partners will see to that."

"The New Year?" Grace raised her perfectly shaped eyebrows. Mercy knew her mother always found Adah's vague pronouncements confounding at best and irritating at worst. Grace looked at her daughter. "We don't have that long. You'll have to do better than that."

CHAPTER TEN

The blazing fire makes flames and brightness out of everything thrown into it.

—MARCUS AURELIUS

"They're getting started," said Tandie, pointing to the Druids inside the garden, who seemed to be taking their places. "Shouldn't you be in there?"

"I'm ready." Adah pulled out a white unlit taper in an old iron candlestick holder from under her voluminous cape. She held it up by the little handle at the side of the plate base.

Tandie laughed. "What kind of bonfire is that?"

"You'll see." Adah smiled.

She had the mysterious smile of the Mona Lisa, thought Mercy, if the Mona Lisa had been a twenty-first-century shaman.

"Blessed Yule!" Adah called to them all as she swept past the two uniforms guarding the entrance to the labyrinth.

"I don't get it," said the teenager.

"It's all part of the ritual lighting of the bonfire," said Mercy. "You see all the logs around the sculpture, right?" She tipped her head toward the Ogham Standing Stones.

Tandie nodded. "I see."

Placed around the sculpture like so many spokes around the fulcrum of a wheel were the longest logs, massive lengths of fissure-barked oak, The spaces between these logs were filled with thinner, shorter lengths of white paper birch, as well as smooth logs of black cherry, with its signature dark potato-chip bark. The effect was a striking pattern of alternating light and dark streaks of wood that resembled rays radiating from a sculpted sun.

"The different woods represent different Yule log traditions," said Mercy. "The English Druids use oak, the Scottish Druids prefer birch, and the French Druids like cherry, with a little wine sprinkled on top for good measure."

"Leave it to the French," said Duncan, with a nod to his wife. Grace came from a long line of Fleury women from the south of France who knew a good wine when they sipped it.

"Wine is bottled poetry," said Grace, quoting Robert Louis Stevenson with the assurance of a sommelier. If her mother ever gave up her beloved law, she could open a winery, thought Mercy. Wouldn't that be *merveilleux*.

Tandie studied the pattern of the logs around the sculpture. "Looks like the sun. I guess it's supposed to, right?"

"Very good," said Mercy. "Go on."

Tandie was a very intelligent girl whose knowledge of languages was surprisingly good for a teenager who'd been kicked out of more than one prep school.

"I'm not a trick dog." Tandie looked down at Elvis. "No offense."

Grace smiled. "I'm sure you can give Elvis a run for his money."

Tandie looked to Mercy for assistance, but she just shrugged. There was no point in defying Grace when the stakes were so low.

"You may as well tell us, show off a little," said Duncan cheerfully. When it came to Grace, if anyone knew that a small surrender could mean a big win later, it was Mercy's father.

The teenager grinned at that. "Solstice, from the Latin *solstitium*. Breaking it down, that's *sol,* meaning sun, and *sesterre,* meaning to stand still."

"Very good," said Mercy. "As you say, solstice literally means standing still. Many ancient peoples all around the world worried every winter as the days grew shorter and the nights grew longer that the sun had stopped moving, that it was, in effect, standing still. The whole point of celebrating the solstice was to get the sun moving again. Once the sun got moving, the days would grow longer again. And spring would come."

"Different cultures honor the solstice in different ways," added her father. "But most involve some version of celebrating the longest night with dancing, feasting, gift giving, and fire. The indigenous Hopi people call their solstice *Soyal,* performing ritual dances, telling stories and singing songs using prayer sticks and kachina dolls. The Chinese Dōngzhì Festival is a tribute to light and dark, yin and yang, the balance of nature. Families get together and celebrate the winter harvest and eat traditional foods, like *tangyuan.*" He paused. "A dessert made of rice balls."

"I love rice balls," said Tandie.

"The Chinese Garden is selling them at their booth over by the town hall," said Feinberg. "Quite good."

"Dad, how do you know all this?" Mercy laughed.

Her father shrugged. "Your mother is the director of the Solstice Soirée. I figured I'd better study up on the subject."

This was so like her father, to support her mother in every way possible. Mercy had once believed that he went overboard in that regard, to the point of negating himself, but now she understood that he was just trying to be a good husband. Troy did the same thing for her. And she'd wised up enough to see it as a mark of his and her father's strength, rather than weakness.

"Don't forget Newgrange." Grace smiled at her husband. "Newgrange is your father's favorite."

"It's a spectacular place," said Duncan. "One of the oldest buildings in the world. Older than Stonehenge and the Pyramids. Grace and I visited the site years ago."

"What's it like?" asked Tandie.

"It's a very grand passage tomb. Stone Age farmers built it on a rise overlooking the River Boyne in County Meath in Ireland. It's a mound-shaped structure of stone carved with megalithic art and topped by a roof of grass. Inside is a passage and small chambers. It was designed to align with the rising of the sun on the winter solstice."

"You mean like a sun dial?" asked Tandie.

"Far more dramatic. Once a year around the winter solstice, as the sun rises a shaft of light shines through an opening above the entrance, illuminating the inner chamber with a flood of sunlight.

"Like in *Raiders of the Lost Ark*. When Harrison Ford holds up the staff in that pyramid and the sun shines through and lights up the map and shows where the treasure is."

"Exactly." Duncan gave her an approving look. Teenagers loved her father, perhaps because he treated them as grown-ups. He treated everyone, regardless of age, like an adult. It made you want to act like one.

"My dad's favorite movie," explained Tandie. "We've watched it, like, a gazillion times."

"I know the feeling," said Mercy, grinning at her own father.

"You saw that happen at Newgrange?" asked Tandie.

"No, it only happens at the winter solstice. We were there in the spring." Duncan glanced at Feinberg. "But I suspect our friend here has seen it."

"Really?" Tandie stared at Feinberg.

"Yes. I was invited as a thank-you for my work on behalf of World Heritage Sites," admitted the billionaire, with a little wave of his hand to indicate that what he'd done didn't amount to much. Mercy knew better.

"What was it like?" asked Tandie.

"It was, it was . . ." In a rare moment of hesitation, the typically self-assured billionaire flushed. "Hard to say, really. Transformative, really. One of the most amazing things I've even seen."

"And it's fair to say that Daniel has seen everything," said Grace.

"Cool," said Tandie.

"It was very cool." Feinberg gazed over at the Ogham Standing Stones in the solstice garden. "You know, a circle of large standing stones surrounds the passage tomb at the Newgrange. I suppose that's why I was driven to donate this sculpture for our village green."

"Thanks to Daniel, we've got a little bit of that Newgrange magic right here in Northshire," said Mercy, although she couldn't help but think of another set of stones, the sloppy slabs of granite at the crime scene. Which may or may not be a stone chamber built by Celtic Druids long, long ago.

"Indeed we do." Adah was back, and she carried a woven basket full of mistletoe. "If you don't believe, give it a try. Once we have completed our rituals inside the circle and the bonfire has been lit, we'll open the garden to everyone here. You can make an offering and toss it onto the bonfire."

"Like what?"

Adah handed Tandie a sprig of mistletoe from her basket. "Some people toss sprigs of mistletoe onto the fire. To attract love and make babies."

"Like kissing under the mistletoe," said Mercy.

"No thanks," said Tandie.

"You're much too young for babies," agreed Adah. "But surely a pretty girl like you has admirers."

"No." Tandie blushed.

"You will soon enough."

"Don't encourage her, Adah." Grace pursed her lips.

Adah nodded, her black velvet hood falling over her forehead. "Or you can burn a bough of holly and an oak branch, to honor the past and welcome the future. That's what our Druids here will do. You can use evergreen branches, too. Or an entire Yule log."

"I heard that some people write down whatever is holding them back on a piece of paper and throw the note onto the fire to burn," said Mercy, "allowing them to let go and move forward."

"It works." Adah laughed. "I know one unhappy divorced woman who burned her wedding dress on her Yule log. She had a new husband by the spring equinox. And a lot of smoke stains on the ceiling in her living room."

"Intense," said Tandie.

She leaned toward the teenager. "We don't allow the burning of clothing here. But you can always burn a picture of you and your ex instead."

"I'm good—no exes here," said Tandie. "But maybe my dad should do that. Help him get over my mom."

Grace coughed. "Speaking of moving on. Why not make a wish for the New Year?"

"One evergreen bough for every wish," added Adah. "Keep your Yule log burning, and you can make a new wish every night until New Year's."

"Twelve wishes coming true," said Tandie, grinning. "I like the sound of that."

"May your wishes all come true. . . ." Adah passed each of them a sprig of mistletoe. "But be careful what you wish for."

CHAPTER ELEVEN

*There are two ways of spreading light: to be the candle
or the mirror that reflects it.*

—EDITH WHARTON

THE CARNYX WAILED AGAIN, EVEN MORE LOUDLY THIS TIME. Mercy could see the Druid playing the ancient horn now, standing next to a large boulder near the outermost ring of the labyrinth. The burly man held up the long skinny tube of the instrument with thick arms. The bronze bore rose a dozen feet into the air, topped by the open-mouthed dragon that served as its bell.

"It's starting," said Grace.

Oisin the Arch-Druid swept up onto the boulder, his long, heavy, white wool robe trailing behind him. The thick cuffs and hood of his robe were trimmed in gold fabric and embroidered with ancient Celtic symbols—triskeles and spirals and shields—much like Adah's garments. He wore a long similarly ornamented stole around his neck, altogether a far cry from the plain white tunic and gray cloak Mercy had always seen him wear before. These must be his special occasion vestments, she thought.

"Who's that?" asked Tandie.

"That's Oisin, Arch-Druid of the Cosmic Ash Grove, Order of the Bards, Ovates, and Druids."

Oisin was very tall and thin, with a slight stoop that did not at all diminish his stature. His silver-white hair fell past his shoulders, in partnership with his long, white beard. He grasped a carved maple staff in his right hand. An impressive presence overall, any night of the year.

"Epic," said Tandie. "Like Santa Claus and Merlin and Dumbledore all rolled into one."

Mercy laughed. At a glance some might mistake him in his flowing robe and beard for Saint Nicholas, but to her, Oisin always looked every inch the pagan priest, no matter where he was or what he was doing or what he was wearing.

He raised his staff, and his fellow Druids fell silent. The crowd outside the garden also quieted. There was a moment of hushed anticipation, broken only by the booming baritone of Oisin himself. "Hail and welcome."

Behind the Arch-Druid, the burly Druid blew the carnyx again. He was now flanked by two bagpipers, who played along in a mournful counterpoint to the primeval howling of the ancient horn. A fiddler and a Celtic harpist stepped up to join them, forming a little band of sorts. The Druids' eerie music took a more melodic turn. It reminded Mercy of some of the more haunting Celtic ballads she'd heard in pubs in Boston.

"Here we go," said Grace.

The remaining Druids—around fifty or so, by Mercy's count—removed small crowns of antlers from under their cloaks and placed them on their heads. In the growing gloom of dusk, the antlered Druids looked like stags moving in and out of the mist of the deep forest.

They moved to the edge of the Yule logs, creating a circle within a circle within a circle. Now Mercy could see the straps that they wore over their robes to secure their frame drums to their sides. Steadying the goatskin drums with one hand, they held their double-headed tippers in the other.

"It's a *bodhrán*," Mercy whispered to Tandie before she could ask. "The native drum of the ancient Celts. And traditional Irish music."

"And Druids," Tandie whispered back as the members of the Cosmic Ash Grove began to drum, adding a pulsating beat to the music of the solstice. "I like their antlers."

The Arch-Druid tapped his staff on the rock in time to the music. The drumming continued, and one by one the other instruments dropped out of the performance, until only the drums beat on in a firework of percussion—faster and faster and faster—as the last of the sun's rays disappeared below the horizon.

As the sky darkened around them, torches illuminated the four corners of the garden, casting shadows on the Druids and the Ogham Standing Stones. The drumming slowed, and again one by one, the drummers stopped beating their *bodhráns*. Now the sun had truly set, and it was time for the ceremony to begin.

Oisin began to speak again, his rich and sonorous voice echoing across the solstice garden and beyond to the town common. He called upon the four elements of nature. *Earth. Air. Water.* And finally, *Fire.*

The Druids beat their drums again, punctuating the pagan priest's words.

Next, Oisin addressed the four directions. North. South. East. And, finally, West. Where the sun had gone. "Hail the darkness," he intoned. "Life and light will be reborn."

"Life and light will be reborn," chanted the Druids.

"Life and light will be reborn," echoed the crowd. The people outside the garden were enjoying themselves, drinking the mead sold at the Druid Spirits booth and drumming and chanting along with the true celebrants. Many wore plastic crowns with antlers.

One of the Druids handed Oisin a candlestick much like the one Adah had shown them earlier. Mercy recognized Liath the Bard, one of the Arch-Druid's aides. The fiddler played a short solo, a lovely, melancholy tune of such longing that it nearly brought Mercy to tears.

As the last poignant chord faded, Oisin began to speak again, this time in a voice so commanding that the sun itself could surely not ignore him. As he delivered with compelling intensity each line of his solstice prayer, his fellow Druids repeated each line. And as they recited, the rest of the people on the common joined in, and every stanza of the pagan poem rang across the village green in a resounding chorus.

> *Hail to all who came before*
> *Hail to all who follow,*
> *The wheel of life and death spins on*
> *And day succumbs to shadow.*
> *While the Sun stands still*
> *The sacred fire burns until*
> *The Oak King smites the Holly King,*
> *And the Sun returns; and with it, Spring.*
> *Now we endure the longest night*
> *And await the coming of the light.*

For come the dawning of the morn
Life and light will be reborn.

At the end of the recitation, the Arch-Druid raised his staff. "Let the winter solstice begin!"

All together the torches went out, and the solstice garden was plunged into darkness. All together the lights on the common went out, and the village green was plunged into darkness. A reverent hush descended on the crowd, perfectly still in their silence.

Mercy looked up. Above them all, the waxing crescent moon shimmered with earthshine and the stars glimmered in the darkening sky. Tandie reached for her hand. Mercy squeezed the teenager's slim fingers. Elvis curled up at her feet, unimpressed by the spectacle.

And they waited. For a long moment, Northshire held its breath, and time seemed to stand still.

Like the sun.

With a roar of reverberation, the beating of the drums began again, piercing the night. A bright light appeared, a flame of hope in the darkness. It was the candle, now burning, that Oisin the Arch-Druid held in his hand.

As the drums beat on, the Druids lined up. In single file, one by one they approached Oisin. Each holding a candlestick, each lighting its taper from the candle in the priest's hand, each returning to their place along the radius of the Yule logs. Candle after candle, light after light, until every Druid held a burning candle. A circle of light.

Out in the crowd beyond the garden, people flicked on their lighters or their phone lights in solidarity. The common was now glowing with candlelight, twinkling in the dark like fireflies on a summer's night.

"It's beautiful," whispered Tandie, flicking on her own phone light.

"Yes, it is." Mercy flicked her phone light on, too. She looked from her mother and her father to Feinberg and Lillian Jenkins, their faces shining in the glow of natural and artificial candlelight.

"Happy Solstice," said Feinberg.

"Everyone's a pagan tonight," said Mercy.

The carnyx sounded again. They all watched as Oisin lit a dry stick of oak kindling with his lighted taper and tossed it onto the logs. Liath the Bard followed suit, tossing a flaming bit of birch bark onto the logs. Druid by Druid, each added their lit branches to the logs.

Little fires burning all around the circle. Burning most brightly at first out by the edges, where the Druids stood and played the siren songs of the solstice with their drums and bagpipes and fiddle and harp and the surreal call of the carnyx.

Slowly the fire spread along the logs, flames streaming toward the center of the garden, where the Ogham Standing Stones loomed. The lighting of the bonfire had begun.

Outside the sacred circle, people started clapping and whooping and shouting, "Happy Solstice! Happy Solstice! Happy Solstice!"

Elvis jumped upright. He pulled at his lead, nearly yanking Mercy off her feet. "Whoa, boy."

"What's wrong with him?" asked Grace.

"Maybe it's the crowds," said Duncan. "Easy, boy."

"Calm yourself," Mercy ordered the shepherd.

The dog sank down on his haunches briefly, then leapt up again. Beseeching Mercy with his eyes. *Wailing. Whining. Wheedling.*

"Something's wrong." Mercy reached down to let him off leash. "Go."

And Elvis drilled through the crowd like a heat-seeking missile.

Looking for the target only he could see. Or smell.

Mercy hustled after Elvis. The shepherd disappeared from view, but she could hear people yelling at him as he whipped around lawn chairs and camping stools and blankets, startling solstice revelers.

"It's a wild dog," cried someone who obviously did not know a working dog when they saw one.

Mercy cursed under her breath. She didn't want Elvis getting hurt by some moronic partier drunk on mead and a false sense of danger. "Elvis!"

"Elvis!" echoed Tandie.

The teenager was right behind her, never one to miss a call to adventure, however misguided. There was no stopping her, and Mercy had stopped trying. Tandie reminded her of herself at that rebellious age, itching for new and novel experiences, the more unconventional and perilous, the better.

Which was probably why Tandie kept getting kicked out of all those boarding schools—and why she liked living with Mercy's family. For her part, Mercy hoped that having Tandie around would help prepare her for the challenges of raising her own daughter.

She heard Elvis yelp, a fierce summons that rose above the noise of the crowd. Somewhere north of the solstice garden. She hurried on, finally spotting him about twenty yards away at the base of Northshire's Civil War monument. His triangular ears lay back flat against his sleek skull and his hackles were standing up at attention. Not a good sign.

The "Single Soldier" monument was typical of those found on village greens all over New England. Cast in bronze, the Union infantryman stood still and silent in his cape and kepi, cartridge box and bayonet slung on his belt, the butt of his rifle on the ground before him, his hands folded around the barrel.

She raced toward the Single Soldier, veering around what appeared to be a group of singers. They were dressed in the black cassocks and white surplices of a church choir. The backs of the gowns were emblazoned with white satin lettering that read THE TEMPLE OF THE END OF DAYS.

They were surrounded by people in everyday clothes carrying signs that read "Heathens Go to Hell" and "Paganism Is Evil." A pastor in a black pulpit gown with a black velvet panel held a bullhorn to his mouth and shouted something about the devil in a thick Midwestern twang. The choir belted out the opening verses of "What a Friend We Have in Jesus."

The choir's rather ragged performance was somehow amplified by a speaker Mercy could not locate. She scanned the area, but didn't see anything. Their voices swelled, and their hymn boomed out over the common in a seeming attempt to drown out the Druids and their ceremonial music. The age-old battle reborn between two groups of conflicting believers, note by note, in a musical face-off. Like "Dueling Banjos," with God.

What next? thought Mercy.

And where was Elvis?

CHAPTER TWELVE

There is no fyre without smoke.

—JOHN HEYWOOD

Orlov watched Reverend Fitz through his binoculars. They'd arranged to meet after this little protest of his, but the so-called minister couldn't stop preaching long enough to take care of business. Fitz kept on wailing about the wages of sin while his choir sang backup and Orlov smoked his cigarettes and thought of interesting ways to kill this wannabe Rasputin.

All religion was ridiculous, but at least in Russia religion was dignified. Incense and icons and chanting, the way worship should be. Not all this bleating with a bullhorn about the devil.

Orlov was getting tired of waiting for Fitz. He wanted to go home. If he left now, he could make it back to Moscow by Christmas. His mother would like that. He'd done his job, but others had not. There was still the matter of the missing money and the missing evidence. Not his problem before, but his problem now.

Reverend Fitz was supposed to help resolve these issues, but so far, the man had been completely useless. Whether out of stupidity or duplicity, Orlov was not sure. But he was duty-bound to find out.

This self-proclaimed man of God couldn't even show up on time for a meeting. More interested in saving souls than doing business. As if Fitz had that power. His only power came from his father. Stupid little rich boy.

Blyat. That dog again.

Orlov spotted the Malinois, whose name he'd learned was Elvis. Americans and their obsession with rock and roll. Who names a dog after a singer? Russian dogs have strong warrior names. Alexander (the liberator). Peter (the great). Ivan (the terrible).

Still, this rock-and-roll dog was fast. The shepherd bounded toward the soldier statue. Mercy Carr raced after him. Woman and dog headed right for him.

Forget Fitz, Orlov thought. Time to go. He stamped the cig butts into the snow. As he headed back to the black SUV, he considered Mercy and Elvis. They were far smarter than that moron Fitz. And they were always where they shouldn't be.

Maybe they were the ones to watch.

MERCY HAD TO ADMIT that the noise was deafening. No wonder Elvis had taken off. He might simply be reacting to the cacophony, his ears far more sensitive to sound than hers. Maybe he was just finding a place to hide, as he did when he first came home from his service as a bomb-sniffing dog and his PTSD kicked in. It had been a long time since he'd reacted this way, but Mercy knew all too well that the scars of war stayed with you. Even when you thought you'd put those experiences behind you forever, they could return with a vengeance, sometimes when you least expected it.

Amidst the drumming of the Druids and caroling of the choir and the clapping and whooping and shouting of the spectators came a cracking rattle. A series of pops pierced the air. Mercy listened hard, trying to isolate and identify the sound in all the noise around her.

It could have been the backfire of a car rambling down a side street by the common. Or fireworks set off by a tourist unfamiliar with Northshire's bylaws, which plainly prohibited pyrotechnics on the common during the Solstice Soirée, and every other time of the year.

But Mercy had a terrible feeling that the sound was a gunshot, although the rhythm and the tone didn't quite match with any weapon she knew. And it didn't ring any bells from her combat duty, either. But it made her nervous all the same.

Few people seemed to notice. And if they did, they ignored it. The Druids went on drumming and the choir went on caroling and the pastor went on preaching and everybody else went on celebrating the lighting of the bonfire.

"Did you hear that?" Tandie yelled, jogging up beside her. "I think it was firecrackers. Do you think it was firecrackers?"

"I don't know. But get down." She pointed to a cooler on the edge of a blanket where a young man and woman were making out, oblivious to the goings-on around them. "Stay there until I get back."

"But—"

"Stay there," Mercy ordered the teenager in her MP *You're under arrest* voice. She might no longer be a military policewoman, but she could still wield the authority of one when it suited her purpose. And her purpose now was to keep the girl safe until she figured out what the hell was going on. Tandie did as she was told, squatting down behind the ice chest.

Mercy closed the gap between her and Elvis and came upon the Civil War memorial, which sat in the shadow of a small crescent of tall juniper trees.

Elvis had moved behind the broad-based monument; she could see his spiked tail and hear his low growl. She stepped carefully around the side of the bronze soldier just in time to see a man dressed like one of the Druids slip between the trees and out of sight.

The shepherd blazed after him. She called for Elvis to come back, but he ignored her. She followed him, squeezing through the thickly planted junipers. On the other side she found herself at the edge of the common, on the sidewalk that ran along Elm Street. Elvis stood in the open space between two parked cars, barking at a dark SUV tearing down the street, slipping in the freshly fallen snow. The vehicle swung wildly as it careened around the corner onto Main Street and disappeared from view.

"Elvis, come."

The shepherd obeyed, reluctantly returning to her side.

"Whoever he is, he's long gone." She patted the dog's sleek head. "What did he do, boy, to get you so riled up?" She clipped the leash on him again and walked him back to the stone monument. There weren't as many lights illuminating this out-of-the-way niche of the common, so she pulled out her phone and switched on the light.

She squatted down, examining the ground around the bronze soldier, which was a muddle of tracks, although she could see a set of Elvis's paw prints in the snow, as well as impressions left by her own winter boots. There were a couple of larger prints as well, typical of men's Timberland boots. Every other guy in Vermont wore boots like this.

Elvis watched her, tipping his head as if to say, "You're wasting your time."

"Nothing here, boy." Mercy scrambled to her feet. "If you've got something to show me, let's see it. We've got to get back to the bonfire."

The shepherd trotted to the far side of the monument and scratched at something in the snow with his claws.

"What is it?" She knelt down, shining her cell light on the churned-up snow. There she spotted what looked like a couple of cigarette butts. Sort of.

As she reached out with her gloved fingers, she heard the crunch of footsteps in the snow. She looked up to find Officer Josh Becker standing over her. Josh was Mercy's friend and Alma Goodlove's partner.

He scratched Elvis's head. "Mercy."

"Josh! Aren't you supposed to be back in the churchyard keeping the public out of the woods?"

"They've mostly moved on to the bonfire. Except for the press, but that's Detective Harrington's problem now." He waved a uniformed arm at the monument. "What are you doing over here?"

"I'm not sure. I just followed Elvis."

Josh smiled. "When I saw Elvis bolt into the crowd and you on his tail, I figured I'd better see what you were up to. Find anything?"

"There was a guy here dressed like a Druid, but he took off in a dark SUV. And no, I didn't get the license plate number." Mercy stood up, holding one of the sort-of cigarette butts in her open palm. The cig did not have a true filter, but rather a cardboard tube which had held the tobacco. "But I think he left this behind."

"What is it?" Josh peered down at the object in her hand.

"I think it's a butt from a *Belomorkanal* cigarette. Russian soldiers smoke this brand. Maybe he was Russian."

"You could be right," said Josh. "But not necessarily. Some weed smokers use them, too. They empty the cigarettes and fill the tubes with tobacco and marijuana. It's like a built-in roach."

"I thought they all used cones now."

"Not everybody."

Mercy shrugged. "There are a few of these down there in the snow. He must have been here awhile. Waiting."

"Waiting for what?"

"I don't know. All I know is that there was something about him that Elvis didn't like very much."

"Well, if you don't like him, boy, I don't like him." Josh smiled at Elvis, and the shepherd thumped his tail in response.

"That's my rule, and it hasn't failed me yet," said Mercy. She watched as the officer pulled a small bag from his pocket. Together he and Mercy collected the remainder of the butts and deposited them into the bag.

"I'll keep my eye out for men with smokes like these," said Josh, pocketing the bag. "You never know."

"So will we." Mercy paused and turned her gaze back toward the Ogham Standing Stones. No one seemed to notice them here at the monument. The attention of the crowd appeared to remain on the bonfire. The choir had moved closer to the solstice garden, and people were milling around them now. Something more was going on, but Mercy couldn't tell what from where she was. "If we're done here, I really need to get back to my family and the bonfire."

"You've had a long day." Becker frowned. "First, the victim in the woods and now whatever this is."

"If it is anything."

"You doubt your dog?" Becker raised an eyebrow.

"No, but I don't know exactly why Elvis alerted to this guy. I thought it was those noises at first." She looked at Becker. "The ones that sounded like gunshots, but weren't."

"Oh, that." He shook his head. "Kids with firecrackers over by the Fountain of the Muses. We disarmed them and wrote them tickets. Their parents will not be pleased when they pay those fines."

"Elvis does hate firecrackers."

"But that doesn't explain why he went for the Druid in the SUV."

"No, it doesn't." Mercy thought about it. "Maybe it was just these cigarettes—he hates cigarette smoke."

"Why is that?"

"I think it reminds him of his military service."

"Soldiers smoke."

"Yep." Mercy knew that more people smoked in the military than in the civilian world. And even those who managed to avoid the habit at home were apt to start smoking once they were deployed overseas. She'd known too many who'd survived their deployments only to succumb to cancer and worse once they returned home.

"Never tempted myself," said Josh.

"Me either." She was glad she'd avoided the temptation. For her sake and for Felicity's sake. And Elvis's. Still, she wasn't convinced that it was the cigarettes that set off the shepherd's alarms, and she told Josh as much. "I'm guessing Elvis took off to get away from all the noise on the common and then came upon this Druid dude and alerted to something. Maybe the cigarettes, but more likely something on his person."

"Understood." Becker scratched the sweet spot between the shepherd's ears. "I thought you knew everything this boy was thinking. Like a dog whisperer."

"Dogs are just like people. You only know for sure what they let you know."

"And the rest is speculation," said Becker, with a final pat on the shepherd's head.

"Yes." Mercy smiled. "Just like people."

CHAPTER THIRTEEN

*The bigger you build the bonfire,
the more darkness is revealed.*

—TERENCE McKENNA

As Mercy made her way back across the common with Elvis, she noticed local law enforcement ushering the pastor and his choir along with the protesters away from the event. As they shuffled along arm in arm, the choir members continued to sing, belting out "We Shall Overcome" without benefit of a speaker.

They were all going peacefully with the police officers, for the most part. The pastor kept his bullhorn, however, and he pontificated on the dangers of paganism and Satan, punctuating his sermon with shouts of "Resist the devil, and he will flee from you!"

The pastor droned on, but from what Mercy could tell, no one apart from his own flock was paying him any attention. Everyone else was too focused on merrymaking, enjoying the bonfire at the height of its blaze. Finally, one of the uniforms relieved the clergyman of his bullhorn, and he was reduced to leading his choir in a rousing rendition of "The Devil Is a Liar."

As they approached the solstice garden, the shepherd suddenly pulled on the leash and veered off toward a couple on a blanket deep in lust with one another.

Mercy spotted the cooler and remembered Tandie. "Good boy, Elvis."

The teenager jumped up from behind the ice chest to intercept them.

"You were gone so long. I thought you forgot about me."

"We could never forget about you." She slipped the dog a peanut butter treat from her pocket.

Tandie hooked her arm in Mercy's. "Is everything all right?"

"Fine."

"Everyone's lining up to make their wishes. Still got your mistletoe?" Tandie dangled her sprig in front of her nose.

"I don't need to make any wishes. All my wishes have already come true." Which was actually the truth.

"Lucky you," said Tandie.

"Lucky me," agreed Mercy, thinking of her husband, her child, her family and friends, Grackle Tree Farm.

"Well, I could use some of that magic or luck or whatever you want to call it."

Mercy's mother and father were still there near the entrance of the solstice garden, watching the bonfire with Feinberg and Lillian. To Mercy's surprise, Harrington was now part of the little group. She thought the detective would still be in front of the cameras, dismissing sensational rumors about the Yuletide Killer. Maybe even he'd had enough of the so-called limelight during this eventful Solstice Soirée. Enough of the relentless Cat Torano and her colleagues. For now, he was safe, but Mercy would bet money neither he nor she and Elvis had seen the last of Cat.

She turned her attention back to the bonfire. The entire radius of logs surrounding the sculpture was now ablaze. The Ogham Standing Stones towered over the conflagration, anchoring the sea of fire. Oisin and his grove were unpinning the mistletoe sprigs from their robes and tossing them into the bonfire.

A large piling of evergreen and holly boughs covered the large boulder where the Arch-Druid had led the ritual, and the Druids were also tossing those into the fire. With the Temple of the End of Days shuttled off the common, the night took on a sacred silence, the only sounds being the crackle of the fire and the hooting of the owls and the murmuring of an admiring audience.

"Good job getting rid of those religious fanatics, Detective. We couldn't let them ruin tonight," said Lillian. "The way they've tried to ruin everything else."

"What do you mean?" asked Tandie.

Lillian crossed her arms. "Those people are determined to destroy this town. More than a hundred of them showed up at our town meeting and tried to cut our education budget to the bone."

"They tried to eliminate the library altogether," said Grace.

"I thought Vermonters loved their libraries." Mercy had missed most of the recent local dramas and traumas, cocooned at home as she'd been so happily and obliviously since the baby was born.

"They're *not* Vermonters," said Lillian. "They're from the Midwest, mostly. An Ohio billionaire named Ephraim Frost helped the church—and I use that word loosely—buy the land and move their followers here to set up their community. That so-called spiritual leader you see leading the group is his son Fitzpatrick. They call him Reverend Fitz."

Mercy turned to Feinberg. "Do you know the father?"

"The Soybean King." Feinberg folded his gloved hands at his trim waist. "I don't know him personally. We travel in different circles."

"But . . ." said Mercy, sensing that he was holding back.

Feinberg shrugged. "He's really into fire and brimstone. Just like his son."

"He's got the money and he's spending it," said Harrington. "We're following the group's activities very closely."

A crescendo of drums announced the last of the Druids' offerings for the bonfire. All of the evergreen and holly boughs that had blanketed the large boulder were burning bright now, sweetening the air with the scent of pine and smoke.

The members of the grove once more took up their places around edge of the Ogham Standing Stones circle. Oisin mounted the large boulder, and raised his staff. The carnyx sounded again, and the Arch-Druid's sonorous voice rang out.

"Hail the Holly King, Father of Winter. We thank you for the stillness of winter, the sleep of the night, and the silence of the darkness. We wish you farewell until the wheel of the year turns anew. Farewell to the Holly King." He lowered his staff.

"Farewell to the Holly King," chanted the Druids.

Again, Oisin lifted his staff. Again, the carnyx sounded. Again, Oisin's sonorous voice rang out. "Hail the Oak King, Father of Summer. We thank you for the return of the sun, the rebirth of spring, and the ripening of summer. We welcome you back after the long nights of winter and look forward to the long days to come. Welcome to the Oak King." He lowered his staff.

"Welcome to the Oak King," chanted the Druids.

"We call upon the citizens and friends of Northshire to celebrate the winter solstice with us. On this night of greatest darkness, we usher in the days of greatest light. We invite you to cast your fears and obstacles into the dying darkness, and name your hopes and dreams as they burn."

The drums began again and the Druids retreated into the shadows. Spectators from all over the common began heading toward the solstice garden, armed with Yule logs, branches of evergreen and boughs of holly, and papers on which they'd written their biggest regrets of the past and their dearest wishes for the future.

"Time to make that wish, Tandie." Mercy gave the teenager a gentle push. "Go on, you can be first in line."

Tandie reached for Mercy's hand. "You come, too."

"Sure."

"Really?" Her mother gave her an amused look.

"Really," she told her mother with a wink.

Grace smiled and mouthed a *thank you*.

Her mother always knew when her daughter was on a snoop, and for once, she approved. Mercy smiled back, and headed into the labyrinth to find Oisin, the Arch-Druid. She hoped he was in the mood to talk.

CHAPTER FOURTEEN

The pieces were placed in a fire under the copper, and they quickly blazed up brightly, while the tree sighed so deeply that each sigh was like a pistol-shot. . . . But at each "pop," which was a deep sigh, the tree was thinking of a summer day in the forest; and of Christmas evening, and of "Humpty Dumpty," the only story it had ever heard or knew how to relate, till at last it was consumed.

—HANS CHRISTIAN ANDERSEN

"Go ahead," Mercy told Tandie. She handed her the sprig of mistletoe that Adah had given her. "Now you can make two wishes."

"Are you sure?" asked the teenager as if Mercy had given up the last seat on a lifeboat lost at sea.

"Yes." She waved her on with a smile.

"Thank you," whispered Tandie as she stepped up to Liath the Bard, who was guiding the solstice revelers to the bonfire.

"Have fun."

Mercy was now free to seek out Oisin. The Arch-Druid stood at the far end of the labyrinth behind the Ogham Standing Stones, next to several stacks of two-foot Yule logs, the wood the Druids would use to keep the bonfire burning through the night.

"Mercy," said Oisin. "Blessed solstice."

"Blessed solstice." Mercy shook the man's hand.

He squeezed her hand gently. "I suppose you're not here to make a wish."

"No."

"I heard about the incident in the woods."

"You mean the murder of our mayor."

"Terrible business." He leaned toward her, eyes gleaming in the reflection of the bonfire. "You know we had nothing to do with that."

"I know that. But not everyone is going to see it that way. Lazlo Ford was dressed as Santa Claus, and the body was topped with a Yule log."

"A desecration." The Arch-Druid held out his carved maple staff, bending it toward the people and wielding it back and forth, encompassing the common. "There are Yule logs everywhere this time of year." He pointed his hallowed walking stick at the people lining up to throw their offerings into the bonfire, many of them carrying Yule logs. "And they're for sale everywhere, too."

"Like at Rory Craig's booth."

Oisin tapped the ground lightly with his staff. "Our friend Rory is only one of the many tradesmen selling Yule logs in Northshire."

"That's true." Mercy reminded herself to talk to Rory before she went home tonight. Tomorrow at the latest.

"The fact that there was a Yule log at the crime scene does not necessarily point to us." Oisin fingered his long beard with his free hand. "Why add the log, anyway? Why set a dead man on fire?"

"That's what we're trying to figure out," she said. "I thought you might be able to shed some light on that."

"Is that supposed to be a solstice joke?"

Mercy could feel her face flush. "No pun intended."

"It's not particularly humorous, but it is appropriate." Oisin folded his hands around the knob of his staff. "Only a dark soul could murder a man that way. And on such a night as this."

"Do you know anyone with a grudge against Lazlo Ford?"

Oisin smiled sadly at her. "I know he was a good friend of yours, and your family. I'm so sorry for your loss." He was quiet for a moment, eyes closed, lips moving in silent prayer. He opened his eyes, looked at Mercy, and went on. "I didn't really know him well. What I did know of him was his generous support of the Solstice Soirée. He and his predecessor Jim Drake worked tirelessly with us on the expansion of the festival. Jim with the planning and execution, and Lazlo with the funding. The man was a genius with money."

Mercy gazed at the sculpture, which appeared to glow in the warmth of the bonfire. "It's beautiful. You did a good job." She looked back at Oisin. "The body was found in front of a structure that could be one of those old stone chambers."

Oisin raised his thick white eyebrows. "And you think that's another link to our grove."

"I don't know. Maybe. If they really are Druidic in origin." She waved her arm at the Ogham Standing Stones. "Do you think the cairns were built by Celts?"

"I think they're a mystery to be solved." The Arch-Druid smiled at her. "Although many have markings some believe to be Ogham symbols. Did this one have any?"

"Not that I know of."

"Either way, it has nothing to do with us. Jim and Lazlo were good friends to our grove. We will miss them both."

"That's what everyone says. It does seem odd, doesn't it, two mayors dying in rapid succession."

"Unlikely at best." Oisin reached out with his carved maple staff to tap her gently on the chest. "I fear you will have your work cut out for you with this one."

"I'm leaving it to local law enforcement. They've got this."

Adah appeared at the Arch-Druid's side, her black velvet cloak swirling around her. With the flames of the bonfire flickering behind her, she looked as if she'd stepped right out of the fire. The good witch, emerging from a fairy tale. She handed Mercy a twisted bunch of switches tied with a silver ribbon.

"Hawthorn, elder, and birch," she told Mercy. "The guardians of the forest. They will protect you."

"Thank you," said Mercy. "But why do you think I need protection?"

Adah and Oisin exchanged a look.

"Whether you wish it or not," said Oisin, "you will be pulled into the maelstrom. You cannot avoid it."

"But you can survive it." Adah pointed to the bonfire. "Take your bundle and make your wish."

"And what do I wish for?"

"For the light to overcome the darkness," said Adah.

"For protection," added Oisin. "And peace."

The seriousness of their intent moved Mercy. She didn't always understand Adah or Oisin, but she'd learned to heed their advice, however puzzling. She regarded the long switches in her gloved hand. What could it hurt?

She approached the labyrinth of fire. She considered what wish to make, and settled on the one that had marked prayers for millennia. "Peace on earth, goodwill to men," she whispered, and tossed the tied knot of slim bare branches into the flames.

She stood there with Adah and Oisin in silence. They watched as a burst of brightness flared where the bundle hit the burning logs before it was consumed by the conflagration.

The church bells rang out the hour. Time to get home to Felicity. She'd been gone too long already. She'd have to talk to Rory tomorrow, after all.

She said her goodbyes to Adah and Oisin and went back to join Tandie and her family.

"What did you wish for?" asked Tandie.

"Peace on earth. Goodwill to men."

"Not very original."

"No," admitted Mercy.

But Tandie wasn't listening. Her eyes were trained on the Druids. One by one, the white-robed men and women of the grove sank into seated positions around the bonfire. "What are they doing?"

"They're settling in for the long wait until sunrise," said Mercy.

"We're going to be here all night?"

"No, we're going home."

"But it's not over."

"It soon will be, for all intents and purposes," said Grace firmly. "The Solstice Soirée runs until ten o'clock. Then the common will be closed to all but the Druids. They stay while the fire burns. Well, some of them, anyway. Many go home, and regroup here at dawn to watch the sunrise. Only the stalwarts stay the course all night."

"Like Oisin," said Tandie.

"Like Oisin," confirmed Grace.

"We're going home," said Mercy. "Now."

Tandie protested, but her heart wasn't in it. Together Mercy and the teenager and the shepherd walked through the thinning crowds across the common. In the wake of the lighting of the bonfire, many were leaving. Even on holidays, the village of Northshire was not a 24/7 party town. Besides, they'd all be back tomorrow for the Singing Christmas Tree concert.

Peace on earth. Goodwill to men.

If only.

DECEMBER 22

O Christmas Tree, O Christmas tree,
Of all the trees most lovely;
O Christmas Tree, O Christmas tree,
Of all the trees most lovely.
Each year you bring to us delight
With brightly shining Christmas light!
O Christmas Tree, O Christmas tree,
Of all the trees most lovely.

—ERNST ANSCHÜTZ

CHAPTER FIFTEEN

Now, the tree is decorated with bright merriment, and song, and dance, and cheerfulness.

—CHARLES DICKENS, "A CHRISTMAS TREE"

DOGS AND BABIES ARE LIKE FARMERS—THEY'RE UP WITH THE SUN every morning. Felicity typically slept through the night these days, but was always up by dawn. Just like the dogs.

Cats, not so much. As soon as Mercy got out of bed, Muse had jumped up to take her place, curling up on her pillow. The kitty was dozing now, obliviously indifferent to the usual early morning antics of the Carr-Warner household.

Mercy sat cross-legged on the bedroom floor, watching Felicity play hide-and-seek with Elvis. The baby, snug in her pink-and-white-striped designer onesie, was crawling toward the walk-in closet after the shepherd as he bounded into the clothes-lined space.

The closet opened onto the master bath of the en suite as well, allowing Elvis to slip from bedroom to closet to bathroom and back to the bedroom again. He snuck up on Felicity's flank, the clicking of his nails on the old wide-planked oak floors giving him away. Felicity turned, shrieking with joy as she spotted the shepherd.

Elvis perked his ears and trotted off again, out of sight, the baby wriggling as quickly as she could after him, only to be thwarted again when he reappeared behind her. This endless loop of fun was how every morning had begun here at Grackle Tree Farm since Felicity had gone mobile. Right now, crawling was her superpower.

Soon she'd be walking, and Felicity would give Elvis a run for his money. Not that she'd ever really outrun him. The Malinois could clock in at thirty-five miles an hour when he was really motivated. But that was okay. The shepherd seemed to understand that the point of this game was not to win, but to entertain. And Felicity was nothing if not entertained.

Elvis skidded to a stop. Perked his ears, and barked just once. Felicity stopped, too, mid-crawl. She tumbled onto her baby butt, sitting up and clapping. That could mean only one thing.

"Daddy's home!" Mercy scooped the baby up into her arms, bouncing her up and down as she moved from the floor to the bed. Troy and Susie Bear had been out on patrol, and she knew they'd be tired. They were always beginning or finishing a shift as the sun came up.

The haphazard clomping of the Newfie as she plowed up the stairs was echoed by the slap of Troy's field boots on the steps as he followed in the wake of the big dog. The shaggy canine clown bounced into the room, exchanged a hello sniff with Elvis, and then plopped her huge head onto Mercy's knee so Felicity could pat her broad, furry nose.

"Good morning!" Troy poked his head around the doorjamb and pulled a Punch and Judy face. Felicity laughed, a high-pitched tinkle that only grew in intensity as he played peekaboo with her, hiding his mug and then showing it again several times before coming into the room. He sat down on their four-poster bed to join the family cuddle.

"Don't you need to get some sleep?" asked Mercy.

"I'll take a nap before my next patrol." Troy kissed the top of his wife's head, and then his daughter's.

The poor child had inherited Mercy's unruly curly red hair. Mercy felt guilty for passing along the curse of the redhead, but Troy claimed he was thrilled Felicity was a ginger like her mother. And as far as she could tell he really meant it.

He reached for Felicity and she giggled with joy. Her daughter was a daddy's girl, just like she was. Mercy had always found her father much easier to get along with, mostly because he was much easier to get along with.

But now that she was a mother of a daughter herself, Mercy was beginning to understand—and sympathize with—her own mother more than she would ever have believed possible. Her mother understood what it meant to be a woman in the world, and felt honor-bound to prepare her daughter for that reality.

When it came to Mercy, her father didn't carry that burden. But he had taken a firmer role with her brother Nick, presumably to help him navigate what it means to be a man—and she supposed should they ever have a son together, Troy would step up to prepare their boy.

But for now, it was all about Felicity—and her baby girl had her daddy wrapped around her little finger. Just like Mercy had wrapped her own father around her little finger. Which was as it should be.

"How was your night?" she asked her husband quickly, before he could ask about hers.

"Not as interesting as yours." He waited.

But she didn't take the bait. "Go on."

"If you insist. And I see that you do."

She listened carefully as Troy told her about the poacher he and Gil caught red-handed and the bones he'd stumbled upon. "That's quite a story."

"Your turn."

"I'm sure you've heard most of it already." The dead Santa in the woods was the talk of the town—and the business of local law enforcement, which included Troy.

"I want to hear your version."

Mercy filled him in while he tickled Felicity. As she spoke, she was struck by the contrasts that marked their lives: crime and crib, poaching and playtime, murder and motherhood. Just like life—the good and the bad thrown together in a seemingly random and yet eternal cycle of hope and despair, happiness and sorrow, light and dark.

"Are you all right?" Troy drew her into a group hug with their baby.

"I'm fine. It's just not how I imagined Felicity's first Solstice Soirée to go. Not how I wanted it to go."

"It's been a weird twenty-four hours." Troy kissed her again, and pulled Felicity onto his lap. He removed his warden cap and placed it on the baby's head. "For all of us."

"Two murders," said Mercy. "Strange, to say the least."

"One old and one new. Probably not related."

"No." Mercy shook off the feeling that bad things come in threes. Time to get back into the Christmas spirit. "How about we forget all about murder and focus on what really matters."

"Let me guess." Troy laughed as the baby grabbed his hat with her fingers and tugged. It tumbled onto her chubby little legs and she reached for it. "Felicity's first Christmas."

Mercy smiled. "Got it in one."

"No argument from me. You know I love Christmas."

"You have no choice. It's in your genes."

"That's right."

Troy came from a family whose devotion to Christmas rivaled the Griswolds'. Every year his father and his brothers transformed the grounds of their hundred-year-old Dutch Colonial into a Christmas wonderland. His mother, Lizzie, chose the theme and the design, and the Warner men—all in the construction business, apart from Troy—built it to her specifications.

Themes ran the gamut from *Blue Christmas* complete with singing Elvises to *Ugly Christmas Sweater Party* complete with, well, ugly Christmas sweaters, all bigger than life, all awash in lights. So excessive were their efforts that the Warner family had won the "Most Exuberant" prize in the annual Northshire Holiday Outdoor Decorating Contest a record six times.

This year's theme was—surprise, surprise!—*Baby's First Christmas*. To say Lizzie was excited for another girl child in a family full of men was to downplay her enthusiasm. The thought of what was to come was truly terrifying. Thank goodness it was their yard, and not hers.

"We could try to keep it simple," said Mercy.

"Simple is good," said Troy solemnly, then gave her one of his sweet crooked smiles. "Probably not going to happen."

"No." She sighed. Truth be told, Mercy's mother was as obsessive about the holidays as Troy's mom—even though their respective styles were completely different. If Lizzie were the Dolly Parton of Christmas, then Grace was its Audrey Hepburn. And never the twain shall meet.

Mercy and Troy were going to have to find their own style, preferably somewhere between the extremes. "If we don't do it, our mothers will do it for us."

"Perish the thought."

"We have to find a way to make it our own."

"We found a way to do that when it was just us." Troy smiled at her, and she smiled back.

Her husband was more sentimental than he let on—and more of a romantic than she'd ever be. Even in the whirlwind of activity that characterized their family holidays, he always carved special alone time for them as a couple. For their first Christmas together, he'd surprised her with a sleigh ride on Christmas Eve, champagne under the stars. For their second, they'd gone to an ice-skating dance party. They'd both played ice hockey as kids, but learning to dance with each other on the ice made for one of the loveliest evenings they'd ever spent together.

This year would be their third Christmas together, and their first with the baby. The end of an era—and the beginning of a new one.

"But it isn't just us anymore," she said. "And baby makes three."

They both watched as Felicity tried to put the cap back on her little head. Tried and failed. Tried and failed again. The third time it fell to the floor.

"Then we'll just come up with some family traditions of our own." Troy retrieved the hat, parked it back on his own head, and rose to his feet, the baby still in his arms. She reached for the hat, and he ducked away. She giggled. "*This* family."

"Like what? Between your mother and mine, there are hardly any family traditions left."

"You're not giving us enough credit. Christmas is in our DNA." He dropped his head and let the baby steal the hat once more. "Right, little girl?"

Mercy laughed. "True enough. We're bound to think of something."

"How about we start with a tree." Troy drew the three of them together in a hug. "A tree we cut from right here on Grackle Tree Farm."

"A tree we cut from our own woods every year." She gave her husband a kiss. "The perfect ritual for a simple, down-home family Christmas."

Troy took Felicity downstairs for her morning oatmeal and the dogs went with him, giving Mercy time for a leisurely shower. She was thrilled to slip into a turtleneck and a pair of her old cargo pants, having finally shed the last stubborn five pounds of baby weight. She pulled her tangle of red hair into a loose knot at the back of her head, then tugged on her hiking boots and grabbed a parka and her pack. Ready for the woods.

Not quite.

She went to the nursery and gathered the essentials she couldn't risk being caught without: diapers, wipes, pacifier, blanket. And her baby's two favorite stuffed animals, a miniature Malinois and a black Newfie. Dubbed "El" and "Sue" by Felicity, the first and only two words she'd spoken so far. Forget "Mama" and "Dada," endearments which their baby had yet to utter. For Felicity, it was all about "El" and "Sue."

The beloved toys were gifts from Captain Thrasher and his love, Wyetta Wright. Wyetta was a brilliant textile artist, and she'd made the adorable little doggies herself. The sweet furry creatures could comfort Felicity when nothing else could, and Mercy dared not forget to keep them close by. Into the backpack they went.

Downstairs, she joined Troy and Felicity at the white marble island. Her husband had made coffee and brought out what was left of Patience's Bûche De Noël. The cake was going fast.

She prepared a bottle for the baby, gulping down some coffee and gobbling down a piece of cake while her husband finished airplaning small spoonfuls of cereal into Felicity's pink little mouth. Elvis and Susie Bear flanked the high chair, tails wagging as they waited for the inevitable dribbles of food to fall to the floor.

"Good to go?" Her husband cleaned Felicity's face and hands and lifted her out of the high chair.

"Yep." She replaced the cover on the cake stand.

"What about Tandie?"

"Let her sleep in." Mercy smiled. "She'd rather decorate the tree than cut it down."

The teenager couldn't bear to see trees felled, even when it was necessary. Mercy understood that reaction, but here on the old farm they'd been growing Christmas trees since the limestone manor house was built back in 1866. The previous owners had let much of the property go over time, but Adah Beecher's brother Levi had done the best he could to keep the surrounding forest from encroaching on the gardens and orchards during his longtime tenure as caretaker.

He was less successful with the Christmas trees, which were planted at the far end of the cleared ground, and over the decades in which the house stood empty the neat rows of evergreens were gradually swallowed up by the woods. Still, Levi had done what he could to promote the health and growth of the remaining stands of fir and spruce that could still be found among the pines and hemlocks and maples and oaks that dominated the forest. He was thrilled when Mercy and Troy bought the place, and even more thrilled when they renewed the tradition of cutting a tree from the grounds to grace the old Victorian's parlor every year at Christmas.

"What about Levi?" asked Mercy.

"He'll be along," said Troy with a grin.

"No doubt." Mercy laughed. Both Levi and Adah had a knack for showing up when they were needed most. As if they could somehow commune with the house and the land and their inhabitants—and maybe they could.

Elvis and Susie Bear barreled out of the kitchen. Felicity pumped her legs and arms furiously, trying to wriggle out of Troy's grip. It was only a matter of time before she was toddling after the dogs at warp speed whenever they sensed the doorbell was going to ring.

The doorbell rang.

"I'll go," said Mercy, thinking it must be Levi.

But it was Troy's boss, Captain Thrasher, who stepped into the house when she opened the front door to a blast of cold air and snow flurries. Warmly dressed in his winter field uniform, he nodded at her as he removed his gloves and his blaze-orange cap.

"Good morning," he said, stooping to greet Elvis and Susie Bear.

"Good morning." Mercy waited while he rubbed their bellies.

Floyd Thrasher was a dog person, and they loved him. Mercy suspected that one of the reasons he'd devoted his life to protecting the flora and fauna of the great state of Vermont was because Mother Nature didn't swoon whenever the extraordinarily handsome man walked into a room, like most humans did. Out in the woods, the creatures didn't care what the captain looked like—and even here indoors, the dogs only cared what he smelled like. And, like most game wardens, he smelled good. Like earth and sky and trees.

"Come on through." Elvis and Susie Bear led the way back to the kitchen, where Troy waited, Felicity ready and suited up for the snow in the carrier on his back. Levi was there, too, a bright orange chain saw case in his hand and a tool belt slung around his hips. He wore jeans and a light barn coat and work boots, his only concessions to the winter weather being a pair of gloves and a lumberjack-plaid scarf around his neck. He'd told her once that scarves were the secret to staying warm in a Vermont winter. She'd never seen him in anything else.

"Looks like I'm interrupting something," said Thrasher, regarding Troy apologetically. "I know it's your day off."

"We're just going to cut down a Christmas tree," explained Mercy. "You're welcome to join us."

"Got the saw," said Levi.

"I can see that," said Thrasher. "I'm here to pick up your contribution to Toys for Tots."

The captain had served in the Marines—once a Marine, always a Marine—before joining the Vermont Fish & Wildlife Department, and every year he helped run the service's cherished charity.

"Amy and Tandie have been wrapping lots of books and toys," said Mercy. "They're stacked in the entryway by the hall tree."

"Great. Thanks." He cast a longing look at her grandmother's Bûche de Noël. "I should get going."

"Stay where you are." Mercy didn't want the captain to leave before he'd filled them in on the case. *Cases*, she corrected herself. Plural. "You've got time for coffee and cake."

She poured him and Levi each a cup of coffee. "Help yourself to the cake." There wasn't a man alive who could resist Patience's desserts.

The two men stood at the island, drinking their coffee and eating their cake. Nobody said anything. Even Felicity was quiet, already tired from her romp with the dogs and Daddy, her little eyelids fluttering as she dozed off to baby dreamland.

What was it about a sleeping child that grabbed your heart and wouldn't let go? Mercy smiled at the sweet sight of her baby snug in her carrier, her red curls tucked under her blaze-orange knit beanie, her little head nodding on her father's broad shoulders. Mercy reached for her phone in her cargo pants pocket, to snap yet another photo of Felicity.

"Can't have too many of those." Thrasher grinned at her, breaking the baby spell.

"True enough," said Troy.

Mercy snapped the photo, pushed her cell back into her pocket, and focused on the captain. She figured Thrasher was really here to tell them the latest about the bones or Lazlo or both. But he wasn't talking with Levi there.

Levi didn't say much, but he never missed a nuance. He swallowed the last of his coffee and placed the cup in the sink, heading for the porch. "I'll be outside."

The dogs took off again, not to follow Levi but to greet another guest at the front door.

"Must be Patience," Mercy said, given the level of yelping, which they could hear all the way in the kitchen. They might like Thrasher, but only Patience merited that kind of welcome. Even the kitty Muse would come out eventually to say hello to Mercy's grandmother.

"Let's hope she brings another one of those cakes," said Thrasher.

Her grandmother bustled into the room, the dogs at her heels and two casserole dishes in her hands.

"More cake?" asked the captain hopefully.

"Lasagna and lemon squares."

Thrasher gave her grandmother a thumbs-up. "Works for me."

Patience ignored him. "I thought you could use some help with dinner. I understand you've both been very busy."

"We were just on our way out to get a tree."

"I just need a minute of your time." Patience opened the fridge and placed the covered dishes inside, then closed the door and stood with her back to it. She still wore her white bibbed puffer coat, and made no move to take it off.

"Aren't you supposed to be at rehearsal?"

Patience didn't answer.

"Something's wrong."

"I'm fine."

"No, you're not." Mercy studied her grandmother's face. "Tell us."

CHAPTER SIXTEEN

Christmas waves a magic wand over this world, and behold, everything is softer and more beautiful.

—NORMAN VINCENT PEALE

Not really 'wrong.'" Her grandmother unzipped her coat and pulled a thick cream-colored envelope from an inside pocket. She stood there, holding the envelope between her fingers as if it were about to blow up. "Just odd."

"What is it?"

Her grandmother frowned. "Lazlo left something for me."

"You were his best friend."

"Yes." Patience held the envelope out to Mercy. "But not his confidante. Lazlo did not confide in anyone, as far as I know."

"Intriguing." Mercy noticed the engraved name of one of the most prestigious law firms in Northshire in the left-hand corner: *Roland & Roper*. Her lawyer parents knew them well—and sometimes referred people to them when for whatever reason they couldn't represent them themselves.

But more often than not, the two firms were rivals. As far as Mercy knew, her parents had been Uncle Lazlo's attorneys since forever. Why would he use Roland & Roper?

"'Weird' is more like it," said Patience. "According to Jules Roland, Laz wrote this letter and instructed him to give it to me in the event of his death. Jules delivered it to me in person this morning, along with Boris."

Boris was Lazlo's cat. "Poor Boris."

"Boris is fine. He's a white Maine Coon cat, a very rare specimen, and he knows it. Not too thrilled about living in a houseful of other felines and no Lazlo, but he'll be okay."

"Uncle Laz knew you'd take good care of him." Mercy pointed to the envelope containing the letter. "What does it say?"

"I don't know." Her grandmother looked tired. "I mean, I know what it says, but I have no idea what it means. I thought maybe you could help me figure it out."

"I can try."

"Go ahead." Patience nodded at her.

Mercy opened the unsealed envelope and drew out a folded sheet of thick cream-colored paper. She unfolded the letter. A handwritten scrawl of one word appeared in the middle of the page:

Snegurochka

"It's a word I've never seen before." To the best of her ability, Mercy read the word out loud. The dogs barreled out of the kitchen again. Probably not due to her poor pronunciation. She ignored them.

"Sounds Russian," said Troy, ignoring the dogs, too.

"Something about snow," said Patience.

They all looked at her.

"*Sneg* is Russian for 'snow.'" Her grandmother shrugged. "One of my patients is named *Sneg*. Lovely Samoyed, with the breed's characteristic fluffy white double-layer coat." She paused. "Nice dog."

"What does it mean?" Mercy pulled out her phone.

"Don't bother googling it." The colonel appeared in the kitchen like the ghost of Christmas Past, Elvis and Susie Bear at his side. "I know what it means."

"Of course." Thrasher smiled. "The old man speaks Russian."

Colonel Hugo Fleury was Patience's brother. Mercy's great-uncle. An inscrutable character who'd lived many lives in many tongues, most of them straight out of a John le Carré novel. *Tinker Tailor Soldier Spy Hugo.*

After years conducting military operations all over the world—from Vietnam to the Cold War to the Middle East and beyond—he now ran a highly successful and secretive security firm. No one really knew what he'd done in the past, what he was doing now, or what he might do in the future. And he liked it that way.

"I see the gang's all here," Uncle Hugo said with a nod to the captain. He slipped off his black cashmere coat, revealing his civilian uniform of double-breasted navy blazer and gray trousers. This Savile Row uniform never varied, except that he swapped out the white turtleneck he wore under his blazer now for a crisp, white cotton shirt come summer. His black boots were highly polished regardless of the season. Or the weather. He tossed the coat over the back of one of the kitchen stools, as if planning to stay awhile.

Mercy wondered why her great-uncle was here. He never just dropped by, and he never did anything without a reason. He was up to something. He was always up to something.

"I'm just here picking up Toys for Tots," said Thrasher.

"Right." The colonel smiled. "And I'm from the Salvation Army."

The two men stared at each other like two Dobermans fighting over the same bone. Mercy wondered what the bone was. She was betting on Uncle Laz. She glanced at Troy. She could tell he was thinking the same thing. He raised his eyebrows at her, code for *This is getting interesting*.

"Go ahead, Hugo," said Patience with the impatient affection only a little sister could muster. "Enlighten us."

"I have a feeling that this is going to take a while." Mercy waved an arm at the island. "We may as well all sit down."

Patience sank onto a stool, and Muse appeared as if from nowhere, meowing and leaping into her lap. Mercy and Troy took side-by-side seats, he perched at the edge of the stool, Felicity now asleep in the carrier on his back. The dogs curled up at their feet.

The colonel settled onto his own stool, folding his hands on the white marble. "That looks like one of your justly famous Bûche De Noël cakes, Patience."

"Go ahead."

"It's the last piece."

"I'll make more," said everyone in unison.

"You know I will." Patience laughed.

The colonel helped himself while Mercy poured him a cup of coffee and the rest of them waited for the old man to tell his story. He always had a story to tell. The question was, How much of it were they to believe?

In between bites, the colonel talked. "*Snegurochka,* from the Russian word *sneg,* meaning snow."

"I've already told them that, Hugo," said Patience. "Tell us something we don't know."

"I'm getting there." The colonel breathed deeply in and out, then launched into a lecture. "*Snegurochka* is the Snow Maiden, the heroine of several Russian folktales. Most are variations of the same story." Uncle Hugo paused for dramatic effect, sipping his coffee before continuing. "An old childless couple praying for a child of their own builds a girl out of snow and a miracle brings her to life. She's a lovely creature, with eyes like stars and red lips. She longs for admirers like the other maidens, but she has a heart of ice. Only when she falls in love with the right man, the man who truly loves her, can she find happiness. She finds true love at last, and her heart of ice melts. And she with it."

"She dies in the end," said Mercy. "So much for happily ever after."

"Not a very cheerful story," said Patience.

"Russians love an unhappy ending," said Thrasher.

"Not completely unhappy," said the colonel. "When her heart of ice melts, it means that the long winter is over. And that spring will come again."

"*The Snow Maiden,*" said Patience.

The colonel smiled. "I knew you'd remember eventually, Sissy."

"What are you talking about?" Mercy loved it when Uncle Hugo called her grandmother "Sissy." It amused her to picture them as the small, precocious, argumentative siblings they once were. And in many ways, still were today. Only bigger. And even smarter.

"It's a Russian folk song that's sung around Christmastime," said Patience. "My mother loved Christmas carols, and she collected them from all over the world. She played the piano and the organ beautifully, you know. She found *The Snow Maiden* when Hugo here brought home a girl from Kiev to spend Christmas with us. Mom played it for her." Patience frowned. "What was that girl's name?"

"Svetlana."

"That's right. She was a beauty."

"What happened to her?" asked Mercy, knowing her uncle's reputation as a ladies' man, even now.

"Hugo broke her heart," said Patience. "He broke all their hearts."

"Not true." The colonel shook his head. "Not true at all."

"She loved you," said Patience, with a small smile. "They all loved you."

"Water under the bridge. It was all a very long time ago."

Something in his voice caught Mercy's attention. She suspected that there was more to Svetlana's story than Uncle Hugo was telling. There was always more to the story than Uncle Hugo was telling.

Patience shifted on her stool and changed the subject. "Why would Lazlo leave this message for me?"

"Snegurochka is also the heroine of the opera *The Snow Maiden*," continued Uncle Hugo, as if he hadn't heard his sister's question. "Composed by Nikolai Rimsky-Korsakov in the late 1800s. He also wrote the libretto, based on the play by Alexander Ostrovsky. Interestingly, Tchaikovsky was first tapped to write the opera, but the Bolshoi Theatre turned to Rimsky-Korsakov to develop the full opera. Tchaikovsky went on to repurpose some of his *Snow Maiden* score in his *Hamlet*."

"A Russian opera?" asked Mercy.

"Yes," said the colonel with a contented look.

Uncle Hugo was an opera aficionado of the first order. He had box seats at the Met and La Scala, and attended performances all over the world. He especially loved the Russian operas. Mercy had never understood how such a melodramatic and sentimental art form, however beautiful, could appeal to the colonel. Opera seemed an odd passion for such a disciplined man. But then Uncle Hugo was nothing if not a man of contradictions.

"What does any of this have to do with Lazlo?" pressed Patience, checking her watch.

"Probably nothing," admitted the colonel. He eyed his sister sharply. "You have a train to catch?"

"It's Grace. I promised her I'd be on time."

"On time for what?"

"You need to get to that rehearsal," Mercy guessed. Her cell and Troy's cell pinged simultaneously, and they both retrieved their phones to take a look. "Mom," they said in unison. They looked at each other and sighed.

The colonel paid no attention. "Rehearsal?" He looked from Mercy to Patience.

"Let me guess," said Patience to Mercy. "Christmas decorations?"

"Yes," she admitted. Her mother and Troy's mother both wanted to know who was in charge of decorating Grackle Tree Farm. Each coveted the role. It didn't seem to occur to either of them that it might be Mercy and Troy.

"One conversation at a time," ordered Uncle Hugo.

"I'm taking Laz's place as the organist for the Singing Christmas Tree," Patience told her brother.

"And for the Christmas services at the First Congregational Church," added Mercy.

"Don't remind me."

"You'd better get going."

"I'm leaving already," said Patience. "Hugo, I know that you know more than you're saying. Tell them everything. Help them figure this out. And let me know what if anything I'm supposed to do about it."

"You don't have to do anything about it," said Thrasher. "We'll look into it."

"Lazlo left this message for me for a reason," said Patience. "Even if that reason escapes me."

"We're on it." Mercy put her arm around her grandmother and gave the men a grave look. "Right, guys?"

"Right," said Troy.

"I'll hold you to that," said Patience.

The colonel bowed to her smartly. "Anything for more of your Christmas cake, Sissy."

Halfway out the kitchen door, Patience turned and looked at Mercy. "If you want my advice . . ."

"Always," said Mercy, her grandmother being the one person other than Troy whose guidance she was most likely to appreciate.

"Give the dueling grandmothers what they want."

Mercy looked at her blankly. "How?"

"Let Grace do the inside, and Lizzie do the outside."

"What?" Mercy could feel her pale face flush to a deep red at the very thought of giving her mother and her mother-in-law free rein over the decorating of her home. "You're not serious. We're planning a simple, down-home family Christmas." She looked at Troy. "Right?"

"Right."

"You know that's never going to happen," said Patience. "You're hosting the entire family Christmas here. Mothers included. But you can control the madness if you give them a mission."

"A mission. For Christmas. What does that even mean?"

Patience laughed. "Come up with a theme. Neither Grace nor Lizzie can resist a good theme."

Troy laughed, too. "That just might work."

"It's a good plan," agreed Thrasher.

"They'll never go for a simple, down-home Christmas theme," said Mercy.

"No, they won't, but that's okay," said Patience. "Choose something a little grander that's still something that you can live with. The decorating mission will distract them, and while they're distracted, you can do your own simple, down-home Christmas thing."

"Like cutting down your own Christmas tree," said Thrasher.

"The captain gets it," said Patience.

"It's just like we talked about," said Troy. "We save some Christmas for ourselves. Just as we always have."

Mercy thought about it. "It would have to be one heck of a theme."

"You'll think of something," said Thrasher.

"You always do," said the colonel.

"Imagine the possibilities," Patience said, and swept out of the room.

CHAPTER SEVENTEEN

*The frost had grown more severe...
but, to make up for this, everything had become
so still that the crisping of the snow under foot
might be heard nearly half a mile away.*

—NIKOLAI GOGOL

"Start talking," Mercy told her great-uncle as soon as she heard the front door slam behind her grandmother as she left the house.

"I have no idea what you mean by that," the colonel said with a slight smile.

"Come on, Uncle Hugo, we don't have all day. We're supposed to be out in the woods cutting down our Christmas tree. We need to get it up and decorated, pronto."

"I never thought I'd see you in a hurry to decorate anything," said Uncle Hugo dryly.

Thrasher laughed at that. So did Troy, waking Felicity. She stuck her thumb in her mouth and Mercy grabbed the pacifier from the bowl on the counter—they kept spares all over the house—and swapped it out for her little thumb. The baby sucked at it contentedly, and dozed off again.

"Very funny," she told the colonel. While it was true that she was now going to delegate most of the decorating of their old Victorian manor to Grace and Lizzie, Mercy still bristled at what she took as an affront. This was different. "It's Christmas, Uncle Hugo. Felicity's *first* Christmas."

"Indeed." He turned to Troy and Thrasher. "Fascinating how even the most undomesticated female turns into Martha Stewart once she has a baby."

"I'd quit while I was ahead if I were you," warned Thrasher.

"I'm not turning into Martha Stewart. I'm turning two Martha Stewarts loose on Grackle Tree Farm."

"And you'll be the better for it," said the colonel thoughtfully.

"Why are you here, Uncle Hugo?" said Mercy. "I know you're holding out on us. Do I have to call Daniel and ask him?" Feinberg and Uncle Hugo shared an interest in antiquities and sometimes worked together to retrieve and restore stolen treasures from all over the world. She could only imagine what other activities the billionaire and the old spy shared.

The mention of Feinberg seemed to hit home.

"I'm not holding out on you. But this is a very delicate matter."

Mercy thought about Lazlo Ford. What she actually knew about the man, which was in truth very little. "Tell them everything," Patience had told her brother before she left. Apparently, they knew far more about Uncle Laz than anyone else did. Except maybe Feinberg. "Who was Uncle Laz, really?"

"I can't tell you much, because I don't know that much." The colonel sighed. "But I can assure you that he was a good man who did not deserve to die that way."

Mercy, Troy, and Thrasher all waited. With their military and law enforcement experience, they knew how to wait. Of course, so did Uncle Hugo. When it came to waiting, spies played the longest game of all.

Felicity roused again, and started to cry. Mercy retrieved her from the carrier on Troy's back, rocking her against her chest. Her baby kept on crying. "Uncle Hugo."

"Here's what I do know," he said. "Sixteen years ago I got a call from an old friend. He needed me to help someone disappear."

"And that someone was Lazlo Ford." Mercy deposited Felicity back into the high chair, pulling a kitchen drawer open and retrieving a set of lettered plastic blocks. She dumped the blocks on the high chair tray, and the baby stopped crying mid-sob, grabbing a block. "Go on, Uncle Hugo."

"That wasn't his name then." The colonel leaned forward. "And don't ask me what his real name was, because I never knew. I only knew that he'd risked his own life to expose some very bad people. And that he needed to disappear."

"Witness protection," said Thrasher.

"Not exactly."

"What does that mean?" asked Mercy.

"It means that's all I can say."

"You think whoever Lazlo Ford helped put away finally found him and killed him," said Troy as he stacked up the blocks with Felicity.

The colonel nodded. "Looks like it."

"That's a long time to nurse a grudge," said Thrasher.

"These people have long memories," said Uncle Hugo.

"That's what you always say about the FSB and the KGB and the Stasi," said Mercy.

The colonel closed his palms together prayer-style and pressed his index fingers against his chin. "Yes, but they're not the only ones who'll go to great lengths to exact vengeance. Most evil people are narcissists determined to get their revenge. They bide their time and wait for the right moment to strike—no matter how long it takes."

"And you have no idea who these people are."

"No," said the colonel.

"And your old friend?" asked Thrasher.

"He died three years ago. Cancer." The colonel lowered his hands. "And before you ask, he left no instructions or information concerning Lazlo. We checked."

"I'm sorry for your loss," said Mercy, wondering who he meant by "we." FBI, CIA, NSA, MI6, Mossad . . . it could be anyone from any intelligence organization anywhere in the world. There was no end to the man's contacts.

"We're still trying to track down his widow to see if she knew anything. It's a long shot—these guys usually don't confide in their wives or anyone else in their private lives for that matter. It's strictly *need to know*."

"Maybe his secret identity died with him." Troy caught a block as the baby swatted it off the tray. Fetch for grown-ups—a game Felicity loved.

"Then no one else will be at risk now," said Mercy, completing her husband's thought.

"That would be good news for Northshire and the Solstice Soirée," said Thrasher.

"I'm not sure we can count on that," said Uncle Hugo. "The message he left Patience worries me."

"And you really don't know what it means," said Mercy.

"No. The obvious answer is something to do with Russia or Russians, but I know of no such connection to Lazlo. Or what they might have to do with the people he was hiding from. My impression was always that the threat against him was domestic."

"Find the connection, and maybe we find Uncle Lazlo's killer," said Mercy. "I'm going to talk to Rory Craig about the Yule log this afternoon when we go to see Patience and the Singing Christmas Tree. But first we have to get our own Christmas tree." She rose to her feet in a not-so-subtle signal that it was time for her guests to leave unless they wanted to come along.

"I'll keep digging at my end." The colonel popped the last bite of cake into his mouth. "Go ahead, I can let myself out."

THRASHER AGREED TO ACCOMPANY Mercy and Troy on their tree-cutting outing. Which was fine by Mercy. The captain was family, after all, and she knew that he was wise enough to keep any decorating thoughts he had to himself.

Perched happily once again on her father's back in the carrier, Felicity laughed as Elvis and Susie Bear bounded out of the house, dancing around Levi, who stood ready with the chain saw. As a precaution against trigger-happy hunters, they all wore blaze-orange vests, including the dogs. Even Levi pulled a blaze-orange cap from his back pocket and slipped it over his silver ponytail.

The lean outdoorsman led the way past the barn and the fallow vegetable garden, past the new greenhouse and the old orchard, into the woods. The dogs ran ahead, weaving in and out of the trees that flanked the narrow trail. Their tracks appearing and disappearing in the deepening snow.

It was cold, but sunny and bright. No more flurries, at least for now. The best kind of winter day.

"Do you think the two crimes are related?" Mercy asked Thrasher.

"I don't see how. Dr. Darling says the body Troy and Gil found had been there a long time, at least a dozen years or more. Hard to be exact given the state of decomposition, but she's guessing between fifteen and twenty years."

"No ID yet?"

"No."

"Any relevant missing persons reports?" asked Troy.

"Not so far." Thrasher tugged on a low branch blocking the path and held it for Mercy, Troy, and the baby to pass. "But Darling says the teeth may reveal something. Unusual dental work. Maybe foreign. She's working on it."

"So someone shoots a foreign guy wearing antlers right between the eyes and stuffs him in a rotting snag and leaves him there."

"Something like that."

"A professional kill."

Thrasher shrugged. "Could be."

"What about poor Uncle Laz?"

"Nothing much in terms of forensics. We'll see what turns up."

"We need to figure out the motive. What the torn piece of the Christmas carol means."

"It may mean something, or it may mean nothing. He was an organist—it could be as simple as a torn sheet from the hymnal that stuck to his glove."

"Or not."

"Or not," admitted Thrasher.

"That *Snow Maiden* note he left for Patience must mean something."

"Yes. Let's hope Hugo can clear that up. Or you."

Mercy couldn't see how she could decipher the obtuse message. At least not yet. She needed to know more. More of what remained unclear.

Up ahead, Levi took a sharp turn through a copse of aspen and they followed single file, Troy and Felicity, Mercy, and Thrasher taking up the rear. The dogs circled back from wherever they had roamed and stood waiting for them in a patch of new-growth forest that still bore the traces of the old Christmas tree farm planted years before. There were uneven rows of red and white spruce, black and blue spruce, noble fir and balsam fir and Fraser fir, white pine and Scotch pine—all growing alongside their neighboring hemlocks and maples and oaks.

"So many beautiful trees," said Mercy. "How will we ever choose?"

"Depends on what you want," said Levi. "If you want a tree that smells good, get a balsam. They're the most fragrant."

"Fragrant is good," said Mercy.

"Everything smells good out here in the woods," said Thrasher, inhaling deeply.

Spoken like a true game warden, thought Mercy.

"The firs are bushy and full," Levi pointed out. "Great shape, but less room for ornaments."

He went over to a tall red spruce. "The spruces have a nice shape, too. And their upturned branches make them easier to decorate than firs."

"My mother will like that," said Mercy. "When it comes to Christmas, she believes that more is more."

"My mom, too," said Troy.

"That may be the only thing besides a fierce love of their families that the two women share," said Thrasher.

"You got that right," said Troy.

"What about the baby?" asked Thrasher. "Seems to me that the fewer the ornaments, the safer the tree."

"She does put everything in her mouth," Troy said.

"No worries," said Mercy. "We have a fix for that. We just put the tree in the middle of a large wooden playpen. That way, she can see but not touch."

Thrasher grinned. "Brilliant."

Mercy laughed. "You can thank Patience. It's what she does to keep the puppies out of the Christmas tree at the clinic."

"What about the cats?"

"The cats do whatever they want."

"Of course," said Thrasher.

Levi stomped through the snow over to a massive Scotch pine. "The Scotch pine is the most popular Christmas tree in the country. It's very durable and retains its needles for a long time. And its branching pattern allows for lots of ornaments."

"Which tree lasts the longest?" asked Troy.

"The firs can last up to six weeks. The pines, three weeks. Two weeks for the spruces."

"Well, it's nearly Christmas now. And we'll take it down after New Year's. So any of these should work." Mercy looked at Troy. "What do you think?"

He walked over to join Levi at the Scotch pine. "I like this one. There's plenty of room for ornaments. Like your mother says, more is more."

Felicity reached up and tugged on the needles, giggling.

"I guess that clinches it," said Mercy, smiling. "It seems Felicity has made her choice. More is more."

LEVI AND THRASHER CARRIED the monster pine back through the woods while Mercy and Troy and the baby and the dogs trailed behind. Mercy started singing "O Christmas Tree," and they all joined in as they made their way back through the woods and the gardens to the house.

As they finished the last verse, Levi surprised them with a solo, belting out "O Tannenbaum" in the original German in his rich baritone. They clapped in approval, to little Felicity's delight. She loved to clap. She kept on clapping all the way home.

"Better than a bear bell," said Mercy to Troy.

"Yep."

As they tramped through the patches and piles of snow toward home, Mercy felt the Christmas spirit fill her heart, a seemingly physical lifting of the soul. As much as she might resent the commercialization of the holidays, she loved the simple rituals and traditions that made all the hustle and bustle worthwhile. The snowy woods, the comfort of friends and family, love and light and laughter, carols and cake and the sound of her baby daughter clapping. This was what Christmas meant to her.

When she was in Afghanistan, she'd suffered the usual low-grade homesickness that plagues all soldiers, barely noticeable as she went about her mission in theater. But this time of year, the subliminal longing for home became an active ache—even for those who joined the military to get away from home.

For soldiers like Mercy, whose holiday memories were rich with good company and great food and an abundance of affection and appreciation, Christmastime took on a sacred luminance worthy of Dickens, whether you believed in God or not. And most soldiers did, at least while the bullets were flying.

If you made it home, then every Christmas thereafter was a gift. A gift of joy, of love, of home. Mercy and Troy had both made it home, and they wanted to share this jubilant gift with their family, friends, and, most important, their daughter. That's why this year, for the first time, everyone would gather at their house for the holidays.

Dickens. Maybe Dickens was the answer. Maybe when it came to Christmas, Dickens was always the answer, Mercy thought.

"How about a Victorian Christmas theme?" she asked Troy. "An old-fashioned Christmas. That's probably as simple and down-home as our mothers will get."

"Perfect," said Troy. "You tell your mother and I'll tell mine."

"A Dickensian Christmas in your Victorian manor," said Thrasher. "I can't think of anything better."

"I will honor Christmas in my heart," chanted Levi, from *A Christmas Carol*.

"Exactly," said Thrasher with a conspiratorial grin, seemingly unsurprised that Levi was quoting Dickens.

The woodsman is a wonder, thought Mercy. It was a good omen. As was this Christmas tree.

The magnificent pine from their own woods was just the start of what Mercy was beginning to think of as the Best. Christmas. Ever.

And nobody was going to ruin that.

CHAPTER EIGHTEEN

See the blazing yule before us Fa la la la la la, la la la la
Strike the harp and join the chorus Fa la la la la, la la la la
Follow me in merry measure Fa la la la la, la la, la la
While I tell of Yuletide treasure Fa la la la la, la la la la

—"DECK THE HALLS"

WHILE MERCY CHANGED THE BABY AND GAVE HER LUNCH, Thrasher and Levi helped Troy put the tree up in the living room. Grace and Lizzie had been informed of the holiday theme and their respective decorating responsibilities, and the dueling grandmothers had retired to their respective corners to plan their respective campaigns. Let the Christmas wars begin.

Tandie was up, and she played with Felicity while Mercy searched the guest room closet for the boxes of ornaments that she and Troy had collected over the years. She brought down the modest collection—positively meager by Grace's and Lizzie's standards, no doubt—to show Tandie.

"Not nearly enough for that huge tree," said Tandie.

"Don't worry, this is just the beginning." Mercy explained the grandmothers' inside/outside decorating strategy and the Victorian theme.

"Cool," said Tandie. "It's like *National Lampoon's Christmas Vacation* versus *Christmas in Connecticut*."

"*Christmas in Connecticut*?"

"Barbara Stanwyck. Dennis Morgan."

"I know," said Mercy. The Christmas film about a phony food writer entertaining a soldier home from the war over Christmas was one of her favorite old movies. "How could you possibly know that?"

"Dad and I watch it every year. Along with *It's a Wonderful Life*, *Elf*,

White Christmas, The Bishop's Wife—both the Loretta Young and the Whitney Houston versions—and *Love Actually*."

"What? No *Die Hard*?"

Tandie laughed. "That, too. And all of the *Home Alone*s."

"*Christmas in Connecticut* sounds about right. My mother has hired Tammy's Good Tidings, and they'll be dropping off decorations for the interior of the house. So you should have plenty to work with."

Tammy's Good Tidings was Vermont's most prominent holiday decorating service. Every year, her mother hired Tammy to bedeck her own home and office, and the results were always chicly gorgeous. This year, Grace had offered to do the same for Grackle Tree Farm.

Initially Mercy demurred. She had intended to host a decorating party, with friends and family bringing ornaments and decorating the tree together. But now that the grandmothers were stepping in, she'd leave them to it.

Still, Mercy didn't want strangers in the house, and she and Troy had made it clear to Grace and Lizzie that they drew the line at having outsiders do the actual decorating. So Grace was enlisting the help of Tandie, Amy, and Amy's boyfriend Brodie, while Lizzie of course had the Warner men at her disposal. Mercy hoped the old house could withstand the onslaught.

The more she thought about the Dickensian theme, the more she liked it. It suited the old Victorian manor better. But it also meant more work. So as much she might balk, she needed the help.

Especially now that she'd been charged with solving Lazlo's murder. His death and its aftermath coupled with Troy's patrol duties meant they were running out of time to prepare this perfect Christmas. They'd all be going to a funeral tomorrow instead of a party, and people would be going to Patience's place afterward instead of coming here.

Mercy was glad about that, because she wanted their house to become the default setting for the *happiest* of events in the lives of their circle of friends and family. Not the saddest. As tomorrow's event would be.

In the meantime, Christmas here would go on. Armed with Grace's good taste and Tammy's Good Tidings' expertise, Amy and Tandie and Brodie would have the pleasure of doing all the inside decorating themselves. Levi had already volunteered to help Lizzie and Troy's father and brothers with whatever they were planning for the outside of the old limestone manor. Who knew what the place would look like by the time Mercy got back?

The massive Scotch pine filled an entire corner of the large living room, standing tall and proud next to the exposed brick fireplace with the lovely carved mahogany surround and mantel, lovingly restored by Tandie's carpenter father, Ed. Levi plugged in the lights that he and Troy and Thrasher had strung along its branches, a mix of old-fashioned colored bulbs and tiny white twinkle lights.

"It's a beautiful tree," said Tandie, handing a squirming Felicity to Mercy.

"Nice job, guys." Mercy held on to the baby, who was desperate to go for that tree.

"Grace asked me to cut some live greenery for the mantel and sills and stair railings," said Levi. "I'll bring it in for you, and get started on the outside."

How very Victorian, thought Mercy. "Thank you, Levi."

Levi loped off, only to return to make an announcement. "There's a big truck outside. Tammy's Good Tidings." With that, he left again.

"Right." She glanced at Elvis, who like Mercy did not always look kindly on strangers being in the house. "Stay."

"That's my cue," said Thrasher, who promptly said his goodbyes and was gone.

"Mine, too." Troy kissed Mercy and Felicity as he headed out with Susie Bear to work.

As soon as her husband shut the front door behind him, Mercy heard it open once more. She and Tandie and Felicity all watched in equal parts delight and dismay as two burly guys in "Good Tidings" sweatshirts brought in carton after carton of decorations. Mercy stopped counting after twenty boxes.

The guys bellowed "Merry Christmas!" as they deposited the last of the stuff and left the building.

Tandie looked around at the mound of decorations. "I don't even know where to start."

"You're in charge now. Use it any way you want."

"This is a lot of stuff."

"Think Dickens," advised Mercy. "If it doesn't say Dickens, it doesn't belong."

"I can't do this alone."

"Amy and Brodie will help." Mercy slipped Felicity back into her snowsuit. "I texted them and they're on the way."

"Okaaaaay," said Tandie, as she watched Levi drag in a big tarp full of freshly cut evergreen and holly branches and pine cones. "That's *more* stuff."

"You've got this." Mercy tugged on her coat, slung on her pack, and tucked Felicity under one arm and the carrier and diaper bag under the other. Elvis ran for the door, knowing an exit when he saw one. "It'll be great. Just remember Grace's Number One Rule of Christmas Decorating."

"No." Tandie slumped to the floor in the middle of the mess of boxes and branches and berries. "Don't even say it."

Mercy smiled at the teenager as she headed out after the shepherd with Felicity. "More is more."

THE TOWN COMMON WAS even more crowded than it had been the day before. Gentle flurries filled the air, and all the lights bathed the Christmas markets in the hazy glow of contentment. Felicity giggled as a giant snowflake landed on the tip of her tiny nose. Out of the corner of her eye, Mercy could see her daughter reach up with her mitten-clad little hands to catch the dancing stars of ice.

It wasn't that cold—just barely below freezing—and the tower heaters lining the paths kept everyone toasty and warm. Mercy headed across the misty green, Elvis on the lead at her side, weaving through the throng of people. She steered clear of the candied apple booths and gingerbread chalets and stuffed animal huts, where Felicity was apt to reach out and snag a treat or toy when she wasn't looking. Elvis, she didn't have to worry about. The dog was too well-trained and too well-disciplined to give in to such temptation without an invitation. The baby, not so much.

Rory Craig's WoodWorks Shed was one of the largest and most charming chalets in Northshire's Christmas market. Craig himself was a stocky man with a big head, made bigger by a leonine head of curly salt-and-pepper hair. He had arms as thick as the tree trunks he carved into sculptures, the muscles clearly visible even under the blue-gray Shetland sweater he wore over jeans and brown work boots. Swap out his chain saw for a double-bitted axe, and the man would have made a first-rate Paul Bunyan.

"Mercy Carr. And baby. And dog." Ignoring his other customers, he headed straight for them. He gave Mercy a big smile, and Felicity an even bigger one as he favored Elvis with a good scratch between his perked ears.

Craig had been a fixture of village life for years, but Mercy had really only gotten to know him when she asked him to carve a standing bear like the one Patience had at her clinic, to mark the entrance of the outbuilding that Troy was turning into a small shop back home at Grackle Tree Farm. She'd been impressed with his workmanship, and so had Troy, who'd loved the gift.

At Rory's chalet, he sold all kinds of large wooden sculptures like Troy's black bear, carved with a chain saw with strong cuts that favored the wood. There were sheep and goats and foxes and owls and turkeys and hounds, turtles and snakes, frogs, trout, moose, deer, and even a raccoon. Of all his larger works, the pièce de résistance was the nearly full-sized Nativity scene with Joseph and Mary and the baby Jesus, attended by a couple of sheep and a cow.

He'd also carved smaller pieces, delicate creatures like butterflies and birds and dragonflies, all whittled with a wood-carving knife and a talented hand. There was a kids' section, too, and at the side of the booth, there was a small display of Yule logs, neatly stacked.

"Take your time and look around. But don't miss the toys. It is Christmas, after all." He waved a beefy arm at the display at the front of the booth, which held a delightful collection of hand-carved wooden toys and puzzles. There were pull toys shaped like cars and trucks and bunnies and puppies, puzzles that spelled out names and numbers and maps of the United States and the counties of Vermont. "The little girl is bound to like one of these. And they're educational, too."

"They're lovely." Mercy pointed to the Enchanted Forest, a cleverly designed wooden tree trunk whose branches held individually carved leaves and birds and animals—a kind of stacking game for toddlers. "We'll take that one."

Felicity reached for it, starting to cry. Rory handed her a small giraffe on wheels and the baby babbled with joy. "Merry Christmas, little one."

"We couldn't."

"The giraffe will keep her busy while I wrap up the Enchanted Forest for you." He cradled the toy in his large hands and carried it to the counter.

"Thank you." Mercy followed him and watched as he folded plain brown paper around the puzzle.

"Now tell me why you're really here." He brightened the brown-papered package with a red satin ribbon. "I'm guessing it has something to do with the murder of the mayor."

"Yes." Mercy smiled.

"I liked Lazlo Ford. He was a good man, but a terrible Santa Claus. Why would anyone want to kill him?"

"That's what we'd like to find out."

"I heard you found the body." Craig gave her a bemused look. "The police say he was set on fire with one of my Yule logs."

"The maker's mark certainly looked like yours. The ox."

"Very strange."

She walked over to examine his selection of Yule logs. "There aren't that many left."

"We'll be sold out by this afternoon. And then I'll make more."

Just like Patience and her cakes, Mercy thought. "People are still buying Yule logs after the solstice?"

"Yep. Right up until New Year's Eve. They buy one, they burn it up, and then they come back for another one."

"The Yule log at the crime scene had your maker's mark. But it also had decorative carvings on it." She pointed to one of the Yule logs on display. "Holly, like this."

"Like I told the police, that's a popular design. I've sold at least a hundred of those this season. And I'll sell a hundred more before the season's over."

"And you don't remember who bought a log like this yesterday."

"Lots of people bought a log like this yesterday. And the day before that."

"No one who seemed suspicious in any way?" Mercy glanced around at the other shoppers examining Rory's offerings, none of whom seemed suspicious.

Rory spread his arms wide. "All kinds of people are out here. I don't pay much attention, as long as they're careful with my carvings. You break it, you buy it, you know?"

Mercy nodded.

"And as long as their money's good." He shrugged his thickset shoulders. "If you're asking if anyone who looked like a Santa slayer dropped by and bought a Yule log from me, then no." He smiled. "Not that I remember. I don't mean to sound like a jerk. But that's an impossible question."

"Where do you keep your stock? There's not much here."

"I got a truck parked down the side street full of the logs, keep them locked up in the enclosed bed. But I suppose if you wanted to *bad* enough, you could just break in and take one. Or you could buy one here or at one of the many other shops around town that carry my Yule logs."

Mercy could see that pinpointing where the killer got the log might indeed be impossible. At least with what little they had to go on right now. "Why do you think the murderer put a burning Yule log on the victim?"

Rory drummed the counter with sausage-sized fingers. "He was shot, right?"

"Yes. He was already dead when the Yule log was placed on his body and set ablaze."

"Overkill." He stopped the drumming, and looked at Mercy. "Unless it was a message of some sort."

"Exactly. The question is, what kind of message does a blazing Yule log send?"

"*May the log burn, May the wheel turn,*" chanted Rory. "*May evil spurn, May the Sun return.*"

"Who wrote that?"

"Nobody knows for sure. They say it's an old Celtic chant." He placed his meaty fists on his hips. "There are a lot of rituals and superstitions around the Yule log. My Scottish gran Nessie used to burn a piece of the Yule log every night during the twelve days of the solstice and then put what was left under her bed. She said she did it for luck, as protection against evil spirits, disasters, especially fire. Which is kind of funny when you think about it." He placed the Christmas present for Felicity in a brown paper bag. "Not that any of this is funny."

"No."

"Maybe the killer used the Yule log as a talisman against his own evil." Rory looked up as if heaven may have heard him. "Gabriel be my breastplate, Michael be my belt, Raphael be my shield. . . ." He looked at her sheepishly. "You can never be too careful around evil."

"No, you can't." Mercy had learned that in war. She'd also learned that people would invoke the evil of Satan when it was really only the meanness of man. "Maybe it wasn't a talisman at all. Maybe the killer just figured it was a good way to destroy evidence."

"Except you came along."

"More like Elvis came along."

"Right." He gave Elvis another good scratch. "Handsome dog. He'd make a good subject."

"No argument from me."

"I'm sorry that I wasn't much help."

"I wouldn't say that. Thanks again for the giraffe."

"Merry Christmas!" Rory waved to them from the entrance to his booth, where he stood by the Nativity scene, surrounded by all his creations, a sculptor among the creatures of the forest. And the baby Jesus.

Even if the Yule log that blazed on top of poor Uncle Lazlo was one of Rory's, Mercy knew that the sculptor had nothing to do with it. Still, the log had to mean something. To the killer, if no one else.

May the log burn, May the wheel turn, May evil spurn, May the Sun return.

Words to live by, thought Mercy.

CHAPTER NINETEEN

The bear tilted his head back and pointed to a cluster of stars low in the sky, and with the same deep and rolling voice said, Look. That is my ancestor. The Great Bear. Do you see her?

—ANDREW KRIVAK

Troy pulled the Ford F-150 up to the small cabin deep in the woods not far from the Temple of the End of Days compound. This was the widow Edith Tupper's place. Edith was a retired midwife who'd helped deliver most of the babies born in the county over the past fifty years. Troy among them.

A compact woman whose energy belied her age, she marched down a recently shoveled walkway to greet Troy and Susie Bear. She wore a green parka and ski pants, and a pair of binoculars hung around her neck; gray pigtails bounced underneath her orange knitted toque.

"Troy Warner. As I live and breathe." She gave him a sharp look, like that of a crow eyeing a grasshopper. Like crows, Edith didn't miss a trick. Which was good news for Troy and bad news for her neighbors. "And your loyal Newfie." She ruffled Susie Bear's shaggy head. "Such a lovely girl."

"Hello, Mrs. Tupper. You're looking well."

"How's your baby daughter?"

"She's great," said Troy. "Growing like a weed. Starting to talk. She'll be walking soon."

"Splendid." She paused. "Now on to today's business. The bastards are at it again."

"I assume we're talking about the Temple of the End of Days."

"Come this way." Edith stomped off through the snow without a backward glance, her knee-high duck boots crunching in the new-fallen snow. Susie Bear shambled along behind her, Troy taking up the rear, as they navigated a rough, narrow path too overgrown to qualify as a trail.

"Domestic animals on the loose." She pointed to recent cow pies peeking out of the snow. "Hunting out of season." Another wave of her arm at an illegal trap.

That's two violations already, Troy thought, as he snapped photos of the manure and trapping materials.

"Dumping." Edith stopped at a small clearing, where a slight ridge overlooked a shallow gully. What runoff remained from warmer weather was frozen now, and pocked with trash. Tires, tipped-over barrels, plastic bags torn to shreds by predators, revealing what was left of the contents. Chicken bones, rotting produce, tin cans, used boxes, and more.

Troy hated anyone who spoiled the woods. "And this is your own property?"

"Yes. Theirs is the other side of the gully. So technically the border runs right down the middle of the water."

"Right. But either way, it's dumping."

"They push it into the gulch and then claim it's my problem."

As she went on, he caught it all on camera.

"They have sanitation and sewage issues out there," she said. "They brought in too many people too fast. They don't have the infrastructure they need."

"They claim to be working on it."

"Ha." The woman picked up a random beef rib that some animal had brought to chew on and then abandoned. She tossed it toward the temple property.

He watched as the bone sailed across the icy trench, landing in the snow on the other side. "Nice pitch."

She ignored that. "Not to mention the bears."

"Bears?" Troy didn't like the sound of that.

Edith scraped her boot at a bump in the snow marked by a long, straight maple twig. With the snow gone, the bear scat was readily visible. He took more photos.

"I'm worried about them," she said. "They'll end up nuisance bears, and you know what happens to them."

"A fed bear is a dead bear." It was Troy's job to take care of nuisance bears, which could mean relocation, but more often meant death. "People are always the nuisance. They attract the bears with their bird feeders and unsecured trash cans and then they're surprised when the bears act like the wild animals they are."

Trash and birdseed were the black bears' gateway drug to becoming habituated to humans. Associating people with food, losing their fear of humans, and potentially causing harm. Which had only happened six times in the history of the state. The only person actually killed was a hunter in 1943 who shot a black bear, assumed it was dead, and then got mauled by it when he went up to take a closer look. Without his firearm.

"You can see that this goes way beyond bird feeders and trash cans," Edith said. "Between the crops they're planting and the problems with waste, they're just asking for bear trouble. May as well hang out a welcome sign."

"The bears end up paying the price." He sighed. Nearly half of the bear calls that came in to their department were related to trash and the issues that arose when people didn't dispose of their trash properly.

"Such a waste," she said. "Pun intended."

"Yes." This was one of the reasons Troy often preferred animals to people.

The wind picked up, bringing with it a malodorous waft from the gully. Susie Bear sniffed the air, and ventured very close to the brink of the ridge.

"Stay," he told the dog.

'Smart move," said Edith. "You don't want her rolling around in that."

"Is that what I think it is?"

She handed him her binoculars. "See for yourself."

He trained her binoculars on the barrels. Human waste overflowed from them, frozen solid. "It sure is." Bears were attracted to the smell of human poop. He gave her back the binoculars and snapped more photos.

"Can't you shut down their wannabe church?" She stood with her gloved fists on her hips.

"What do you mean, wannabe?"

"You don't go to church anymore," she said primly.

"We're going on Christmas Eve," said Troy.

Edith scoffed. "Christmas and Easter don't count. If you were still a churchgoer, you'd know that Reverend Fitz is a fraud."

"Why do you say that?"

"I looked him up." She gave him her smart-as-a-crow stare. "On the internet. His 'divinity *degree*'"—here she used air quotes—"is from some scam religious organization. You know, the kind you can buy for a hundred bucks from an ad in the back of a magazine. He's no real preacher."

"Really," said Troy neutrally.

"And the Temple of the End of Days is as phony as he is." She leaned toward him. "All you need to start a religion in this country is three founding members, a mission statement, and a bank account. Can you believe that?"

"I didn't know that. But I'll definitely check that out. Along with these alleged violations."

"You'd better. I'd hate to have to take matters into my own hands."

Edith sounded like she would be thrilled to take matters into her own hands. And if she was half as good a shot as she was a pitcher, the Temple of the End of Days could be in trouble.

"We'll take care of it," he told her. "You did the right thing in calling us. We'll get to the bottom of this. You have my word."

They turned away and began the snowy slog back toward the house, Susie Bear alongside them, cavorting in the drifts. They hadn't gone fifty yards when the Newfie stopped mid-prance and spun around, ready to bound back toward the gulley.

"With me," ordered Troy. Quietly they stalked back just far enough to spot what Susie Bear had smelled in the air.

A large black bear was happily rooting through the trash at the bottom of the gulch. He lifted his head and sniffed the air, but after a long stare in their direction went back to his rummaging.

"Told you," whispered Edith. "Male, no doubt, given his size and the time of year."

"Safe bet." This guy was big, close to four hundred pounds, and he needed all the calories he could get to survive the winter.

Black bears didn't hibernate, as most people thought. They entered a state of torpor, retreating to their dens for most of the cold season, typically from December to April, conserving their energy until spring. But they'd venture out for good eating. Like this bear was doing. He may even have delayed his winter retreat until he could ravage this dump thoroughly.

They left the bear to his feast.

"There are a few simple things you can do to deter the bears. First, soak some rags in ammonia and toss them down there on your side of the gully. Bears hate that smell." He reached into his pocket and pulled out a black device shaped like a small walkie-talkie and handed it to her. "For now, I'll lend you my Critter Gitter, which uses heat and motion sensors to detect bears, and scares them away with flashing lights and high-pitched sounds. If that doesn't work, you can always get an electric fence. The shock discourages bears without hurting them."

"Thanks, I'll give it a try," said Edith. "But what about the cult next door? They won't bother with ammonia or Critter Gitters or electric fences. They'll just shoot."

"That would be illegal. Don't worry, I'll be talking to your neighbors," Troy assured her. "You can count on that."

CHAPTER TWENTY

Jolly old Saint Nicholas, Lean your ear this way;
Don't you tell a single soul, What I'm going to say. . . .

—EMILY HUNTINGTON MILLER

Mercy and Elvis left the Wood Works Shed behind. Felicity played with her new toy, tapping it against the carrier and babbling to herself. The shepherd was on alert, ears perked and tail up, as they made their way toward the First Congregational Church. Mercy wondered if whatever had caught his attention yesterday would capture it again today.

They joined her parents Grace and Duncan at the life-sized crèche that flanked the church, not far from the Singing Christmas Tree.

"The tree looks great, Mom," Mercy told Grace.

"It does, doesn't it?"

The tree was in fact a structure that looked much like the Singing Christmas Tree in Macy's Thanksgiving Parade. Ascending bleachers built on a wheeled platform in the conical shape of a tree, with railings covered in greenery and lights. The effect was striking.

The singers all wore jeans and snow boots, topped with bright red knit sweaters trimmed with white faux fur and red knit beanies with white faux fur pompoms. The only exceptions were Bob Cato, the crime scene tech/choir director, who looked more like Scrooge in his black woolen overcoat and top hat, and an enormous man who stood to Bob's right, in full-on Santa suit.

Mercy couldn't help but think of poor Uncle Laz. She shook off the feeling and went to greet her grandmother. Northshire's new organist was seated at a digital organ at the base of the tree on its own platform.

"I wondered how you were going to play for Singing Christmas Tree from the pipe organ inside the church," said Mercy.

"Daniel donated the digital organ to the town for this and other outdoor activities," said Patience, looking stunning in a red cape trimmed in white faux fur, her blond-gray hair tucked under a matching white faux fur pillbox hat. White fingerless gloves covered her hands.

"Nice outfit."

Patience smiled. "I have your mother to thank for that."

"You look like Julie Christie in *Dr. Zhivago*," said Mercy.

"You must mean Geraldine Chaplin," said Grace. "She wore the most elegant clothes in that film."

Mercy laughed. "I stand corrected."

Bob clapped his large hands.

"It's time," said Patience. "Off with you." She placed the talented fingers that typically handled animals with such care onto the organ's keys.

Felicity waved bye-bye to her great-grandmother as Mercy and her parents stepped back from the Singing Christmas Tree and joined the crowd gathering for the concert. Many in the audience wore Santa hats as well, in keeping with the spirit of the occasion.

Santa's elves moved among the crowd, handing out song sheets. Mercy took one with an inquiring glance at her mother.

"There are three acts," explained Grace. "In the first, the choir sings classic hymns and carols, then they switch to more modern songs, and they finish strong with a sing-along of perennial favorites."

"Fun."

Patience began to play and the powerful, floaty chords of "Angels We Have Heard on High" rang out across the town green. The choir began to sing, and people drifted over to the church from all corners of the common, drawn by the familiar melody, the dulcet tones of the instrument, and the ringing voices of the Singing Christmas Tree.

Felicity dropped her giraffe as she clapped her hands to the music, but Mercy's quick-thinking father caught it midair.

"Thanks, Dad."

"She'd rather clap," he said. "She's very musical."

"Right." Mercy got such a kick out of the way her folks, and Troy's folks as well, attributed sterling qualities to their baby with virtually no evidence to back it up. Or maybe she was totally wrong, and there was something to it. It was true that they had far more experience in parenting than she had.

She pulled the carrier off her shoulders and released her baby into Duncan's open arms. Felicity immediately pulled his goatee, and he laughed.

"She's playing beautifully," Mercy said to Grace, with a nod toward Patience.

"Of course, she is," said her mother. "The woman is a wonder."

"Look who's talking."

Grace smiled. "You know she plays at home every day."

"It's good to see her playing in public again."

Patience had played the organ at church every Sunday when her husband Red was alive. Mercy's grandfather sang with the choir, and had a beautiful bass voice that stole the show every time he sang a solo. But since his death several years ago she'd played only in the privacy of her own home. Mercy figured that her grandmother was only playing now to please Grace, and to honor Uncle Laz. Patience made a practice of saving the day, whether you were a horse with bloat or a Singing Christmas Tree without an organist.

The lilting strains of "Gloria in excelsis Deo, Gloria in excelsis Deo" echoed through the crowd, fading as the song drew to an end. Patience swept on to "Carol of the Bells," as Bob the choirmaster moved his graceful hands—the same hands that carefully processed crime scenes—to guide the singers through the four-part harmonies of the haunting "Ding Dong" carol. Felicity was mesmerized by the scene: the lights and the singers and the music. And Bob.

Even Mercy was mesmerized by this charismatic, dynamic choirmaster Bob, with his dancing hands and his passion for the music. He bore virtually no resemblance to the cranky man of forensics that she thought she knew. People surprised you—and the ones you thought you'd figured out were often the ones destined to surprise you the most.

She wasn't alone. The magic of Bob and Patience and the Singing Christmas Tree had entranced most everyone on the common by now. The concert area was filled with people standing shoulder to shoulder, faces shining and bodies swaying to the music. Many were singing along already in muted voices, since the sing-along had not officially begun.

After a lively medley of "The Little Drummer Boy," "Greensleeves," "God Rest Ye Merry Gentlemen," and "Hark! the Herald Angels Sing" drew raucous applause from the audience, Bob stopped conducting long enough for a quick bow, acknowledging both the choir singers and Patience, who all took a bow as well. Then, tapping his top hat for quiet, he tipped his top hat to Patience and she began to play once more.

"Here he comes," said Grace proudly.

"Who?"

"Our star soloist. Timothy Carter. He's a plumber from Rutland County." Grace smiled up at the platform as the large man in a full-on Santa suit stepped up to a freestanding microphone next to Bob. "Lovely baritone. They call him The Singing Plumber."

"They do not."

"Ladies and gentleman," boomed Bob, leaning in to the microphone. "Let's give a warm Northshire welcome to our special guest, The Singing Plumber, Vermont's own Tim Carter!"

"They do." Her mother placed a gloved finger on Mercy's chest. "I'll have you know that he sang the national anthem at a Red Sox game last summer." She moved her finger to Felicity's little neck, and tickled it. Her granddaughter giggled. "He's wonderful. You'll see."

Bob certainly seemed to think so. He pivoted back to his place in front of his choir and paused, waiting. Hands raised, ready to begin.

The Singing Plumber stood in front of the Singing Christmas Tree. He removed his long, red, fur-trimmed stocking cap from his silver-haired head and tucked it into his broad, shiny black belt. Smoothing his long white beard, he unhooked the microphone from its stand and looked over at the choirmaster.

"That beard is real," said Grace.

"*Shush*, love," said Duncan. "It's 'O Holy Night.'"

Patience played on, and Mercy realized that her father was right. She recognized the opening chords of the beloved sacred hymn and hoped that Tim Carter would do her favorite carol justice. She knew it was not an easy song to perform.

Bob dipped his hand at Tim Carter. The Singing Plumber closed his eyes for a moment, then opened them and began to sing, in a voice so rich and resonant it nearly brought Mercy to tears. But she did not recognize the words. She glanced over at her mother.

"He's singing it in the original French," Grace whispered. "'*Cantique de* Noël.'"

You didn't have to speak French for the carol to cast its spell. A blissful calm fell over the common as the baritone's voice swelled along with Patience's organ. Dusk was falling, and snow was falling, and the people of Northshire were falling.

No one moved. Not even Felicity. Not even Elvis. They just listened as the spirit of Christmas descended on them all. "*Noël, Noël, voici le Rédempteur.*"

Mercy realized that she was holding her breath. She exhaled as Bob swung his long arms up into the air and the entire ensemble of singers joined Tim Carter as he sang the carol again, this time in English. Together they sang the moving hymn, the choir's melodious tones the perfect complement to The Singing Plumber's sonorous baritone. By the time they rang out the last lines—"*O night, O holy night, O night divine*"—and Patience pounded out the last chords, the silence of the audience was complete . . . until everyone broke out in a roar of approval.

"Told you," said Grace, as the applause died down.

"You did," said Mercy.

"More," said Felicity, clapping her hands.

Mercy stared at her baby girl. "What?" She turned to her parents. "Did you hear that?"

"More," said Felicity again. Louder this time. Clapping harder.

"She said 'more.' Her first real word!" Mercy clapped, too. "Clever girl."

"I thought she already knows the name of the dogs," said her father.

"El and Sue. I don't count that, Dad."

He smiled. "I bet the dogs do."

"Your first word was 'No,'" pointed out Grace. "I'd considered this a win."

Mercy kissed Felicity, and bounced her up and down. "More! More! More!"

"More!" her brilliant baby said again.

"But Troy missed it." Mercy felt bad about that. "He missed her first *noun.*"

"Don't tell him," advised her mother. "She'll say it again when he's around. Let him have his fun."

"They're starting up again." Duncan nodded toward the Singing Christmas Tree.

"'O Holy Night' was the big finale for the classic hymn part of the show. They'll sing some more modern songs now," said Grace.

Of course, her mother was right. Bob once again tipped his hat to her grandmother. And Patience once again tinkled the organ keys . . . well, as much as you could tinkle organ keys. The choir broke into "Feliz Navidad," followed by "Dreidel, Dreidel, Dreidel," both bringing the audience to its feet, dancing along to the lively songs. Felicity loved it.

When the last *"dreidel, dreidel, dreidel"* faded into the air, Patience began to play the ever-popular "Santa Claus Is Comin' to Town." Still at the mike, Tim Carter pulled his long stocking cap out of his belt and placed it back on his head. Smiling broadly, his white beard bouncing, he began to sing, this time in what Mercy could only think of as a holly, jolly baritone. The choir stood in as backup singers, doo-wopping it up behind The Singing Plumber, complete with a bit of hand jive.

As he playfully cautioned children young and old not to cry and not to pout, the crowd sang along. Many began to dance, doing hand jive moves as well. Mercy held up Felicity and she played patty-cake with her grandfather. Elvis remained perfectly still, seated by her side. The shepherd did not play patty-cake.

"Santa Claus is comin' to town," sang the choir, as one of Santa's helpers brought out a big red bag and set it down next to The Singing Plumber. The audience roared their approval, and the elf took a bow, then scampered off. Disappearing into the throng.

As the Singing Christmas Tree launched into "Here Comes Santa Claus," Tim Carter replaced the microphone, picked up his bulging sack, and headed into the crowd. As he greeted his audience, he dipped his hand into the bag, pulling out jingle bells and candy canes and red and green glow-in-the-dark bouncy balls and passing them out to all the kids.

As the deep-voiced St. Nick wove through the crowd toward Mercy and her family, Elvis rose up and leaned forward, ears perked. Dark eyes trained on The Singing Plumber.

"Merry Christmas!" Santa said to Felicity, who reached out and tugged at his beard.

"It's the real thing," he told her as he held up a pair of jingle bells and shook them gently. The jinglejangle delighted Felicity. She released the poor man's beard and reached for the bells.

He let her take the bells, and then put a finger to the side of his nose and winked at Mercy. "Lovely baby."

"Thank you. Great performance," Mercy said, and her parents murmured their agreement.

Elvis raised his nose at Tim Carter.

"That's some dog," he said.

"He's a good boy," said Mercy.

Tim Carter saluted Elvis, smiled at Felicity, and then set his bright blue eyes on the next child. As the choir caroled the last verse, he quickened his pace, tossing bells and balls and canes deep into the crowd. His bag empty, The Singing Plumber returned to Bob's side, waving to the audience before taking a final bow.

Everyone clapped and whooped and whistled as he took the microphone once again. "Thank you, thank you, thank you." He smiled a big Santa smile. "One more, and then I've got to get back to the North Pole. Very busy time of year, you know."

Everyone laughed, and then settled down as Patience played the intro to "Have Yourself a Merry Little Christmas." Bob flicked his fingers with a flourish at Tim Carter and the audience once again seemed to hold its breath, Mercy included. Waiting for his glorious baritone to bring the wistful tune to life.

But The Singing Plumber did not sing. He stood there, as still as snow, his mouth open but issuing no sound. Everyone waited.

"He missed his cue," whispered Grace. "What is he doing?"

"I don't know, but don't worry," said Mercy. "Bob's got this."

She'd barely uttered the words when the choirmaster gestured to Patience, who without missing a beat seamlessly transitioned from the main melody back to the introduction. Mercy could feel everyone rustle around her in anticipation.

That anticipation turned to anxiety when Tim Carter missed his cue again. People began to mutter, shifting and shuffling closer to the Singing Christmas Tree to see what was going on.

"What's wrong with him?" asked Grace.

Tim gasped for breath. Once. Twice. Three times. The microphone slipped from his hand, dropping to the ground with a terrible thud that echoed out over the common.

A discordant chord followed. Patience stopped playing the organ, rising to her feet. Bob stopped conducting, hands in midair. The choir members stopped singing, a staggered dwindling of notes.

Someone screamed. Elvis barked. Felicity cried.

The Singing Plumber teetered and tottered and clutched his chest, his face crumpled in pain. Bob moved in front of him just as he pitched forward. Falling, falling, falling.

Right into the choirmaster's arms.

CHAPTER TWENTY-ONE

Sire, the night is darker now
And the wind blows stronger
Fails my heart, I know not how
I can go no longer.

—"GOOD KING WENCESLAS," FOURTH VERSE

Mercy stood with her parents watching Officers Becker and Goodlove keep the throng of onlookers at bay as the EMTs carried a prone Tim Carter away. The ambulance had arrived within minutes, but they all knew by then that it was too late. Tim Carter had suffered an apparent heart attack, and efforts to resuscitate him had failed. The Singing Plumber would sing no more.

Bob and Patience and his choir tried to soldier on with the sing-along, but it was clear that no one's heart was in it. After a rather pitiful rendition of "Good King Wenceslas," Grace made an executive decision. "I'm pulling the plug on the Singing Christmas Tree."

Mercy watched as her mother marched up to Bob, whispering in the choirmaster's ear. Declaring the concert over, no doubt. Grace stood by Bob's side as he made the announcement, using the same microphone with which the magnificent baritone had sung his last song.

Bob removed his top hat, just as The Singing Plumber had removed his stocking cap when he sang "O Holy Night." He told the audience, "Given tonight's tragedy, we've decided to wrap up our concert now. But before we go, let's have a moment of silence, please, while our organist Patience Fleury O'Sullivan performs Sir George Thomas Thalben-Ball's *Elegy*. Our thoughts are with Tim Carter and his loved ones."

As Patience played the meditative piece, the crowd fell into a poignant silence. Many tapped on their cell lights, the bouncing beams brightening the gloom as dusk fell.

As her grandmother sounded the final notes of the piece, Bob replaced his top hat and the choir quietly closed their songbooks. Patience bowed her head and folded her hands in her lap. The Singing Christmas Tree disbanded, the crowd dispersed, and the organizers removed the organ.

Patience and Grace rejoined Mercy and the family. Her grandmother's face was pale. "I can't believe it. The poor man."

"It's terrible," said Mercy, her mind racing to the worst-case scenario. A worst-case scenario that was truly too terrible to contemplate.

"But?" Her father gave her an apprising look. "I am sensing a 'but' here."

"That's two dead Santas in two days," said Mercy.

Her grandmother shook her head. "I may only be an animal doctor, but I know a heart attack when I see one."

"Let's hope so," said Mercy.

"Our Mercy doesn't believe in coincidences, do you?" observed her father in the quiet, professorial manner in which he addressed juries in the courtroom. In his way, he was just as effective an attorney as her mother was, the yang to her yin.

"Of course it was a heart attack," said Grace with such force that no one dared defy her. "Anything else is unthinkable."

"Or something lethal that presents as a heart attack," said. Mercy.

"Possible," said Patience. "Something like digoxin could do it."

"Digitalis," said Mercy. "Foxglove." Thanks to her herbalist neighbor Adah, Mercy was learning all about the beneficial—and lethal—aspects of plants. Adah used all kinds of plants and herbs in her popular line of organic beauty products.

"Yes." Patience gave Elvis a head scratch. "In humans, digoxin is prescribed to treat heart failure and atrial fibrillation. It's not approved by the FDA as a veterinary med, but sometimes vets do use it off-label to treat congestive heart failure and arrhythmia in dogs and horses. It's a tricky medication, in humans and in animals. You have to be careful with it, and monitor patients closely."

"Our Singing Plumber died of natural causes," said Grace, only slightly less vehemently.

"Dr. Darling will figure it out, one way or another," said Patience. "She's very good."

"If they even bother with an autopsy," said Mercy. "If it looks like natural causes"—at this she gave her mother a reassuring smile—"and there's no apparent motive, they may not."

"I don't think Detective Harrington believes in coincidences, either," said Duncan.

Mercy nodded. "No cops do."

"Whether it's murder or bad luck or coincidence or fate doesn't matter," said Grace. "What matters is that it's only December twenty-second, and we still have ten more days of the Solstice Soirée to go. We cannot afford any more of these unfortunate incidents."

"It's not your fault, love," said Patience.

"I don't know what's happening here, but it must stop," said Grace. "It simply will not do. Not on my watch." She straightened her spine, and smoothed the front of her burgundy wool trousers.

One of her mother's classic moves. *Here come my instructions,* thought Mercy, biting back a smile. And wondering if Felicity would learn to read her as well as she could read her mother.

Grace turned to her. "Mercy, take my granddaughter home to see her first Christmas tree." She smiled at Felicity, tucking her red curls back under her knitted cap just as she'd done countless times for Mercy when she was little. "And once she's in bed, you can sit down and do whatever it is you do with that singular brain of yours to figure out what is going on here. Before the next catastrophe."

"They say bad things come in threes," said her father.

"What happens twice, happens three times," added Patience.

"You are not helping, either of you," admonished Grace. But to Mercy she said, "They could be right. Which is why we need *you*."

"Let me see what I can do," Mercy said, stealing her mother's trademark line, the one she used on clients with impossible cases, even though she had no idea what she could do at this point apart from continuing to dig into Uncle Laz's past. And maybe The Singing Plumber's, if it came to that. "You're all welcome to drop by to see the tree. And have some supper. Patience made lasagna. And lemon squares."

"We'll see," said Grace. "We've got damage control to do here."

"Can't keep me away." Patience slipped her arm through Mercy's. "Let's go."

Mercy blew her parents kisses and Felicity followed suit. Her baby girl loved blowing kisses. "Come on, Elvis."

The three of them—grandmother, granddaughter, great-granddaughter—cut across the common together, Felicity shrieking as snow once again began to fall. Elvis stayed close to Mercy, nose at her hip, ears perked. There were few people in this part of the town green now; most had moved on to the Christmas markets for the food and drink and shopping. Only three shopping days left before Christmas, after all.

They passed the structure that supported the Singing Christmas Tree, which a couple of men in work clothes were busy dismantling. Others were erecting a sign that advertised the next big entertainment of the Solstice Soirée, *A Christmas Carol*, to be performed the very next night by one of Vermont's most esteemed theater groups, the Green Mountain Players. Mercy hoped for her mother's sake and the sake of all Northshire that the play went off without a hitch. At least there was no Santa Claus in Dickens's holiday tale. Just ghosts.

Elvis whined and pulled at the lead. Trying to go back in the direction from which they'd come.

"With me," said Mercy firmly, ordering the shepherd to heel.

But Elvis did not listen. He simply sat down on his haunches. Refusing to move. And barking.

"Let him go," said Patience.

Mercy looked around. She had the feeling that someone was watching her, but there was no one else here but the workers, and they were busy doing their job. No one was paying any attention to her—or to Elvis.

She couldn't imagine what he was going on about, but then she rarely could. The brilliant shepherd operated in a world that was mostly invisible to Mercy, a world of sounds and scents beyond her ken.

She unhooked his lead, wondering what he'd find this time. Hoping it was just the odd cigarette butt, like yesterday, and not a corpse, like the day before.

He veered away, toward one of the beams that had supported the structure of the Singing Christmas Tree.

"And he's off," said Patience.

"El!" cried Felicity. "El!"

She handed Felicity to Patience. "I'll be right back."

"Always trust your dog," her grandmother reminded her.

Mercy followed Elvis as he darted through the workmen disassembling the Singing Christmas Tree to the farthest pile of pieces used to build the tree structure. The beams and bleachers were sitting right about where Tim Carter had stood while performing his lovely solos. Beyond that space was a long hedge of holly bushes that flanked the steps that led up to the entrance of the First Congregational Church.

To the right stood the stable that housed the church's Nativity scene, crudely fashioned out of wood. The life-sized sculptures of Mary and Joseph—along with a donkey and a couple of sheep—were made of metal painted so cleverly as to appear three-dimensional. A star twinkled over the stable and an angel floated above the scene. Spotlights shone on the Holy Family, the brightest bathing the manger—empty but for a red blanket—in light. The effect was dazzling.

Even if the Baby Jesus had yet to make his appearance.

Elvis did not seem impressed. He easily leapt the fence separating the Nativity scene from the path and bounded into the stable.

"Elvis!" Mercy called for the shepherd to return, but he'd sunk into his Sphinx position, alerting to something. Not moving a muscle.

"I'm going to hell," she muttered to herself as she climbed over the fence and headed into the stable. She knelt down next to Elvis, who remained steadfast in his mission. She studied the scene before her, but she could see nothing of interest, nothing that might trigger the dog.

"What are we looking at here, boy?"

He tilted his head, triangular ears up, as if to say, "Duh."

"I don't get it. Spell it out for me."

The Malinois leaned forward, and nudged the red blanket in the manger with his nose.

Mercy slipped her winter gloves out of her coat pocket and slipped them on. She squatted down, pulling the blanket out of the small wooden trough, scattering straw as she did. As the blanket unfurled, she realized that it was not a blanket, per se, but rather a large sack.

Santa's sack. The bag Tim Carter used to carry the toys he passed out among the crowd. "Nicely done, Elvis."

The dog thumped his tail in acknowledgment of his justly earned praise.

"But why is it in the manger?" She ran her gloved hand around the inside of the sack, and felt a slim object at the bottom. "There's something here."

Mercy pulled it out and held it under the light where she and Elvis could see it.

It was a used syringe. The better to inject someone.

"Good boy, Elvis."

But the shepherd was paying no attention to her. He pivoted gracefully and barked. A single bark. His signal bark.

"What is that?"

Mercy looked up to find the reporter Cat Torano hovering over her. Elvis growled.

"Step back," said Mercy.

Cat stood her ground, training her cell on Mercy. "Let me see that."

Elvis growled again, lips curled. This woman was either really intrepid or really stupid, thought Mercy. Few people failed to retreat when confronted with a snarling Malinois. She rose to her feet. "Step back," she warned again.

Cat hesitated. Elvis leaned forward, his sleek body an arrow tipped with bared teeth pointing right at the reporter's gloved hand. Staring at her as if she were a bullseye.

"That's Malinator for 'back off,'" she warned the reporter.

"What's a Malinator?" Cat looked more curious than cowed.

"You don't want to find out."

"Then call him off," the reporter said, a challenge in her voice.

"Put the cell away first."

This was a game of chicken Mercy knew she would win. After all, she had Elvis on her side.

Cat sighed and tucked her cell into her coat pocket.

"Down, Elvis."

The shepherd dropped to the ground, still staring at the reporter.

"This is a crime scene now." Mercy texted Officer Becker, one eye on Cat. "You need to leave."

"That's a syringe." Cat gazed at the shepherd with admiration. "He found it, didn't he?"

Mercy ignored the question. "The police will be here shortly."

"That's one smart dog. I knew he was onto something."

"Have you been following us?" That feeling that someone was watching her had not been her overactive imagination at work, it had been Cat. Mercy was equally annoyed and amused. Wait till Harrington heard that reporters were abandoning him for Elvis. Although that could not last. She couldn't have this journalist or any other tailing them. She'd put a stop to that.

Cat shrugged her narrow shoulders. "I go where the story goes. Seems like that means going where your dog goes."

"That sounds like stalking to me." Mercy pointed toward the common. "Out. Now."

"But—"

"Elvis, come on." With the help of the shepherd, she ushered the woman out of the crèche and back over the fence.

"Is that syringe what killed The Singing Plumber?"

"I don't know." A ping on her cell. Mercy glanced down to see an otw text from Becker. "The cops are on their way."

"At least let me get a photo of you and Elvis and the stable."

"No."

"What are you, one of those cops who don't believe in freedom of the press?"

"I'm not a cop."

"Once a cop, always a cop."

Mercy sighed. "One photo. Of Elvis. Not me."

Cat nodded, her black bangs bobbing, making her look even more like a Tibetan terrier. A self-satisfied canine who'd caught a big find on the mountainside.

Mercy ordered Elvis to sit in front of the fence, the crèche in the background.

Cat aimed her cell camera lens at the Malinois. "Smile, Superdog, smile."

DECEMBER 23

I have always thought of Christmas Time, when it has come round—apart from the veneration due to its sacred name and origin, if anything belonging to it can be apart from that—as a good time: a kind, forgiving, charitable, pleasant time: the only time I know of, in the long calendar of the year, when men and women seem by one consent to open their shut-up hearts, freely, and to think of people below them as if they really were fellow-passengers to the grave, and not another race of creatures bound on other journeys.

—CHARLES DICKENS,
A CHRISTMAS CAROL

CHAPTER TWENTY-TWO

Every winter,
When the great sun has turned his face away,
The earth goes down into the vale of grief,
And fasts, and weeps, and shrouds herself in sables. . . .

—CHARLES KINGSLEY

Just about the time Troy figured that Mercy would be heading toward the funeral, he got a text from Gil asking him to meet him at Leland Hallett's place. It turned out that the Mainer had inherited his dad's place here in Vermont, and went back and forth between the two residences. They'd gotten a search warrant and they were ready to execute that warrant.

Hallett lived in a single-wide on the north fork of Terry Brook, not far from Egg Mountain near the town line between Sandgate and Rupert. The fact that the poacher lived so close to the critical ecological area that local residents and the Vermont Department of Forests, Parks, and Recreation were so eager to acquire and protect was not lost on Troy. No doubt it wasn't lost on Gil either.

The Ford F-150 jounced along the unpaved road that led to the trailer. Snow was falling at a slow but steady pace, big fat flakes that stuck to most surfaces like glue. At the end of the road on the bank of the brook perched the old single-wide. It was a long box covered in a mishmash of siding, all painted a sad-looking brown the color of mud, with small windows set so high on the walls that they looked like eyes. You could see the rust on the metal roof despite the snow. A sagging screened-in porch jutted out from the trailer, enclosing the front door.

Troy sat in his truck, Susie Bear by his side, and scanned the premises.

The small yard was cluttered with steel barrels and old tools and discarded car parts half buried in the snow. No one seemed to be around. He heard a dog barking somewhere from within the single-wide, but he saw no canine head popping up in the windows. The yapping had a pathetic ring to it, the sound of an unhappy dog rather than an aggressive one.

Susie Bear barked back. That silenced Hallett's miserable hound, at least for the moment. Since the perp had yet to post bail, and as far as Troy knew he lived here on his own, the poor dog had probably been alone in that tin can a while, and was hungry by now.

Susie Bear gave Troy a sorrowful look, as if she were thinking the same thing. Maybe she was. He looked at the Newfie. "It's okay, girl, we'll take care of your pal."

Gil drove up, and together with Susie Bear they trudged through the snow, making their own path since Hallett didn't seem to be into shoveling. They slipped on gloves and knocked on the flimsy storm door to the porch, but no one answered. A gust of wind flapped the door open and they went on in. The small space served as a sort of mudroom, crowded with boots and coats and hats, dog food and fishing rods and boxes of canned goods. The only possible hunting paraphernalia were a couple of empty pet cages that might or might not have spelled poaching.

"We can tag the cages, but there doesn't seem to be anything else incriminating here," said Gil. "Let's go on inside."

Troy told Susie Bear to stay. Gil knocked on this door, too, and the only reply was a frenzy of yowling and a scramble of scratching on the other side of the door.

"I think that's dog for 'Come in'," said Gil, pushing open the unlocked door.

"Hang tight," said Troy to Susie Bear as he closed the door behind him, her dark eyes watching him mournfully.

Hallett's dog was a jumper. The English springer spaniel bounced up and down, desperate for attention and company. Troy's cousin raised spaniels; he knew they were a nervous breed prone to separation anxiety. Certainly, this lovely girl was a shivering, slobbering wreck. He stroked her long silky ears and spoke to her in a calm, firm voice, slipping her a doggy biscuit from his pocket.

The spaniel calmed down but the racket continued. More noise was coming from what Troy assumed was the bedroom.

Troy and Gil exchanged a look. They moved toward the door, and the cacophony of growling, hissing, and squealing increased exponentially as they approached.

"You've got to be kidding me," said Troy.

"Merde," said Gil. "Skunks."

Troy sighed. The ranger was right—odds were that what was behind that door were skunks. At least a pair of them, maybe more, from the sound of it. "Let's hope they've been de-scented."

Gil crossed himself. "Please, God."

"Do you see a pet cage anywhere?" They both glanced around the room.

Cleanliness was not exactly a priority for Leland Hallett. Dirty dishes in the sink, clothes littering the floor, empty beer cans and fast food wrappers scattered across the threadbare couch in the corner. The small kitchen table doubled as a desk; there was a stack of mail and papers tucked messily into a shoe box and an assortment of sophisticated computer equipment. Troy snapped photos on his cell, documenting the disarray. "I didn't see Hallett as a tech guy."

"Me either." Gil looked around. "That seems to be the only stuff here from the twenty-first century."

"No cages," said Troy.

"Except for the ones on the porch. Which we'll need for forensics." Gil pointed to the wall and whistled. "Look at that."

The only decorating touch, if you could call it that, was the gun rack hanging over the flat-screen TV in the tiny living room. The rack was empty but for an old M1 Garand semiautomatic rifle, the kind issued to American soldiers in World War II.

"Been a while since I've seen one of those," said Gil.

"My great-grandfather had one," said Troy. "He gave it to my granddad when he passed on. My dad has it now, locked up in the gun safe."

"Right place for it."

They stared at the M1 Garand on the gun rack for a moment. Hallett's old rifle was a souvenir, no doubt, or a sentimental hand-me-down from an older relation. The rest of the perp's weapons were probably the hunting long guns they'd confiscated from the man's truck when they arrested him. Unless they found more somewhere else on the property.

"We're going to have to take those skunks in," said Troy finally.

"I'll fetch a cage and some bait," said Gil.

The ranger left the house. Troy could hear him talking to Susie Bear, who was waiting patiently outside. Troy found the dog dishes, filling them with water and kibble from the porch for the spaniel. The dog scarfed down her food, and while she was eating, he took the opportunity to check out the postage-stamp kitchen. There were some photos on the fridge door held in place by John Deere magnets featuring the leaping stag logo: one of Hallett and the sad-looking older woman Troy would bet was his mother; a beach shot of a pretty girl, no Hallett in sight; and a trophy pic of Hallett and another hunter hunkered over a dead moose. The hunter looked familiar somehow, but Troy couldn't place him. He snapped photos of all the pics, and then started going through the few cabinets in the kitchen and the box of mail on the table.

Just the usual bills and advertisements, including a stack of religious pamphlets, *The Watchtower* and the *Adventist Review* and *The Friend*, along with local church bulletins from the First Congregational Church, the Temple of the End of Days, the Baptist Fellowship of Northshire, Ascension Episcopal Church, and St. Mary of the Mountains.

Troy was surprised; he hadn't figured Hallett for a religious man. But if these publications were any indication, he was a seeker. Although with those boxes of canned goods on the porch he could see the guy as a survivalist—and that often went hand in hand with religion.

Gil lugged in a metal spray-proof skunk trap, a pet cage, a baggie full of marshmallows, and a catch pole. He handed the pole to Troy. "Backup."

"Right." With any luck, they would not need the backup. The good news was that skunks moved clumsily and relatively slowly; they relied on their stink rather than their speed to deter predators. That's why so many ended up as roadkill, because they hadn't run off quickly enough.

Still, trapping an unknown number of unhappy mammals who'd been holed up in a trailer for God knows how long could end up being a very smelly comedy of errors. Snaring a surfeit of skunks could make even the most experienced game warden feel more like a Keystone Cop than a law enforcement professional.

"Find anything in here?" asked Gil.

"Not really." Troy pointed to the electronics. "We can tag those and have the techies go through them." He spotted a leash hanging by the door and tied the spaniel to a kitchen table leg. "That should keep her while we round up the stinkers."

"*Bien.*" Gil placed the long PVC pipe–style trap on the floor against the bedroom door, and armed it with the marshmallows. He paused, his gloved hand on the doorknob. "Ready?"

"Ready." Troy stood behind the ranger, pole poised.

Swiftly Gil threw open the door and shoved the trap inside. Two skunks assailed the door, stomping and hissing and puffing. Gil slammed the door shut, pounding their little snouts in the process. The spaniel whined.

"*Ouf,*" said Gil.

"You can say that again," said Troy.

"*Ouf.*"

"How many of them did you see?"

"Two."

"That was my count, too."

"No spray."

"So far so good."

They heard a thump coming from the bedroom, the sound of the trap-door slipping down into place.

"One down," said Gil. "One to go."

"If we're lucky." They only had the one trap, so they had to move the trapped skunk from the trap to the pet cage and try again for the second skunk. But his pal might or might not fall for the same trap, no many how many marshmallows they used as bait. Depending on how smart this particular skunk was. And skunks were pretty smart, smart enough to grow trap-shy quickly.

Gil lured the trapped skunk into the pet cage with more marshmallows. The skunk obviously preferred the open-air cage to the dark tunnel trap. The little guy went willingly into the cage and did not spray them.

"De-scented and cage-trained," said Troy. "Outstanding. Let's do it again."

Gil armed the trap with marshmallows a second time.

"On three," said Troy.

"*Un, deux, trois.*" Gil pushed open the door again, grabbed the trap, and yanked it toward him. As soon as the trap cleared the threshold, Troy reached for the doorknob and jerked it closed.

Too late.

A blur of black and white galloped awkwardly past Troy's legs. Gil grinned at him as he spun around, catch pole in hand. He looped the little animal's neck in one toss.

"Yippee ki-yay," said Gil.

Troy gently lifted the skunk into the cage along with his friend.

"I'll search the bedroom," said Gil.

The spaniel yowled as Troy took the skunk cage out to the truck. Susie Bear watched, tail whomping in the snow as he came back to the trailer.

"Anything?" he asked Gil.

"Our boy liked his weed, but other than that there's not much in there but old porn magazines and unopened packs of condoms. And a Bible, with an inscription from Reverend Fitz."

"Nice," said Troy. "I'd like to see that Bible."

Gil gave him a knowing look. "Knock yourself out."

Troy fetched the Bible. Reverend Fitz's inscription read:

> *Proverbs 18:22 Whoso findeth a wife findeth a good thing, and obtaineth favor of the Lord.*
>
> *Yours in Christ, Reverend Fitz.*

He flipped through the stiff pages, but found nothing to indicate that Hallett had ever read any of the good book he'd been given by the good reverend.

"We need to search the outbuildings."

Troy nodded. "Susie Bear can help."

Gil gathered up the rest of the evidence while Troy gave Susie Bear the command to search. The Newfie shambled around the yard, sniffing at the piles of snow-covered junk. She loved her job; for her, hide-and-seek was even more fun in the snow.

Gil caught up with Troy and together they followed the snow-happy dog around to the back of the house, where an old wooden shed with peeling white paint stood at the very edge of the bank, leaning so sharply toward the water that the next strong wind might toss it right over into the water. The brook was fast-moving; even with the cold only patches of the surface were frozen in ice.

Susie Bear danced through the snow, dropping down with a heavy plop in front of the shed door. A combination lock hung at an angle from a rusted latch.

"No sounds of crazed skunks coming from inside."

"*Bon.*" Gil pulled a pair of bolt cutters from his utility belt and lopped off the lock. "Talk about making it easy for us," he said, replacing the cutters and pushing the door open.

"Bingo," said Troy.

Inside was a tumble of illegal traps of all kinds, from snares and foothold traps to toothed traps and even explosives. Pelts hung from hooks; Troy spotted bobcat and marten pelts among them.

Gil and Troy snapped photos and began to gather the evidence. But Susie Bear wasn't finished yet. She shimmied through the snowdrifts, following the brook.

"And she's off again," said Troy.

They followed her. About a hundred yards from the house, they came to a Conex container tucked under a towering pine. The Newfoundland dropped onto her belly, sniffing at the edges of the steel box. She barked.

And a wailing answered her.

The pained cries of foxes in distress.

Troy looked at Gil. "What *won't* Hallett catch."

Gil shook his head. "We'll pack them up on the way back."

They continued their search of the property, and with Susie Bear's help, they located a dozen illegally set foothold traps. The most disturbing find—the one that would earn Susie Bear a rare treat: a steak dinner—was a five-gallon bucket full of corn and illegally rigged with a snare designed to trap bear.

"Bastard," said Gil.

"Yep," said Troy.

They photographed everything they found and called in backup to expand the search and remove all the evidence.

"I can wrap this up," said Gil. "You need to get to that funeral."

Troy checked his watch. "I'm missing the funeral. But if I leave soon I might make the reception at my mother-in-law's house."

"Never miss an event hosted by your *belle-mère*," said Gil solemnly.

"I'll take the spaniel. I'm sure Patience will take good care of her."

"Deal." Gil smiled at Troy. "Good day's work. This should put Hallett out of business for a while."

"Hope so." Troy called Susie Bear, and she shambled over. "Come on, girl, let's go free the foxes."

CHAPTER TWENTY-THREE

Snow beneath whose chilly softness
Some that never lay
Make their first Repose this Winter. . . .

—EMILY DICKINSON

THEY DIDN'T WASTE ANY TIME BURYING LAZLO FORD. MERCY SAT on a hard pew at the front of the nave of the First Congregational Church, half turned in her seat so she could watch the people as they gathered for the funeral. Her mother and her great-uncle sat with her, waiting for Uncle Laz's service to begin. Elvis was under the oak bench, snoring lightly.

"I can't believe they arranged this so quickly," whispered Mercy. "Especially this time of year."

"The town council wanted it over and done with immediately," said Grace. "Better for all concerned."

"And the better for Solstice Soirée," said Mercy.

"No one wants to go to a funeral during the holidays."

Mercy didn't want to go to a funeral anytime. She'd left the baby at home with Tandie, who was on Christmas break. Amy and Brodie would be there, too, as the decorating continued. And Troy's family, if they hadn't come to the funeral. She suspected they would come; she hadn't seen them yet, but they could be here somewhere in this crowd.

Troy and Susie Bear were out on patrol, their last before Christmas. She wished they were here with her. Mercy hated funerals, even as she recognized the importance of the ritual. But she'd attended too many of them—and to her mind, too many of them fell far too short of a proper farewell.

Maybe this one would be different. She spotted Lillian Jenkins up by the altar, outfitted in a black dress with her trademark peplum, the ministerial white collar at her neck. Lillian was an ordained minister—she'd married Mercy and Troy—and she filled in from time to time for local ministers.

And where the grande dame of Northshire went, the townspeople followed. Mercy looked behind her. The church was overflowing at this point, the funeral service for Lazlo Ford having attracted so very many people. Mourners crowded the pews and the aisles, with standing room only in the back. More spilled out the double oak front doors onto the steps outside.

It was snowing in earnest this morning and everyone was in full winter gear, tramping into the sanctuary in wet boots and leaving puddles on the red rug runners that ran along the old plank floors down the center aisle up to the altar.

"Where's Reverend Jane?" Mercy asked her mother. Reverend Jane Williams was the minister here at the First Congregational Church. As much as she loved Lillian, Mercy was surprised not to see Reverend Jane here. It was, after all, her parish, and Lazlo had been the organist.

"She was already booked for a service at the assisted living center and a Blessing of the Animals over at the local shelter," said Grace. "Besides, Lillian really wanted to do it. She adored Lazlo."

"Really?" Mercy was very fond of Uncle Laz, they all were, but "adore" was a very strong word that was usually not applied to men as unassuming as he.

"Laz advised her on the restaurant accounts. His financial acumen kept The Vermonter from going under more than once."

"I had no idea."

"Lazlo was very generous that way," said Grace. "Lillian wasn't the only one in town who benefited from his advice."

"Interesting." Mercy looked around the church, wondering how many other upstanding Northshire citizens owed their fiscal solvency to Lazlo.

"That's why so many local business owners are paying their respects," said her mother. She tipped her perfectly coiffed blond head toward the stained-glass windows on the other side of the church, then leaned in to whisper. "There's Adele Dantas of Adele's Boutique and Rupert Percy of Percy's Antiques & Collectibles and Barry Abalos of the Northshire Credit Union. And of course you know Jillian Merrill the Realtor and Brooklyn Kennedy the hairdresser and Monique Simon the hostess at *Eggs Over Easy*. Practically everyone with a business license picked Lazlo's brain at one time or another. Even if it was just over a cup of coffee at a Chamber of Commerce meeting."

"I see Doris and Maureen, too." The tiny silver-haired sisters ran a feline rescue organization called the Cat House, endowed by their great-aunt Clara, the Grand Cat Lady herself, who'd left her sizable fortune and her eighteenth-century Northshire saltbox to cats in need, care of Doris and Maureen.

"Lazlo loved cats," said Grace. "But he was just as generous with his time with other nonprofit organizations as well. Every nonprofit director in the county is probably here."

So it wasn't just his work for the town government that endeared him to the villagers, thought Mercy. That seemed to be the real reason there were so many here to remember such a self-effacing man. As a tribute to his financial acumen and largesse.

It was a lovely place for such a tribute. The church was beautifully decorated with freshly cut evergreen and holly and mistletoe and white candles. A simple crèche stood on a small table to the right of the altar and brightly colored felt banners with silhouettes of the Holy Family proclaiming "Peace on Earth" and "Hope Is Born" hung on the walls between the simple stained-glass windows. Mercy smiled at the realization that apart from the banners and the crèche, the Christmas decorations were not much different from the Druids' winter solstice decorations.

The smell of damp wool and fresh snow mixed with the clean scent of pine and candle wax to sweeten the air of the nave. Even with the front doors open, the usually drafty church was warm thanks to all the people gathered here to honor and remember poor Uncle Lazlo. For a quiet loner of a man with few close friends and no family to speak of, apart from Mercy's, Lazlo had obviously won the hearts of the people of Northshire—and they'd all come out to see him off into the great unknown.

Except for his murderer. Who'd hated Lazlo enough to kill him in such a brutal way.

Mercy scanned the faces in the pews. Everyone seemed appropriately respectful if not altogether somber. She wondered if the killer was here. Watching and gloating and believing they'd gotten away with murder. For Christmas.

She spotted Fitzgerald Frost near the back. "I'm surprised to see Reverend Fitz here."

"Where?"

Mercy tipped her head in his direction.

"How inappropriate." Grace glared at the preacher. "Lazlo hated him and his father and their ersatz evangelism."

Fitz shrank against the wall of the church, as if he could feel the prick of her mother's pointed disdain all the way across the nave. Other mourners pushed in front of him, and he was lost to view. When the crowd thinned again, he was gone.

"Good riddance," said Grace.

Mercy leaned toward the colonel. Uncle Hugo had *The New Century Hymnal* open on his lap, but he wasn't looking at it. His eyes were closed and his hands were clenched at the base of the book. She knew this meant not that he was sleeping, as he might want onlookers to believe, but that he was thinking. Dark thoughts, by the look of those fists.

Mercy checked the numbers on the hymn board that hung from a pillar on the left at the front of the church: 438, 99, 606. She checked the spread of the pages in her great-uncle's hymnal: "O Little Town of Bethlehem." Hymn number 133 in the thick volume that held some six hundred hymns.

Uncle Hugo appeared to be thinking along the same lines that she was. He wasn't convinced that the torn sheet of music Dr. Darling had found in Uncle Lazlo's gloved hand when he died was just a coincidence, either. He believed that it meant something, that it was a message of some sort, planted by the killer or provided by Uncle Lazlo in a desperate attempt to identify his attacker.

"You can't let it go." Mercy tapped the page of the hymnal on her uncle's lap. He acted as if he were startled, but she knew better. The colonel was a light sleeper, as most soldiers were and always would be, long after they'd left the battlefield. He knew what she was doing.

"Can *you*?"

"No. Have you learned anything else about Uncle Laz?"

He frowned. "I've been asking around, but everyone is very tight-lipped."

"But we're talking years ago. What about the Freedom of Information Act?"

He ignored that. "I think it must have something to do with the Cold War and its aftermath."

"You heard about The Singing Plumber."

"Yes."

"And the syringe." Mercy paused. "Even I know that's a classic KGB move."

"Not just KGB. Drug addicts. Doctors. Nurses."

"Do we know what was in the syringe?" If anyone outside law enforcement knew, it would be her uncle.

"The official word is digoxin. But they haven't announced it yet."

Digoxin. The drug that could save your heart—or stop it altogether.

The colonel pulled out his phone from his coat pocket, tapping and scrolling before handing it to Mercy. "Here's the autopsy report."

"That was fast, even for you."

"Coming on the heels of Lazlo's murder, people are motivated. These deaths have triggered some very important people."

"Like who?"

Uncle Hugo chose not to answer that one. *Interesting. Who was Tim Carter, anyway?* Mercy wondered as she skimmed the report. She tried another question. "What do you know about him?"

"On paper, he appeared to be your typical Vermonter outdoorsman. He liked to fish, hunt, trap." The colonel gave her a wry smile. "And he actually *was* a singing plumber. He did a lot of plumbing, mostly commercial work but also some residential. Remodeling and restoration work as well as new build."

"Who kills a plumber?"

"Indeed. Although he did have a reputation as a ladies' man. They called him the Rogue of Rutland."

"They did not."

"No, they did not." He laughed, earning a disapproving glance from Grace. "But they will now. Apparently, he was very active on Tinder."

Ironic, thought Mercy, since her great-uncle was also known as quite the playboy. She kept a straight face as she said, "Really."

"And he applied for more than one fiancée visa."

"Really," Mercy said again. She'd known several guys in the army who'd applied for fiancée visas for foreigners they'd met abroad—and all to a man had gone on to marry them. "But he never married any of them?"

"Not that we know of."

"Shush," admonished Grace. "It's starting. Your grandmother is playing."

The opening notes of "It Was Well with My Soul" sounded throughout the church. Mercy stole a glance back up at the gallery, where Patience reigned at the spectacular antique pipe organ. There was no choir in attendance; presumably they were all too traumatized by the night before. But Patience being Patience, the show went on. And she played.

The pallbearers—Feinberg, Thrasher, Harrington, her father, Rory Craig, and Pizza Bob—began the long walk up the aisle with the coffin carrying Uncle Laz. Elvis raised his head, his muzzle sniffing the air by her feet, no doubt catching the enticing scent of Pizza Bob.

The chosen pallbearers were an interesting group of men, in terms of their relationship to the deceased. Feinberg had worked with Laz on civic projects for the town; no doubt, given their mutual gift for finance, they bonded over their moneymaking genius. Thrasher and Harrington would have known Laz through work as well. Her father knew him through Patience and family gatherings. She wasn't sure why Rory and Pizza Bob were chosen to be pallbearers; maybe as small business owners they, like Lillian, had Lazlo Ford to thank for staying in the black.

Most everyone in the church stood up and began to sing. Elvis pulled his nose back under the pew. Mercy stood but did not sing along to the moving lyric poem calling for hope and resilience in the face of loss: "When peace like a river attendeth my way, When sorrows like sea billows roll."

Her mother elbowed her gently, and Mercy joined in. "Whatever my lot, thou hast taught me to say, It is well, it is well with my soul."

Given the way Lazlo Ford had died, she couldn't believe that all was well with his soul. If ever there were a case for ghosts haunting this world until justice was served and they could move on to the next, Lazlo's murder would be it. In lieu of a vengeful specter, Mercy would step in and see to it herself that Uncle Laz could rest in peace.

The hymn ended in a crescendo of voices and chords as the pallbearers reached the front of the church. They bowed their heads, retreating to their seats in the front pew and leaving the forlorn wooden box alone in the aisle.

Lillian approached the pulpit. It had stopped snowing and the clouds had cleared and the sun shone through the stained-glass windows, casting a golden glow over the little woman. Her russet-colored hair glinting like a halo, she welcomed everyone, said a few sweet words about Lazlo, and then asked Feinberg to step up and say a few words.

With the grace of a lion, Daniel moved across the church and up to the lectern. He told the story of Lazlo's life—what they knew about it, anyway, which did not seem like much.

"Lazlo Ford was a private man," said Daniel, his calm and confident voice echoing through the nave. "He was a genius with numbers. Given this extraordinary gift, he could have had a career in mathematics or finance or data science and become a billionaire, but instead he chose to serve our little village, paying off our past debts, stabilizing our present, and securing our future. It's thanks to Lazlo that we were able to restore the Fountain of the Muses on the common and acquire the Ogham Standing Stones and rebuild the elegant spire on this very church. Not to mention balance the budget every year."

Daniel wrapped up his eulogy with a nod to Lazlo's parting gift to Northshire, a legacy that would fund local cultural events for the rest of the century and beyond. The mourners burst into spontaneous applause.

"I didn't know about that," said Mercy. "What else was in Uncle Lazlo's will?"

"I could have told you a week ago," said Grace, pursing her lips. "But the will we drew up for Lazlo is now obsolete. He wrote a new will. Roland and Roper handled it."

"Like they presumably handled the Snow Maiden message." She pictured the page of Roland & Roper stationery with the Russian word *"Snegurochka"* scrawled in the middle that had been delivered to Patience. Mercy stared at her mother. "Weird."

"Indeed," agreed Grace.

"What was in the will he wrote with you?"

"He left most everything to a trust dedicated to good works, namely in Northshire. To cultural and educational causes, like the library and the Arts Council. Two separate bequests, one to the Cat Ladies, and one to Patience. She was his dearest friend."

"Of course she was." Mercy figured at least half of Northshire counted her grandmother as their dearest friend. Maybe more. "And he loved the Cat Ladies. That's where he found and adopted Boris."

"Laz did love that cat." Grace frowned. "You know, your grandmother has his monster feline now. Like she needs another cat."

"What's one more?" asked Mercy with a smile. Patience had a houseful of rescued cats. Some she found homes for, but the ones no one wanted stayed with her. "Cats, the arts, Patience. That's it for his will?"

"Daniel remains the executor. He can tell you more. But my understanding is that now it's more complicated."

"What do you mean, complicated?"

"Banque Beutel is involved."

"Banque Beutel?"

"Arguably the most secretive of the secretive Swiss banks." Grace smiled at Mercy. "You might ask Daniel. Or Uncle Hugo."

"Indeed." If anyone knew their way around secretive Swiss banks, it would be the billionaire and the spy.

Grace put a manicured finger to her lips. "After the sermon."

Lillian was back in charge at the pulpit. She launched into a moving reading of Psalm 23, her voice ringing out over the congregation as clearly as a bell. "*The Lord is my shepherd, I shall not want. . . .*"

The congregants bowed their heads, and many muttered the plaintive verses along with the minister. Mercy closed her eyes when Lillian read "*Yea, though I walk through the valley of the shadow of death, I will fear no evil. . . .*" It was a line that always reminded her not of death, but of war. Even as she knew that they were often the same thing.

A rustling at the back of the church roused Mercy. She opened her eyes, and turned around to see what was happening. Elvis came out from his hiding place under the bench, and slipped into the pew, startling the people seated behind them.

By now nearly everyone in the church was casting discreet and not-so-discreet glances toward the entrance, where a tall, blond woman in a long, luxurious fur coat and knee-high, brown leather boots muscled her way through the front doors. She strode through the standing-room-only crowd and down the main aisle as if she owned not only the church but God, too. A buzz of speculation followed her, murmurs rising like bees swarming toward a new hive.

"That doesn't look like faux fur to me," Mercy whispered to her mother, arbiter of all things haute couture.

"That's a real lynx coat," said Grace. "The genuine article."

"Lynx?"

"Designer. Parisian." Her mother studied the woman as she swept up the aisle toward them.

"In Northshire?"

"Dior," Grace said definitively. "One of the most expensive furs in the world."

"And the most endangered," said Mercy.

"And that's a Dior Book Tote she's carrying."

"I can tell," said Mercy of the large toile-patterned shoulder bag, emblazoned with the words "Christian Dior." She asked her mother, "Who is she?"

"I don't know, but she's late," said Grace as the young woman came to stand right next to the pew where they were sitting.

The blonde paused dramatically, as if she were a high-fashion model stopping at the end of the runway for a final round of applause. She looked up and down the first few rows of pews on both sides of the aisle.

From the pulpit Lillian stared down at the interloper, and raised her voice in an effort to be heard over the muttering crowd. "Please join us now in *The Lord's Prayer*."

The woman in the lynx coat stepped into the pew where Mercy, Grace, and Uncle Hugo were sitting. Elvis growled softly, and Mercy ordered him down with a flick of her hand.

The woman gestured at Grace to move over.

"This pew is reserved for the family of the deceased," Grace told her.

"I *am* family," the woman said.

Grace gave her the same look she reserved for unreliable witnesses on the stand while interrogating them. The woman did not budge. Standing tall and proud, she stared down at Mercy's mother with gunmetal eyes and a confidence that bordered on arrogance.

Frowning, Grace glanced at Mercy and Uncle Hugo. The colonel shrugged, and moved down the pew. Mercy and Grace scooted over, too, to make room. The woman drew her fur coat around her and glided gracefully onto the hard, oak bench. She was very beautiful, in that well-tended, *I can afford a Dior lynx coat* kind of way that many very rich women have.

"Thank you," she said in English tinged with a faint foreign accent Mercy could not place.

Lillian began to recite the prayer—"Our Father, who art in heaven"—and the congregation joined in. Mercy chanted along, sneaking quick peeks at her mother and Lazlo's long-lost relative.

It was going to be a long service.

CHAPTER TWENTY-FOUR

This being human is a guest house.
Every morning a new arrival.
A joy, a depression, a meanness,
some momentary awareness comes
As an unexpected visitor.

—RUMI

AFTER THE FUNERAL SERVICE, EVERYONE GATHERED AT PATIENCE'S house, the graceful Queen Anne Victorian where Lazlo Ford had spent so many holidays with Mercy and her family. Mercy loved the restored white two-story home, with its gingerbread trim, elegant turret, and wide front porch. This jewel of a house, set on a hill not far from downtown Northshire, was Mercy's home away from home.

It was also her grandmother's veterinary clinic. The Sterling Animal Hospital—named after her late grandfather Sterling "Red" O'Sullivan, himself named for Sterling Mountain up in Lamoille County, where he was born and raised and served as sheriff—was located in a new wing built behind the original 150-year-old dwelling.

The clinic was closed today in honor of Lazlo and his love for animals, namely cats. But the parking lot for the clinic was still full of SUVs and trucks and Subarus driven not by patients and their humans but by mourners. The long driveway leading up the hill to the house and clinic compound was also packed with vehicles.

Both the driveway and the parking lot had been plowed recently, but Mercy worried that if it started to snow heavily again, they'd all be digging out. She pulled the Jeep by the shoulder of the road at the bottom of the hill as close as possible to the old stone wall that marked the property.

She and Elvis tramped up to the house, the shepherd leaping through the deepest of the snowdrifts on purpose, just for the fun of it.

Mercy was glad she was wearing the fancy après-ski boots her mother had given her last Christmas, which may have been dressier than her steel-toed Timberlands but were surprisingly waterproof. She wondered how the woman in lynx would make it through the snow in her spiky heeled boots. The bold blonde had disappeared right after the funeral service, but Mercy had a feeling they had not seen the last of her.

Mercy and Elvis followed the neatly shoveled gravel pathway up to the porch and through the front door. People in black were everywhere. She and Elvis wove through the mourners standing around talking and drinking champagne in the entry. Mercy peeked into the parlor, her grandmother's lovely formal sitting room done in elegant shades of lavender and blue. She spotted her parents sitting on one of the gray velvet love seats across from Uncle Hugo and Feinberg, but short of tackling the guests who stood between them, there was no getting over there anytime soon. The same was true of the dining room, where more people milled around the antique cherry French farm table laden with casseroles and sandwiches and salads.

Elvis obviously agreed, or maybe he just headed for the kitchen out of hunger and habit. Patience's kitchen abounded in treats for two-legged and four-legged creatures alike. The shepherd swiveled around the hips of the unsuspecting guests as smoothly as an eel in reedy waters. All Mercy could do was make her apologies and follow him.

Patience was holding court at the white marble island, which was filled with platters of hors d'oeuvres and glasses of champagne. Mercy loved this room, with its cheerful, golden-yellow walls and antique baker's rack and Provençal pottery and the scent of sugar and flour and cinnamon. Mercy's own kitchen at Grackle Tree Farm came as close to its identical twin as her cousin Ed and Troy's father and brothers could make it. A warm and happy space. Even on a sad day like today, maybe especially on a sad day like today, Patience's kitchen was a comfort to people. Just as the woman herself was.

Captain Thrasher and Bob Cato were standing at the far end of the island, talking to Troy. Susie Bear was curled up in the corner by the baker's rack, her nose balanced on her thick paws, eyes on the gleaming oak floors, watching for a wayward shrimp or pig in a blanket. Elvis settled down on the other side of the rack. Two canines at the starting line, waiting for the next drop.

Mercy joined Troy, who'd come straight from patrol. Still in his field uniform, looking tired but very pleased to see her. He helped her out of her coat, hung it on one of the top brass knobs on the baker's rack, and returned to her.

"It was a lovely funeral," Mercy told her grandmother.

"Yes. Lillian says that Lazlo left very specific instructions, right down to the readings and the hymns."

"Lillian did a great job."

"Yes. You should tell her that when you see her."

"I will."

Troy leaned in and kissed her forehead, whispering in her ear, "How soon can we leave?"

"Very soon," she whispered back. "Promise." They just needed to put in an appearance here and then they could go home to Felicity.

Elvis lifted his head and growled softly. Susie Bear followed suit, sans the growl. Mercy followed the dogs' line of sight to the dining room, where people were standing agape as the tall blonde who'd interrupted Lazlo's service appeared like a vision from another world. She slipped the lynx coat from her pale shoulders with the subtlety of Marilyn Monroe, revealing a curve-clinging black jersey dress that left very little to the imagination. She slung the heavy coat over one slim arm and smiled at the struck-dumb mourners, sashaying into Patience's kitchen.

She tossed the lynx coat over the back of one of the stools at the island. Plucking a glass of champagne from the nearest silver platter, she lifted the flute with a manicured hand. "To Lazlo!"

Everyone stared. Mercy recovered first, lifting her own glass. "To Lazlo!" she said, and the people around her echoed the toast.

Mercy moved toward the woman, determined to find out who she was and what she was doing here. But Patience beat her to it, wiping her hands on her *La Cuisine Française* apron and welcoming the woman warmly.

"I'm Patience O'Sullivan. Thank you for coming." Her grandmother paused, waiting for the funeral crasher to identify herself.

"I know who you are," said the woman with an imperiousness that rivaled

Mercy's mother's when she was in a mood. And this blond amazon, whoever she was, was in a mood. Or maybe she was always this way.

"Good," said Patience, her bright blue eyes darkening with the same displeasure she displayed when dealing with people who abused their pets. "Now, since you are a guest in my home, and I like to know the guests in my home, perhaps you'd care to introduce yourself."

"I am Tasha Karsak." She tossed her shoulder-length blond hair, flipping it with beringed fingers before going on. "I am the daughter of Lazlo Ford."

Patience frowned. "We were not aware that Lazlo had a daughter."

Tasha ignored that, sipping her champagne. "I am here to mourn my father."

"Of course. We're all here to mourn Lazlo." Patience pointed at the stool where Tasha had deposited her lynx. "Why don't you have a seat. We'd love to hear all about you and your connection to Lazlo. And get to know you."

"I am not here to talk to you. I do not want to get to know you." She slipped onto the stool, revealing long legs as she crossed them at the high split in the dress.

Her fancy boots were somehow completely devoid of snow. Mercy wondered how she did that.

"That's unfortunate," said Patience. "We have always considered Lazlo family, and always will."

"You are not family." Tasha tipped her now-empty flute at Patience. "Blood is family."

"Blood may be thicker than water," said Patience, "but I've known Lazlo for nearly twenty years." She pulled the open champagne bottle from the silver ice bucket on the island and poured Tasha another glass of Veuve Clicquot Brut. "And he never mentioned that he had a daughter."

Tasha raised her glass to Patience. "I was his secret."

TASHA SAID NO MORE. She simply sipped her champagne in silence, ignoring all attempts at conversation. When the flute was empty, she placed it on the marble island, pushing it away from her. Then she left as dramatically as she had arrived, blond head held high, the costly lynx tossed casually over her shoulders, the spiky boots clicking along the parquet floors.

The colonel sidled up to Mercy and Troy. "Meeting in the Rufus Ruckus Room."

Mercy glanced around the kitchen, and realized that Patience, Feinberg, Thrasher, and her parents were nowhere to be seen. "Guess we better go," she told Troy. She snapped her fingers and Elvis left his post by the door and came to her side. Susie Bear lumbered to her feet, reluctant to leave all those hors d'oeuvres behind.

"Come on," said Troy.

They all followed the colonel down the hallway to Patience's veterinary clinic in the new wing. They passed through the double doors that marked the transition from the old building to the new building and stepped into the reception area, where the spaniel from Leland Hallett's place was asleep in a crate.

"Poor thing's exhausted," said Troy.

"She's in good hands here," said Mercy. "Where's Hallett?"

"Still in jail. But he'll probably make bail."

"He'll want his dog back."

"That's not going happen."

They went on to the Rufus Ruckus Room, a large space that served as the indoor play area for the clinic, home to a brightly colored riot of dog toys and tunnels and cones and box jumps. Usually the Rufus Ruckus Room was indeed a ruckus of dogs of every shape and size and breed, scrambling around, enjoying the doggy amenities. But today it was empty of canines. And full of fury.

Patience and Grace sat on one of the box jumps, surrounded by Mercy's father and Feinberg and Thrasher. They were a tight circle, talking in tight voices.

"She's not who she says she is," announced the colonel as they joined the group. "This much we know. Lazlo did not have any children."

"That we know of," said Patience.

"If he had, he would have insisted that she be protected from whatever and whoever he was running from," said Uncle Hugo. "He would have brought her with him to Northshire."

"Maybe he didn't know that he had a child," said Mercy.

"It's easy enough to establish paternity," said Patience. "All we need is a DNA test."

"She has to agree to provide that DNA," said Thrasher. "Which she may or may not do."

The colonel smiled, and pulled a champagne glass in a plastic bag from one of the generous side pockets of his cashmere coat.

"You carry evidence bags on your person?" asked Mercy.

The colonel smiled. "Don't you?"

"Good point," said Troy. He looked at Mercy, and she shrugged. He knew that she always tucked a few plastic baggies and paper sacks in her backpack.

She knew that her husband was thinking that she was more like her great-uncle than she liked to believe. Although she preferred to think that her talent and skill for investigation came from her grandfather the sheriff and was honed by her training and service as a military policewoman in the U.S. Army, not from her great-uncle the clever covert operative.

"We should be able to get her DNA from this flute," said Uncle Hugo.

"And his?" asked Patience.

"We have his from the crime scene," said Thrasher.

"Have we run it through the system yet?" asked Grace. "Maybe it will tell us who he really was."

"No hits on our database," said Thrasher. "We're checking with Interpol."

"That's smart." She turned to the colonel. "I know you thought the threat against him was domestic, but maybe it wasn't. Maybe Lazlo Ford was on the run from abroad."

"I'm beginning to think you may be right," said the colonel. "Consider her name. Tasha Karsak. The surname 'Karsak' comes from the word 'corsac,' a kind of fox found on the Eurasian steppes. It's fairly common in Russia, Belarus, Ukraine. But I'd put my money on Russia."

"Maybe Interpol can tell us if this Tasha Karsak really is who she says she is," said Troy.

"If that's even her name," said Grace.

Mercy thought about Tasha Karsak and what they knew about her. Which was practically nothing so far. "Just as important as who she is is what she's after. If she's not his daughter, why is she here?"

"And if she is his daughter, why wait till he's dead to visit?" asked Patience.

"It could simply be a matter of the money," said Feinberg.

"You saw that lynx coat. Money is not a problem for her," said Grace.

"Mom says you're the executor of the will, Daniel."

Feinberg smiled, giving away nothing but his amusement. "Let's just say the account in Banque Beutel is substantial."

Mercy wondered what kind of fortune a billionaire would consider substantial. "How substantial?"

"I can't give you an exact number," Feinberg demurred. "Let's just say it's larger than the GDP of some countries."

"That's a lot of money." Troy looked at Grace. "Even for a woman with a lynx coat."

"Where did Lazlo get that kind of money?"

"He's very good with money," said Duncan.

"Nobody's that good," said the resident billionaire with confidence. "Even Lazlo couldn't build that kind of wealth on his salary." Feinberg paused. "Either he already had the money and it's been sitting in Switzerland all this time multiplying unchecked, or he's been doing something else on the side."

"Something illegal," said Thrasher.

"Not necessarily," said Duncan.

"Legal or illegal, doesn't much matter," said Feinberg. "The threat against him, whatever it was, was real enough for him to hide away in a village in Vermont living a very low-profile life. Drawing very little attention of any kind to himself."

"Until he was thrust into the role of mayor," pointed out Grace.

"And Santa Claus," added Duncan.

"Do you think Tasha could be our Snow Maiden?" asked Troy.

"She does look like she has a heart of ice," said Mercy.

"All Russian women have hearts of ice," said Uncle Hugo with a wistful smile. "That's part of their appeal."

"Wistful" was an emotion Mercy had never before associated with her great-uncle. She remembered his old flame Svetlana. Maybe she'd been the one woman to break the colonel's heart, rather than the usual other way around.

"Tasha is beautiful, Russian, and dresses like a snow queen," said Grace. "Maybe she is your Snow Maiden."

"'Tasha' is short for 'Natasha,'" said Mercy. "And 'Natasha' is a diminutive form of—"

"'Natalya,'" interrupted the colonel. "Which means born on Christmas Day."

"And 'The Snow Maiden' is a popular Christmas song in Russia," said Patience.

"So maybe Tasha Karsak is the Snow Maiden," said Thrasher.

"Or maybe she's just one of the millions of females around the world named Natasha or Natalya," said Grace. "There must be hundreds of thousands in Russia alone."

"Let's say she is the Snow Maiden," said Duncan. "What does that tell us about her?"

A very thoughtful question, thought Mercy. You could always count on her father to ask the most thoughtful questions.

"I'm not sure," she told her father. "We don't know the significance."

"We're only guessing," said Grace, frowning.

Mercy smiled. Her mother hated guessing. She was the sort of woman who preferred certainties.

"Maybe the answer is in the song itself," suggested Patience.

"Or the opera," said the colonel.

"You'd like that, wouldn't you?" Mercy laughed. "I'll do some digging."

"Meanwhile, what do we know about Tasha Karsak?" asked Grace. "Tomorrow morning is the reading of the will. No doubt she'll be there, since she insisted on having one."

"What do you mean?" asked Troy.

"The so-called tradition of the reading of the will is outdated," said Grace. "It rarely happens that way anymore."

"Beneficiaries are typically contacted by email or snail mail these days," said Duncan.

"Then why has Jules agreed to it?" Mercy sked her mother. Grace had been to law school with Jules Roland, and knew him well.

Grace smiled. "Jules is never opposed to a bit of drama. And if there's one thing we actually know to be true about Tasha Karsak, it's that she's a drama queen. It should prove quite the reading."

"There's a reading of the will on Christmas Eve?"

"She's pushed Jules to do it right away," said Grace. "Apparently, she needs to get back to wherever she came from."

"Why not today?" asked the colonel wryly.

"Oh, she asked," said Feinberg, with another one of his enigmatic smiles.

"Jules refused," said Feinberg. "Tonight's 'A Christmas Carol' at the arts center. One of the highlights of the Solstice Soirée. Jules's wife is the director."

"He doesn't dare miss it," said Feinberg.

"We can't miss it, either," said Mercy. "It's Henry's big moment."

Henry was Lillian Jenkins's grandson. A very smart little boy Mercy had gotten to know quite well a couple of years ago on a case. They'd become fast friends, she and Henry and Troy and Elvis and Susie Bear. With Patience's help, they'd found Henry a dog of his own, a sweet and smart Great Pyrenees and Australian shepherd mix. The devoted dog gave the boy the emotional support he needed to navigate the world. Including the theater, where he'd discovered a talent for acting.

"Of course," said Patience. "We'll all be there for Henry."

"And for the rest of the cast," said Grace. "Half of Northshire is in this play." She looked at Mercy. "And do feel free to bring Felicity. There will be lots of kids there, on and off the stage."

"Today's quite the busy day. And tomorrow will be, too." Mercy counted off the next day's many obligatory activities: "Last-minute shopping, Christmas Eve dinner at our house, and the midnight Christmas service."

Uncle Hugo turned to Thrasher. "Any chance we could have answers from forensics by morning?"

"Maybe. Due to the holidays, we're short-staffed and it might take even longer than usual."

"Two deaths in as many days," said the colonel.

"Three bodies, if you count the bones in the woods," said Troy.

"We're counting them," said Thrasher. "I'm sure everyone is working as quickly as possible. The pressure is on Harrington for results."

"Which means pressure on us all down the line," said Troy.

Mercy thought about that pressure, and who was applying that pressure, from the top down. "Who'll be the new mayor now?"

"I hear Harrington has his eye on the office," said Thrasher.

"He'd give up being head of the Major Crime Unit?" asked Patience. "He seems to revel in his position."

"He does like his job, and he's good at it." Thrasher nodded. "But the man is nothing if not ambitious. Being mayor could lead to state senator, even governor."

Mercy looked at her mother. "You should be the mayor, Mom."

Grace frowned.

"You'd be great," said Duncan. "And then *you* could run for governor."

"I'd vote for you," said Troy earnestly.

"And I'd finance your campaign," said Feinberg.

"Thank you both, sincerely, but I think my daughter is getting a little ahead of herself." Grace favored Mercy with one of her most exasperated expressions.

"You're very good at running things," said Mercy. Because her mother really *was* good at running things. And running people. Other than her daughter, who resisted being run by anyone. Especially her mother. Mercy wondered if *her* daughter would resist her in the same way.

"You can't tell by the Solstice Soirée," said Grace. "People are dying."

"Not your fault," said Duncan.

"You could rule the world, Mom. And the whole planet would be better for it."

"True enough," said Feinberg.

"Right now, I'd settle for running a drama-free event for the remainder of the Solstice Soirée."

"We're going to figure this out." Mercy looked at Troy. "Time to go home. We've got some digging to do. Not to mention we need to see how the decorating is going."

"You're going to love it." Grace beamed at her. "Just remember, more is more."

CHAPTER TWENTY-FIVE

Had I power to give to you
Many a rich and costly gem,
Fit, in brilliancy of hue,
To adorn a diadem, I'd bestow the jewels rare . . .
Many a merry Christmas. . . .

—VICTORIAN CHRISTMAS CARD POEM, 1883

IT WAS DUSK BY THE TIME MERCY DROVE HER JEEP THROUGH THE tunnel of snowy branches formed by the trees hugging the shoulders of the road leading home. Levi had plowed the long drive that led up the wooded rise to the house, and the snow was piled high along the verges. More snow was on the way; she just hoped that the storm would hold off until after the play tonight. Theatergoers might be deterred by bad weather, or at least the tourists among them might be. And Henry deserved a full house.

At the top of the hill, the oaks and maples and beech and birch gave way to a long line of junipers that hid the house from view. All she could usually see of the two-and-half-story limestone manor from here were the tall chimneys of the main house and the enormous sugar maple beyond it—and she could see that only during daylight hours.

With the sun sinking beyond the mountains, she shouldn't have been able to see much of anything in the growing gloom, but now that same obstructed view seemed to glow. Presumably thanks to whatever holiday illumination Troy's family had added during their absence. She wondered what transformation awaited beyond those junipers.

Troy was right behind her in his truck, and as she parked in the large gravel lot on the side of the house, he pulled in next to her. Susie Bear bounced from the truck and shambled over to Elvis to exchange a quick hello sniff before bounding after the shepherd as he disappeared into the juniper hedge.

Her husband took her hand. "Are you ready for this?"

"How bad could it be?" she asked, thinking uncharitably of ugly Christmas sweaters and singing Elvises.

"Knowing my family, it could be pretty bad. Let's hope that I don't have to disown them all after this."

"Surely it won't come to that."

It was snowing again, and even though Levi had plowed the gravel driveway that morning, the white stuff was already piling up again. They tramped over to the opening in the hedge where a shoveled brick path led the way to the house.

Troy held out his arm and bowed. "After you."

She stepped onto the path into the yard and stared up at the spectacle before her. She heard Troy behind her.

"Wow," she said.

"Is that a good wow or a bad wow?"

"It's a good wow."

And it was. The Second Empire Victorian had always been a handsome limestone pile, with its classic gothic lines, arched dormers, and slate-shingled roof. They'd cleaned it up when they bought the property, and the results were good.

But never had she dreamed it could look like this. Like something out of a Christmas storybook. Or a Victorian novel. Or a Russian fairy tale.

Evergreen bedecked with red ribbon topped the keystone lintels of the many tall, multi-paned windows. Candles glowed at the sills. Strings of white lights illuminated the bones of the house, running along the roof lines, tracing the outlines of the dormers, and highlighting its most distinctive architectural feature—a grand three-story tower crowned with a widow's walk that anchored the entrance.

The entrance itself, with its massive carved arched door, was trimmed in evergreen and wrapped in red satin ribbon and flanked by two beribboned spiral spruce topiaries. Like a present to open up and call home.

All along the brick path black cast-iron urns filled with evergreen and holly and pine cones marked the way to the front door. Twinkling rattan deer brightened the raised beds of the garden, now covered in snow.

Best of all, the massive sugar maple, home to the multitude of grackles that gave their name to the property, rose over the house like an angel over a Nativity scene, its enormous trunk wrapped in little white lights, dozens of silver and gold wind spinners and shiny round baubles hanging from its bare branches. The few grackles that had not flown south for the winter didn't seem to mind.

"It's beautiful," she said. "Your mother is a genius."

"I can't believe she's shown such restraint."

"We must be missing something," she teased.

Troy frowned. "You know we are." He scanned the house and the grounds. "Up there." He pointed at the top of the tower. "Wait for it."

They stood there together, gazing upward, snowflakes falling all around them, glimmering in the glow of Grackle Tree Farm. A burst of brightness appeared on the roof, bathing the widow's walk in a glare of light—and Santa Claus appeared. This was a Victorian St. Nick, dressed in an old-fashioned long red velvet cape and capelet trimmed in white faux rabbit fur straight out of "'Twas the Night Before Christmas." Clement C. Moore would have been proud.

St. Nick raised a white gloved hand in welcome, and "Have a Holly, Jolly Christmas!" blared from a hidden speaker somewhere, echoing across the lawn.

Mercy laughed. "How did you know?"

"No Warner Christmas decoration is complete without a surprise automated component," said Troy.

They watched as Santa continued to wave his arm up and down and Burl Ives continued to "Oh, by golly" to the last verse. At which point the widow's walk spotlight went out, Santa disappeared, and the only sounds were the whining of the dogs at the front door, a signal for Mercy and Troy to join them at the house.

"We should go see what's waiting for us inside," said Troy.

"Let's hope my mother took her cue from yours."

Troy laughed. "I can't imagine that happening."

"I know, wishful thinking."

They walked along the brick path up to the front door, and let the dogs rush ahead into the house. Together they stepped into the large entryway and found themselves in a sea of sparkling stars and poinsettias.

Now it was Mercy's turn to say, "Look up."

Troy looked up and smiled. They were standing under the chandelier in the foyer, from which dangled a large mistletoe kissing ball. He took her in his arms and kissed her. "I like what your mother has done with the place."

She kissed him back. "Let's wait to pass judgment until we've seen the rest of the house."

Kicking off their boots, they shrugged off their coats and hats, and deposited them on the now-beribboned antique hall tree.

The entry was adorned with freshly cut evergreen and pastel-colored ornaments trimmed in Victorian frippery. Elaborate garlands of freshly cut cedar, pine, eucalyptus, fir, ivy, holly, and juniper, with accents of feathers, berries, and pine cones graced the doorways and the carved handrails and spindle balusters of the elegant staircase that rose to the second floor.

A portent of Christmas excess, thought Mercy, feeling a full-on complement of fussy if fabulous bric-a-brac coming on. She hoped she was wrong.

She wasn't. They walked into the living room, which until this very moment had been one of their favorite rooms in the house. When they first moved in, her mother Grace had decorated this room for them in jewel colors that complemented the graceful lines of the elegant room, with its high coffered ceilings and brass and crystal globe chandeliers and long rosette-trimmed windows. They loved the large deep blue velvet L-shaped sectional Grace had chosen, along with the marble coffee table and the easy chairs. All gathered around the original brick fireplace with the ornately carved mahogany surround and mantel, lovingly restored by Tandie's father Ed.

Now that same lovely room looked like it was going to prom. Or at least the winter formal. The windows and fireplace and chandeliers dripped with garlands of evergreen and pearls and feathers much like the ones in the hallway, although the living room versions definitely upped their game. Bowls of pomander balls graced every table.

Talk about gilding the lily, thought Mercy.

Amy and Tandie were putting the finishing touches on the soaring Scotch pine Mercy and Troy had harvested with Levi and Thrasher that morning. In her slim hand, Amy held a raspberry-and-gold ornament as extravagantly bejeweled as a Fabergé egg. Tandie perched on a small stepladder, swathing long strings of luminous white, ruby, and rose-gold pearls around the tree. Twice as many lights now glittered on the massive pine, casting colorful glints on what seemed like—and probably was—hundreds of opulent ornaments like the one Amy was hanging on an already crowded branch.

Amy's little girl Helena was asleep on the couch, surrounded by opened boxes of decorations. Felicity sat upright on a baby mat in a brightly colored plastic play yard, tossing soft baby alphabet blocks at the dogs, each of whom had stretched out along the outside of the pen like two guardian Sphinx. Neither canine moved, even when one of the squishy blocks hit home.

Troy scooped the baby up and together he and Mercy covered her in little kisses. Felicity squealed and giggled in equal measure.

"We're almost finished," said Amy, reaching for another ornament. "There were so many boxes to go through. But I promise you that we curated the decorations carefully. What do you think?"

"Isn't it epic?" asked Tandie. "You know it's epic."

"Epic," repeated Troy, with a grin at Mercy.

"You're not saying anything." Tandie hopped off the stepladder, twirling a long rope of pink pearls like a cowboy about to lasso a steer. "How can you not say anything? I mean, this is awesome. It's like *Moulin Rouge* and *Bridgerton* had a baby."

An unfortunate description, but not a wholly inaccurate one, thought Mercy.

"Say something," begged Amy. "Say we didn't spend all day decorating every inch of this living room for nothing."

Mercy looked at Troy.

"I like it. It looks like a cupcake explosion." Her husband threw Felicity up into the air, and caught her in his strong outdoorsman's hands. The dogs watched this favorite father-daughter pastime, which always unnerved Mercy, with a calm but vigilant air.

The baby jiggled with laughter. Troy looked at Mercy. "And our little Felicity loves cupcakes."

Cupcakes. Moulin Rouge. Bridgerton. Throw in a little Marie Antoinette and Lady Gaga and you might begin to describe her mother's over-the-top holiday design. Not Audrey Hepburn in *Breakfast at Tiffany's*, which is what Mercy had in mind. This was Audrey Hepburn in *My Fair Lady* and *Funny Face* on steroids.

And here she'd been worried about Dolly Parton. Who knew that Troy's mother Lizzie would prove the subtler of the two grandmothers.

And yet.

Mercy did a slow turn, taking in every nuance of the Victorian Christmas Extravaganza that her living room had now become. *The Painted Ladies*. That's what they called that resplendent row of restored Victorian houses in San Francisco, the ones with the gingerbread trim and elaborate tricolor palettes. Of course, the name referred to the exteriors of those famous homes, but what her mother had done here was turn the interior of the old limestone manor into a Painted Lady. *Christmas style*.

"More is more," Mercy said.

"More is more," agreed Troy, as he tossed their daughter into the air again.

"More!" cried Felicity as she hit the top of her trajectory.

Troy caught her handily as she dropped back down into his arms. He turned to Mercy, grinning. "Did you hear that? She just said 'More'!"

Mercy laughed, silently thanking her mother. "She did!" She kissed her baby's nose. "You did! Such a clever girl." She kissed Troy. "Just like her daddy."

"Her first real word!" Tandie whooped.

Amy whooped, too. "That's practically an entire sentence!"

Elvis and Susie Bear abandoned their posts and joined Mercy and Troy and the baby, tails wagging, part of the celebration.

All the excitement roused Helena from her nap on the sofa. She sat up, rubbing her eyes. "What's going on?"

As if in answer to the little girl's question, Elvis raced out of the room, Susie Bear on his heels.

Mercy looked at Troy. "Now what?"

CHAPTER TWENTY-SIX

The giant trees are bending
Their bare boughs weighed with snow.
And the storm is fast descending. . . .

—EMILY BRONTË

It was snowing harder now, and when Mercy opened the front door, damp gusts heavy with snow whipped into the house. Elvis and Susie Bear sat on either side of her, big shaggy black head and sleek blond head both tilted at the glamourous woman on the threshold.

Olga Volkov.

Olga ran a Russian tea shop in nearby Sunderland. Mercy had met her a few times, mostly at Chamber of Commerce functions that her mother insisted she attend from time to time, but she didn't know her very well. She wondered what the tea lady was doing here.

The woman never failed to impress. Today, despite the inclement weather, she was the picture of winter chic, in a long, shiny silver parka trimmed in white fur. She stood before them, bright blue eyes framed by platinum-streaked bangs. She was thin and tall and beautiful in the way of Eastern European supermodels, and her Russian-accented English only enhanced her exotic appeal.

"Mercy Carr," she said, her voice tinged with anxiety, an emotion Mercy didn't associate with the cool beauty who'd always seemed so poised when they'd met before.

"Hi, Olga."

"Hi." She stood there uncertainly, the snow whipping around her like something out of a Tolstoy novel.

Mercy hesitated, crossing her arms against the cold, her mind on *Anna Karenina*. The woman crossed her arms, too, mirroring her. Waiting.

Elvis stiffened. Susie Bear simply stayed put. The snow kept on blowing.

"May I come in?"

"Of course." Mercy stepped back. "I'm so sorry, I guess I'm just surprised to see you here."

"You were not expecting me."

"No." She had no idea why Olga was here, especially so close to Christmas. Didn't she have a tea room to run? "I thought you'd be at the shop. Busy time of year. All those tourists . . ."

"I closed the shop today. I needed to see you. About Lazlo."

"Okay. Of course." That made two Russian women showing up uninvited with Lazlo Ford's name on their lips. She wondered what this one would have to say. And how she knew Lazlo. Although now that she thought about it, if she'd seen her at the Chamber mixers, Lazlo would have, too. They must have been friends. Which still did not explain what she was doing here.

"Come on to the living room." She ushered the woman into the house, crossing the entry to the hall and expecting Olga to follow.

She didn't. Mercy looked back to find her backing away from the dogs, who'd come to their feet to greet their guest.

"I do not like dogs," she said, her voice trembling.

Maybe she's a cat person, thought Mercy. Like Uncle Laz. "They won't hurt you. Come on."

Olga hesitated, looking down at the dogs.

Mercy retraced her steps, waving the dogs away, reaching gently for the woman's elbow, leading her through the entryway into the living room. Elvis and Susie Bear brought up the rear, Olga glancing back nervously as she sidled up to Mercy.

Troy, Amy, and Tandie all looked up at their unexpected visitor, seemingly as taken by surprise as Mercy had been.

Tandie stared at her. "Who are you?"

Mercy jumped in. "This is Olga Volkov."

"You're the tea lady," said Amy.

"Tea lady?"

Mercy could tell that the teenager was thinking that the elegant young woman didn't look much like a tea lady. And she'd have been right.

"It's a lovely shop on Pleasant Street in Sunderland," said Amy. "Very good tea."

Olga gave Amy a grateful smile. "Russian tea is the best in the world. That's why all the Eastern Europeans in Vermont come to my shop. The only place to serve Russian tea."

"I'm sure," said Tandie.

"You said you've come about Lazlo," prompted Mercy.

"Yes." Olga pursed her perfectly glossed lips, seemingly reluctant to go on.

Mercy didn't remember seeing her at the funeral; she surely would have remembered if she had. "You weren't at the funeral."

"No." Her face flushed, but she did not explain herself.

"Why don't you sit down," said Amy, with a *You know we've got to hear this* look at Mercy.

Troy smiled at Olga as he bounced Felicity on his knee. "Have a seat."

"Nice baby." She smiled back at him and Felicity, a quicksilver curving of the lips that came and went in an instant. But instead of sitting down, she looked at Mercy.

"Of course, do sit down," said Mercy. "Please."

Olga floated into one of the easy chairs. She pulled the hood off her head and slipped the midi-length silver parka off her shoulders. Underneath she wore jeans and an oversized blue cashmere sweater that made her eyes seem all the bluer.

Her silver UGG boots were wet with snow. She tugged them off, revealing matching blue cashmere socks. Tucking her feet under her, she folded her manicured hands on her lap, her long nails painted the same shade of blue.

"Make yourself at home," said Tandie, rolling her eyes.

"Now, what's this about Lazlo?" asked Mercy. "How did you know him?"

Olga raised her chin. "I am Lazlo's intended."

"His intended?" Amy asked, looking to Mercy for confirmation. "Like, fiancée?"

"This is news to me," said Mercy.

"Uncle Laz was a confirmed bachelor," Tandie said.

"Tandie," warned Mercy.

"Everybody says so. That his only true love was his cat."

"Boris." Olga smiled a very small, very sad smile. "Lazlo loved Boris."

"Did you come here on a fiancée visa?" asked Tandie.

"Certainly not," she said, her accent thickening with anger. "I am not one of *those* desperate souls. I have an aunt in Brooklyn—she helped me come to this country."

"I'm sure Tandie meant no offense," said Mercy.

"I didn't, really," said the teenager.

Olga's face softened. "I feel so sorry for those women. They come to my shop, for a little taste of home. If they marry their rich Americans, they stay and they are homesick. If they do not marry them, then they get deported. Which can be very bad for them."

"How so?"

"If they met their man through a legitimate company, then they are okay. But if they are working for gangsters, they must make as much money as possible—and the lion's share goes to the mob. This means getting the guys to give them money, jewelry, stocks and bonds. . . ." Her voice trailed off.

"And once they're married?"

"Then they must"—here she used air quotes with her blue-painted fingernails—"send money home."

"What if they don't want to marry the guy?" asked Tandie.

"Then they are . . ." She lapsed into Russian: "ежду молотком и наковальней. Between the hammer and the anvil."

Mercy smiled. "Between a rock and a hard place."

"Yes." Olga smiled back, but she said no more.

Mercy looked over at her husband, and he took the hint.

"So back to you and our confirmed bachelor," Troy said, returning to a happier subject. "They say a confirmed bachelor is only confirmed until he meets the right woman."

"We were engaged," Olga said.

First a secret daughter, now a secret fiancée, Mercy thought.

"Really," she said. Even dead and buried, Lazlo continued to astonish. The man they thought was a bachelor by choice was courting a woman at least fifteen years his junior. Up until now, it would have seemed far more likely that he'd have a secret daughter than it did that he'd have a secret fiancée. Besides, a secret daughter you can keep under wraps, especially when she lives abroad. Keeping a secret fiancée under wraps in the villages of southern Vermont seemed nearly impossible. But the amazing Uncle Laz had done just that.

"How did you meet?" asked Troy.

"We met at a Chamber of Commerce meeting. Six months ago."

Of course, thought Mercy, they would have known each other. But the jump from friends to lovers was a big one. Lazlo hadn't wasted any time making that jump. Good for him. And now terrible for her.

"And then?" asked Troy, smiling again. Mercy admired her husband's easygoing manner, which could calm victims even as it tricked perpetrators into a false sense of security.

"Lazlo came to my shop. He liked my tea."

"Everyone loves tea," said Amy.

"He helped me with my accounts. My Lazlo is—was—very smart with money."

"That's true," said Mercy.

"One day a Russian girl came in for tea. Zoya. Good customer." Olga paused. "She had a black eye. She wore a lot of makeup to cover it up, but still I could see it. She told me her fiancé did it, and that she could not marry him. But she could not go home to Russia either. I didn't know what to do, so I asked Lazlo for help." She gazed at the Christmas tree, seemingly lost in her memories.

"What did Uncle Laz do?"

"He helped her get away."

"Where did she go?" asked Amy.

"I do not know. Lazlo said she was safer that way. That I was safer that way." She looked at Troy, her blue eyes dark with sorrow. "That is the day I fell in love with him. August second."

No one spoke for a moment.

"I'm so sorry for your loss," said Mercy finally. "How can we help?"

Olga pushed the velvet throw pillow on the chair behind her back, sitting up straight in the easy chair. "I've come about the impostor."

"Imposter?" asked Troy, bringing his bobbing knee to an abrupt stop. Felicity wailed.

"You mean Tasha," said Mercy, "the woman who says she is Lazlo's daughter."

"Yes." She shook her head, and her thick fringe fluttered. "She is not his daughter."

"And you know this how?" Troy shifted the baby to his other knee and began the game again.

"He told me when we got engaged. He was never married. He had no children."

"He could have been lying," said Mercy. "Or maybe he didn't know about the child."

"We told each other everything. I know he did not lie." Her blue eyes blazed. "Lazlo is no liar."

Mercy agreed with her. Lazlo may have been guilty of lies of omission, perhaps, but so far no one had accused him of being an outright liar. A man of secrets, certainly, secrets that may have driven someone to kill him. Or not.

And yet. Secrets breed secrets. Everyone around Lazlo seemed to carry their own secrets, hidden deep in their hearts. Mercy wondered what secrets his fiancée was keeping. She watched as the woman placed her slim-fingered hands on her belly in the protective way of pregnant women everywhere.

"You're pregnant." A secret which explained a lot, thought Mercy. But not everything.

"Yes."

"And Lazlo is the father." She wished poor Uncle Laz had lived long enough to welcome his child into the world—assuming Olga was telling the truth, which Mercy believed she was.

"Yes. He was very excited. His first child. He said so."

Mercy thought about that, frowning. "But why would he keep this a secret from us all? Why keep you a secret? Why keep the baby a secret?"

"We were going to tell you all on Christmas Eve. At your family party. Our big Christmas surprise." Olga twisted her hands into a tense prayer. Her blue eyes filled with tears. All signs of anxiety were gone. Only grief remained. "Lazlo was very proud."

Mercy knew something about grief. She went to Olga, perching on the arm of the velvet chair and drawing her into a hug. She felt her stiffen at her touch, then shudder and collapse into her arms, sobbing.

She stroked the crying woman's platinum-streaked hair. She could only imagine the pain she would have suffered if she'd lost Troy while she was carrying Felicity. If she lost him *ever*. She looked over at Amy and Tandie. "Maybe you could bring us some tea and lemon squares."

"We're on it," said Tandie. She and Amy left, little Helena trotting after them.

"Sorry," said Olga, as she pulled out of Mercy's embrace. "This is why I could not go to the funeral."

"Don't apologize. It must be so hard." Mercy joined Troy and Felicity on the sofa.

"It. Is. Hard." She looked at Troy, Felicity wriggling on his lap. "A baby needs a father."

"Of course," said Mercy. "And I'm sure Lazlo would have been a wonderful father."

"He would do anything for the baby. For me." Her glossy lips tightened, her jaw set. "That is why I will not let the phony daughter take his money. That inheritance is for my baby."

"Yes, well, you're going to have to tell his lawyers about your relationship. And your baby. Right away."

"Roland and Roper. Lazlo said he would talk to them, but then he . . ." Her voice caught and she paused before going on. "No time."

Mercy thought it was odd that Lazlo had not changed his will to include Olga and the baby. Or maybe that was what Banque Beutel was all about.

"We know the executor of the will. Daniel Feinberg. I'm sure he will help."

Olga did not seem convinced. Frowning, she rubbed her belly, and now Mercy could see her baby bump. She looked to be about four or five months along.

"My mother can help you approach them," said Mercy. "She's an attorney, and Lazlo retained her for years before using Roland and Roper."

"I do not trust lawyers."

"I understand. But this is my mother we're talking about. She's very good at what she does." Mercy smiled. "She's good at everything."

"Lazlo told me. His friend Patience, your mother, you. Good people, he said."

"Daniel Feinberg is also a good man. Lazlo trusted him."

"Lazlo liked him. He said that Daniel is a good man even though he is very, very rich." She hugged herself as if she were cold. The fire was burning strong and the room was warm, but pregnant women often reacted unseasonably to room temperature, Mercy knew. And Olga might still be in shock over Uncle Lazlo's death.

Mercy reached behind her and pulled the knitted afghan Patience had made for her off the sofa. She tucked it around the shivering woman.

The girls came back from the kitchen with a tray bearing tea and lemon squares and placed it on the coffee table. Helena was already munching on a lemon square.

Amy poured a cup of tea for their visitor. "Here. I'm sure it's not as good as yours. . . ."

Olga smiled at that.

"But it will warm you up," said Mercy.

"Thank you." She sipped her tea and accepted the lemon square wrapped in a napkin from Tandie.

"You're welcome," said Amy, concern creasing her brow. Mercy knew that the young mother had a soft spot for pregnant women, especially those with absent fathers.

"Lazlo told me to come to you if anything bad happened." She stared at Mercy and Troy as if she were not sure putting her life and the life of her unborn child in their hands was a good idea, no matter what he had told her.

"So Lazlo was worried that something bad was going to happen to him," said Mercy.

"Yes."

"Did he tell you why?" asked Tandie.

"Not really. But he was worried. I could tell." Olga pulled a postcard from her jeans pocket. "He told me that if anything happened to him, I should give you this." She held it out to Mercy as reverently as if it were an offering to the gods.

Mercy scrambled off the couch and gently plucked the card from the woman's open palm. The address side was blank, but for a notation at the upper-left hand corner, which was in Russian. On the other side was an enchanting work of art: a pale beauty dressed in a silver-white coat made of snowflakes, set against the purple shadows of snow-laden evergreens. She held it up for Troy and the others to see, too.

"What is it?" asked Tandie.

"It is a Russian painting," said Olga. She'd stop shivering now, and her pale face showed a little more color.

"It's beautiful. She is beautiful." Mercy pointed to the Russian script on the flip side of the postcard. "And what does this mean?"

Olga tapped a blue fingernail on the top line. "It's the name of the artist, Mikhail Aleksandrovic Vrubel. A famous Russian painter. Lazlo loved his work. He has his art in his house."

"This painting?"

"No. Another. In his office. It is called *The Lilacs*."

"Right." Mercy pointed to the next line of text on the card. "And the next line?"

Olga moved her blue fingernail down. "This is the name of the painting, Снегурочка."

Mercy remembered the delicate snowflakes that sparkled in the woman's hair on the other side of the postcard. "*The Snow Maiden*."

CHAPTER TWENTY-SEVEN

O Father Winter, what evil you have done me?
O Mother Spring, be kind, and give to me
A bit of ardent sunshine and of flame.
To warm again this poor cold heart of mine!

—NIKOLAI RIMSKY-KORSAKOV, THE SNOW MAIDEN

"Why do you think that Lazlo wanted you to give this to me?" Mercy asked Olga.

"I do not know." Olga pulled her knees up to her belly and wrapped the afghan tightly around herself, a cocoon of mother-to-be and child-to-be-born. "But you must know."

"I don't know. But I will try to figure it out." Mercy told her about the envelope with the note reading *"Snegurochka"* that Lazlo's lawyer Jules Roland had delivered to her grandmother Patience.

"It is a message," said Olga.

"A message meaning?"

"I do not know."

"Okay, let's think this through. Was Lazlo very fond of opera?"

Olga shrugged. "He has a big collection of classical records. Vinyl. Maybe some opera. I don't know. When we were together, we listened to jazz. We both loved jazz."

"You had that in common. What else did you have in common?"

She smiled a sly smile. "You think I was too young for him."

"I didn't say that."

"You think I loved him for his money." Olga shook her head, patting her belly as if to reassure her unborn child it was not true. "I do not need his money. I have money of my own."

"But you don't want Tasha Karsak to have it."

"Lazlo would want his baby to have it. Not this . . ." Here Olga seemed to struggle for the right word and then settled for her native tongue. ". . . *Provokator*." She pronounced it neither the French nor the English way, but the Russian way.

Mercy suspected she meant it the Russian way, too. She knew from Afghanistan that when Russians used that word, they could be talking about a troublemaker, sure, like when you used it in English, but they could also be talking about a sting or false-flag operation. Russians were very fond of false-flag ops, usually designed to create a pretext for war. From Olga's perspective, Tasha Karsak's insistence that she was Lazlo's daughter was indeed a pretext for war. *The War of the Blondes.*

"Understood," said Mercy.

"Okay then." Having delivered her whopper of a revelation, Olga untangled herself from the chair, pulled on her boots, and glided to her feet, a swan about to take flight.

"You will find who killed my Lazlo," she said, looking from Mercy to Troy.

"We will," said Mercy. "We loved him, too."

Olga pulled a card from her back jeans pocket and handed it to Mercy. "When you know something, call me."

"Sure." The thick cream-colored card featured a pretty blue-and-rose logo with a samovar and the words "Mystic Chai / A Tea & Coffee Shoppe." The card also listed Olga as the proprietor and the address, hours of operation, and phone number.

She leaned in and gave Mercy a quick hug. "I will wait to hear from you."

"I'll be in touch."

Olga zipped her silver parka over her blue cashmere sweater and tugged the fur-trimmed hood over her long hair.

Mercy accompanied her to the entrance, the dogs following at a discreet distance. "If you need anything," she said, looking down at the woman's baby bump, "just let me know."

"Thank you," Olga said simply.

And then she was gone, a long silver streak disappearing into the storm of snow. Mercy stared after her, then pulled the postcard from her pocket.

She studied the postcard in her hand, with the blue and silver shadows of snow swirling around the Snow Maiden.

Olga Volkov was a dead ringer for the Snow Maiden.

Half an hour later, Amy and Tandie were in the living room packing up the remainder of the leftover decorations, to be stored in a spare guest room until Christmas had come and gone. Troy and Susie Bear were upstairs putting Felicity down for a nap.

Snow was falling again, waves of soft flakes that shimmered in the glow of the Christmas lights strung along the branches of the massive sugar maple. Mercy settled onto the sectional with Elvis at her feet, laptop on her crossed legs. Time for a deep dive on *The Snow Maiden*. She found the entire book of the opera by Nikolai Rimsky-Korsakov, who'd composed the music and written the libretto, online and downloaded it, printing a copy as well.

Looking for clues, she read the entire libretto, searching for anything that might explain why Uncle Laz would be steering her to explore *The Snow Maiden*. The libretto detailed the story of the girl with the heart of ice who falls in love only to melt away like the last of the winter snow—complete with fauns and fairies and choruses of birds and flower spirits.

Mercy enjoyed the reading, although she would always prefer fairy tales in which the heroine lives happily ever after. The story of the Snow Maiden reminded her too much of those nineteenth-century novels where if the heroine has any fun at all she must throw herself in front of a train at the end. Those novels, however beautifully written, always depressed her.

She knew it wasn't enough to read the libretto. To understand the full impact of the story, she was going to have to watch the opera in full. Otherwise she might miss something.

There was a video of an entire production of *The Snow Maiden* opera online, and Mercy began to watch it. It was lovely and lively and long. She really enjoyed the "Dance of the Tumblers," the composer's fiery tribute to Russia's talented and energetic street performers. It was the first song in the opera that sounded familiar to Mercy. The one she knew for sure she'd heard before.

Somewhere about halfway through the three-and-a-half-hour production, Mercy grew sleepy. *Sleep when the baby sleeps,* she thought, and dozed off to the sound of the Blind Gusli-Players singing a soaring melody that began as a lullaby and grew in force and power over the course of the piece.

As *The Snow Maiden* played on, she dreamed of blazing Yule logs and dead Santas and singing Christmas trees. Maidens with glistening halos of giant snowflakes danced through snowy forests while poachers caught lynx in snapping traps and tall blondes sipped chai from etched silver and gold demitasse cups. . . .

Felicity's cry awakened her. Something tugged at the edges of her consciousness. Something important. Mercy tried to remember what it was as she changed the baby. But whatever it was, it eluded her.

Downstairs, she made lunch for her little girl—tricolor rotini and slices of soft cooked sweet potatoes and banana. While Felicity gleefully smeared a palette of orange and yellow and green mush on the high chair tray, Mercy googled Eastern Europe and researched the past several decades there, from the Cold War and the fall of the Berlin Wall to the post-Soviet years and the rise of the oligarchs.

She was hoping that she would find something that might explain Tasha Karsak and the Russian cigarettes and *The Snow Maiden*. Something that could be the key to Lazlo's mysterious past.

"What are you doing?" asked Tandie, joining them at the marble island.

Troy came in, too, from the porch, Elvis and Susie Bear on his heels. He'd been out with the dogs and Levi, shoveling the paths from the parking lot to the house. The Newfie was a giant dripping snowball, thanks to her penchant for rolling in the white stuff. Elvis, on the other hand, was already curled up in the corner by the pantry, licking himself clean of it.

"What are you doing?" said Troy, repeating Tandie's question.

Mercy tried to explain the links she was looking for, and couldn't seem to find.

"You'll find it."

"I need to know more about Lazlo. He had so many secrets." Mercy paused. "What have Thrasher and Harrington found out about him?"

"Not much that I can tell," said Troy. "Thrasher said Becker and Goodlove searched his house and came up with nothing."

"And Interpol?"

"Still waiting on the DNA results." Troy laughed as Felicity flung a rotini down to Susie Bear. Elvis immediately roused himself and joined the Newfie at the base of the high chair. Waiting for the next pasta toss.

"I bet you could find something, Mercy," said Tandie. "You always find stuff the cops miss." She looked at Troy. "No offense."

"None taken." He grabbed a wet paper towel and cleaned the tray while Mercy used a baby wipe to clean up Felicity's hands and face. "It's true."

"Sorry, guys," Mercy told the dogs, who shuffled off to their respective corners of the kitchen now that their favorite food game was over.

"Tandie's right. You should take a look at Laz's house."

"Harrington would never approve." Mercy handed the baby her wooden giraffe and the stuffed Elvis and Susie Bear doggy toys. This was the triad that now accompanied Felicity wherever they went. Or else.

"Not if Thrasher's there, too." Troy pulled out his phone and texted his boss. Seconds later his cell pinged back. He grinned. "The captain will meet us there in thirty minutes. We can go right from Laz's place to the village green for *A Christmas Carol*."

"Cool," said Tandie.

Troy gave the eager teenager a sympathetic look. "Just Mercy and me, I'm afraid. We'll take Felicity with us and you can ride with Amy and Brodie and Helena. We'll see you at the theater."

"Not fair," said Tandie.

"I'm sorry, but you know Harrington."

"What about the dogs?" asked Mercy.

"Harrington said no to the dogs."

"That's just dumb," said Tandie.

"Agreed," said Troy. "But we can't take them into the theater anyway, so they'll stay home."

"They'll keep me company," said Tandie, brightening. She didn't often get both pups to herself. She turned to Mercy. "What's Lazlo's house like?"

"I don't know," said Mercy. "I've never been."

"Me either," said Troy.

"You really didn't know him at all, did you?" asked Tandie.

"No," said Mercy, realizing that what she'd always thought of as reserve on Uncle Laz's part may very well have been subterfuge. "Jillian says she can tell you everything you need to know about a person by their home. That every house is a secret waiting to be discovered."

"Spoken like a true Realtor," said Troy.

"Let's hope she's right."

Outside, Troy belted Felicity into the baby carrier in the backseat of the Jeep while Mercy slipped her Glock into the glove compartment.

"Anticipating trouble?" asked Troy, peering over the headrest.

"Not really." She smiled at Troy. "There won't be any Santa Clauses at Laz's house. Our perp seems fixated on St. Nick."

"True," said Troy. "And Thrasher will be there."

"And Thrasher will be there." There was no better man to have by your side than Thrasher, apart from her husband. "I'm sure it'll be fine. But better safe than sorry."

"Agreed."

"I just can't shake the feeling somebody's watching me. You. Us."

"I know that feeling. And I trust it." He shut the back door and walked around to the driver's side of the vehicle. He slid into the seat and handed Mercy his Ruger LC9. "Like you say, Better safe than sorry."

This was a soldier's sixth sense, honed in theater, that protected you long after you left the battlefield. If you listened to it.

Mercy was listening. So was Troy. Two listeners were better than one.

And two guns were better than one.

Better safe than sorry.

CHAPTER TWENTY-EIGHT

*We shout for gladness, triumph o'er sadness,
loving and praising*

—CATHERINE WINKWORTH

THIRTY MINUTES LATER TROY PULLED THE JEEP UP TO THE NEATLY restored nineteenth-century Greek Revival home on a side street lined with oak trees about a dozen blocks east of the town common. *Even here the roads are lined with parked cars,* thought Mercy. With only two days till Christmas, Northshire was packed from end to end with locals and visitors alike. The snow had stopped, at least temporarily, and a winter sun shone on the village.

Her husband turned the Jeep onto the narrow driveway that led up to the small detached garage on the east side of the house, parking behind the captain's shiny black Chevy Silverado 2500. Even in the snow, Thrasher's truck gleamed, being as well-groomed and polished as the captain himself, no matter what the weather.

Thrasher was leaning against the tailgate of his pristine vehicle. He wore a shearling-lined bomber jacket over a gray turtleneck cashmere sweater and dark denim jeans. The picture of off-duty elegance.

He smiled and raised a sleek leather-gloved hand in welcome, then started toward them.

Mercy stepped out onto the snow-covered drive, and Troy did the same, coming around to her side to meet the captain.

Thrasher greeted Felicity with a tap on the window, and she happily tapped back. He handed the keys to the house to Troy. "They've already gone over the place pretty thoroughly. Harrington is desperate enough for some progress on the case that he agreed to this search. But you'll have to make it fast. I'll stay with the little one in your vehicle."

"Thank you, Captain," said Mercy. The man was a wonder with babies, just like her mother was. Both blessed with the magic of baby whisperers. Both marked with the mystery of hidden depths.

"Shall we?" Troy raised his arm as if to escort her. She paused as her skin began to tingle, not from the cold but from the sense that she was being watched. She glanced up and down the street, but saw nothing. And the feeling dissolved.

"What is it?" asked Troy.

"Nothing." Maybe it was just Thrasher, she thought.

Mercy and Troy made their way onto the white-columned porch to the red front door. A Christmas wreath bedecked in red satin ribbon hung on the door, crisscrossed in crime scene tape.

Mercy and Troy slipped on gloves. Troy unlocked the door, lifting the yellow tape to allow them to pass.

And here she was, entering the sanctuary of another man with hidden depths. Dark currents that might hold the answers to his death. If only she could navigate the undertow.

They went inside, stepping into an entryway anchored by a round burl-topped center hall table with lion-shaped feet. On the table stood two silver candlesticks and a silver tray that held mail. The techs had already removed anything of interest; all that was left was direct mail ads. Mercy rifled through them, but didn't see anything worth reading.

They moved into the large living room, simply decorated in grays and blacks and yellows. One long wall of ceiling-to-floor black shelving held books, magazines, and the extensive vinyl record collection Olga had told them about.

But the centerpiece of the room was a beautiful pipe organ that would have been the pride of any chapel.

"Wow." Mercy snapped a photo of the magnificent instrument. "That organ is nicer than the one at the church."

"I don't know much about organs," said Troy, "but it's certainly as big as the one at the church."

There was a lovely antique maple folio cabinet where Uncle Laz had kept his sheet music, and that, along with his books and records, had all been sifted through by Harrington's team already. There didn't seem much point in spending much time doing it again. Unless they came up short in the rest of the house.

"Let's come back to this room," said Mercy. They'd started toward the hallway when they heard a loud thump coming from deeper into the house. *Guess my sixth sense was right,* she thought.

Troy lifted his index finger to his lips.

Another *whack!,* like someone slamming shut a cabinet or banging closed a drawer.

"Kitchen," he mouthed to Mercy.

She nodded.

Like Thrasher, Troy was in civvies, dressed for the theater, not for the field. He was unarmed. As was Mercy, who wore black velveteen leggings and a burgundy silk tunic under her rose-colored cashmere wrap coat, all gifts from her mother. Room for weaponry not being a prime consideration for Grace. Ever.

Their firearms were in the glove box of the Jeep. Mercy had even left her pack in the car. *Damn.*

Quietly Troy texted the captain.

10–70.

Home invasion. He motioned to Mercy to stay behind him, and together they moved silently through the entryway toward the kitchen. The noises banged on.

Whoever it was, she thought, they were not even trying to keep it down. Either they didn't know anyone else was here—or they didn't care.

Mercy and Troy parted as they approached the kitchen, each grabbing a silver candlestick from the round table, each heading for the opposite side of the kitchen door, each flattening their back to the wall.

"On three," whispered Mercy.

One, two, three.

Mercy slipped through the doorway. Troy was right behind her. There stood Olga Volkov on the far side of the room, beyond the antique trestle dining table. She was rummaging through the drawers of an Amish-style antique pine hutch.

"What are you looking for?" asked Mercy.

Startled, Olga spun around, her long platinum-streaked hair flying. With her hands behind her back, she closed the open drawer, recovering her composure. She lifted her chin. "What are *you* doing here?"

This was a side to Olga that Mercy had not seen. She was cornered, and not happy about it. Whether from embarrassment or guilt or both, Mercy wasn't sure.

"We're here on behalf of law enforcement," said Troy. "You are trespassing."

"I am not trespassing. I have a key."

"A key," said Mercy. Not unheard of between partners. But still, questionable timing.

"Yes. I have a key to his home, and he has a key to mine."

"Key or not, this house is a crime scene," said Troy. "You should have known that from the crime scene tape."

Olga said nothing, but her pale face reddened.

"You can't miss it," said Mercy. "It's all over the entrance to the house."

"I used the back door." Olga pointed to a back door at the opposite end of the room where tall multi-paned windows revealed a nicely landscaped backyard surrounded by an eight-foot wooden privacy fence.

"There's tape on the back lock, too," said Troy.

"I thought you were finished doing whatever it was that you were doing, so I took it off and came in."

"That's a crime," Mercy said gently. "Why would you do that?" She wanted to be on the pregnant woman's side, she *was* on her side, but . . .

Olga didn't answer that either.

"To avoid law enforcement," said Troy.

"Which is why I didn't see her." Captain Thrasher barreled into the kitchen. Mercy could see the bulge of his pistol under his jacket at his hip.

Olga tried to protest but sobbed instead. She sank into one of the Windsor chairs. Mercy crossed over to her, and placed her arms around her. They sat there for a moment, until Olga wriggled out of her arms, rising to her feet. Mercy did the same.

"Looks like you've got this under control. But just in case." Thrasher handed Troy his gun. "Collect her key before you leave, and lock up. I'm going back to Felicity. Becker's on the way."

"Thank you." Mercy leaned toward the captain, lowering her voice so Olga couldn't hear. "Guns in the glove box."

"Roger that."

With tired eyes, Olga watched the captain leave. She handed the key to Troy. "Why is this a crime scene anyway? Lazlo did not die here."

"The victim's residence is a crime scene that may yield evidence critical to the investigation." Troy stuck the house key in his pocket and the gun in his belt.

Olga tapped one of the stacks of paperwork that littered the kitchen table. "The police looked already. So why are you here?"

"You first," said Mercy.

The woman sighed with the resignation Mercy was beginning to expect of Russians. "I want to know his secrets. Why he was killed. Why he did not tell me he had a daughter. If she *is* his daughter. I want to know who is this man whose child I carry."

"I understand." And Mercy did understand.

"Your turn."

"I'm here for the same reason you are. I hoped that if I were here in his home I would come to know him better, and that would help me—us—find out who did this to him. And why."

Olga clenched her fists and placed them on the table, as if to hold herself up.

"Are you all right?" asked Mercy.

"Fine." The pregnant woman straightened, her brow creased with resolve. "We can look together."

Mercy glanced at Troy. He shrugged.

"All right." She looked around the neat kitchen, with its clean, uncluttered black granite counters and neatly stacked dishes on open pine shelves. There didn't seem to be much to find in here—and odds were that it would have been found by now if there were. She turned to Olga. "You said he had an office."

Olga led them upstairs, where there were three bedrooms. The master bedroom and en suite bathroom were as sparely furnished and decorated as the downstairs rooms had been. A king-sized bed dominated the space, with built-in end tables topped with modern sidelights. Over the bed hung a lone artwork, a landscape oil painting of an isolated barn set among the trees in winter. The effect was that of a kind of lyrical loneliness. Nothing like the Vrubel painting, which evoked more of a fairy tale aesthetic.

Mercy peered closely at the signature but couldn't make it out. She couldn't speak or write Russian, so she wouldn't necessarily be able to read it even if she could decipher it. It seemed like an artist's signature was often as indecipherable as a doctor's. "Do you know who painted it?"

"It's an Ivan Sorokin," said Olga.

"Did he ever paint a Snow Maiden?"

"I do not think so. He was famous for landscapes."

On to the walk-in closet, which revealed half a dozen suits, a dozen button-down shirts, and a collection of sweaters, jeans, and shoes. All very good quality, if a little on the staid side. Like Uncle Lazlo himself. Or at least that was how he always presented himself.

The en suite bath was simply designed in black and white subway tiles, a shower built for two, double sinks, and a large bevel-mirrored medicine cabinet that held a minimum of toiletries. Uncle Lazlo had never been a vain man, and his bathroom bore that out.

The guest bedroom was as spare as a monk's room: a bed, a dresser, a chair, and a closet that held only linens. It didn't seem like Uncle Laz had many people sleep over. Except maybe Olga.

The third bedroom was Lazlo's office, and it was only here that you got some sense of the man. The antique rolltop desk and wooden file cabinets looked like they were straight out of a nineteenth-century lawyer's office. Bookshelves were filled to overflowing with books on finance and accounting and trade journals; another long table held a computer stand, two large screens, and a printer. The computer was gone, taken for evidence by the crime scene techs, no doubt.

It was a space dedicated to work. Just the kind of room Mercy and her friends and family would have expected of Lazlo Ford—a man they knew as dedicated to work.

Hanging above the desk between the flat-screen monitors was a painting of a raven-haired girl in front of a lilac bush that filled the background from top to bottom and side to side. Mercy stepped in for a closer look.

"*The Lilacs*," said Olga, coming to stand beside her. "By Mikhail Aleksandrovic Vrubel."

Like Vrubel's *The Snow Maiden*, this was a haunting genre painting in which the deep purple lilacs enveloped the raven-haired girl as if guarding her from a great and terrible fate.

The Lilacs was the only artwork in the room. Nothing else was on the walls other than a calendar and a small whiteboard. The whiteboard was blank; a red marker sat on a ridge at the bottom of the board's frame, unused.

The painting struck an odd note in the business-as-usual office.

"One of these things is not like the others," said Mercy.

"What?" asked Troy.

"This painting—it doesn't really go with the rest of the room. Or with the rest of the house. Which is very American. Filled with early-American antiques. I'd bet even the organ was made here."

Olga reached across the desk, tracing the gold frame that bordered *The Lilacs* with a blue fingernail. Grief shone on her face.

"You should be wearing gloves," Troy told her.

She ignored him. "The painting is very Russian. Like Lazlo."

Mercy had never thought of Uncle Laz as Russian. The man she had known was all numbers, all finance, all business—an American capitalist through and through. And his English was as perfectly American as hers was. "He didn't seem that Russian to me."

"You know only the new Lazlo, the American." Olga pulled back from the picture, and crossed her arms, leaning against the desk. "But Lazlo was an old soul. An old Russian soul."

The Sorokin painting in the master bedroom and this Vrubel here in Lazlo's home office were the only real personal touches in the house. Apart from the organ and the records in the living room, but you could make the case that his interest in music was part of his public life, as he had shared it with his fellow churchgoers. Whereas the two most private rooms in this very private man's residence were hidden away upstairs, away from prying eyes.

Presumably he shared his master bedroom only with Olga, who over the course of their relationship had grown to know this secret side of him. But with whom did he share his office? Who knew that secret side of him? Mercy figured no one. And she figured he liked it that way.

"If Uncle Laz had secrets to find, they'll be here," she told Troy.

Mercy studied the room again, from the books and journals to the file cabinets. And finally, to *The Lilacs*.

"Excuse me." She motioned Olga to move away from the desk. With a gloved hand, she traced the gold frame of the painting as Olga had done. But she did it twice, and the second time she ran her fingers under the frame. "Here we go."

"What?" asked Olga.

Mercy said nothing; she simply pulled gently on the right edge of the painting. The artwork angled forward, and she opened it as if it were the mirrored front of a medicine cabinet. Revealing a built-in wall safe with an electronic lock.

"Good work, sweetheart," said Troy.

"Ничего себе!" said Olga.

"Huh?" asked Troy.

"Wow," Olga translated, smiling. She patted Mercy on the shoulder. "Very good."

Mercy examined the safe. "It uses fingerprint technology for quick access."

"A little late for that," said Troy.

"There's a keypad, too, so we should be able to get in with the right PIN," said Mercy. She turned to Olga. "Any ideas?"

"You mean like birthdays," said Olga.

"Worth a try," Mercy told her.

Olga grabbed the red marker and began to write down numbers on the whiteboard.

"You two figure it out and I'll go tell the captain you struck gold," said Troy.

"We won't know that we've struck anything until we get it open," warned Mercy.

"Don't find anything until I get back." Troy laughed and left, heading down the stairs. With Olga's help, Mercy tried Laz's birthday and Olga's birthday. No go. "The system will probably shut us out of we don't get it right on the next couple of tries."

"We can call a locksmith."

"The police will do that. And I'd rather know what if anything is inside before law enforcement takes over, wouldn't you?"

"Yes." Olga's eyes filled with tears. "You are smart. You will find who killed my Lazlo."

"Let me think." Mercy closed her eyes and ran through everything she knew about Lazlo's life and death so far—a mélange of images and impressions, facts and figures and data points. The dead Santa. The organ. The secret daughter. The blazing Yule log. The pregnant girlfriend. The missing pompom. The funeral. *The Snow Maiden*. The torn hymn. *The Lilacs*.

"'O Little Town of Bethlehem,'" she said.

"What do you mean?"

"Lazlo had a strip of the sheet music in his hand when he died."

"Lazlo loved that Christmas song. His favorite." Olga smiled. "But these are words, not numbers."

"Exactly." Mercy grabbed the woman by her shoulders. "Olga, you're brilliant."

"What did I say?"

Mercy remembered the hymn board at the church. "Laz was an organist. Hymns and carols are all listed in the hymnal, and they have numbers." She pulled out her cell and texted her grandmother.

What's the hymn number for O Little Town of Bethlehem?

Her cell pinged back almost immediately.

133

Leave it to Patience not to ask any questions, but to just give her what she needed without explanation.

"Okay. 133. We're still three numbers short. Most of these PINs are six numbers long." Mercy considered the hymns Lazlo had chosen for the funeral; Lillian said he planned every aspect of his memorial in advance.

But there were three numbers on the hymn board. She counted them off for Olga: #438: *It Is Well with My Soul*; #99: *Abide with Me*; #606: *Nearer My God to Thee*. "Which was his favorite?"

Olga shook her head. "I do not know. I do not go to church. Lazlo wanted me to, but . . ." She wiped at her eyes with the sleeve of her sweater. "I should have gone with him. For him."

"That's okay. We'll figure it out." Mercy couldn't try them all without getting locked out. "Maybe Patience knows." She texted her grandmother again, to ask her which was Lazlo's favorite hymn. Her cell rang and she picked up and put it on speaker.

"Try number 438 or number 99," her grandmother said. "I chose number 606 myself because BWV 615 was too hard for me to play."

"BWV 615?" *This was no ordinary hymn number,* thought Mercy. "What is that?"

"Bach's chorale prelude to *In Dir Ist Freude*."

"English, please."

"*In Thee Is Gladness*. It's one of those hymns that Bach wrote a chorale prelude for. Playing it may have been a piece of cake for Lazlo, but it's a very challenging piece. At least for me."

"So you didn't play it."

"No, I substituted *Nearer My God to Thee*. I reckon he'd forgive me."

"And it was to be the last hymn of the service."

"Yes. Mercy—"

Mercy cut her off. "Thank you. If this works, I'll explain it all later."

"You certainly will."

Patience rang off. Mercy looked at Olga. "Let's try this again. 133 for 'O Little Town of Bethlehem' and then 615 for the Bach prelude."

Olga wrote the numbers down on the whiteboard, repeating them as she scribbled.

Mercy held her finger up to the pad. "Ready?"

"Ready."

Mercy punched in the numbers as Olga read them off the board. She held her breath. Olga did, too.

And there it was. The lovely sound of an electronic lock unlatching.

"We're in."

"You were supposed to wait until we got here." Troy stood behind her,

Felicity in his arms, playing with the captain's hat, the hatless Thrasher at his side.

"Well done," said Thrasher.

"You want to do the honors, Captain?" asked Mercy.

"Go ahead. I'll just shoot it." Thrasher pulled out his cell and recorded her as she cracked open the safe and looked inside.

"Well?" asked Troy.

She reached in and retrieved the only object in the safe. A thumb drive. She held it up for her observers to see.

Thrasher slipped his phone into his pocket. "I'm afraid I'll have to take that."

"Why?" asked Olga.

"It's evidence," said Troy.

"If you insist." Mercy dropped the drive into the captain's open palm. "Although it's probably encrypted." She shot the captain a meaningful look. "I'm sure we know who could get into it for us."

Mercy was referring to Brodie, who was twice the accomplished techie of anyone in local law enforcement. In the past, he'd been instrumental in solving several tech challenges that allowed Mercy and Troy to bring more than one killer to justice.

Even Harrington was forced to acknowledge his expertise, to the point where Brodie now served as a consultant to the department from time to time. *This should be one of those times,* Mercy figured.

"Your boy Brodie." Thrasher smiled. "I'll talk to Harrington."

"I hate to spoil all the fun," said Troy, passing his boss's pistol back to him. He checked his watch. "But are we done here? We need to get to that play."

As soon as they stepped outside onto the porch, Mercy felt that telltale tingling along the back of her neck. The sun had slipped behind the clouds, and it was very cold. She did a quick 180-degree surveillance of the front yard, from the stone wall separating Laz's house from its neighbor on the right to the long spruce hedge that bordered its neighbor on the left. She saw nothing but snow and spruce, rock and oak, Becker and his black-and-white.

"What is it?" asked Troy.

"Nothing." Maybe she'd been a civilian too long and her sixth sense was finally failing her. She hoped not.

She and Troy said goodbye to Olga as Thrasher consulted with Becker. Mercy belted the baby into the car seat, and climbed into the front passenger seat while Troy made his way to the driver's side. She rolled the window down despite the cold. Still listening. Still observing. Still tingling.

Mercy heard Thrasher instruct Becker to accompany Olga to her vehicle, and she watched as Becker guided the pregnant woman carefully along the snow-covered path to the slushy sidewalk and down the street toward her Ford Bronco.

The sun came out again, and the snow sparkled in the light. The captain headed for his own vehicle. Troy punched the ignition, and the Jeep roared to life. As he eased the vehicle in reverse, the wheels spun a bit in the snow before gaining traction and rolling back down the narrow driveway to the street. As the Jeep swiveled onto the road, swerving in the slush, Mercy gave the graceful Greek Revival home and grounds one last look.

A glint in the spruce hedge caught her eye. Light on metal. Maybe the barrel of a gun peeking through the evergreen, maybe tinsel on a twig glittering in the afternoon sun, maybe nothing at all.

She was taking no chances. "Stop," she told Troy as she reached for the glove compartment. Her eyes still trained on the spruce hedge.

Troy braked, hard. The Jeep skidded to a stop. Felicity started to cry.

Mercy pulled out her Glock. Troy lowered his seat and dove into the back behind her, shielding the baby.

She aimed the gun at the glint in the hedge. Waiting for whatever came next. Ready to fire.

A subtle flash and the glint was gone.

"What is it?" Troy asked from the backseat.

"Nothing. Yet."

They waited. Thrasher had sized up the situation and was now in position behind his SUV, waiting as well.

The glint did not reappear.

They waited some more.

"False alarm," said Mercy finally, putting the Glock back in the glove box.

"Maybe," said Troy, texting the captain. "He and Becker will do a search. If anyone's here, they'll find him."

ORLOV HAD CUT IT close, as the Americans would say. He'd stayed too long at the Lazlo Ford house, thanks to the satisfied look on the captain's face and the way the man patted his breast pocket when he talked to the uniform. They'd obviously found something, something his associates had missed—and the sharp-eyed Mercy Carr had not.

He thought he could just wait until the uniform was down the road and the Jeep had pulled away and then relieve the captain of whatever they'd found. But Mercy Carr had spotted the titanium suppressor of his pistol in the hedge and aimed her gun at him. He had no doubt she would pull the trigger. And no doubt that she was a good shot.

He was not going to die at Mercy Carr's hands. Nor in a gunfight with cops at the O.K. Corral.

They were not paying him enough to kill cops.

Orlov cursed. This was what came with working with morons. He'd have to find another way.

CHAPTER TWENTY-NINE

> *If I could work my will, every idiot who goes about with "Merry Christmas" on his lips, should be boiled with his own pudding, and buried with a stake of holly through his heart.*
>
> —CHARLES DICKENS, *A CHRISTMAS CAROL*

THE VILLAGE GREEN WAS EVEN LIVELIER AND MORE CROWDED than it had been the evening before. Tomorrow was Christmas Eve, and everyone was out doing their last bits of Christmas shopping and decorating and caroling. The ice rink was full of skaters, the Christmas market chalets were full of customers, and the labyrinth was full of larger-than-life gleaming ice sculptures of reindeer and dragons, angels and unicorns, knights and elves and princesses. The Druids and the bonfire were now replaced by the annual winter ice art installation, the winning piece to be announced on New Year's Eve.

Troy and Mercy went on to the theater. Thrasher texted Troy to let him know that they'd found evidence that there had indeed been someone by that hedge, but a search of the neighborhood revealed nothing and no one.

"Good to know I didn't imagine the whole thing," Mercy told Troy. "I guess my sixth sense is still operational."

"I never doubted it for a minute."

"What do you think the guy was after?"

"Captain Thrasher appeared to be the target. Maybe someone's got it out for him," said Troy, his voice worried. "Harrington's got people on that already."

"Or maybe it's the thumb drive," she said, glad that the drive was now safely in the hands of law enforcement. Several copies of the encrypted files had been made and secured.

"Who else could know about it?"

"Good question." One to which she did not have an answer.

The arts center was in the far corner of the village common, away from the labyrinth and the town hall and the church. Mercy hadn't been here since the most recent restoration of the arts center, which drew its inspiration from the nineteenth-century building's glamorous days as a movie palace in the 1920s, when an ambitious conversion had transformed the Quaker meeting house into an Art Deco showplace.

Entering the theater was like walking back in time. Clara Bow and Rudolph Valentino wouldn't be out of place here, drinking gin martinis, framed by the silver and gold wallpaper embellished with zigzags and lightning bolts and the scrollwork of stylized peacock feathers and trumpet-shaped florals, their dancing feet clicking on the black-and-white tile floors.

The reality of twenty-first-century Vermonters dressed for a blizzard was a little less glamorous. Mercy and Troy made their way through the ticket booth, Felicity in her father's arms, mesmerized by the crystal chandeliers and the shiny wallpaper.

"There's Harrington with Daniel," said Troy.

"With Cat Torano on his tail," said Mercy.

The journalist dogged the detective, calling out questions as he stalked away from her. "Who's the Yuletide Killer? What are you doing to protect the public? How soon will he strike again?"

"No comment," repeated Harrington. "No comment."

Poor Harrington, thought Mercy. She knew he'd never want "No comment" to be known as his mantra. He was a man of action, not avoidance.

A security guard blocked Cat's way. "No unauthorized entry." She moved forward, and he took her by the arm.

"Let go of me!" Cat twisted in the man's grip.

"No unauthorized entry," he repeated.

"I have a ticket." With her free hand she held up a ticket for the world to see. "I have every right to be here."

While she argued with the guard, Daniel opened a side door along one of the lobby's walls and he and Harrington disappeared inside. Into the bowels of the theater, where nosy reporters could not follow.

"Wait!" Cat yelled after them. But she was too late.

"Settle down, miss," said the guard, "or I'm going to have to ask you to leave."

"'Miss'?" she said to him. "Really?"

The security guard released the journalist, and she made a show of readjusting her coat. She glanced around the lobby, looking for her next story. Spotting Mercy.

"Incoming. Two o'clock," warned Troy.

Cat barged up to them. Mercy introduced Troy, then turned toward the stairs that led to the balcony level. "See you later."

Cat pivoted so that she was once again face-to-face with Mercy. "I'm surprised to find you here. I thought you were on the case. Anything new on The Singing Plumber and that syringe?"

"Our family has long supported the arts," Mercy said imperiously, channeling her mother.

Cat ignored that. "Where's your dog?"

"At home. This is a theater—no place for dogs." She was on the verge of saying, "Or journalists," but Troy saved her.

"You must be here to review the play," he said to Cat.

"Uh, right." Cat nodded insincerely.

"I do hope you'll be kind," said Mercy.

Cat smiled, not sure if they were mocking her or not. Mercy wasn't quite sure either. She was a staunch supporter of the First Amendment, and as much as the woman annoyed her, Mercy admired her determination. In some ways, Cat reminded her of Elvis. And herself. A dog with a bone.

The lights blinked on and off, the signal that the play was about to begin.

"That's our cue," said Troy, and expertly ushered Mercy and the baby away from the reporter. "Enjoy the show."

Mercy could feel the reporter's eyes on them as they climbed the elegant staircase. "She's not giving up that easily."

"Nope," said Troy. "Like someone else we know."

"Very funny."

As patrons of the arts, Mercy's parents had season tickets for box seats for the entire family. Grace and Duncan were already in the box waiting for them, along with Patience and Tandie. Amy and Brodie were down in the orchestra seats, close to the stage, where most of the parents with small children were sitting, the better to see the show and keep their restless charges occupied.

Mercy and Troy settled into their red velvet–padded seats, her mom and dad on one side and her grandmother on the other. Felicity sat happily on her father's lap, playing with the wooden giraffe Rory Craig had given her.

"Great seats," said Troy.

"Best in the house," said Mercy. And they were. Their box was right between Lillian Jenkins's and Feinberg's boxes—stage left, very close to the stage, with unique views of both the performers and the audience.

"And it's so beautiful," said Grace approvingly. "They did a great job with the restoration."

"They sure did," said Mercy.

As with the lobby, the stage and house sections of the theater had been elaborately restored to their former Art Deco glory. Mercy wondered what the Quakers who built the place two hundred years ago would think of it now. This building had lived as many different lives as the generations of people who'd come here to find God, or to find knowledge, or to find entertainment. All forms of escape and refuge, one way or another.

Patience smiled. "Just the place for our little Henry to make his stage debut."

Mercy smiled back.

She looked over at Lillian's box, where the eleven-year-old boy's family had gathered to watch the show. Sitting there were Lillian; her son, Ethan Jenkins, Henry's father; and Ethan's fiancée Yolanda Yellowbird, the sweethearts looking as happy as an engaged couple should.

Mercy looked to the other side of the loge seats, where Feinberg held court in his own box with Uncle Hugo. Thrasher and his lovely partner, the talented artist and café owner Wyetta Wright, were there, too. And Harrington.

Mercy nudged Troy. "There's Harrington with Feinberg."

"No surprise there. He's angling for mayor."

"If he doesn't arrest the Yuletide Killer soon," said Duncan, "he'll be lucky to keep the job he has."

Patience nodded. "The press is all over him and the public outcry is growing."

"No chance at higher office for Harrington, then," said Troy. "At least for now."

"Speaking of mayors, who's sitting for Laz as acting mayor in the meantime?" asked Mercy.

"Nathan Moore," said Grace. "Senior town selectman."

"You know him, Troy," said Duncan. "He's the building inspector for Northshire. A solid citizen, but no politician. Just a stand-in until the town can hold a special election after the New Year."

Troy nodded, but Tandie rolled her eyes. "Dad says he's let that weirdo cult get away with all kinds of building code violations."

"How does that happen?" asked Mercy.

"He just looks the other way." Tandie shrugged. "Dad says it happens all the time."

Grace squared her shoulders. "Well, it shouldn't."

"How'd he get to be the acting mayor then?"

"Seniority," sniffed Grace. "I'm all for Harrington as mayor if he can beat Nathan Moore."

"But if he can't?" asked Mercy.

"We'll cross that bridge when we come to it."

"Where *is* your dad?" Troy asked Tandie, changing the subject.

"Oh, he's backstage," she said. "He's the stage carpenter."

"We can count on good sets then," Troy said, rocking Felicity, who was half asleep already, her red head bobbing gently against his chest.

"I still think Mom should run for mayor," said Mercy. "You'd whip them all into shape, Mom."

Tandie laughed. "Like it or not."

"Please stop." Her mother's voice was an uncharacteristic plea.

The lights blinked on and off, a second signal that the show was bound to begin and people should take their seats.

"Saved by the bell," said Duncan cheerfully.

The lights went down, the orchestra began to play, and a hush settled over the crowd.

As the red velvet curtains began to rise, Mercy heard a *swoosh* to her left. She glanced over at Feinberg's booth. And there she was, the woman in the lynx coat.

Smiling at Harrington, who stood to welcome her. Leaning forward to greet the handsome detective in the traditional triple-cheek air kiss bestowed by Russians on family and friends. Gazing into his dark eyes for a moment too long before retreating into the shadows.

"Did you see that?" Mercy elbowed Troy. She watched as Harrington introduced Tasha Karsak to Feinberg and the others.

"I saw it," said Tandie. "What's up with that?"

"Tasha Karsak knows Harrington." Mercy wasn't sure what to make of that. She tried to catch Feinberg's eye, but failed. All eyes were on Tasha, as she settled into the seat next to Harrington. She crossed those long legs and patted the open seat next to her. Harrington did not look especially pleased; in fact, for once he looked nonplussed. But he sat down.

"Looks like they're way more than friends," said Tandie.

"I'm not so sure," said Mercy. Tasha reminded her of a Siberian goshawk, all snow and silver and feathers and claws. She had her eye on Harrington, all right, for better or worse.

"Shush," said Grace again, as the orchestra began to play Mozart's *Sleigh Ride*. "It's starting."

CHAPTER THIRTY

"I wish to be left alone," said Scrooge. "Since you ask me what I wish, gentlemen, that is my answer. I don't make merry myself at Christmas and I can't afford to make idle people merry...."

—CHARLES DICKENS, *A CHRISTMAS CAROL*

THE CURTAINS ROSE AND THERE WAS VICTORIAN LONDON, A ROW of shop fronts ringed in evergreen, cobblestone streets dusted with snow, people in nineteenth-century dress milling about the stage, and ladies and gentlemen and street hawkers selling roasted chestnuts and flowers and newspapers. Gaslight streetlamps cast a warm glow over the foggy scene, thanks to a fog machine billowing smoke from one of the wings.

Church bells tolled as a tall man wearing a waistcoat and trousers stepped forward into a spotlight on the stage's apron. From her perch in her parents' box above, Mercy could see him plainly. "That looks like Levi."

"It *is* Levi." Troy grinned. "He looks good."

"I had no idea he was an actor. It must be Adah's doing."

"Shush," repeated Grace.

"Old Marley was as dead as a doornail," said Levi in a British accent. "This must be distinctly understood or nothing wonderful can come of this story I am going to relate."

"Levi does accents," whispered Mercy in wonder.

"Who knew," said Troy.

They sat in thrall as a chorus of carolers sang "I saw three ships come sailing in, on Christmas Day, on Christmas Day" as the street vendors and costermongers and barrel-traders pulled the shop fronts apart and with lightning speed and precision transformed the London street into the countinghouse of "Scrooge & Marley." A bleak space with high desks and ledgers and bookcases and that small, cast-iron, coal-burning stove that burned so little coal, thanks to stingy Ebenezer Scrooge.

And there he was, Scrooge himself. An imposing figure with long white hair and an impressive pair of white muttonchop sideburns dressed all in black, brass-tipped walking stick in hand. He removed his gray top hat as he stepped up to his clerk, Bob Cratchit.

"Scrooge looks familiar, too," said Mercy, borrowing her mother's opera glasses to peer down at the lead character.

"It's Oisin," said Troy, consulting the program.

"It can't be," said Mercy, picturing the trademark foot-long flowing white whiskers of the Arch-Druid. But her husband was correct; as she looked more closely she could see that it was indeed Oisin. "He shaved his beard. I can't believe he shaved his beard."

"A method actor," said her father dryly.

"It'll take him a long time to grow it back," said Tandie.

"He's still got those muttonchops," said Troy. "Not a total loss."

"Who's Bob Cratchit?" At this rate, the actor must be somebody else she knew, thought Mercy.

"Cal Jacobs," said Patience.

"The psychiatrist?" Mercy had met Cal when he was working with Henry. Nice guy and a consummate professional; but in the end, it was really Elvis who'd won over Henry, earning his trust, and by extension, hers. A trust that helped them solve a murder, and apprehend the killer.

"Having Cal onstage must help Henry play his part," said her father.

"Keep watching," advised her mother.

They kept watching. Scrooge bah-humbugging Christmas with Bob Cratchit, his nephew Fred, and the portly gentlemen collecting for charity.

"It's about time for Henry to make his entrance," said Patience.

As if on cue, the chorus and the street hawkers appeared, singing and moving the set pieces to create the London street again. The spotlight followed Scrooge as he left the countinghouse, moved across the narrow lane, and yelled at a small boy in a newsboy cap and knickerbockers. He was leaning on a crudely made crutch. Accompanied by a dog.

"It's Henry." Mercy smiled. "And Robin." Robin was Henry's support dog, a sweet and strong Great Pyrenees and Australian shepherd mix. Henry had named her in honor of Robin, sidekick to his beloved hero Batman.

"Merry Christmas, Mr. Scrooge," said Tiny Tim in Henry's clear, bright voice.

Scrooge yelled at the boy again. "No begging on this corner, boy!"

"I'm not begging, sir. I'm waiting for my father. I'm Tim Cratchit." Tiny Tim beamed his big, beautiful Henry smile at Scrooge. An audible *awwww* ran through the audience.

"Are you indeed." Scrooge raised his cane at the dog. "Be gone, cur!"

"This is my dog, Mr. Scrooge. His name is Robin." Tiny Tim patted the big dog on her fluffy head.

Another *awww* from the audience.

"That is not true to the original," said Mercy's father with a smile.

"Between Dr. Jacobs playing his father and Robin playing his dog, Henry has all the support he needs," said Patience.

"The little guy is good," said Tandie.

"He's a natural," said Mercy. "He's got the audience eating out of his little hand."

And so it went. The chorus and the street hawkers set up Scrooge's dark and dreary house, where the curtains ruffled and the wind rattled and the dark spirits moaned and groaned, ushering in Scrooge's dead partner, Marley, an appropriately creepy Rory Craig looking like a Victorian zombie.

"Is everyone we know in this play?" asked Mercy.

"Almost," said her grandmother. "Looks like we're the only people in town who aren't in it."

"Maybe next year," said Duncan.

"I don't think so," said Grace.

Marley aka Rory warned Scrooge of the ghosts who would haunt him that night. The church bell tolled one o'clock, heralding Oisin's wife, Elisabeth, now appearing as the Ghost of Christmas Past.

"It's *'Elisabeth with an S,'*" said Troy, recalling the way the professor and poet Elisabeth Bardin, PhD, always introduced herself.

"That fits," said Mercy. Elisabeth's poetry was often rooted in the past, and the hold the past held over us, like it or not. She was also deeply involved with the Northshire Alliance of Poets, a local nonprofit dedicated to preserving and protecting the town's literary heritage, including Euphemia Whitney-Jones, Vermont's most famous poet—who'd lived and worked at their own Grackle Tree Farm. Another reason Mercy loved the place she was lucky enough to call home.

"It's Jillian," said Troy, as Belle, Scrooge's long-lost love, glided onto the stage in a swirl of hoops and petticoats.

Jillian was not only their friend but their Realtor, the one who'd helped them buy their beloved property. Mercy was used to seeing the petite blonde clothed head to toe in Talbots, but she was completely believable as a Victorian lady corseted in silk and satin. Jillian's husband played the young Scrooge. They were a cute couple, on and off the stage.

It was fun and instructive watching people she knew play roles so different from themselves. Mercy had no desire to perform herself, but she loved that her friends were killing it tonight. Dickens wasn't her beloved Shakespeare, and the Green Mountain Players weren't the Royal Shakespeare Company, but this production was so entertaining that the untimely deaths of the past few days faded into the background, at least for a while.

The clock chimed again, and Pizza Bob bounced into Scrooge's world as the Ghost of Christmas Present. Just as he'd been a perfect Santa Claus, he was now the perfect personification of the Christmas spirit. His enthusiasm and love of life were as contagious onstage as they were offstage.

Everyone loved Pizza Bob. The audience roared their approval when he quoted the famous lines, *"There is never enough time to do or say all the things that we would wish. The thing is to try to do as much as you can in the time that you have."*

Mercy loved that speech about the nature of time. In the military, time either felt like it was standing stock-still while you waited for something to happen—or like it was moving at the speed of light when something did happen and you found yourself in the heat of battle. Now that she had a child, time had morphed once again for her, moving lightning fast and glacially slow at the same time. Past and present swapping places like musical chairs. With the future lying just out of reach.

But not in *A Christmas Carol*. As the clock struck midnight, the stage once again undulated with waves of fog. The Ghost of Christmas Yet to Come appeared in a silver-shrouded costume that glinted under the stage lights. When the hood slipped off the ghost player's head, Mercy identified the ghost as their neighbor and friend, the mystical and often prescient Adah Beecher.

Adah's ghostly pale painted face, eyes ringed with kohl like black holes, was barely recognizable. She looked like Edvard Munch's *The Scream* brought to life. Mercy only knew it was Adah because of the long salt-and-pepper-hair that hung wildly over her draped form. And of course her name was in the program.

"Northshire's resident shaman," said Troy. "Typecasting."

"The dark side of Adah," said Tandie pensively.

"The dark side," agreed Mercy. The real Adah was friendly and compassionate; this Adah-as-spectre was eerie and intimidating.

Adah did not speak. She simply raised her arm and pointed into the gloom with a long, bony finger. More fog rolled in. Scrooge walked with the Ghost of Christmas Yet to Come into the bleak destiny that might await him.

Oisin and Adah. The Druid and the wise woman. The doomed and the doomsayer. Love or despair—that was the choice left to Ebenezer Scrooge. *That's always the choice,* thought Mercy.

When the mist dispersed, the Ghost of Christmas Yet to Come was gone with it. Scrooge was left alone on the stage to face the truth of his wasted years, his lonely life, and the possibility of an even lonelier death. The truth that finally melted the old miser's heart, and triggered his transformation.

Oisin played Scrooge's epiphany with humor and passion. His beautifully enacted emotional journey from self-centered obstinacy to charitable good nature won over the audience. All of the Green Mountain Players—from Levi and Adah to Oisin and Jillian—performed well.

But it was Henry who stole the show. The little boy stood in the spotlight, Robin by his side. He removed his cap and proclaimed, *"And God bless us every one."*

The audience leapt out of their seats. Whistling, whooping, applauding. Felicity clapped too, and kept on clapping. When it was time for the curtain call, Henry and Robin took their bows together, the dog as graceful as the boy.

A Christmas Carol was a triumph.

And no one had died.

Mercy glanced at her mother, and saw the relief flood her fine features. *One for the Solstice Soirée,* she thought.

"Let's go see Henry," said Patience.

Troy slipped Felicity into the sling. The baby girl was still clapping, and Mercy and Tandie were clapping right along with her.

They piled out of the theater boxes, and moved with the lively crowd down the stairs to the lobby, where the actors were mingling with the audience. Henry and his loyal canine Robin stood in front of a fan-shaped Art Deco mirror with Cal Jacobs, surrounded by fans, while his grandmother Lillian and his father Ethan and Yolanda looked on with pride. Henry, who once balked at being touched, especially by strangers, shook hands easily with his admirers, his other hand planted on Robin's thick furry head. Henry's canine rock, the better to handle all the fuss.

"Congratulations, Henry. You're the star of the show," Mercy said, smiling.

"It's not me," Henry said, "it's my dog Robin."

"You make a good team."

"Congrats, Henry," said Troy, ruffling the young boy's hair while Lillian and Yolanda cooed over Felicity.

"Thank you," said Henry seriously. He always took Troy very seriously. A salute to the uniform and the fact that Troy protected the woods and the wildlife that the little boy loved so much.

A group of young well-wishers around Henry's own age approached, and Troy and Mercy excused themselves to go talk to Thrasher and Wyetta.

Hugs all around, an extra-long one from Wyetta, who whispered, "Thank you" into Mercy's ear.

"Nothing happened," said Mercy.

"But it could have." Wyetta squeezed her tight.

Thrasher got right down to business. "Gil and the uniforms finished their search of Hallett's property. They found three more of those bucket-rigged bear snares and a number of additional illegal traps designed for other mammals as well."

"Hallett has been busy." Troy nodded. "But it seems like too big an operation for a lone poacher. We think he may be poaching on other properties as well. We'll be keeping an eye on him once he's made bail."

"*After* Christmas," said Wyetta, raising her eyebrows at Mercy.

"After Christmas," agreed the captain. "Nothing's going to interfere with Felicity's first Christmas."

CHAPTER THIRTY-ONE

*"Men's courses will foreshadow certain ends, to which,
if persevered in, they must lead," said Scrooge. "But if
the courses be departed from, the ends will change."*

—CHARLES DICKENS, *A CHRISTMAS CAROL*

It was growing late, and by now Thrasher and Wyetta and most of the theatergoers had left the building. The cast was leaving as well, headed for Pizza Bob's, where the after-party was being held.

"We need to get going," said Ethan, taking his son Henry by the hand. "You should come to the party. It will be fun."

"And the food will be good," promised Henry, a boy who loved Pizza Bob's pies as much as he loved his grandmother's burgers and shakes. Just like everyone else in town.

"Thanks, but we really should be getting home," said Mercy.

"Please," said Henry.

"It can't hurt to drop by for a minute," said Troy. "Felicity's sound asleep—she won't even notice." Her husband leaned over to kiss her, and whispered in her ear. "We don't get that many nights out these days. And Thrasher and the colonel will be there, along with Harrington and Tasha."

Mercy kissed her husband back and smiled at Henry. "We wouldn't miss it for the world."

They decided to walk to Pizza Bob's Wood Fired Pie Company, which was down on Main Street about a quarter of a mile from the town green, not far from the police station where Troy had parked his truck. The snow was falling steadily, heavily, coldly, big fat flakes that stuck to their coats and their noses and little Felicity's pink knit beanie.

"We can't stay long," he said. "Not with this weather. But I knew you'd want to see Tasha Karsak again."

"Like you don't." She knew he was as determined to get to the bottom of Lazlo Ford's and the Singing Plumber's murders as she was. Even though her husband had his own murder—the bones with the bullet hole in the skull hidden in the dead log—to solve. Not to mention the Hallett investigation.

"Why do you think Harrington was with Tasha?" She tucked her arm under his as they strolled past the lighted storefronts, dodging last-minute shoppers.

"She could be his prime suspect, and he's trying to get under her skin. He's good at doing that."

"He is indeed, but from what I could see it looked *she* was getting under *his* skin. Hopefully we'll get a better look at them at the party." Mercy thought about the play they'd just seen, the theater and the sets and the costumes. "*A Christmas Carol* reminded me of the murders."

Troy laughed. "Everything reminds you of the murders."

Mercy laughed with him. "I know, but think about it. The first two murders were performances really. The Santa costumes. The Solstice Soirée. The public display."

"There is a theatricality to both crime scenes. But not the third crime scene."

"Antler Man." Mercy shrugged. "If there is a connection, we haven't found it yet."

"The victim was hidden in that old log in the forest for years. And he might have remained there undiscovered indefinitely if that poacher hadn't stumbled over him. Whereas one of our murdered Santas was found on fire in the woods in close proximity to the village green. And the other died virtually in the middle of a song. Both dramatic deaths bound to attract attention."

"And an audience." Mercy paused, thinking about the old bones. "But the antler headdress could qualify as theatricality. "What do you think?"

"Maybe," said Troy. "But then why hide the body?"

"If a man wearing antlers falls in the forest and no one is around to see it . . ." Her voice trailed off.

A lady, laden with shopping bags full of presents, stood at the edge of the sidewalk. Mercy and Troy stopped, letting her cross over to her silver Subaru, parked right there on the street behind a black SUV. She thought about the black SUV she'd seen pulling away from the village green when

Elvis chased down those Russian cigarettes. This probably wasn't the same one; black SUVs were as ubiquitous in New England as silver Subarus.

She glanced up and down Main Street and spotted two more of each vehicle. In the wake of the incident at Uncle Laz's house, she was seeing trouble everywhere. When she'd seen the glint of the winter sun on the barrel of the gun peeking through the evergreen, her training had kicked in—she'd grabbed her gun from the glove box without a second thought. Now she couldn't turn off her hypervigilance. She sighed and tried to put the thought of black SUVs and pistols in spruce hedges out of her mind. And failed.

Troy opened the car door for the lady and helped her unload her bags. Reminding Mercy that she still hadn't come up with a good gift for her husband yet. Hoping that he wasn't expecting much this year, and more important, that he wasn't planning one of his perfect surprise gifts for her.

"Merry Christmas," called the lady as she drove off.

Mercy took Troy's arm once more and they trudged on through the snow. It was a beautiful night. Not too cold, the air clear and bright. The lights of Northshire shimmering all around them. You'd never know this winter wonderland was now being hailed as "winter murderland" on social media. Bringing her right back to solving the puzzling crimes.

"What about motive?" she asked Troy.

"No real motives that I can see. Other than the Russian blondes fighting over Lazlo's inheritance."

"Olga didn't want him dead. And Tasha, well, who knows what that woman really wants."

"I guess you don't like her much." Troy grinned.

"I don't know what I think of her, really. But I don't trust her. There's something about her that screams 'player' to me."

"I can see that." Troy steered her around a snowman that someone had knocked over onto the sidewalk.

"Who knocks down a snowman?"

"Kids."

"And when they grow up, they knock over Santa?"

Troy frowned. "Maybe Tandie's serial killer theory is not far off."

"A shrink would say that the killer suffered a childhood trauma associated with Christmas. Or maybe he—or she—was abused by a man who looked like Santa Claus. Older, white hair and beard, outwardly jovial.

Or maybe"—here Mercy smiled slightly—"maybe the perpetrator was targeting them because they were both musicians. Lazlo Ford the organist and Timothy Carter, The Singing Plumber."

"Maybe he just hates Christmas carols." Troy smiled.

"Not." Mercy scooped up a snowball and smashed his shoulder with it, careful not to wake Felicity in the sling.

"No fair. I can't fight back."

"When we get home, we'll have a proper snowball fight." She brushed the snow from his jacket, and gave him a quick kiss.

"Deal." He kissed her back.

"Seriously, maybe whoever did this is some kind of killer narcissist who likes to show off."

"Yes. This may be his way of thumbing his nose at authority." Without a hitch in his rhythm, Troy cocked his head slightly at a shop window of a clothing store as they passed. Just for a second, but long enough for Mercy to notice. In the window was a shearling-lined leather bomber jacket much like the one Thrasher wore. A little more rugged, a little rougher around the edges, just like Troy himself.

"You mean authority like law enforcement," she said, continuing the conversation as if she hadn't just found the perfect gift for Troy. But she had. Her husband's wardrobe was strictly practical, utilitarian, serviceable. He might admire Thrasher's style in general, and his coat in particular, but he'd never get one for himself. Yet in that split-second approving glance at the shop window, her humble husband had revealed a secret yen for a little luxury. And she could make that Christmas wish come true. That's what wives were for.

"Or authority of any kind," said Troy. "We see it more and more all the time now. Our perp could hold a grudge against the police, the government, the military, the deep state, whatever. His father, his teacher, his boss, his commanding officer, his selectman. Even his spouse."

It was snowing again now, and a sudden gust of wind blew a curtain of the white stuff in their faces. Troy twisted his torso toward the street, protecting the sleeping baby from the brunt of the gale. While his back was turned, Mercy texted her mother about the coat for her husband.

"What's up?" he asked when the wind died down and they continued on their way.

"Just Mom, wanting to know what's keeping us."

"Nearly there." Troy pointed down the street.

Mercy spotted the Pizza Bob sign. A beacon of good food and drink.

"Looks like they're busy," he said.

"Yes," she said absently. Her mind was back on motive, not pizza.

Troy grinned. "What? What are you thinking?"

"Maybe the staging of the crime scenes is just a ruse to distract us."

"From what?"

"From the real motive. Whatever that may be." She looked at Troy. "There's a reason the victims were killed in such careful, premeditated ways."

"The killer was making a point, if only to himself."

"Exactly." Mercy sighed. "We really need a motive."

The closer they got to the restaurant, the bigger the crowd became. She'd never seen so many people there. Surely they weren't all there for the cast party.

"We don't have enough to go on yet," said Troy.

"We need to keep on digging."

"You'll figure it out," said her husband, squeezing her shoulders. "You always do."

PIZZA BOB'S WAS A madhouse. Even though a big sign on the door read "Closed for a Private Party," the sidewalk fronting the restaurant was besieged with would-be customers hungry for the best pizza in town. Officer Becker stood at the entrance, waving away uninvited guests.

In the small strip of lawn between the sidewalk and the building sat a red-and-gold, four-seater, nineteenth-century sleigh. A surprisingly lifelike Santa Claus sat in the upholstered driver's seat, his big sack perched on the back bench. The effect was worthy of Dickens himself.

Children were taking turns climbing up to sit next to St. Nick while their parents captured the moment with their cell cameras. The perfect photo op. Although whether Pizza Bob would approve of the interlopers Mercy wasn't sure. At least it was good advertising, and the sleigh appeared sturdy enough. In its years of service, it must have seen many lively children come and go.

Mercy thought about getting a photo of Felicity in the sleigh next to the stuffed Santa, but before she could suggest it, Becker beckoned to their little group, much to the grumbling of frustrated diners told to go elsewhere tonight and come back tomorrow. At least they got their pictures, she thought, as the officer ushered them inside the joint.

And a joint it was. Not much to look at, even at Christmastime. Outside, just classic white clapboard outside brightened by strings of lights and the sleigh. Inside, dark red walls decorated with faded pop art posters from the sixties and seventies—the usual Peter Max rainbows and Andy Warhol soup cans and Pauline Boty collages—a décor that had not changed since Mercy was a little girl. A faux Christmas tree stood in one corner and plastic poinsettias served as centerpieces on the old scarred wooden tables—decorations that seemed as old as the place itself.

But the interior did boast the one thing true pizza aficionados appreciated most: a massive one-of-a-kind pizza oven, also adorned with graffiti art from the sixties and seventies. *Flower power. Go with the flow. Give peace a chance.* The menu drew its inspiration from that era as well. Troy and Thrasher's favorite: *The Howl,* an enormous hand-tossed pie with pepperoni, sausage, bacon, meatballs, and ham.

Even more than the good vibes, though, were the good smells that assaulted you when you stepped into Pizza Bob's. Garlic. Oregano. Freshly baked bread dough. A savory heaven that never failed to comfort Mercy. And all the pizza parlor's fans, no doubt.

The party was in full swing. Her parents were at the bar, martinis in hand, hobnobbing with Jules Roland and his wife, who'd directed the play. Her mother raised her glass at Mercy, her version of a thumbs-up. Which meant she'd gotten that text and approved. One less thing for Mercy to worry about.

She looked around as Troy and Felicity went on to greet Levi and Adah. It was fun to see all the cast members in contemporary dress, minus the crinolines and bonnets and ringlets for the women and the cutaway coats and cravats and muttonchops for the men. Except of course for Oisin, whose muttonchops were real, just as his trademark beard had been.

Mercy met the Arch-Druid of the Cosmic Ash Grove with compliments on his performance as the cranky and crotchety Scrooge. He looked as odd to her in jeans and a sweater as he had in his Victorian costume onstage. She'd only seen him in his Druid robes. "You were fabulous."

Oisin beamed. "Thank you."

With the beard gone, Mercy could see more of his face. He still cut an imposing figure, but he was handsomer than she'd realized, with craggy good looks befitting a spiritual leader moonlighting as an actor. "Although it took me a minute to recognize you."

"I do miss the beard, and I will grow it back." Oisin stroked his considerable sideburns. "The sacrifices one makes for art."

"Indeed." She took him aside. "Have you met Tasha Karsak?" She nodded in the blond woman's direction.

"The one who says she's Lazlo's daughter."

"You don't believe it."

Oisin tucked his large hands in his jeans pockets, leaning back on his heels. "I suppose it's possible, although he never mentioned her to me."

"You and Uncle Laz were friends?" This was news to Mercy, and if it were true, she wondered why he hadn't told her that earlier.

"'Friendship' would be putting it too strongly," said Oisin. "Lazlo came to me from time to time for advice."

"Advice? What kind of advice?"

"Spiritual advice."

"Really?" Mercy could believe that some people relied on Oisin for guidance; certainly the members of the Cosmic Ash Grove did. And by all accounts he was a wise and thoughtful man. But as far as she knew, Lazlo was not a Druid. He belonged to the First Congregational Church. Where he was not just a parishioner, but the organist as well. "Why didn't he confide in Reverend Jane?"

"I don't know," said Oisin. "He might have been more comfortable coming to me because I *didn't* know him. He was a troubled man with a difficult past."

"What did he tell you?"

"Nothing specific. Just that he was worried about his past coming back to haunt him."

"The Ghost of Christmas Past." Mercy looked over at Tasha Karsak, tickling Felicity as Troy held her in his arms. Harrington was there too, with Thrasher and Wyetta. The detective appeared decidedly uncomfortable.

"I told you these were shadows of things that have been. That they are what they are, do not blame me . . ." said Oisin, quoting the words the

Ghost of Christmas Past had thrown at him as Scrooge in the play just an hour before.

"Do you think Tasha was part of that past?"

"I'm sure I don't know," said Oisin. "But her showing up here just as the poor man is killed hardly seems like coincidence."

"Right." She knew how the past could raise its ugly head in surprising ways, even in the form of a beautiful woman in a lynx coat. "What did you advise him? When he came to you for guidance?"

"I told him to let the past go." Oisin smiled at her. "As your beloved bard would say, '*To mourn a mischief that is past and gone is the next way to draw new mischief on.*'"

"A Druid who quotes Shakespeare," said Mercy, adding this to the long list of reasons why she liked Oisin so much.

He shrugged. "I like to think that Shakespeare was a Druid at heart, no matter what the scholars may say."

Mercy considered the mischief that had come to their woods. "You think that whatever was haunting Lazlo finally caught up with him. *The past is prologue.*"

"I don't know. But it seems likely."

"How well did you know him?" She thought that maybe if Lazlo had revealed the troubles of his soul to Oisin, he may have revealed other preoccupations, too.

"Not particularly well. He kept himself to himself."

That seemed to be everyone's experience, including his fiancée's. "Did you know he'd gotten engaged?"

"No," he said evenly.

"But you're not surprised."

"No." Oisin rubbed his now-bare chin. "I knew he was happier, and I suspected it was due to a woman. When a man is happy, it is almost always due to a woman."

"A heaven on earth I have won by wooing thee."

"That's right." Oisin smiled as his wife Elisabeth came over to join them, carrying two glasses of red wine. "Here comes my heaven on earth."

Elisabeth handed her husband a glass of wine. "There's more where that came from," she told Mercy. "The Chianti is flowing over there at the bar."

Pizza Bob's wine menu was known for its good Chiantis, all imported from the Mediterranean. "Thanks. I'll get some in a minute."

"We were just talking about Lazlo." Oisin raised his glass, and Elisabeth clinked her glass against his. "To Lazlo."

Elisabeth and Mercy echoed his toast. "Lazlo."

"Terrible business." She sighed, her brown eyes troubled behind her wire-rimmed glasses. "There's been so much terrible business lately. And right before Christmas, too. When is it going to stop?"

"I'm sure Mercy will figure it out." Oisin drew the small woman into his tall frame and hugged her tight. "Let's not ruin Henry's party."

"Of course." Elisabeth removed her spectacles and wiped her eyes with the back of her hand. "Tonight, we celebrate." She tipped her Chianti toward Mercy, then downed the wine in one long sip. "Tomorrow, you find his murderer." She replaced her glasses and untangled herself from her husband. "I'm getting another glass."

Oisin and Mercy watched her head for the bar.

"I'm afraid Elisabeth has taken Laz's death badly. And Timothy Carter's."

"She knew The Singing Plumber?"

"He was her student at Northshire Valley College." Oisin sighed. "She takes all her students under her wing. To the point where I worry about her sometimes."

Mercy knew that Elisabeth was an academic as well as a poet, serving as the chair of Women's Studies at the local community college. "He was majoring in women's studies?"

Oisin smiled. "Introduction to Poetry. Students take it because they think it'll be an easy A. They don't know Elisabeth."

"With a voice like that, how did he end up a plumber?"

"My understanding is that he studied music at college while he was working for the family plumbing business. Elisabeth liked him. He did well in her class, and as a singer he was especially interested in poetry put to music. He did a paper on it for her."

Mercy thought about Lazlo and The Singing Plumber. If Elisabeth knew them both, other people outside chorales might have, too. The two victims may have had more than church music in common. More connections that would explain why they were both targeted. "No wonder Elisabeth is upset."

"I admit I'm a little upset as well."

Oisin was not a man easily upset. Mercy thought of him as a kind of Zen Druid. Like Yoda, only much taller. "What is it?"

"That skeleton Troy and Susie Bear found in the forest. Could it be related to these other murders?"

"Why do you ask?"

"I heard they found an antler headdress with the bones. That, along with the Yule log . . ." He sipped his wine. "It all strikes a little too close to home."

"Home being the Cosmic Ash Grove."

"Yes."

"Did Timothy Carter have any Druidic affiliations?"

"Not that I know of." He drained his glass. "But I know that he was an avid hunter. It's probably nothing, but I keep hearing that speech from *The Merry Wives of Windsor* in my head: *There is an old tale goes that Herne the Hunter, Sometime a keeper here in Windsor Forest, Doth all the wintertime at still midnight, Walk round about an oak with great ragg'd horns.*"

Mercy recited the second bit for him. "*And there he blasts the trees, and takes the cattle, And makes milch-kine yield blood, and shakes a chain, In a most hideous and dreadful manner.*"

Together they finished it: "*You have heard of such a spirit, and well you know, The superstitious idle-headed eld, Received and did deliver to our age, This tale of Herne the hunter for a truth.*"

They were both silent for a moment.

"I should find my better half," he said finally.

"Of course. I should, too." She'd kept him long enough.

"One last thing." Oisin trained his sharp eyes on her.

"What's that?"

"What's happening here is all very strange," he said, his voice dark with worry. "And sinister."

Mercy couldn't disagree. Talking to Oisin helped her realize that a part of her had been holding her breath all through the performance of *A Christmas Carol*. She'd been expecting something bad to happen.

But it didn't. And still she felt a trepidation she could not shake. Apparently, the Arch-Druid did, too.

Oisin placed a large hand gently on her arm. "Be careful, Mercy."

ORLOV HADN'T LEARNED WHAT went down in Laz's house, what they'd found or if it pertained to his mission. All he'd learned was that Mercy Carr was a force to be reckoned with. So here he stood, again in the shadows, observing the people at the cast party. All of this village's most important personages were here, including Daniel Feinberg and Colonel Hugo Fleury. He'd been warned to watch out for the two men, both considered threats to the operation here and abroad.

Feinberg was a billionaire with few alliances among the Slavic oligarchs, unlike many of his American peers. Fleury was an old spy running a security firm that exploited the rivalries among the Slavic oligarchs, providing intel that fueled the fierce competition between them. Cashing in on the turf wars, no matter who might win them.

Orlov spotted Tasha Karsak on the arm of the detective, Harrington. Charming her way into the billionaires' circle. Or maybe barreling her way into their little clique. The woman was as bold as she was beautiful.

Tasha was not a trustworthy woman. In Orlov's experience, there were three kinds of untrustworthy women: the pushy ones, the sneaky ones, and the pushy, sneaky ones. The pushy, sneaky ones were the worst. That's what Tasha was, and it was going to get her killed.

He wasn't sure what her game was. He didn't know, and he didn't care. He just wanted her to stop. He needed her to stop. He had a job to do and she was getting in the way. Bringing unwanted attention to Lazlo Ford's past. A past that needed to stay dead and buried. Just as Lazlo himself was now dead and buried.

Tasha needed to let sleeping dogs lie, as the Americans would say. Orlov preferred the Russian version, не буди лиха, пока спит тихо. *Don't awaken Doom while it sleeps quietly.*

A more accurate description of trouble to come.

CHAPTER THIRTY-TWO

One would think that our good old Santa Claus, who devotes his days to making children happy, would have no enemies on all the earth; and, as a matter of fact, for a long period of time he encountered nothing but love wherever he might go....

—L. FRANK BAUM

Troy and Felicity were no longer part of the little group that included Tasha Karsak. That group had dissolved, and new ones formed, as was the way with good parties. People were always moving, shifting, mingling. Mercy should have talked to Tasha when she had the chance.

She found her husband and her daughter seated in a large booth with Tandie and Henry, plus Ethan and his fiancée Yolanda. Felicity was in a high chair, nibbling on pizza crust. Henry's stalwart canine pal Robin was tucked under the bench, waiting for a stray crumb to come her way. Knowing that with a baby in a high chair, crumbs *would* stray her way.

Thrasher and Wyetta were huddled together at a table in a quiet corner eating pizza and drinking Chianti, a happy couple apart. Harrington and Tasha Karsak were nowhere to be seen.

Mercy helped herself to a large slice of *The Howl* pie. Troy pointed to a full glass of red wine. "Saved it for you."

"Thank you." She sipped her wine and observed the crowd, wondering where Tasha Karsak and Harrington were. Maybe the detective had managed to shake her.

"Henry was just telling us about the lynx coat Tasha Karsak was wearing," said Troy.

"Really." Mercy raised her eyebrows. "So what do you know about the woman in the lynx coat?"

"Canadian Lynx is an endangered species," said Henry solemnly. "It is against the law to trap or hunt lynx in the state of Vermont." He looked to Troy for confirmation.

"I don't think Tasha's coat is from here, Henry," said Mercy. "My mother says it's from Dior. A couture designer in Paris."

"She's Russian," said Troy. "The pelts are most likely sourced from Russia."

"Lynx can get caught in traps set for other animals," continued Henry as if he hadn't heard. "Like fisher and mink. You can trap them during trapping season."

"That's true, Henry. But we're watching out for that."

"It's not illegal to *wear* a lynx coat, Henry," said Yolanda.

"It should be. Then you could arrest her." Henry raised his slice of pizza and pointed it toward the entrance of the restaurant.

Tasha Karsak was following Harrington, Feinberg, and Uncle Hugo as they wove through the crowded parlor to the large table where Lillian and Nathan Moore, the acting mayor, were seated with Pizza Bob, Rory Craig, and Jillian Merrill and her husband Richard.

Mercy wondered where they'd all been, and why they'd left the cast party, only to return again. "She's managed to weasel her way into their inner circle. What is she up to?"

"I don't know, but from the look on Harrington's face, he doesn't like it."

The four of them joined the party, but Tasha did not sit down with the rest of them. Instead, she handed Harrington her Dior tote. He held it as if it were old fish, and Mercy smiled. She had never thought of the detective as the sort of man content to carry a woman's purse, and this confirmed it.

Tasha shrugged off her lynx coat, revealing a red sweater dress with strategically placed cutouts. She slung the fur over her arm, plucked her bag from Harrington, hitched it over her shoulder, and headed for the ladies' room.

"I'll be right back," said Mercy. Now was her chance to get Tasha alone. Troy smiled at her. "Famous last words."

Mercy grabbed her pack, excused herself, and wound her way across the room to the hallway at the side of restaurant, where the restrooms were located. She pushed open the door marked "Women." The long narrow room was painted in neon pink and covered in peace signs, rainbows, and flowers. There was a double sink and a large mirror, and three stalls.

She didn't see anyone, so Tasha must have been in one of the stalls. Mercy waited for the woman to come out, biding her time by combing her unruly hair and washing her hands and reapplying her lip gloss. But no one came into the restroom and no one came out of the stalls.

She listened carefully, but all she heard was the sound of her own breathing. Squatting down to peek under the stalls, she spotted Tasha's spiky boots in the middle unit. "Tasha? Are you okay in there?"

No answer.

Mercy waited another minute, then knocked on the door of the stall. "Tasha?"

Nothing.

She pulled at the door. But it was locked from the inside.

"I'm going to count to three and then I'm coming in. One . . ." As she counted down, Mercy entered the stall next to the one where Tasha was hiding. She put the lid down on the toilet, and stepped up on the commode. She peered over the side wall.

No Tasha Karsak. Just her red sweater dress, propped up on the toilet seat like a sack of potatoes, a crumpled lump. And her boots.

Mercy couldn't imagine where the woman had gone. Or why. Tasha's lynx coat and her tote were missing. She must have had a complete change of clothes in her bag, from the shoes up.

She snapped a photo of the stall where Tasha had abandoned her dress and boots with her cell camera. Hopping down from the toilet, Mercy left the stall. She stood there studying the restroom, looking for something she might have missed.

But she saw nothing. There was no window in the restroom, no exit route other than the way in from the dining area. If Tasha had moved quickly enough, she would have had just enough time to change and leave the bathroom, but Mercy would have seen her if she'd gone out through the hallway to the entrance of the restaurant.

Leaving the ladies' room, Mercy ventured into the hallway. To her left was the men's room and the dining area of the restaurant. To her right was a back door. She'd never noticed it before; it was painted the same dark red as the walls and blended right in. There was a dead bolt high on the frame, but it was unlocked.

This was how Tasha must have made her hasty exit. But why?

Mercy pushed open the door, and stepped outside into a snowdrift. An outdoor light switched on automatically to the left of the door. Someone had recently been this same way, given the half-moon groove on the ground left by the door when it opened onto the new layers of fresh snow.

There were footprints there, fast filling with falling snow—the rugged marks left by thick-soled, nubby tread–patterned snow boots. Another larger set of footprints from heavier boots were also visible. Maybe these belonged to whoever Tasha was meeting. There was something sticking out of the snow. Several somethings.

Mercy squatted down, pulling a paper sack and her gloves from her pack, and plucked one of the objects from the drift—the same kind of cigarette butts she'd found by the Civil War memorial on the common. The kind with a cardboard tube that held the tobacco, rather than a true filter.

Maybe the same guy who'd left them there had been smoking here while he waited for Tasha. Sure looked like it. She stood up, tucking the butt into the bag, and left the others, small depressions fast filling with snow.

The exit opened onto a parking lot with room for only half a dozen vehicles, tightly packed into the small space. The outdoor light by the door illuminated only so much, but she could see a large dumpster at the end of the lot where it opened onto the street. A red-and-white sign read: "Employee Parking Only."

Mercy tapped on her cell flashlight and followed the two sets of prints, which led through the lot and around to the front of the restaurant. It was growing late now, and most everyone had gone home. There were few people on the street, and no one nearby. Even Officer Becker was gone from his post.

Here the prints were barely visible in the muddle of slush and sand that slickened the sidewalk. Snow continued to fall, curtains of the white stuff streaming down, glittering under the streetlamps and all the strings of lights that outlined the shops and stretched back and forth across the road. Mercy kept her eyes on the ground, crossing the path that led to the entrance of Pizza Bob's place and onto the strip of snow-laden yard that fronted the building.

There sat the lovely red-and-gold antique sleigh, looking like the centerpiece of a Christmas snow globe. Beautiful. Mercy leaned over as she peered back down at the footprints, impressions so faint in the newly fallen snow that she could barely see them. They'd be gone completely any minute.

The boot treads led right up to the sleigh. Mercy straightened up, coming nearly eye to eye with the eerily lifelike St. Nick in the driver's seat. His eyes were shiny black beads, and his cheeks were painted rosy red, as were his lips. And his fake snow-white beard was bushy and long and nearly as impressive as Oisin's real one had been before his shearing.

This Santa Claus was missing his cap, and his white wig was topped with a layer of snow. Mercy looked beyond the stuffed jolly old elf to his right. For the first time, she noticed another figure splayed next to him on the green-tufted seat.

A woman in a snow-dusted fur coat. A red Santa stocking cap with white fur trim tilted oddly on her blond crown, falling over her brow.

Mercy blinked, pushing a wet tangle of red curls out of her eyes, and looked again. And again. Harder. It couldn't be.

She scrambled around the curled gold blades of the long sled, slipping in the snow, over to the passenger side. There in the sleigh slumped Tasha Karsak, her head leaning against the bulky mannequin of St. Nicholas. Her face pale and wet, her eyes open, the stocking cap grazing her arched eyebrows. She looked very, very cold.

"Tasha!"

The woman did not respond. Didn't move, didn't mutter, didn't even breathe, as far as Mercy could tell. She reached for the carotid artery in the soft hollow of Tasha's neck, brushing the soft lynx coat with her fingers.

She stopped short when she spotted a dark red spot marking the white fur trim on the Santa's cap. A dark spot Mercy recognized as blood seeping through the white faux fur. With a gloved finger, she pushed the edge of the cap up. And there in the middle of Tasha's forehead was a bullet hole.

There was no point in checking her pulse. Tasha was very, very dead.

Another Santa gone to rest.

"Look what you found."

Startled, Mercy turned to find Cat Torano hovering over her, her face so close to hers that her bangs nearly brushed Mercy's cheek. "Back off."

"You really are quite the sleuth," said Cat, hands up as she stepped back an inch. "Even without your dog."

CHAPTER THIRTY-THREE

Dashing through the snow on a one-horse open sleigh,
O'er the fields we go laughing all the way,
Bells on bobtails ring, making spirits bright,
What fun it is to ride and sing a sleighing song tonight.

—JAMES PIERPONT

MERCY AND TROY STOOD WITH TANDIE OUTSIDE THE POLICE tape in front of Pizza Bob's Wood Fired Pie Company, conversing with Thrasher and Harrington. Tandie had insisted on staying with Mercy at the crime scene; Felicity was safe with Patience.

Cat Torano lingered as near to the scene as she could, hoping to capitalize on her scoop. Throwing out questions and comments, advancing and retreating as Harrington warned her off, finally threatening the reporter with arrest.

The adults all continued to ignore her, so Cat was now chatting up Tandie, asking her about her relationship with Mercy and their crime-solving activities. The teenager demurred, but Mercy could tell she was impressed by the determined young woman.

"You never give up, do you?" the teenager asked Cat, with as much wonder as admiration.

"I'm in it for the story. No matter how long it takes." She glared at Harrington. "Even if it gets me arrested."

"Cool," said Tandie.

"You know," said Cat, "I might like to do a story on you: 'Northshire's Nancy Drew'!"

Tandie glanced at Mercy, her face red. "I don't think so."

"Think about it." Cat pressed a business card into Tandie's palm. "Any time."

If this kept up, thought Mercy, her ever-faithful teenage Watson might decide to swap hunting criminals for hunting stories. Or worse, start writing up their exploits herself.

Dr. Darling and the Crime Scene Search Team were hard at work analyzing the victim, the sleigh, and the surrounding area. It was late, and all but the most die-hard of onlookers had gone home, encouraged by law enforcement personnel. Except for the growing swarm of Cat's fellow reporters from all over the state and beyond. Officers Becker and Goodlove were inside the restaurant, taking statements from the guests at the cast party.

Harrington himself had taken Mercy's statement, his intelligent dark eyes shadowed by an emotion Mercy could not name. Concern or grief or irritation, she wasn't sure. Maybe some combination of all three.

Certainly, it did not look good for a woman in his company to die an unnatural death just a couple of yards away from him, separated only by the walls of a pizza parlor. Not to mention that this was the third murder—four if you count the Antler Man bones Troy and Susie Bear found in the woods—in as many days on his watch. The optics, to use one of the detective's favorite words, couldn't have been worse.

The attending members of the press were a circus unto themselves, some making even Cat look restrained. Mercy caught snippets of the stories being broadcast out into the world beyond Northshire: *Santa #3 Slain in Sleigh, Three's a Corpse, Sleigh Ride to Murder, Mrs. Claus Catches a Bullet, Somebody's Killing the Santas of Northshire,* and the internet favorite *Winter Murderland* . . . They went on and on in what appeared to be a contest for the most sensational headline.

And who could really blame them. The so-called Yuletide Killer had struck again, and this time the victim was not a middle-aged man in a Santa suit but a beautiful woman in a lynx coat with a foreign accent, which added an elegantly exotic element to the weirdness. The fact that she was found in an antique sleigh wearing a Santa cap with a bullet hole in the middle of her forehead was just as strange as the bizarre circumstances in which the other two dead Santas had died, if not stranger.

It was a conundrum, thought Mercy. The other set of boot prints led to the sleigh, just as Tasha's had. And then back out to the sidewalk, where they disappeared in the slushy crush of other tracks.

There was no other sign of the mystery man—the size of the tracks indicated a man—who'd accompanied her to the sleigh. And no clues as to where he'd gone next.

The small knot of investigators—Harrington, Thrasher, Troy, and herself—stood there watching the proceedings, each apparently lost in their own murder-related thoughts. Tandie was still talking to Cat, who seemed bent on befriending the girl.

"The key to solving these crimes is what connects the murders," Harrington said finally, in a low enough voice that Cat could not overhear.

"Some of the media say it's some Christmas-obsessed serial killer targeting anyone wearing a Santa cap," said Mercy.

"You don't believe that." The detective regarded her with a respect he'd never quite shown her before. It seemed as if they might be able to move on from enemies to frenemies, if not friends.

At least Mercy hoped so. "I'm not sure what I believe, but I think it must be more complicated than that."

"Most murders are not at all complicated," said Harrington. "Somebody loses their temper and lashes out with whatever's handy, a gun or a knife or their fists, and shoots or stabs or punches whoever has provoked their rage."

"This is not that," said Thrasher.

"No," said Harrington. "This is not that."

"Maybe she was posing for a picture in the sleigh, as lots of people have done tonight. And she wore the cap for the photo," said Troy.

"She pinched it from the mannequin," said Mercy.

"I wouldn't have thought she was the kind of woman who would carry around a Santa cap," Thrasher said. "Much less wear it."

"Good point," conceded Mercy. Her mother would never be seen wearing one either. "Maybe her companion insisted she wear the cap for the photo."

"You mean the guy with the boot prints and the Russian cigarettes," said Troy.

"Yes. Maybe he got her up there for the photo and then he killed her."

"We'll track him down sooner or later," said Harrington.

"From what I saw, it didn't look like the bullet went through the hat.

So either it slipped down over the wound after she was shot, or . . ." Troy looked at Mercy.

"Or the hat was placed on her head after she was shot," she said.

"Copycat?" asked Troy.

"Let's not get ahead of ourselves," said Harrington.

The last thing Harrington needed was two murderers running around loose in Northshire, thought Mercy. "Maybe Dr. Darling will be able to clarify this for us."

As if he could see through it to the dead woman, the detective stared at the tent the forensic techs had erected over the sleigh and the body. "She was photogenic, even in death." He clicked his tongue at the horde of photographers with their long lenses trained on the tent. "Vultures."

"How well did you know her?"

"I didn't." Harrington bristled at the question. "She insinuated herself into our investigation every chance she could. Claiming she wanted justice for her father."

"Was she really Lazlo's daughter?"

"She died before we could do the DNA test." He pursed his thin lips.

"She agreed to it?" Mercy smiled, remembering how the colonel had fingered Tasha's champagne flute for surreptitious DNA testing. At that very moment, he was probably pestering whoever was doing the testing for the results.

"She said she was going to." Harrington nodded. "But we won't need her permission to do one now."

Thrasher avoided Mercy's eyes, and she knew he was thinking about the colonel, too. He shook his head. "No."

Becker and Goodlove came out of the restaurant, and Mercy could tell by their disappointed faces that they hadn't learned much.

"Well?" demanded Harrington.

"Sorry, sir," said Becker. "No one saw anything."

"One of the waitresses said she noticed that one of the stalls in the bathroom was occupied for a long time, but she didn't think anything of it."

"And no one other than Mercy saw our victim go to the bathroom?"

"No."

"And no one saw her talking to a man outside the restaurant?"

"No."

"Check the evening's receipts," said Harrington. "We may be able to track down someone leaving the restaurant about the same time as the murder. Maybe someone saw something."

Becker shrugged. "It was a cast party. Pizza and soda was all paid for by the Arts Council. But there was a cash bar. We'll check with the bartender."

"Let's hope our killer is a drinker," said the detective. "And track down everyone on the guest list who's already come and gone."

"On it," said Goodlove.

Harrington's cell rang and he turned away to answer it, only to swing back around seconds later. "I'm going to have to make a statement. Not that we have much to say at this point. But we need to get in front of this." He stalked off toward the crowd of journalists, their yelling growing louder with his every step. Cat scampered after him.

Dr. Darling exited the tent and stood aside as the crime scene techs carried the corpse away in a body bag. She snapped off her gloves. "Curiouser and curiouser."

"What do you think?"

"Cause of death was the gunshot wound to the head. Shot at close range with a small-caliber bullet, probably a .22 given the size of the entry wound." The medical examiner paused.

"But?" asked Mercy. "I'm sensing a 'but.'"

"But I suspect that she was incapacitated somehow first. I'll know better when I get her on the table."

"So they got her up on the sleigh under the ruse of a photo, shot her, and walked away."

"There's mud on the floor of the sleigh that does not appear to be left by the victim," said Dr. Darling. "The soles of her boots were clean."

"So many people have been in and out of that sleigh today," said Mercy.

"True. And given the cold most were probably wearing gloves." Dr. Darling cocked an eyebrow at Mercy. "I understand she changed her clothes in the ladies' room and left them there."

Mercy nodded. "I saw them there in the stall."

"Our techs are checking it out. And that backdoor area, too, where you found the cigarette paraphernalia. That might lead us somewhere."

"Maybe she thought she'd be back soon, and didn't want to carry her dress and her boots."

"Maybe. Can't say it makes much sense to me right now."

"Did you ever find her purse? She was carrying one of those Dior tote bags. With a toile pattern."

"Nice," said the medical examiner. "But no, we haven't found it. All she had on her was her clothes and that cap. And a lipstick in the pocket of her fur coat. Dior 999."

"Figures." Mercy looked at her. "No cell phone?"

"No."

"Dr. Darling!" Harrington's voice cut through their conversation. He waved her over to where he was addressing the press.

The medical examiner smiled. "I'd better be on my way. Looks like this is going to be a long night."

They watched as she trundled through the snow to join the detective. Cat and her colleagues pressed forward, yelling out questions as spotlights flashed. Many had to do with Harrington and his failure to catch the Yuletide Killer. Mercy almost felt sorry for him, but mostly she felt sorry for Uncle Laz and The Singing Plumber and Tasha Karsak, no matter whose daughter she was.

"We should be going, too," said Troy. "I think it's going to be a long night for all of us."

"I still have presents to wrap."

"You'd rather snoop than wrap." Troy kissed her freckled nose. He claimed to love her freckles, and she loved him for it. "I'm sure you can get Tandie to do it all for you, in exchange for a lot of debriefing and a little sleuthing."

"You know me too well." She kissed his nose in return. "That is my secret plan."

"First up?"

"The Russians."

MERCY SAT CROSS-LEGGED ON one side of the king-sized bed, her laptop on her knees. Troy lay on the other side, with Felicity in the middle, asleep, red curls spilling over her little forehead. Elvis was curled up on his bed in the corner and Susie Bear was stretched out across the bare polished oak floor. She put the laptop aside, pausing her deep dive on oligarchs, as Troy briefed her on the visit to Leland Hallett's place. He showed her the photographs he'd snapped there.

"Skunks, foxes, bears, bobcats, fisher, marten." Mercy counted off the animals, dead and alive, as he scrolled through the pictures. "And one pretty girl and a trophy moose."

"We think Hallett must be part of a bigger operation," said Troy.

"Go back." Mercy thought she'd seen something. "The one with the dead moose."

Troy scrolled back to the shot of Hallett with his hunter pal and their trophy bull. Mercy stared at the hunter.

"He looks familiar, right?" asked Troy.

"I think it's The Singing Plumber. Without the beard."

Her husband looked closer. "Could be. Which means that Hallett knew him."

"If it's him. And even if it is, I'm not sure what that means, if anything." Mercy studied the clean-shaven, younger version of the baritone singer, and the broad-faced Hallett. They didn't look much alike, apart from their large heads and the deep clefts in their chins, which she pointed to as she said, "I think cleft chins are genetic traits."

"Maybe they're related." Troy reached for his cell and texted Thrasher. "The captain will find out."

They went through the rest of the photos together and noticed nothing of import. Troy gathered up the baby and took her off to the nursery to sleep in her crib. Mercy pulled her laptop back onto her knees, ready to resume her research.

Troy's phone pinged as he came back to bed, and he read the text, then reported to Mercy, "Timothy Carter and Leland Hallett were half brothers. Same father, different mothers. Carter used his mother's name. Thought it made a better stage name for an opera singer."

"He was right about that. For all the good it did him." She couldn't help mourning the loss of the man's beautiful voice.

"I can understand why Hallett might end up dead," Troy said, "given his criminal activities. But The Singing Plumber was clean."

"As far as we know."

"As far as we know." Her husband rolled over and promptly fell asleep.

Mercy opened her laptop. "Back to the Russians."

DECEMBER 24

CHRISTMAS EVE

Christmas always rustled. It rustled every time, mysteriously, with silver and gold paper, tissue paper and a rich abundance of shiny paper, decorating and hiding everything and giving a feeling of reckless extravagance.

—TOVE JANSSON

CHAPTER THIRTY-FOUR

The snow lay on the ground, the stars shone bright,
When Christ our Lord was born on Christmas night
Venite adoremus Dominum, Venite adoremus Dominum,
   Venite adoremus Dominum
Venite adoremus Dominum, Venite adoremus Dominum,
   Venite adoremus Dominum.

—TRADITIONAL IRISH-ENGLISH CAROL

By dawn on Christmas Eve everyone at Grackle Tree Farm was up and about: Troy and Mercy, Felicity and the dogs, even the teenager Tandie. Mercy didn't know if it was simply the anticipation that always accompanies one of the loveliest nights of the year or the excitement over Felicity's first Christmas or the invigorating scent of evergreen and oranges and cloves that wafted upstairs from the extravagantly decorated downstairs or some heady combination of all three.

A good thing we're all up already, thought Mercy, the doorbell ringing just as she pressed the button on the coffee maker to get her day started right. The dogs were outside enjoying their morning constitutional, Susie Bear cavorting in the snow and Elvis making his rounds, checking the perimeter for intruders.

Whoever was at the front door, it was someone of whom the Malinois approved.

"I'll get it," muttered Tandie through a yawn, and she shambled toward the entry in her pajamas, her slippers slapping on the parquet floors.

Mercy pulled out the cinnamon rolls she'd been heating up in the oven. Her grandmother had presented them with the pan when they picked up Felicity the night before so they'd have them for this morning. Patience knew they'd be a welcome addition to breakfast as they prepared for what was bound to be an exhausting if exquisite day.

"It's Uncle Hugo and Feinberg and Captain Thrasher," called Tandie.

Mercy fetched more coffee cups and small plates and placed them on the marble island.

"Good morning," said the dapper colonel jovially, dressed for the holiday in his usual navy blazer and trousers, his breast pocket now brightened by a holly-red silk handkerchief emblazoned with bright white snowflakes and leaping reindeer.

"Where's Troy?" asked Thrasher.

"Right here." The dogs scrambled into the kitchen from the back porch to greet the colonel and the captain, bringing with them blasts of cold air and whips of stinging snow. Troy followed, slamming the door behind him. "What's going on?"

"We have some information to share," said Feinberg enigmatically.

"You got the DNA results on Tasha Karsak," guessed Troy.

"That was fast," said Mercy as she placed the coffeepot on a trivet by the tray of cups and saucers and sugar and milk. The cinnamon rolls were already on the island, and several of them were already gone. "Help yourself."

"There are those who are very motivated to wrap up the investigation into Tasha's death," said Uncle Hugo.

"So is she Lazlo's daughter?" Tandie was building little towers of Cheerios on the high chair tray in front of Felicity. There was also some sliced banana and a sippy cup full of water. But the baby was most interested in the Cheerios game.

Feinberg accepted a cup of coffee with a smile of gratitude. "What do you think?"

Mercy thought about it. "No."

"Because?" Her great-uncle regarded her sharply, like a professor with a bright student he hoped would not disappoint him.

"Because Tasha Karsak was not telling the truth. Not about that, not about anything."

"Because?" Uncle Hugo asked again, as he reached for another roll. For such a fit, energetic man of a certain age, he sure could eat.

"Because there was something inauthentic about her. Something of the performer." Mercy sipped her coffee. "But most of all, because she was basically stalking Harrington."

The colonel turned to Troy. "You?"

"Agreed." Her husband smiled at her. "On all points."

"Who was she really, Uncle Hugo?"

He raised a hand to Feinberg. "You do the honors, Daniel."

The billionaire placed his manicured hands on the island. "To begin with, she was not Lazlo's daughter."

"You were right," said Tandie to Mercy. "You're always right."

The colonel harrumphed. "I bet even Mercy did not see this coming."

"Who was she?" Troy caught one of Felicity's Cheerios midair before it fell to the floor.

"She was the daughter of Viktar Mraz, the Russian oligarch," said Uncle Hugo with a self-satisfied smile.

"The one and the same," said Feinberg. "Although technically he's Slovakian."

"Interesting," said Mercy, pulling another pan of rolls from the oven. Funny how talking about murder fueled a craving for sweets. "He has his fingers in a lot of pies."

The colonel nodded. "Money laundering. Smuggling. Arms. Electronics. Drugs. Arts and antiquities."

"Prostitution," added Thrasher. "Human trafficking. You name it. If it's illegal and in demand, he's in it."

"What about Tasha Karsak?" asked Tandie.

"She grew up with her mother in Switzerland," said Daniel, finally succumbing to temptation. "Karsak is her mother's maiden name. Belorussian."

"Switzerland," said Mercy. "Home of the Banque Beutel."

"Exactly. As far as we know she's been living in Europe all her life. Until late summer, when she came here. For reasons to be determined."

"But that's not even the most intriguing part," said Thrasher, turning to Mercy's great-uncle. "Tell her."

"The DNA did come up with a match. But not the one we expected." Uncle Hugo paused dramatically. "Not for Lazlo."

"Way to keep us waiting," said Tandie.

"Mraz . . . ," said Mercy.

"What are you thinking?" asked Troy.

Something about the name nagged at her. Mraz was the Slovakian form of the surname Moroz. *Moroz,* as in *Ded Moroz.* Meaning "Grandfather Frost" in Russian. Also known as "Father Frost." She grinned at her uncle.

Troy laughed. "That's the smile of victory."

"Let's hear it," said Thrasher.

"Tasha is related to your Soybean King."

Uncle Hugo applauded. Felicity, who up until now was completely focused on her Cheerios, looked up from her breakfast and clapped her sticky little hands, too.

"I don't get it." Tandie pulled out her phone and starting scrolling. "It says here that Father Frost is kind of like the Russian Santa Claus. He comes on New Year's to give out presents. Only he expects you to give presents to him, too. If you don't, he kidnaps the kids."

"The dark side of St. Nick." Troy grabbed a baby wipe and started to clean up the little one's messy fingers. "Only in Russia."

Mercy nodded. "Father Frost is a staple in Russian folklore. He appears in many Russian fairy tales. Depending on the translation, he's known as Father Frost or Grandfather or even King Winter."

"*The Snow Maiden,*" said Tandie. "That's how you knew."

"That's correct. Tasha's father's name is Mraz. The Slovakian form of *Moroz.* Meaning 'Frost.' The same name as Ephraim Frost, the billionaire from Ohio."

"By way of Slovakia." The colonel smiled. "Once upon a time."

"How close was the match?" asked Mercy.

"Around three percent," said Feinberg. "Which means they are most likely second cousins."

"I never could keep that straight," said Tandie, building another tower of Cheerios for Felicity. "First cousins, second cousins, first cousins once removed—how does that really work?"

"Your first cousin's kids are your first cousins once removed," said Mercy. "Your second cousins share a great-grandparent with you."

"So Tasha and the Soybean King share a great-grandparent," said Thrasher.

"That may explain the Snow Maiden message Lazlo left for Patience," said Troy.

"*Snegurochka,*" said Tandie, very pleased with herself. "But it still doesn't tell us who killed Tasha." She hesitated. "Does it?"

"No, but maybe it shows us where to look." Mercy poured herself another cup of coffee and helped herself to a roll. At this rate, she was going to need the caffeine and the sugar. "We need to look at the connection between the oligarch's daughter and the billionaire from Ohio."

"What do they have in common besides three percent of their DNA?" asked Troy.

"Money," said Tandie. "Aren't they both, like, super-rich?"

"Yes, they are," said Feinberg.

"Family ties can mean other ties as well. Business, trade . . ." Uncle Hugo's voice trailed off. "Legal and illegal."

"If she's part of her father's enterprise, that could be the real reason she was here."

"Soybeans?" Tandie did not seem convinced.

"We export thirty billion dollars' worth of soybeans every year," said Feinberg.

"Wow. That's a lot of soybeans." Tandie started scrolling again.

"I suspect our Soybean King has other fiefdoms as well," said the colonel.

"Corn and hogs," said Tandie, reading off her phone. "Oil. Solar. Bitcoin."

"Diversification," said Feinberg. "Frost has undoubtedly invested in finance, energy, tech, real estate, even fashion. Those are the big-money industries."

"He's also been pouring money into that religious community," said Thrasher. "That's got to be a money pit."

"What community?" asked Tandie.

"The Temple of the End of Days," said Mercy.

"You mean those people protesting the Druids' bonfire?"

"One and the same," said Thrasher. "Frost bought the old Lutheran summer camp on the Batten Kill River for them."

"Reverend Fitz is his son," said Troy. "He and his followers have been turning it into a year-round commune, for lack of a better word. But there have been complaints. I was just out there at Edith Tupper's place. She shares a property border with them, and she's not happy. She showed me evidence of unsecured domestic animals, illegal trapping, and dumping. The bears are having a field day."

"After they tried to cut the education budget and shut down the library," said Thrasher, "the town got tough and called the state's Agency of Natural Resources. The state slapped a bunch of violations on them, resulting in thousands of dollars in fines, the threat of incarceration and eviction. They claim they're making an effort to clean the place up."

"*Not,*" said Tandie.

"Sounds like it's time for a sting operation," said the colonel.

"Speaking of work." Thrasher stood up. "Troy and I were just leaving. We'll let Harrington know about this connection between Frost and Tasha Karsak."

Troy gave Mercy a kiss and headed for the door after Thrasher, Susie Bear following reluctantly, unhappy to leave the cinnamon rolls behind.

With the Newfoundland gone, Elvis moved right under Mercy's stool at the island, perfectly positioned between Mercy and Felicity.

"We need to know more about Tasha," Mercy said. "Why would she say she's Lazlo's daughter when she's not?"

"She's from Switzerland—maybe she knew about Lazlo's Banque Beutel money and decided to claim some of it as her own."

"She's an oligarch's daughter," said Tandie. "Isn't she rich already?"

"If money isn't the motive, then what is?" Mercy asked Tandie, giving the teenager an opportunity to play amateur sleuth.

"Love, lust, loathing, and loot," said Tandie. "The Four Ls of Murder."

The colonel stared at her. "Indeed."

"Tandie watches a lot of true crime," explained Mercy.

"So not loot." Tandie counted off the Ls on her fingers. "That leaves love, lust, and loathing. We don't know anything about her love life, or who would hate her enough to kill her."

"And what, if anything, her murder has to do with the murders of Lazlo and The Singing Plumber." Mercy frowned. "None of it makes sense."

"It makes sense if this is the work of a serial killer," said Tandie. "Their motives are different. The FBI says their motives are anger, thrill-seeking, financial gain, and attention-seeking."

"The crime scenes are certainly in keeping with the motive of attention-seeking," said the colonel.

"The Yuletide Killer has gone viral big-time," said Tandie.

"Two were shot, one was poisoned," said Mercy, feeling a little over-caffeinated. "Different weapons. That argues against serial killer."

"Olga has a motive for killing Tasha," said Tandie, finishing off another roll and washing it down with milk. "Love and loathing and loot. Maybe lust, too."

"But no reason to kill Lazlo or The Singing Plumber," said Feinberg.

"The Singing Plumber was a player." The teenager licked the icing off her fingers.

"A player?" asked Feinberg.

"He brought all those foreign women over on fiancée visas and then never married any of them," said Tandie, rolling her eyes. "That's just asking for trouble."

"Love and loot," said Mercy, thinking about all those unhappy women. "All their dreams of marriage and money in Vermont dashed."

"Hoisted by his own petard," said Uncle Hugo.

Mercy laughed. "I suppose it's possible." She remembered the story Olga had shared about Zoya and how Lazlo had helped the distraught woman disappear, and shared it with her breakfast visitors. She gave her uncle a sharp look. "You wouldn't happen to know anything about that, would you?"

The colonel demurred. Mercy shifted her gaze to Feinberg. "Daniel?"

"Let's just say she's safe now," said Feinberg. "From everyone."

"Everyone? I'm confused," said Tandie.

"I think what Daniel is trying to say is that she's safe from everyone who abused her."

"Discretion is usually absolute in these cases. With good reason."

"Understood. The last thing we want to do is put Zoya in any danger," said Mercy.

"Best to leave it alone," said Uncle Hugo.

"Agreed." Feinberg paused. "A check of Carter's finances revealed that he was making cash deposits unrelated to singing or plumbing to a savings account at a bank in upstate New York."

"Not his usual bank."

"No," said Feinberg. "No indication of where the cash came from, at least not yet."

"The trades often deal in cash," said the colonel.

"The better to hide income," said Feinberg.

"Or vices," said the colonel. "Drugs. Gambling. Not that there's any indication that our Singing Plumber was into either, at least not yet."

"It could be money he'd made helping his half brother Leland Hallett trap and sell illegal pelts." She told them about the picture Troy had found of the two siblings and the dead moose, and Hallett's poaching operation.

"So gross," said Tandie.

"But they have no evidence directly tying Carter to the poaching," said the colonel.

"Not yet. Troy and Gil are working on it."

They all sat in silence for a moment, each trying to connect the dots in these bizarre murders.

"It all comes down to Uncle Lazlo." Mercy sighed. "He was the biggest enigma of all. For all we know, all of Tandie's Ls could apply to his murder. Let's hope his will clears up some of the man's mystery."

Feinberg checked his watch. "Speaking of the will, we should get to that reading."

Tandie grinned. "L is for loot."

CHAPTER THIRTY-FIVE

*What Child is this, who, laid to rest,
On Mary's lap is sleeping?
Whom angels greet with anthems sweet,
While shepherds watch are keeping?*

—W. CHATTERTON DIX

THE OFFICES OF ROLAND & ROPER WERE DOWNTOWN ON MAIN Street across from Eggs Over Easy in a converted bank. *It's a handsome building,* thought Mercy as she and Elvis went inside. She'd left Felicity at home with Tandie, who along with Amy and Brodie and Helena would be overseeing the preparations for the Christmas Eve party. The caterers would be setting up well ahead of time.

Mercy had brought along Elvis because she had a bad feeling about this will, and the part she—and her entire family—might be expected to play in Uncle Laz's legacy. She figured that in a sense they were all going into battle for Laz, and there was no better comrade in arms than the Belgian Shepherd.

The enormous old vault at the back of the building lent the space a gravity and authority that surely served Jules Roland and his army of associates well. The subliminal message: Your money is safe with us. And at $650 an hour, that money would be going fast.

The conference room was in a corner of the old bank to the left of the huge metal door to the old vault. Seated at the long Le Corbusier black granite table were Jules Roland at the head, her parents and Uncle Hugo on one side, Patience, Feinberg on the other, along with Olga Volkov and a young man Mercy recognized as Jules's grandson Adrien.

She and Adrien were the same age; they'd been under pressure from their families to go to law school and join their respective family firms around the same time. Adrien had agreed, and done just that, while Mercy had balked and joined the army instead. Wearing a smart black-and-burgundy plaid wool suit and a confident expression, Adrien appeared every inch the successful solicitor—content with his choice, as she had been with hers.

Olga smiled at Mercy, and she smiled back. She was wearing another oversized cashmere sweater in a lovely pale rose color that flattered her pale skin and a matching midi-length skirt over tall, fur-trimmed UGGs. Mercy was glad to see the young woman here—and wondered if her presence was thanks to Grace, or someone else.

"Mercy Carr, do please come in," boomed Jules. He rose to his feet, as did all the men in the room. "And Elvis the Wonder Dog."

Mercy released the shepherd from his lead and he trotted over to Patience, hands down his favorite person in the room. Adrien pulled out a black leather armchair for Mercy and she sat down next to him. Elvis allowed the rest of his admirers to give him a nice scratch between the ears before finally settling at Mercy's feet, his muzzle resting on the top of her snow boots.

Jules raised his hands as if in benediction. He was known to be quite the performer in the courtroom, and Mercy was getting a sense of that here. Once he was sure he had everyone's attention, he lowered his arms and began. "We are gathered here together for the reading of the last will and testament of Lazlo Ford. Lazlo took money very seriously, and for that reason he chose to leave some of his money in a trust, and some of it to be distributed directly through his will. As you know, he named Daniel Feinberg executor of the will, as well as trustee of the trust. That has not changed. But before he died, he changed much of the terms for both the trust and the will."

While Jules made his way through the legalese of the document, Mercy watched the faces of the parties assembled. Her parents wore the neutral expressions they'd perfected after years of appearing in court. Feinberg looked engaged, as the executor should. Her grandmother Patience looked like she'd rather be somewhere else, preferably somewhere with animals. The colonel's miss-nothing blue eyes were the only memorable feature in his poker face, the bland expression mastered by the perfect spy. Only Olga revealed her emotions, her striking features drawn, her blue-painted nails pressed into her crossed arms.

Mercy wondered why the young woman was so tense. The person most likely to challenge her claim, Tasha Karsak, was dead. Of course, there was no guarantee that she or her baby would be named in the will anyway, but Vermont law allowed for children born after a parent's death to receive an inheritance, provided the parent had not specifically written the child out of the will. If the child was Lazlo's and if he provided for it in his will and if he didn't expressly deny the child and if . . That was a lot of ifs.

Maybe that's why Olga was so tense. Raising a child alone in a new community on the income from a tea shop wouldn't be easy. Olga said she had money; Mercy hoped that was true, no matter what the outcome here today.

Jules raised his voice, and began to list Lazlo's particular bequests. "In his will, Lazlo bequeathed five hundred thousand dollars each to the First Congregational Church, to the Cat Ladies, and to Patience. He left his home and all his worldly goods to Mercy."

Olga gasped, as did everyone else in the room besides Jules and Adrien and Daniel, all of whom would have known what was coming.

"Does that include the cat?" asked Grace, looking from Patience to Mercy.

"Yes," said Jules.

"Good. Mother has enough cats."

"I don't understand." Mercy was stunned. There was no reason for Uncle Laz to have done that. "That's not right." She didn't dare look at Olga, who by all rights should have been bequeathed Lazlo's home and belongings. "Why would he do that?"

"He had his reasons," said Jules. "Reasons he did not share with me, I'm afraid."

"Or me," said Mercy, appalled.

Jules gazed at Olga, who was now openly sobbing. "Courage, my dear."

Adrien moved to comfort the young woman, for which Mercy was grateful. He had a true warmth about him that surely endeared him to his clients. She hoped that his compassion could penetrate Olga's grief and disappointment. The poor woman.

Jules began to speak again. "Now on to the trust. This is a split-interest trust, meaning that the ten million dollars in assets of the trust are split, in this case, between beneficiaries. The main beneficiary of the trust is the Northshire Arts Center.

"That said, there are conditions outlined here that may affect the distribution of funds, subject to the discretion of the trustee."

Mercy breathed a sigh of relief. "That means you can fix this, Daniel. You're the trustee."

"Let us finish one thing before we embark on another," said Jules firmly.

"Right," said Mercy. "Sorry."

Jules regarded Olga with a solemn look. "If definitive proof of a biological child fathered by Lazlo should come before the trust, the child will be provided for as seen fit by the trustee until the age of thirty, at which time the child would be granted full access to twenty-five percent of the trust."

Olga launched herself out of the armchair. She stood there shaking with rage, her hands cupping her belly. "This is our baby. Lazlo's baby. He knew that." She rubbed her baby bump with her blue-painted nails. "This is the proof. What more do you need?"

CHAPTER THIRTY-SIX

White are the far-off plains, and white
The fading forests grow;
The wind dies out along the height,
And denser still the snow. . . .

—ARCHIBALD LAMPMAN

Troy followed Thrasher down the old river road to the former Lutheran summer camp now owned and operated by the Temple of the End of Days. The captain slowed down and flicked on his turn signal, steering his black Chevy Silverado onto an unpaved road barely visible from the main route, marked only by a large boulder with "Ps 118:5" carved into the stone.

A foot of snow topped the rock, but its face was wiped clean, so that the numerical notation for Psalm 118:5 stood out loud and clear. Troy recalled his Sunday School teacher reciting the psalm. *I called upon the Lord in distress: The Lord answered me, and set me in a large place.*

"I guess this is the large place," he told Susie Bear as he turned the Ford F-150 onto a road that had not been plowed since at least the night before. The truck rumbled through the six inches of snow in the wake of the deep ruts carved by Thrasher's Chevy as it barreled toward the encampment.

They passed cabin after cabin, all in various stages of winterization. Originally built for summer, they had no heat or running water. Everywhere there was evidence of the organizers' attempts to build the infrastructure needed to support a growing community. Thrasher and Troy followed the road along the large loop at the heart of the camp, where the largest of the buildings were located.

The refurbished shingled lodge rose two and a half stories between the loop and the riverbank. Its red metal roof held an impressive array of solar panels and a very large crucifix. There was an expansive cross-beamed porch topped by signage proclaiming "The Temple of the End of Days" in bright red lettering on a bright white background.

It had started snowing again, and the temperature was dropping quickly. Maybe that was the reason very few people were out and about, or maybe they were in the lodge-cum-church, praying. It was, after all, Christmas Eve.

They were there to talk to Reverend Fitz about the complaint filed by Edith Tupper. What Troy had seen in the gully was damning enough. But given the DNA linking Tasha Karsak to the Frosts, Harrington was taking no chances. The Temple of the End of Days was now a priority in a homicide investigation.

Troy and Thrasher weren't taking any chances either. Armed as usual, they were both wearing bullet-resistant vests, a staple of the field uniform. The captain had a search warrant in his pocket. And backup was on the way.

"Where is everybody?" asked Troy as they made their way cautiously to the entrance of the main building. No one was there to meet them.

"I don't like it," said Thrasher. "Good thing backup should be here soon."

The only sound was the crunch of snow under their boots, the *swoosh* of Susie Bear's paws as she sauntered through the drifts, and the thrumming of woodpeckers in the trees. Snow continued to fall silently. There was very little wind.

As they stepped up onto the porch, the green double doors opened and a man in a black suit with a clerical collar and a large gold cross around his neck stepped out. He had black hair slicked back off a high forehead and a long, narrow face that reminded Troy of an opossum. Not a good thing, given the aggressive nature of the species. Not to mention its ability to play dead.

"Fitzpatrick Frost," said Thrasher, under his breath.

The man extended his hand in greeting. "I am Fitzpatrick Frost. Everyone calls me Reverend Fitz."

Thrasher shook his hand and introduced himself and Troy. "There's been a complaint filed about ongoing violations on your property."

Reverend Fitz raised his arms as if he were going to offer a blessing or appeal to a greater power. But instead, he simply shook his head and said firmly, "We have broken no laws. Everything is fine."

"I've seen evidence of the violations myself," said Troy, who didn't believe this guy for a minute.

"Either way, we have to check it out," added Thrasher. "By law." The way the captain said it, Troy knew his boss thought Fitz was lying, too.

"I'm assuming that Edith Tupper filed that complaint. Am I right?" He smiled at them broadly. "You know she's a little overzealous."

An ironic choice of words, thought Troy, *for the leader of a cult.*

"We have a search warrant," said the captain, pulling the document from his pocket.

Fitz examined the warrant. He leaned toward them conspiratorially. "This is all just a misunderstanding. One of our flock serves as our sanitation engineer, in charge of garbage disposal. He was storing it until he could remove it, and it froze to the ground. Winter, you know."

"Winter is not a legal argument."

Reverend Fitz shrugged. "We'll fix it. He'll fix it. He's fixing it now. Here we ask our brothers and sisters to focus on solutions, not problems."

Right, thought Troy.

As if in answer to Troy's skepticism, the pastor went on. "We try to be completely self-sufficient. We grow and harvest our own food, run a woodworking shop and a metalworking shop. We tap our own trees for maple syrup, bake our own bread, milk our own cows."

"Those cows need to be fenced at all times," said Troy.

"Look, we're addressing all the issues the town council raised. Winter has just slowed us down." He stepped forward, as if to usher them back to their respective trucks.

Neither Troy nor the captain moved. Blocking the man's way.

Fitz stopped short, his opossum face reddening. "Surely you can give us more time."

Troy said nothing. Thrasher said nothing. They simply stood their ground. And waited.

The silence unnerved the reverend, as they hoped it would.

Although you'd think a man of God would be comfortable with silence, thought Troy. All that time in prayer and contemplation. Maybe that wasn't true for Fitz's fire-and-brimstone brand of ministry.

"Very well." Reverend Fitz turned back toward the double doors. "Come on in and I'll arrange for you to speak to our sanitation engineer, Brother Leland."

Troy caught Thrasher's eye, and he held back a minute. Long enough for him to whisper to his boss, "Leland Hallett."

"Guess he made bail." The captain raised his voice for the benefit of the reverend. "Join us when you can, Warner. We'll be inside."

"We can wait," said Reverend Fitz, clearly unwilling to leave law enforcement outside unattended. Not that he had a choice.

"I just have to check on my dog," said Troy. "I'll be right there."

Thrasher held up an open palm. "Shall we, Reverend?"

The captain ushered the minister inside, the heavy green doors clattering shut behind them.

Troy jogged to his truck, letting Susie Bear out and grabbing a leash for later but keeping her off-lead for the time being. "Let's wander, girl."

He let her sniff about while he surveilled the area, doing a brief perimeter search of the lodge. Just to get a lay of the land. They were southwest of Edith Tupper's place by about a mile.

Beyond the building ran the Batten Kill River; a large snow-covered deck looked down the ridge into the water. The river was running, ice floes dotting the surface. Upriver he could see several cabins. Downriver there were a number of outbuildings, most as old as the cabins but also a couple of brand-new prefabricated warehouse-style buildings made of steel and outfitted with solar panels like the ones on the lodge roof.

He saw a small flock of wild turkeys scratching through the snow looking for nuts and seeds near one of the outbuildings, but he saw no members of the reverend's human flock. Or anything else of immediate interest. Although he would have liked to get a good look inside those warehouses. Too bad the search warrant only covered the outdoors.

Time to join the captain.

"Come on, girl," called Troy.

The Newfie was watching the wild turkeys. She lifted her big head at him but then turned her attention back to the birds, who were moving along toward the larger of the warehouses.

"Don't even think about it," he told her, reprimanding himself for letting her off the lead. Chasing wild turkeys might be one of her favorite pastimes, but Susie Bear knew she wasn't supposed to do it. Which didn't always stop her.

She lumbered through the snow toward the turkeys, bellowing, and they yelped in return, running for the woods beyond the warehouses, some taking flight. Troy huffed after the dog, whistling sharply.

Susie Bear slid to a stop, plopping onto her backside in the snow. She tilted her shaggy head, now sprinkled with snow, at Troy. But she did not return to him.

The turkeys were long gone, out of reach in their roosts, taking shelter in the trees.

"Party's over," Troy told the Newfie as he caught up with her. "Let's go." He reached down to clip on her lead and she jounced away from him, disappearing around the corner of the larger prefab building.

Whatever Susie Bear was after, it was not the turkeys. Something else had captured her attention. Or some*one* else.

Troy rounded the warehouse, spotting the black dog splayed on the snow at the foot of the large garage doors on the long end of the building. She was alerting to something inside.

To the left of the garage doors was a small window and a standard-sized door. Troy crept toward the window, ducking under it and flattening himself against the side of the building. Twisting to take a quick peek at the interior without being seen by whoever was inside.

There was no one inside that he could see. What he could see was not a bakery or woodshop or a metalworking space. What he could see was row upon row of pelts hanging from hooks.

Lynx. Beaver. Marten. Fox.

Part of the salting process, no doubt. After trappers skinned their catch, they typically salted the pelts thoroughly, at least once and sometimes twice. Then they hung them up to dry in a place like this, somewhere cool and well-ventilated. Depending on how long they needed to store them, they might wrap the pelts in burlap and place them in a freezer.

Troy took another quick look and just as he suspected, he spotted a couple of freezers in a far corner. Next to them were floor-to-ceiling shelves, stacked with burlap and cardboard boxes and other shipping supplies.

From what he could see this was quite the operation—one that screamed illegal activity. Poaching and smuggling, to start. Maybe more. The Lord's work, no doubt.

"Good girl," he whispered to Susie Bear. The dog's alert was sufficient cause to search the warehouse; they didn't need the warrant. He slipped the Newfie a peanut-butter doggy treat from his pocket. She gobbled it down in one gulp.

Troy scratched the sweet spot between her ears, and they headed for the other prefab building. He wanted to see what was going on in that warehouse, too.

They were nearly there when Susie Bear barked. Her signal bark, a kind of burly yelp that always meant trouble. The dog clambered ahead.

Troy trailed after her. He heard the creak of a door, and glanced over in time to see Leland Hallett slip into the warehouse, Susie Bear hot on his heels. Hallett slammed the door behind him just as Susie Bear hurled herself at him. Escaping her by seconds.

The dog stood on her hind legs, her massive front paws on the door, growling. Obviously, she remembered the guy. And she didn't like poachers any more than poachers liked dogs.

"Down," said Troy.

Reluctantly the Newfie abandoned her post.

"Stay," he told her, and she whined her displeasure. "Stay," he told her again, and this time she dropped onto her belly. "Good girl."

Troy drew his weapon and quietly turned the knob, then inched the steel door open, staying well away from the opening.

"I'm coming in, Hallett," he yelled. "Don't do anything stupid."

A bullet pierced the door.

So much for not doing anything stupid, thought Troy.

Susie Bear's plumed tail thumped in the snow, scattering icy flakes and signaling Thrasher's arrival. The captain was usually the only backup Troy ever needed. He hoped that was true this time, too.

"How many?" asked Thrasher, his weapon also drawn.

"Only Hallett confirmed inside."

"Right," said Thrasher. "Exits?"

"Only this door and the garage doors, as far as I know. The windows are small, but he might be able to squeeze through."

"I'll do a perimeter check."

But before Thrasher could move, a terrible crash sounded—metal on metal—as a panel truck slammed into the garage door from the inside and smashed through it to the outside. The vehicle bounced forward, Hallett at the wheel.

Troy and Thrasher both fired, and one of the bullets hit home, nicking one of the tires; Troy chose to think it was his. The truck spun in the snow as Hallett put on the gas and sped toward the loop that would take him out of the commune and onto the river road.

Troy and Susie Bear ran after the truck, Thrasher right behind them. The congregation of the Temple of the End of Days poured out of the lodge. People were yelling and pointing and running for cover.

Sirens sounded, growing closer and closer as backup arrived.

"About time," said Thrasher.

"They'll cut him off."

"Let's hope so."

Hallett careened around the loop, past his Temple brothers and sisters and onto the narrow straightaway.

But he was too late.

Two police cars barreled toward the lodge. Toward Hallett. He swerved to avoid the cop car and lost control of his vehicle. The panel truck fishtailed, swinging right into the nearest tree. Hallett was sidelined.

Edith Tupper stepped out from behind the tree and cocked a shotgun at Hallett's head as he struggled to free himself from the wreckage. "One move and you're dead meat."

Amen, sister, thought Troy. *Amen.*

CHAPTER THIRTY-SEVEN

On the first day of Christmas,
My true love gave to me
A partridge in a pear tree.

—FREDERIC AUSTIN

"So, did the little old lady blow Hallett away or not?" asked Tandie as she reached for a length of red silk ribbon.

They were all gathered in the living room, wrapping last-minute gifts and drinking hot chocolate and snacking on popcorn and chocolate-covered raisins. The floor was stacked with cardboard boxes holding gifts that needed wrapping. And the coffee table was awash in a Christmas-colored rainbow of paper and fabric, bows, ribbon, stickers, tape, scissors, and other paraphernalia—including all manner of stocking stuffers that the Fleury-Carr family preferred to use as present toppers. For Mercy's "more is more" family, just sticking a present in a holiday bag and calling it quits was considered, well, the act of a quitter. A Christmas quitter.

The tree twinkled in the corner, along with all the other lights that glinted in the über-decorated room. Mercy was curled up with Troy and Muse at one end of the velvet sofa; a sleeping Felicity was curled up with a sleeping Elvis at the other end. Tandie sat cross-legged on one of the easy chairs, Susie Bear's shaggy head on her lap. Thrasher sat unaccompanied in another of the easy chairs.

Troy had built a blazing fire in the fireplace, and the flames added a cozy note to the room, so thoroughly costumed in Christmas finery. It had stopped snowing, and now the noontime sun shone on the glittering winter wonderland outside. The scene would have been as pretty as a Victorian Christmas card, if only they hadn't been talking about murder.

They were all catching each other up on their respective morning activities. It was Troy and Thrasher's turn, Mercy having run through the bullet points of the reading of the will and her dismay at the terms of Laz's will and trust.

"Hallett is not dead," said Thrasher. "He is, however, back in jail. And he should be there for a long time."

"All those poor lynx and marten," said Tandie. "Beaver and fox, too. It's a, a"—here the teenager struggled to find the right word—"a *travesty*."

"Agreed," said Thrasher.

Mercy leaned her head against her husband's shoulder. "What was in that other warehouse?"

Troy hugged her to him. "Mostly electronics."

"Like what?" Mercy moved Muse from her lap gently, handing the kitty over to Troy as she roused herself to wrap another present, destined for someone currently not in the room. She was running out of time; the guests would be arriving for their Christmas Eve buffet supper in a couple of hours.

"You name it. Integrated circuits, digital cameras, transistors, transformers, radar equipment, periscopes, even ball bearings."

"Can't you just buy that stuff here?" asked Tandie, using double-stick tape to secure a candy cane to a silver-wrapped box that held a cobalt-blue cashmere scarf for Patience. Mercy's grandmother loved candy canes.

"Yes, you can," said the captain. "And that's what they were actually doing. Buying the products here, and then smuggling them into Russia."

"Don't they have their own?" Tandie placed the finished gift with several others under the coffee table, out of the way.

"Not necessarily," said Troy, stroking little Muse. "Russia relies heavily on imports in these areas. And they're not the only ones."

"There's been increasing criminal activity in this area lately," said Thrasher. "Earlier this year a New Hampshire man was arrested and accused of being part of a Russian smuggling ring. They were buying electronics and sophisticated testing equipment here, repackaging it, and selling it overseas. He pled guilty. This appears to be a similar operation."

"Still," Tandie said as she reached for a stuffed green frog intended for Felicity. "I can't believe anyone from Vermont would do such a thing. We're better than that."

"Doesn't Felicity have enough stuffed animals?" asked Troy before going back to the investigation. "Technically, Frost is from Ohio."

"You can never have enough stuffed animals," said Mercy. "Besides, this one goes in the bath as well as the playpen."

"Sold," said Troy.

"So Frost is behind all this?" asked Mercy.

"We know that he's related to Tasha Karsak and her father, Viktar Mraz the oligarch," said Thrasher. "Oligarchs are often guilty of making their money in unsavory ways. And according to Feinberg, 'unsavory' doesn't begin to describe Mraz."

"Billionaires, too." Tandie enveloped the frog in bright green tissue paper and tied it at the top with gold ribbon, slipping a pink teether in the bow. "Ephraim Frost isn't all about soybeans and corn, after all."

"It is reasonable to assume that Frost and his foreign relations have been working together, probably for years," said Troy.

"Odds are that they started with the poaching," said Thrasher, "selling pelts from endangered species to Russia and China, and that after the sanctions and tariffs were imposed, they moved on to electronics. A very profitable, if illegal, line of enterprise."

"The family that smuggles together, stays together." Mercy chose a long narrow box with a Brooks Brothers tie to wrap.

"Until they kill each other," said the captain dryly.

"If Tasha was part of her father's operation—and I think we have to assume she was—I can't see her dealing in soybeans."

"She did wear that lynx coat," said Tandie. "Maybe she was into the illegal fur trade."

Mercy laughed. "Maybe."

"Do you really get your father a tie every year?" teased Troy.

"A linen tie for his birthday in the summer and a silk tie for Christmas every year," said Mercy. "Dad likes ties."

"If you say so."

"A well-tied tie is the first serious step in life," intoned Thrasher.

"Who said that?" asked Tandie.

"I did." Thrasher laughed. "But Oscar Wilde may have said it first."

Mercy was still thinking about the Frosts. "And you believe the murders are all somehow connected to the Frosts and their smuggling operation."

"One way or another," said Thrasher, serious again. "We know that Hallett is deeply involved with the Frosts, and related to The Singing Plumber. His half brother may have been part of this operation as well. These smuggling rings are typically run by ruthless people. Murder is not unknown to them."

"What will happen to Reverend Fitz and his followers?"

"The good pastor insists he knows nothing about it," said Troy, "but we know that's not true."

"Why kill Tasha? Or The Singing Plumber? Or Uncle Laz?" Mercy wrapped the tie box in silver-and-gold-striped paper, and festooned it with ribbon and a cigar.

"Cigars are gross," said Tandie.

"Dad loves a good cigar," said Mercy.

"I don't get it," said Tandie.

"Sometimes a cigar is just a cigar," mused Troy. "We don't have all the answers yet. But we're getting there."

"Meanwhile, Hallett's in jail, and his compatriots are abandoning ship." Thrasher regarded Mercy with respect. "Speaking of smokers, your mysterious stranger with a taste for Russian cigarettes is probably halfway to Moscow by now."

"He must have been involved somehow, someway," said Mercy.

"I think it's safe to assume that he's part of this criminal operation. He could be part of the Frost family, too."

"Whoever he is, good riddance," said Tandie.

Mercy looked at the captain. "What about the stalker in the hedge at Laz's house? He had a gun trained on you."

"We're checking all the perps who may hold a grudge." Thrasher smiled that movie star smile. "That could be a long list. Either way, he seems to have gone quiet."

"For now," said Mercy.

The captain rose to his feet, maintaining his ramrod posture even after such a long morning. "The good news is, the bad guys are on the run. You can focus now on what really matters: Felicity's first Christmas." He smiled at the sleeping baby. "I'll let myself out. You get some rest while you can. And I'll see you back here at six o'clock for your Christmas Eve party."

Tandie yawned. "Do you mind if I take a nap before the party?"

"Go right ahead. I can finish up here."

"Great." And with that the teenager was gone, up to her room for a long winter's nap. Muse followed her, knowing a good napper when she saw one. The kitty loved Tandie for it.

Mercy couldn't believe how much teenagers loved to sleep. She didn't remember sleeping so much when she was that age, but she must have. As a soldier, she'd learned to sleep whenever she could, but she slept lightly. A habit she could never break now.

"A nap sounds pretty good to me, too," said Troy, wrapping his arms around her.

She gave him a light kiss, and then wriggled out of his embrace. "I still have presents to wrap."

Troy gave her a skeptical look. "You don't believe the Frosts are behind the murders."

"I didn't say that."

"But you're thinking it. I can see the wheels turning in that lovely brain of yours."

"There's just so much that still doesn't make sense."

"There *is* a lot that doesn't make sense. But with Hallett and Fitz in custody, Northshire is safer today than it was yesterday. Harrington is all over this. And the feds will be involved now, too. So try to relax. It is Christmas Eve, you know."

"I know."

Troy bundled Felicity into his arms and went upstairs, Susie Bear shambling after him.

Now it was just Mercy and Elvis alone in the living room, filled with Christmas lights and her own dark thoughts. Elvis was snoring lightly, his triangular ears perked, ever vigilant, even in his sleep.

She focused on wrapping Troy's gift, the rugged shearling-lined leather bomber jacket that her mother had sweet-talked the shop in Northshire into delivering to the house. Her husband was *not* a tie guy, no matter what Oscar Wilde might advise.

She decided to drape the large coat box in pale blue paper marked by prancing merry moose with jingle bell antlers. Which brought to mind the Antler Man that Leland Hallett had fallen upon in the woods when Troy and Gil and Susie Bear caught him poaching. She couldn't help but think that whoever he was, he was somehow connected to the Yuletide Killer murders.

She just didn't know how. She didn't know how any of it fit together, but she had to believe that it did. It was one heck of a puzzle—a puzzle that would haunt her dreams until she solved it.

Christmas or no Christmas.

As she taped up the paper and grabbed a moose lollipop to tie up with the navy ribbon, Elvis jerked awake and leapt off the couch. The dog could go from sleep mode to alert mode in seconds. Before Mercy could even respond, she heard Brodie's signature knock—three short raps—and the opening of the front door. He was always careful not to ring the bell, which would echo throughout the house, upstairs and down, in case the baby was sleeping.

"Come on in," she called.

Brodie came loping in after Elvis, Uncle Hugo by his side. They were an odd couple, the soft-bellied Gen Z geek and the tough, wiry retired military man. But they shared a keen intellect and a gift for problem-solving that had ultimately drawn them together. Making them an unorthodox but effective team.

The colonel hadn't thought much of the young man at first, but Brodie won him over with his techie talents and the good-natured doggedness with which he approached everything he did. Uncle Hugo even took the whippersnapper—his nickname for Brodie—under his wing, giving him both work and career guidance.

Both the whippersnapper and his mentor looked inordinately pleased with themselves as they stood in front of the fireplace, rocking back on their heels, their hands folded behind their backs. *Who's unconsciously modeling whom*, thought Mercy.

"Well, let's hear it," she told them, waving a hand full of ribbon at the easy chairs. "It looks like you've got big news."

Brodie slumped into a chair, backpack on his lap, only to straighten up again as the colonel seated himself in a matching chair with his usual upright military bearing.

"Go ahead," said Uncle Hugo magnanimously.

The young man pulled his laptop from his backpack and joined Mercy on the sofa. "You've got to see this."

"What is it?"

"It's what was on the thumb drive."

What Mercy saw on the screen was row after row of numbers. "I don't get it. What do all these numbers mean?"

"We're not sure. We think it's like some kind of scrambled financial records."

"Harrington has forensic accountants working on it," said Uncle Hugo. "The feds are interested, too."

"Whose financial records? The Frosts?"

"Maybe," said the colonel. "That might be why Lazlo was killed. For these records."

"But how would he have gotten access?"

"Unclear," said the colonel.

"He did advise a lot of the local nonprofits on financial matters," said Mercy, remembering what her mother had told her. "Maybe after the Temple of the End of Days pulled that stunt at the town meeting, he decided to take a hard look at the organization."

"That seems to be in keeping with his character," said the colonel.

"That's not all." Brodie nodded at the screen. "Keep going."

Mercy continued to scroll through the numbers, and finally came to a series of selfies taken by young women. "Who are these girls?"

"We don't know. Maybe part of their 'bride importation' program," said the colonel, using air quotes. "Glorified prostitution and human trafficking."

"Fiancée visas," said Brodie.

Like Zoya, she thought. She went through the photos again. "This girl looks like the one in the photo Troy found at Hallett's place."

"Maybe she's one of their girls," said Brodie.

Mercy looked over at Uncle Hugo.

"We'll find out," said the colonel, with an air of finality that meant the subject was closed. "Which brings me to my news. I finally managed to talk to Rita."

"Rita?" Mercy started on another package, this one a Myrrh & Tonka scented candle from Jo Malone. Buying presents for Grace was always a challenge, but you couldn't go wrong with Jo Malone. Now she just had to find a wrapping worthy of the gift. And of her mother.

"Not her real name. My old friend's widow. The old friend who asked me to help Lazlo disappear."

She chose the silver paper embossed with rose gold Christmas trees. As elegant as her mother. "I remember. What did Rita Not Her Real Name tell you?"

Uncle Hugo smiled. "She told me she'd heard about the Yuletide Killer and his victim Lazlo Ford, and that she was waiting to hear from me."

"She knew his name?"

"She recognized it. Her husband had talked to her about Lazlo only a few days before cancer finally took him. He told her that if, once he was gone, she should hear of a man with that name dying, then she should share certain information with me—and me alone. But only if I asked."

"That's so intense," said Brodie.

"Yes. And highly unusual." The colonel frowned. "The fact that he shared this only with his wife and not his colleagues really surprised me. Of course, once I heard the information, I understood."

"Don't keep us in suspense, Uncle Hugo." The old soldier really did like a bit of drama, Mercy thought as she wrapped the paper around the boxed candle.

"It is quite the story." The colonel crossed his legs, smoothing the crease in his wool trousers.

"And she told you this story over the phone?" Mercy decided on a length of embroidered silver ribbon to embellish her mother's gift.

"No," he said. "She faxed me a copy of a coded letter he'd handwritten and hidden in a safe at their home. One of the simpler codes we used back in the day."

"Fax machines," said Brodie. "So old school."

"Far more secure than email. And easy for Rita to operate."

"Cool," said Brodie.

"Rita didn't know what it meant." Mercy fashioned a bow out of the embroidered ribbon and fastened it to the present, festooning it with silver jingle bells.

"Not at all. All he told her was that if a man named Lazlo Ford died, she might be hearing from me."

"She knew you," said Mercy.

"Once upon a time."

"And she trusted you."

"Yes." The colonel smiled. "Lazlo Ford's real name is Adam Zima."

"Zima," repeated Mercy as she placed her mother's gift with the others.

"Like that weird drink my mom used to drink when I was a kid," said Brodie. "She loved it."

"Right." The colonel frowned. "'Zima' means 'winter' in many Slavic languages."

"Of course it does," said Mercy. "We can add it to 'frost' and 'snow' and 'cold' and all the other Slavic surnames we've heard lately that relate to wintertime."

The colonel cleared his throat, signaling his displeasure with this tangent. "Adam was born in 1975 in Bratislava in what was then Czechoslovakia."

"And is now Slovakia," said Brodie.

"Correct," said Uncle Hugo. "His father was a Slovak engineer and his mother was a Russian nurse."

"When the wall came down in 1989, his parents left Eastern Europe and they settled in Switzerland temporarily, where his father found work as an engineer. Their goal was always to immigrate to the United States, but his parents died in a car accident before they could make the move."

"And Adam?" Mercy thought of the poor boy, orphaned so suddenly.

"Adam was only sixteen, but he was a brilliant guy. He stayed in Switzerland and he went on to college there, where he distinguished himself in linguistics and finance. He spoke his native Slovak, Czech, Russian, French, and English. Maybe more."

"Impressive."

"He got a job at the International Olympic Committee in Lausanne. It was there that an ambitious CIA unit recruited him to infiltrate the organization of an unnamed oligarch, one who made his fortune in the metal trades."

'Wow," said Brodie.

"Wow indeed." The colonel leaned forward, his elbows on his knees, his hands folded together. "This is where the intel gets a little blurry. I'm not sure exactly what information Adam passed to the CIA, but after the recession of 2008 hit, something went very wrong, and he needed to make his escape."

"And that's where you came in," said Mercy.

"Yes. I believe that this was when Adam's CIA handler contacted my old friend, who in turn contacted me. He got him out of there and I set him up in Northshire."

"And that's in 2009," said Mercy.

"Yes."

"But why wouldn't the CIA handle his exfil themselves?" she asked. "Why ask you?"

The colonel gave her a shrewd look. "The handler must not have trusted the company to do it right."

"He suspected a leak." She smiled at her great-uncle. "And he wasn't taking any chances." No surprise the handler had turned to the colonel. Always discreet, Uncle Hugo knew a million secrets, all of which he'd be taking to the grave with him.

Uncle Hugo smiled back. "No, he wasn't."

"And then what?"

"Lazlo made a new life for himself here. And it was a good life."

The terrible sight of Uncle Laz dressed as Santa ablaze in the woods flashed in her mind, and she closed her eyes. "Until it wasn't."

"Until it wasn't."

CHAPTER THIRTY-EIGHT

O! O! O! Who wouldn't go,
O! O! O! Who wouldn't go,
Up on the housetop, click! click! click!
Down through the chimney with good St. Nick.

—BENJAMIN RUSSELL HANBY

"Why would Uncle Laz leave me his house?" Mercy had joined Troy up in the nursery, where he was changing Felicity after her nap. The colonel and Brodie had gone, their briefing mission completed. Tandie was still asleep, and the caterers would be here in a couple of hours to set up for the party. She figured this was her last chance to get her husband alone before the onslaught of guests and gifts and *fa la la la*.

"He must have had a good reason," said Troy. "Probably a reason only you can figure out." He put the baby down on the play rug that covered the middle of the planked floor, and set an open plastic crate of toys at one end of it.

Felicity crawled over and hauled herself up, standing by the crate. She placed one pudgy little hand on the crate's top edge for balance, and used her free hand to pull out stuffed animals and blocks and cloth books, tossing them gaily around the room.

Elvis and Susie Bear flanked the rug, one canine at each end, watching but not moving to fetch the toys. They knew they were Felicity's toys, not theirs. Although there were times when it was obvious that they were desperate to go after them. Still, despite the temptation, the dogs stayed put.

Mercy sat cross-legged on the floor, stacking the blocks so Felicity could knock them down. The inevitability—some would say futility—of this game delighted the little girl. But for Mercy it was simply a metaphor for these baffling murders: Every time she thought she was building toward a solution, some new element came along and scattered her thoughts again. Just like Felicity's blocks.

"Lazlo knew how happy we are here at Grackle Tree Farm," said Troy. "He didn't give it to you because you needed a house. And I don't think he would give it to you just so you could resell it."

"No," said Mercy. "You're right. If he wanted to do that, he would have made it part of the trust, and given it to the Northshire Arts Center. It's such a beautiful house; they could have sold it. Or used it as some sort of gallery space or artist's residency or something."

"Yep."

Together they watched as Felicity wriggled toward the edge of the rug, where Elvis was stretched out like a levee holding back the sea. When the baby tried to go around him, veering off the mat, the shepherd nudged her belly with his nose. She giggled, and he nudged her again. She giggled again.

"He must have had another reason to leave it to you." Troy picked up one of the baby's favorite plushies, a plump hedgehog, and squeezed it until it squeaked. At the sound, Felicity squealed. Elvis's triangular ears perked, and Susie Bear tilted her big square head. Blue eyes trained on the hedgehog, Felicity crawled off toward her daddy. "You of all people."

"What do you mean 'you of all people'?"

"Yes, you." Troy held the hedgehog out to Felicity, and she grabbed it, tugging it away from him. "He could have left the house to anyone, including Patience. Why not just add it to everything else he left her?"

"I don't know."

They watched as Felicity plopped into a sitting position, holding the stuffie in her lap.

"Nice sit," said Mercy.

The dogs looked up at her, and Troy laughed before going on. "I think that he left the house to you because he knew you would know what to do with it."

"But I *don't* know what to do with it."

Troy smiled at her. "Sure you do."

Thirty minutes later Troy and Mercy drove by the crowded village green, taking in all the last-minute shoppers strolling the chalets in the Christmas market. Troy turned down the side street where Uncle Laz had lived and pulled into the narrow driveway of his nineteenth-century Greek Revival home. Well, her home now.

Mercy admired the classic lines of the house. The elegant façade was just that—a façade. This was a house of mystery, lovingly restored by a man of mystery, and now she was called to solve that mystery. To somehow look beyond the façade to the inner workings of the place, to the inner workings of Uncle Laz's mind. And perhaps, as Olga had said, to the inner workings of his old Russian soul.

She thought she'd done that already with the painting and the safe and the thumb drive. And maybe she had. Maybe those were all the clues that he'd left her, and she'd failed to decipher them all. Maybe she'd missed whatever it was she was supposed to discover.

"What if there's nothing else to find here?" She turned to Troy, and she could feel her face flush. "Or if there is, what if I can't find it?"

Troy laughed, and gave her a quick kiss. "Of course you'll find it. That's why we're here. Stay right there." He got out of the truck and came around to her side, opening the door for her. "Let me escort you into your new house."

"This is so weird." She had the keys that Adrien Roland had given her. They went in through the front door, no longer marked by crime scene tape.

They stepped inside, and once again Mercy and Troy made the rounds of the lovely home. This time there was no Thrasher waiting outside, no Olga Volkov trespassing inside, no stalker hiding in the spruce hedge. At least none that she could see or sense at the moment.

This time, the house was empty. Empty of life, empty of spirit. A sadder and lonelier place without Uncle Lazlo. Mercy wasn't sure how she was supposed to fix that. If anyone could.

She stared at the enormous pipe organ that dominated the living room. It really was beautiful. The kind of imposing instrument that demanded your full attention, even when no one was playing it. She slipped off her winter gloves—no point in wearing them now, since it was her house and the crime scene techs had come and gone.

Troy did the same. "What are we looking for?"

"I have no idea." Mercy fingered the organ keys, dusty now. The notes reverberated throughout the space, and at the sound she found herself near tears. She backed away from the instrument, banging her shin against a corner of the organ bench. "Ouch."

"Are you all right?"

"Fine." She regarded the bench with interest. She hadn't thought to look there before, not with all of the neatly filed pages of sheet music in the antique folio cabinet that flanked the pipe organ. Which the crime scene techs had already been through. And had come up with nothing.

Mercy lifted the lid of the bench, but all she found inside were random pages of sheet music. She wondered why this particular sheet music had not been filed in the folio cabinet along with the rest of his extensive library of scores. Uncle Laz was nothing if not meticulous about his music.

She collected the small stack and flipped through it. Most of it seemed to be the sheet music for popular Russian songs. She recognized a few of the song titles. "Kalinka," arguably the most well-known of Russian folk songs; she knew the "snowball tree" song from video games like *Tetris* and *Civilization VI*. Another reference to winter and snow and cold.

There was also one of Russia's most famous and ubiquitous songs, which she recognized because of the last verse, which appeared in English. *"Dorogoï Dlinnoyou,"* better known as the ever-popular plaintive lament "Those Were the Days."

And finally, on the bottom of the pile was the last of the tunes, a song she did not recognize, although certainly the title rang a bell: *"Oi Moroz, Moroz."*

Mraz. Ded Moroz. Moroz.

Here we go again, thought Mercy. *More frost.*

"Did you find something?" Troy sat down next to her, and she showed him the sheet music.

"What does it mean?"

"I'm not sure." She pulled out her cell and searched for the song. "It's supposedly a popular drinking song." She read the English translation of the lyrics aloud:

> *Oh frost, frost*
> *Don't freeze me*
> *Don't freeze me*
> *Or my horse.*
>
> *Don't freeze me*
> *Or my horse*
> *Or my horse*
> *My white-maned horse.*
>
> *My horse*
> *My white-maned horse*
> *I have a wife*
> *Oh, she is very jealous.*
>
> *I have a wife*
> *Oh, she is a beautiful woman*
> *She waits for me at home*
> *She waits, she is grieving for me.*
>
> *I am coming to her*
> *At the sunset of the day*
> *I will embrace my wife*
> *And I will groom my horse. . . .*

"Some drinking song," said Troy. "Maybe if you're drinking yourself to death."

"It's like *Stopping by Woods on a Snowy Evening*," said Mercy. "Written by another Frost."

"Miles to go," said Troy.

"That's exactly how I feel. Miles to go before I figure out what this all means." Mercy stood up. She straightened the stack of sheet music and placed it back in the bench, snapping the lid shut. "Let's do the rest of the house."

They went from room to room, but neither of them noticed anything. They ended up in the kitchen, unremarkable except for the wildly expensive espresso maker and the equally extravagant crystal food dishes for the cat. One for food, one for water, placed on a silver tray on the floor.

"The cat who lived like a king," said Troy. "Looks like Laz really spoiled Boris."

"The cat," said Mercy. "I forgot about the cat."

"Wherever Laz is, let's hope he didn't hear that." Troy bent down to pick up Boris's fancy dinnerware. "We should make sure King Boris eats well."

"No, I mean I forgot about the cat."

"I don't follow."

"The cat comes with the house. Worldly goods and all that."

"Right. So what are you saying?"

"Laz knew I didn't need his house or his worldly goods and that sooner or later I'd sell it or give it all away."

"Yeah."

"But he knew I'd never give away his cat." Mercy laughed. "And that sooner or later, I'd figure out that Boris is the key."

"The key?"

"It's been right in front of us the whole time."

"What has?"

"Uncle Laz's cat." She looked at him and smiled. "Boris."

"I don't get it."

"The one place we haven't looked." She looked at her watch. "If we hurry we might make it."

"Make it where?"

"To my grandmother's house." She texted Patience, telling her they were on the way.

"What about the party?" Troy checked the time on his watch, too. "We've got less than an hour before people start showing up."

"We'll get there. We just have to pick him up first."

"Pick up who?"

"Boris."

CHAPTER THIRTY-NINE

Love came down at Christmas,
Love all lovely, Love divine;
Love was born at Christmas;
Star and angels gave the sign.

—CHRISTINA ROSSETTI

"It's a good thing we didn't bring the dogs," said Mercy as Troy maneuvered his truck through the pretty little village to Patience's house. A light snow was falling, making for a snow-globe perfect Christmas Eve in New England. "Patience says that Boris doesn't much like canines."

"Who names their cat Boris?"

"It's a good name. You remember Boris and Natasha."

"Rocky and Bullwinkle," said Troy. "The squirrel and the moose. My heroes. I loved that show when I was a kid."

"And the little boy who loved squirrels and moose grew up to be a game warden. The End."

"In my mind Boris is a villain's name," said Troy. "But it probably means snow or cold or winter or frost like every other Russian name we've heard lately."

"Very funny." Mercy searched online with her cell. "According to the almighty internet, the etymology of the name Boris is 'mysterious,'" she said, hooking her fingers to indicate quote marks. "It might be Turkish or Bulgarian or Persian."

"Why am I not surprised. Everything about Lazlo Ford is turning out to be a mystery. Even his cat."

"True enough." Mercy kept on reading off her phone. "Boris can mean warrior or godlike, wolf or snow leopard, short or success." She grinned. "Take your pick."

"Boris Badenov was a wolf," said Troy. "But I'm guessing that for Lazlo, Boris was more a snow leopard."

Mercy spotted Patience waiting for them on the porch in a white puffer coat and snow boots—a queenly silhouette under the overhead light against the front door, the snow whirling around her. "Something's wrong."

Her grandmother tramped along the snow-covered brick path to the driveway, where Troy was coming to a slow stop. Mercy jumped out of the vehicle, slamming the door and racing to Patience.

"It's Boris," her grandmother said. "He's gone."

"How?"

"I'm not sure." She nodded toward the house. "Come inside."

PATIENCE PUT THE TEAKETTLE on for them all as she talked. "I got your text and I went to find Boris. He likes the love seat on the second-floor landing. But when I went upstairs, he wasn't there. I've looked everywhere. Even put out some canned salmon to lure him out into the open. All the other cats came, but not Boris."

"Would he go outside?"

"Maybe. Maine Coon cats are built for snow and cold weather. Double coat, large paws, bushy tails." Patience looked worried as she passed around blue-and-white china cups and saucers. "We do have a cat door, so they can all go in and out as they please."

"Maybe he's homesick," said Mercy. "Would he try to go home to Lazlo's house?"

"You mean *your* house?" Patience smiled. "I suppose it's possible."

"Maybe he misses his crystal food dishes," said Troy.

"Maybe. But I'm afraid he may have been stolen."

"Stolen?" asked Mercy.

"Pet theft is on the rise. Two million pets get stolen every year." Her grandmother looked to Troy to confirm.

"That's true," he said. "Mostly small purebred dogs. Although good hunting dogs are stolen from time to time. A hunter up in Stratton had his three Plott Hounds dognapped during a bear hunt."

"It's not just dogs," said Patience. "Cats are vulnerable, too. Especially the rare ones."

"There was that case in Connecticut last year," said Troy. "Two armed intruders broke into a couple's house and demanded they turn over their cat. Law enforcement described it as a 'high dollar value' cat."

"Boris is a white Maine Coon cat." Patience wrapped her fingers around her teacup. The cup shook in her hands. "Very rare. Worth thousands of dollars."

"We'll find him," said Mercy.

"Lazlo left Boris in my care. I'll never forgive myself if anything happens to him." Patience put her cup down, clattering in the saucer. "Boris has a GPS tracker on his collar. But we need Laz's phone to access it."

"We haven't found his phone," said Troy. "Yet."

"You don't necessarily need his phone," said Mercy. "If you know the tracker app and Laz's username and password."

"We don't have that either," her grandmother pointed out.

"We can ask Brodie about it," said Mercy.

"And I'll file a theft report," said Troy. "In the meantime, we need to get to the party."

"One more thing," said Patience. "What did you want with Boris?"

Mercy paused. Her grandmother felt bad enough about the cat already; she'd be even more worried if she knew that Boris may have been abducted by a murderer.

Patience reached across the pine table and squeezed her hand. "You really need to tell me what's going on."

Her grandmother could read her too well. There was no point in soft-pedaling the truth. But she could try. "It's just a hunch."

"Hunch, huh?" Patience raised her eyebrows at Troy. "We know how Mercy's hunches usually pan out, don't we, Troy?"

"Yes ma'am." He gave Mercy a sheepish look. "You may as well go ahead and share your theory."

"And it's just a theory," said Mercy.

"Spill it, please," said Patience.

"I think Boris may be the key to all this."

"I don't understand," said Patience. "How?"

"I'm not sure, but the fact that he's missing now worries me." Mercy stood up. "You go get ready for the party. Troy and I are going to take a look around."

Patience excused herself and Troy and Mercy did a search of her grandmother's house. There were cats in every room—every size and shape and color—curled up on couches, perched on windowsills, hiding under beds. But no white Maine Coon cat.

They did a quick perimeter search as well, checking every window and door for evidence of tampering or trespassing. Each was locked and nothing seemed out of place. Until they reached the library that adjoined the living room.

There they discovered a slick of melted snow on the floor and an unlocked door that led into a large rectangular side garden lined with raised beds. In the summer, the yard served as a lovely cutting garden full of hydrangeas and roses, pinks and peonies, daisies and dahlias. In winter, the unkempt raised beds were a bounty for birds and other creatures.

Troy opened the door and together they peered outside. Gentle floats of snowflakes obscured the sun, which was beginning its long descent into the night.

"There." Mercy pointed to a raised bed of bare hydrangea bushes, their dried flower heads topped with snow.

"What is it?"

"There's something there." Mercy stepped out into the soft flurries, following the bit of pink caught on one of the plant's skeletal branches. She pulled a glove from her pocket and slipped it on, then tugged at the rosy patch on the hydrangea bush. She closed her fist around it and jogged back into the house.

"What have you got there?" asked Troy.

She opened her palm and they both stared down at the torn slip of rose-colored cashmere. The same rose-colored cashmere that Olga Volkov was wearing at the reading of the will.

"I think it's Olga's."

Troy squatted down and examined the snowy ground. "There are some prints here. Boot prints. With an interesting sole pattern."

Mercy dropped down to join him, examining the prints in the glow of his cell flashlight. "It's the famous sun pattern. From UGG boots. Olga wears UGGs."

"Really." He looked at her with affection. "How do you know these things?"

"It's a lovely pattern, but more than that, it incorporates their logo. It's one way you can identify the real thing from all the knockoffs." Mercy pointed to the starburst pattern. "This is the real thing." She held up the rose-colored swatch. "Just like this is real cashmere."

"You are your mother's daughter," teased Troy.

"Not," said Mercy, straightening up again. "Should we track these?"

Troy stood. "Guess we should have brought the dogs, after all."

They followed the tracks out of the garden and down the hill upon which her grandmother's Victorian house stood. There the footprints ended at the tire ruts left in the snow by a small SUV.

"Looks like a Subaru Michelin tire track," said Troy.

"That narrows it down," Mercy said wryly, Subaru being known as the unofficial car of Vermont.

"Do you know where she lives?"

Mercy shook her head. "I have her card somewhere." She retrieved the card and punched the number of Olga's shop into her cell. It went to voicemail.

"It will be closed now," said Troy. "Let me see if Delphine can get me a home address." Delphine Dupree was the dispatcher for the warden service.

They said goodbye to Patience on the porch and went back to Troy's truck, where he called Delphine on the radio. Within minutes she'd found Olga Volkov's residence: a farmhouse off Route 7A near Mount Frost Moon between Northshire and Sunderland.

"Let's stop at Grackle Tree Farm and get the dogs," said Mercy. "If anyone can find that cat, Elvis and Susie Bear can."

"Good idea. Although Boris may not think so."

By the time they got home, Mercy's mother was already at the house, overseeing the caterers, with her father's help. Tandie was playing with the baby in the living room, the dogs in attendance.

"You can't leave now," said Grace. "Everyone will be here shortly. You can't abandon your guests."

"We'll be back soon, promise." Mercy whistled for the dogs and Elvis and Susie Bear roused themselves from their baby vigil and came running.

Troy waved toward the hallway and the eager hounds sank onto their haunches, waiting for the word to leave.

"I don't understand," said Grace with more than a little impatience and irritation. "Where are you going? It's Christmas Eve—Felicity's first Christmas Eve. What could you possibly have to do that's more important?"

Mercy smiled. "Save the cat."

ORLOV REACHED OLGA VOLKOV'S little dacha in the woods before Mercy Carr and her husband Troy did. He'd heard them talking to the veterinarian on her porch. It seemed the cat was missing and that Olga had taken it. He wasn't sure what Lazlo Ford's cat had to do with anything or why the Russian tea shop proprietor would take the cat, but if Mercy Carr believed it was important, it probably was.

He'd learned the hard way over the past few days that he discounted the woman at his peril. He knew she'd been an Army MP in Afghanistan, and it showed. Her husband the game warden, who'd also served in Afghanistan, was very sharp, too. What the Americans liked to call a power couple, in the warrior's sense of the word.

But Mercy Carr would not get the better of him this time. This time he would prevail. He'd find the cat and make the tea lady talk. One way or another.

CHAPTER FORTY

While the moon her watch is keeping,
All through the night,
While the weary world is sleeping,
All through the night . . .

—SIR HAROLD BOULTON

THE MINT-GREEN FARMHOUSE WITH THE ELABORATE WHITE gingerbread scrollwork looked more like a dacha than your typical cabin in Vermont, thought Mercy. Set against the forest, with Mount Frost Moon looming in the background, snowflakes filling the air like fairy dust, the colorful cottage seemed straight out of a Slavic folk tale. The kind of magical place where the Snow Maiden herself might have lived and loved and melted.

A blue Subaru was parked on the gravel road by the house. But despite the cold there was no smoke coming from the chimney. The place looked deserted. And yet the front door was wide open.

"That doesn't look good." Troy handed Mercy his pistol and shouldered his rifle. "Just in case."

Maybe it was overkill, but given the fact that three people had died in as many days here in their perfect little corner of Vermont, her husband had a point. They let the dogs out, waving the canines behind them and making their way along the snowy brick path to the entrance.

The door stood ajar, and the snow flurries swept in and around and through the opening to Olga's home.

"Olga!" called Troy. "Boris!"

Mercy called for the pregnant woman and the cat, but neither answered. All they heard was the silver rush of the snow-laden wind and the quiet whining of the dogs, who were desperate to charge through that door. After what, she didn't know. But there was only one way to find out.

She looked over at Troy, and he nodded. "Search," she told the eager canines quietly.

Off the dogs flew, in a lively scramble of flying snow and ice. Mercy and Troy followed carefully. They stopped at the door, where they noticed the splintered wood that spelled illegal entry. They drew their weapons and went inside.

They found themselves in a cozy sitting room with a Moroccan-tiled fireplace and rustic wood and wicker furniture piled with green and gold and blue blankets and pillows. The floor was strewn with books and papers and small objects; the drawers of the antique sideboard were hanging open, their contents scattered.

But the most disconcerting sight was the dark red splotch staining the pine-planked floor. A large hand-painted Russian doll clotted with the same dark red smears lay about a foot from the pool of blood.

"It's one of those *matryoshka* dolls," said Mercy. "You know, the nesting kind. This one looks like it's modeled on a winter fairy tale." She pointed to the snowy scene on the belly of the traditionally dressed Russian lady.

"Not *The Snow Maiden* again?" asked Troy.

"I don't know."

Troy motioned to Mercy and they split up, each taking a side of the house and clearing the rooms on their respective side. But they did not find Olga or anyone else. The place was empty. Devoid of animal life, human and feline and otherwise.

They met back at the bloodied doll.

"I'll call it in." Troy pulled out his cell. No service. He tried the radio. No service. "You?"

Mercy tried her cell, but she couldn't get a signal either.

"Maybe when we're outside," he said.

While she had her cell out, she figured she might as well take some photos of the doll. "Somebody used this as a weapon. It's just made of wood. Do you think you could really kill someone with it?"

"Hard to say. Maybe that's why no one's here. Maybe both victim and perp got away. Maybe they're after each other. Or maybe one of them is already dead and the other is disposing of the body."

"Let's ask the dogs." She glanced around. "Where'd they go?"

"They must be outside."

"Elvis!" yelled Mercy, and the shepherd barreled through the front door, Susie Bear on his heels. He barked once, then swung around and raced back out again, disappearing into the snow.

Susie Bear tilted her big head at Troy, as if to say, "Now what?"

"Come on, girl, let's go find him."

The three of them left the house, Mercy shutting the front door quietly behind them. She hoped that wherever Olga and Boris were, they were safe.

Troy tried his cell and his radio again. "I've got one bar. I'm texting Captain Thrasher." He cursed. "Zero bars now. Let's hope he got it."

Both dogs sniffed their way across the narrow strip of backyard between the house and the forest, Elvis in the lead. The shepherd reached the edge of the woods, twisted his long neck back toward Mercy, and barked once again. Then he turned, leaned toward a copse of white pines, and shot into the trees and out of sight.

Susie Bear clambered after him, and Mercy and Troy took up the rear.

"We're missing our daughter's first Christmas," she said.

"Thrasher will send backup when he gets the message."

"*If* he gets the message."

"Either way we're going home as soon as we check this out." Troy stopped and took her gently by the shoulders. "If we don't find anything, we report it and let whoever pulled the short straw for the holidays take care of it. Deal?"

"Deal."

He kissed her and let her go. They trudged along behind the dogs, Elvis racing ahead and circling back, Susie Bear shuffling and snuffling her way along toward something Mercy and Troy couldn't see or smell. They did find drops of blood dotting the snow, standing out against the swaths of white among the fallen leaves and the deadfall. Whether the blood belonged to Olga or Boris was unclear. Either way it was not a good sign.

It wasn't a lot of blood, just enough to worry Mercy. She wanted Boris to be all right. And she wanted Olga to be all right, too, even if she was a cat snatcher. Olga must have had a very good reason to take Boris. Maybe the same reason she herself had. Maybe Olga also believed that Boris had something to tell them about Laz's murder.

If only cats could talk.

They moved deeper and deeper into the woods, farther and farther away from the little dacha and Grackle Tree Farm and Felicity's first Christmas party. She looked over at Troy. His handsome face was intent on the trail. He was an easygoing guy, her husband, but when he was on a mission he was as intensely tenacious as she was, despite his good-natured temperament. The perfect combination of Elvis and Susie Bear. Whereas she was all Elvis all the time.

The shepherd was back, and he was excited. So excited it seemed like he'd jangle right out of his body. He whipped his tail, yelping at Mercy, and took off with the sleek power of a ballistic missile. Back to wherever he'd come from. Where he'd found something. Something he was very determined to show her. If she could just catch up.

Mercy jogged after him, Troy by her side. They huffed up a hill covered in bare maples and birch and beech and pine. There in a small clearing in front of a snow-covered mound of earth were the dogs, Elvis in his Sphinx position and Susie Bear splayed out on her belly. Alerting to something.

She didn't see anything at first. "What are they alerting to?"

Troy pointed to a small hole in the mound. "Something in there."

They stepped up for a closer look. That's when Mercy realized that the opening might actually be much bigger than she'd thought. She kicked at the snow and dead leaves and debris with her boot, and years of erosion and deadfall fell away, revealing a much larger entryway.

"This is one of those old stone chambers," said Troy. "This one looks like a granite igloo."

Mercy brushed away some of the snow from the surface of the massive slabs to reveal the stonework underneath. "They say these cairns are astronomically aligned with the movements of the sun, like the solstices and equinoxes. Some said they were marked with Ogham script, too. Other people say they're just scratches made by tools." She thought of Tandie and *Raiders of the Lost Ark*. She'd have to show her this sometime. Provided it wasn't a crime scene. She prayed it wasn't a crime scene.

Elvis whined again. The dog was aching to get in there.

"Go on," she told the shepherd, and he crawled over the entryway and wriggled through it, disappearing inside.

"Susie Bear and I will stand guard, you go on in after Elvis," said Troy.

"Are you sure?"

"You know you want to. Just take your gun."

Mercy dropped down to her hands and knees, grateful for her gloves and her flannel-lined cargo pants. She crawled through the narrow opening into a space much wider than she'd expected. Although she couldn't stand up; it was no more than five feet tall.

She flipped on her cell flashlight to illuminate the gloom. The walls were a masterpiece of perfectly set stones and the ceiling was made from enormous stone slabs. She was struck by the precision with which whoever built this structure had placed the stones, without benefit of machinery or mortar. She spotted markings on the walls, too; whether they were Ogham or not she couldn't say.

She spotted no Olga. She did see Elvis in the far corner of the chamber, head high, ears perked, long tail curled up. She crouch-crawled over to him. "What you got there, boy?"

He nudged a pile of debris with his long muzzle. Mercy examined the leaves and saw tufts of white fur peeping through all the brown foliage.

Boris!

OUTSIDE THE STONE CHAMBER Troy waited impatiently with Susie Bear. He leaned over toward the opening of the cairn and called her name into the void.

Nothing. He wished Mercy would at least try to yell at him. Let him know she was okay.

The woods were quiet. The snow was falling more heavily now, and they needed to get back to Grackle Tree Farm while the roads were still navigable. He didn't want to be stuck on the road with Mercy and the dogs, unable to get home to Felicity.

Not this Christmas Eve. He and Mercy had a party to host. More important, Troy had his own Santa duties to perform tonight. It was the first time he would play that role for his little girl. He wanted to get it right.

He heard the crack of a gunshot. He leaned into the stone chamber and yelled to Mercy, "Stay back. Sending in Susie Bear!"

"Roger that!" came her muffled answer.

Troy was relieved to hear her voice. He focused now on getting Susie Bear into the stone chamber with Mercy and Elvis, knowing that she'd be safer in there with them.

"In you go," he said, "go find Elvis."

The big Newfie was not crazy about small spaces. Whining, she didn't budge.

"Go on, girl." He heard the sound of boots crunching through the snow, and pushed the heavy dog halfway into the cairn. Elvis barked in encouragement, and she scrambled inside, disappearing from view.

Twigs snapped. The shooter was closer now. Leaves shuffled. Too close.

Troy dove for cover. Squeezing himself into the space between two large boulders that sat to the north of the east-facing stone igloo.

He could see the entrance to the stone chamber from where he was positioned, and he had a good 360-degree view of the little clearing. Giving him the opportunity for a clear shot at the perpetrator should he show up. When he showed up.

Dusk was approaching and snowflakes danced in the fading light. He heard a crashing through the forest. A little farther away this time. But not far enough. Yet.

Another shot rang out.

Whoever they were, they were not shooting at Troy. Or his wife. Or the dogs.

At least as far as he could tell. He steadied his rifle, resting it on the relatively flat top of the granite boulder. Ready to aim, ready to shoot, ready to protect his family to the death.

He caught a glimpse of pale pink running through the forest. *Olga*. Was she friend or foe? Troy didn't know anymore.

The tall woman stumbled into the clearing, her streaked hair flying out behind her, wet with snow. She was unarmed. And more than a little dazed.

To his horror, Mercy poked her head out of the entryway. Troy realized that she'd been watching at the edge of the chamber opening the whole time. Instead of staying back like he'd told her to do.

Mercy waved at Olga to come inside the stone igloo with her, and the woman lurched forward. Disoriented, she tripped over a downed limb covered in snow and fell onto her knees. Troy watched as Mercy pitched herself forward and out of the chamber, grabbed the woman's arms, and pulled her roughly inside.

That was his wife. Always the hero. Always taking risks she'd be wiser not to take. It was his job to make sure she survived those risks. Now and forever, amen.

Troy focused his attention on the two slim birch trees where Olga had slipped into the clearing. Odds were whoever was chasing her would come into the clearing at the same place.

He listened hard, but heard nothing but the wind rustling the snowy branches of the trees, the skittering of the small woodland creatures, the whistling of the hermit thrush, and the wailing of the loon.

It wasn't long before he heard Olga's pursuer gaining ground and getting closer. Troy steeled himself for the man's arrival. He promised himself he'd wait until he had a clear shot—and then take it without thinking twice.

A heavy pounding on the forest floor. A large man burst into the clearing, his pistol drawn. He had red hair and wore a steel-gray winter scarf knotted around his forehead splashed with what could only be blood. Olga's handiwork with the nesting doll, no doubt.

The man skidded to a slippery stop in the middle of the small glade. He looked around. Troy waited for the guy to realize that he'd lost track of Olga.

Which he did. The wild, red-haired man cursed. Letting loose a torrent of dramatic expletives you didn't have to speak Russian to understand.

The Russian ceased railing midstream. He stared directly ahead, his eyes focused on the stone chamber. A grin spreading across his face as he noted the opening. He stalked toward the granite cairn, his gun aimed at the entryway.

Troy trained his firearm on the big man. "Game warden. Drop your weapon."

The man spun around toward the sound of Troy's voice.

Troy knew that the man could see the barrel of his rifle. "Drop your weapon," he ordered again. "Don't make me tell you twice."

The burly man hesitated. His mistake. Maybe his last.

Troy prepared to fire. Out of the corner of his eye he caught the flash of blond fur as Elvis leapt out of the stone chamber.

The fierce Malinois descended upon the man, clamping his jaws around his shooting arm. But this guy was strong, and he was not going down without a fight. He struggled with the shepherd, but Elvis held fast as a vise.

Troy couldn't get a clear shot from where he was. He couldn't chance hitting Elvis.

The man went down, Elvis still gripping his arm with his sharp teeth and steel chomps. The man fired wildly at the dog. He missed. The bullet struck the boulder to Troy's right, ricocheting into the trunk of a nearby pine. Troy tore out of his position, rifle aimed right at the man on the ground.

"Call off the dog," the man said in heavily accented English as he lay prone on the forest floor, Elvis still bolted to his wrist.

"Drop your weapon," Troy repeated, standing over the guy. "Or you're going to lose that arm."

The man looked at Elvis. Troy could hear Mercy exiting the stone chamber behind him. She held Troy's pistol in her hand. He knew she was debating whether or not to shoot this guy right here and now.

"If you shoot my dog, you die," she told the man plainly, pistol aimed at his head.

The Russian lifted his head, looking from Mercy to Troy to Elvis. He sighed in resignation, dropping the gun. Troy kicked it away. Mercy retrieved it.

"*Blyat,*" the man said, dropping his head back to the ground.

"Come here, Elvis."

Elvis released the man's forearm and trotted over to Mercy.

"Good dog," said Troy and Mercy in unison.

CHAPTER FORTY-ONE

Joy, joy, joy! Joy, joy, joy!
Angels are singing,
And Christmas is bringing us joy, joy, joy!
Joy, joy, joy! Joy, joy, joy!
Merry bells ringing,
And Christmas is bringing us joy, joy, joy!

—WILLIAM EDIE MARKS

THE PARTY WAS IN FULL SWING BY THE TIME MERCY AND TROY and the dogs arrived, with Olga and Boris in tow.

"It's about time," said her mother, intercepting them in the entryway. She favored the two uninvited guests with a piqued look.

"You're here now, that's all that matters," said her father. "Everything all right?"

"Yes, fine." Mercy plucked Felicity from Tandie and smothered her in little kisses, Troy at her side.

"Tell us everything."

"They need to change their clothes first," said Grace severely. "And then greet their *invited* guests."

"The caterers seem to have everything under control," said Mercy, peering into the living room, where dozens of people milled around, laughing and eating and drinking. There was a definite air of Christmas love and joy here tonight. "Thanks, Mom, for overseeing all this."

Her mother rolled her eyes, but before she could say anything else, Patience interrupted her.

"You found him!" Her grandmother reached for the enormous Maine

Coon and whisked the monster cat from Olga into her own arms. "I knew you would."

"He's had a rough day," said Mercy, holding a squirming Felicity, who would have liked nothing better than to play with all that fuzzy white fur. "We'd like to examine him, if we could."

Patience gave her a knowing look. "Okay. Let's take him into Troy's room."

"We're coming with you." Thrasher and Wyetta joined them from the living room. In his red cashmere sweater and gray wool trousers, the captain was as handsome as ever, matched only by Wyetta in her matching red silk dress and heels. Mercy sighed, knowing that they were setting a standard her mother would applaud and that she and Troy could never meet.

"How's our perp?" asked Troy.

"Becker and Goodlove have him in custody," said the captain. "He's not talking. He's lawyered up, but that shouldn't matter." He smiled at Mercy. "Seems he likes Russian cigarettes. According to Interpol, the DNA on those butts matches a former FSB agent named Maxim Bychklov. Gun for hire, operating under a number of aliases. Wanted in connection with multiple murders on multiple continents."

"So he killed Tasha Karsak," said Tandie.

Mercy shook her head slightly.

"Or maybe not."

"I'm sure Mercy has a theory that explains all," said Troy.

"I'm working on it. But we need to check out Boris."

She led them all into the den, aka Troy's room, where the foosball table and the billiards table and the dartboard shared equal billing. Patience plopped the big cat on the billiards table and began to examine him. They all watched while she went over the giant purring cat from head to toe.

"He seems no worse the wear for his misadventures," said Patience.

"Great." Mercy turned to Olga, who'd grabbed the easy chair by the bridge table. She looked pale. "Why did you take Boris?"

Olga flushed. "I did not mean to hurt him. I would never hurt him. Lazlo loved him."

"He seems to be fine," said Patience.

"I took Boris because Lazlo loved him. The cat is all I had left of him.

His cat and his baby." She rubbed her belly, tears gathering at the corners of her eyes.

"It will all be fine, Olga. You'll see." Mercy helped Felicity stroke the lovely feline's long white hair. Boris purred loudly. Together, she and the baby scratched the feline's neck and fingered his pretty snow-white collar.

"What is it?" Troy took Felicity from her.

Mercy unhooked the collar and held it up to them all to see. There was a rectangular box hooked to the collar.

"That's his GPS tracker," said Patience. "The one we couldn't use because we didn't have his phone or his username and password for the app."

"Yes and no."

"What do you mean?"

"Yes, we'd need that access if this were a GPS tracker. But I suspect it's not." Mercy retrieved her Swiss Army knife from a cargo pocket and opened up the mini-screwdriver. She unscrewed the little box and opened it up, placing it on the billiards table. It was some sort of device with what appeared to be a lens on one side.

"It's not a GPS tracker," confirmed Troy.

"Then what is it?" asked Wyetta.

Mercy smiled at Brodie, who'd made a late entrance with the colonel and Feinberg. "Brodie? Would you care to enlighten us?"

"Very cool." Brodie carefully placed the electronic device in his open palm for all to see. "It's a biometric code generator."

"In English," said Grace. "Please."

He pointed to the lens. "This is an iris scanner. You activate the code generator with an iris scan. So only the person with the correct iris can activate it."

"But what does the code provide access to?"

"Probably a secret bank account." Brodie grinned at Feinberg. "In a very secretive bank."

"Banque Beutel!" Feinberg grinned back. "The most discreet bank in Switzerland."

"Huh," said Tandie. "I'm not following."

"An iris scanner is a biometric tool," said Brodie. "It makes a mathematical record of the iris, the colored ring of the eye. Your iris pattern is as unique as your fingerprint. It's formed when you're young, and it doesn't change as you grow older."

"But Lazlo is dead," said Tandie. "Will the iris scanner still work?"

Brodie shook his head. "I think it's been too long. After around sixteen hours, the iris of the deceased changes so much that AI can tell the difference. And the scanner won't work."

"Which means you can't get the code," said Tandie. "And you need the code to get into the account. So . . ."

"So all that money . . ." Patience looked at Olga. "That money that should by all rights be for Olga and his baby is . . . gone?"

Everyone started talking at once. The colonel rapped the billiards table sharply, startling Boris. The huge cat stretched out luxuriously, and then leapt gracefully to the floor, disappearing under the bridge table.

The room was quiet now. You could hear the guests in the rest of the house enjoying themselves, but everyone in the den was waiting for the colonel to speak.

"Go ahead, Uncle Hugo."

"Let's not underestimate Lazlo Ford. He was a careful man with a hidden past. He wouldn't let his money sit in a Swiss bank forever, unavailable to his heirs. He'd plan for contingencies like this somehow." He smiled at his young protégé Brodie. "What would he do, whippersnapper?"

"Of course!" Brodie drummed his hands on the top rail of the pool table. "It's not *his* iris that unlocks the code generator."

"Then whose?"

"The Snow Maiden's," said Mercy.

"Olga," said Troy.

They all looked at the pregnant woman.

"I don't understand," she said.

Mercy went to Olga's side. "He didn't forget you. Or your baby. He just wanted you to be safe. He wanted your inheritance to be safe."

"Safe from whom?" asked Grace.

"His enemies," said Thrasher. "And it seems like he had more than a few."

"Let's hear it, Mercy," said her father, who like all lawyers loved a good summation.

One of the caterers poked her head into the room. "Old New England Egg Nog, anyone?"

"Sure." New England Egg Nog was a holiday tradition that couldn't be beat, given the fact that it was spiked with brandy, whiskey, rum, and bourbon.

While all the adults in the room partook in a little eggnog, Mercy summed up the past, present, and future of Laszlo Ford as best she could.

"A lot of this is circumstantial," she said, "but eventually I think the evidence will support it. Or most of it, anyway." She paused for a sip of eggnog. "We know that Laz made some enemies in international banking while he was working for the CIA. When Uncle Hugo helped him come here, I think Lazlo hid the money he'd made, or somehow appropriated, working with these criminals."

"Banque Beutel," interjected the colonel.

Mercy smiled. "Yes. And there the money stayed, multiplying and multiplying over the years." She paused. "Meanwhile with your help, Laz settled here. Around this same time, someone killed Antler Man in the forest."

"You think the two are related." The colonel frowned.

"The timeframe fits," said Mercy. "And Dr. Darling said judging by his dental work, he was a foreigner. I suspect that Antler Man was sent to retrieve what Uncle Laz had taken from them. He may even have been a Mraz himself."

"Here's hoping they're able to retrieve some good DNA from those old bones," said Thrasher. "They're working on it, but it may take a while."

"You think Laz killed him," said Uncle Hugo.

"I believe Laz killed him in self-defense."

"To protect himself and his new friends here in Northshire," said Troy.

"Exactly," said Mercy. "And there the foreigner remained, hidden in the woods all these years, undisturbed and undiscovered."

"Until the Ohio billionaire named Frost comes here with his son Fitz to establish his fire-and-brimstone commune in Vermont," said the colonel. "His Slavic cousins think it's the perfect place to run a smuggling operation and the billionaire Frost and the oligarch Mraz combine forces. They start off supplying rare pelts to the black market, mainly Russia and China. But then they begin to expand into most of the areas Mraz is already exploiting. Electronics, money laundering, prostitution, human trafficking, and more. Very lucrative." He looked at Mercy. "And then?"

"Fast forward to the Solstice Soirée," said Mercy. "One of the Mraz people over from Eastern Europe realizes that Laz is the man who killed their long-lost relative. Maybe Tasha, maybe someone else."

"Very bad luck for Uncle Laz."

"Or maybe inevitable, given the growing web of criminal activity around here," said Thrasher, shaking his head. "Either way, you're thinking that Mraz hires your Russian gun for hire to exact his revenge, and he kills Lazlo."

"Yes," said Mercy.

"A contract killer, not a serial killer," said Tandie, disappointed but not daunted. "What about the Yule log?"

"Some kind of Russian irony, perhaps," said the colonel.

"But what about The Singing Plumber?" asked Tandie.

"We did a search of his place and found a large stash of sniper bullets hidden in some of his piping," said Thrasher.

"It's not just electronics," said the colonel. "These bullets are export-controlled, too. The Russian Federal Security Service and the Russian military are doing everything they can to get their hands on them."

"The Singing Plumber was a traitor," said Brodie with disappointment. "And a jerk. I checked out his laptop, and there were dozens of emails between him and a woman named Zoya. He brought her over here on a fiancée visa. He wasn't very nice to her. And then she disappeared."

"Bride importation," said the colonel. "Looks like she was one of Mraz's girls. Maybe they don't appreciate their girls being manhandled."

"And the gun for hire got rid of him. That would explain the digoxin," said Brodie. "One of the Russians' favorite poisons."

"I don't think so," said Mercy. "He's a sniper first and foremost."

"Mercy is right. All the crimes he's suspected of are shootings," said Thrasher.

"I think that Tasha was running the bride importation part of their operation, and he hurt one of her girls. When her girl went missing in August, Tasha came over here to find out what happened to her. She blamed Timothy Carter. So he had to pay."

"Месть сладка, когда она долгожданна," said Uncle Hugo. "Revenge is sweet when it is long-awaited. Not that Tasha waited that long."

"She pretended to be Laz's daughter to get close to the investigation. And she tried to ingratiate herself with Harrington to see how much we knew about the family business in general and her girls in particular. She suspected that Laz was the one who helped her missing girl disappear," said Thrasher. "She wanted him dead as much as her uncle Mraz did."

"Revenge should have no bounds," quoted Mercy.

"Is that Russian, too?" asked Brodie.

"*Hamlet*," said the colonel, with a nod to Mercy.

"Then who killed Tasha?" asked Tandie.

Mercy turned to Troy. "Why don't you tell them?"

"Leland Hallett," said Troy.

Tandie clapped. "Mercy! How did you figure that out?"

"Troy found a picture of a pretty girl on a beach at Hallett's house. We know from the photos on that thumb drive that she was one of Tasha's girls."

"Mercy recognized her," said Troy.

"Turns out she was Carter's girl. The one who went missing."

"Tasha went after Carter, and then Hallett went after Tasha."

"We already had so much evidence against him," said Troy. "Poaching, smuggling, attempted murder. When Harrington showed him the photo of the girl, he knew they had him."

"Hallett is hoping for a deal," said Thrasher.

"Will he get a deal?"

Thrasher shrugged. "A lot of people want to know everything there is to know about the Frosts and their Russian cousins. FBI, CIA, Interpol, and a number of other three-letter agencies around the world. But they may not need even Hallett, thanks to that thumb drive you found at Lazlo Ford's place."

"I was totally wrong," said Tandie. "No serial killer. Just revenge. All of these murders were about vengeance. So much for the Four Ls."

"The Russians also have a saying, Не рой другому яму, сам в нее упадешь," said the colonel. "If you dig a hole for someone, you'll fall in it yourself. Not that such a prospect ever stopped a Russian."

"It is all too much," said Olga, her hands massaging her pregnant belly. "My poor Lazlo."

Mercy squeezed the young woman's shoulder. "Lazlo loved you. He did everything he could to protect you and the baby."

Olga smiled through her tears. "And you did everything you could to protect me. Lazlo was right to trust you. To trust your family. You are all good people."

"We just tried to do the right thing by Uncle Laz, and now by you." Mercy shook off the praise. "Shall we try that iris scan?"

They all watched as Brodie held the device up to Olga's right eye. Mercy held her breath, and then it happened. The code clicked on.

"It's working," said Brodie. "Whatever is there is yours,' he told Olga. "And it looks like it's a lot."

"Welcome to the billionaires' club," said Feinberg.

"I can't believe it," said Olga.

"Believe it," said Mercy, raising her glass of eggnog. "Here's to Lazlo. And to you, Olga. Merry Christmas."

"Merry Christmas," said everyone happily.

MERCY AND TROY SPENT the rest of the evening with Felicity, enjoying all their family and friends in the overdecorated Victorian they called home. When it came time for the midnight service at the First Congregational Church, they were there in the second row to cheer Patience on as she played her first Christmas midnight service in years.

Joy to the world. . . .

CHAPTER FORTY-TWO

Come all you weary wanderers beneath the wintry sky.
This day forget your worldly cares and lay your sorrows by.
Awake and sing! The church bells ring! For this is Christmas morning.

We'll tie the fresh green holly wreath, and make the yule log glow.
And gather gaily underneath the winking mistletoe.
All blithe and bright, by glad fire-light for this is Christmas morning.

—EDWIN WAUGH

CHRISTMAS MORNING DAWNED BRIGHT AND COLD. FELICITY AND the dogs were up with the sun, pouncing on Mercy and Troy's bed, eager for the day to begin. Elvis was smart enough to know that there would be presents under the tree for him; he was no stranger to the gift-giving rituals of the holidays. Susie Bear was smart enough to know that if Elvis was excited she should be, too. And Felicity was excited because for her, every new day was exciting.

Tandie was at her dad's house and Amy and Brodie and Helena were in the guest house. All of Mercy and Troy's relations would be over later for a late potluck brunch. But for now, the morning was theirs and theirs alone. Just Mercy, Troy, Felicity, and the dogs.

And Muse, the cat, who did not deign to rise at dawn for any reason, Christmas included. They found the little munchkin kitten curled up on a pile of quilts on one of the easy chairs in the living room, snoring lightly.

The room looked lovely, even in the wake of last night's festivities. The white wooden playpen still encircled the tall Scotch pine, a towering vision shining with lights and garlands and ornaments. The only presents left under the tree were the ones for the animals, and for the three of them, from Santa and from each other.

Elvis trotted over to the Christmas tree, followed by Susie Bear. They knew the drill from Christmases past. Both dogs sniffed the air around the tree, settling down across from two large gift bags tied with ribbons adorned with doggy treats.

Felicity crawled after them, wriggling toward the playpen. She squeezed her little body between the sleek length of Elvis and the furry bulk of Susie Bear. The baby grabbed two of the slats with pudgy little fists and pulled herself up to a standing position.

"Good job, love." Mercy pulled a throw pillow from the couch and sat cross-legged on it, within reaching distance of the baby.

"She'll be walking soon," said Troy, squatting next to her.

"Our clever girl." Mercy smiled at him.

Pointing at the pink baby balance bike, Felicity babbled, "Mine, mine, mine."

"Mine!" Mercy grinned at Troy. "She said 'mine.'"

Troy rose to his feet, leaned over the playpen, and snatched up the bike. He placed it on the floor next to Mercy, and she balanced Felicity on the seat. They watched as the baby banged at the floor with her feet, figuring out how to make the bike move forward. Squealing with glee when she did.

And she was off.

Troy tracked her as she careened around the living room. Mercy lifted the two presents for Elvis and Susie Bear and placed one in front of each dog.

"Merry Christmas," she said. "Go for it." The dogs tore into the bags, retrieving the grass-fed marrow bones approved by Patience herself.

Elvis dragged his bag of bones over to a corner of the living room and settled in for a good long chew. Susie Bear stayed right where she was, already chomping away.

Mercy dropped a small cloth mouse filled with catnip next to the sleeping Muse, then presented Troy with his gift. Her husband sat down on the couch, and unwrapped it solemnly. He smiled when he pulled out the bomber jacket.

"Fancy," he said, giving her a kiss.

"Put it on." She lifted a squalling Felicity from the bike, and positioned her on the sofa. Mercy handed the baby the Noah's ark full of wooden animals that Rory had whittled—and she stopped mid-cry to play with it.

Troy stood up, slipping on the coat. "Very warm. Feels good."

"Very handsome."

"If you say so." Her husband blushed. He was not a vain man, but it was clear that he liked wearing it. She could tell he was pleased.

Together they helped the baby open the rest of her gifts: a push/pull duckling toy, a set of nesting blocks, and a xylophone. She loved them all. Especially the xylophone, which she banged on with great enthusiasm.

Mercy stuffed the spent wrapping in one of the gift bags. There were no presents left under the tree. And no gift from Troy. Yet.

"That's it." She regarded her husband and her baby and the dogs and the cat with the unconditional love that filled her heart. "Our Baby's First Christmas is in the bag."

"Not quite." Troy smiled. "Let's take a walk."

At the word "walk," Elvis leapt up and Susie Bear lumbered up and both raced for the kitchen door. Troy stood, reaching for the shearling-lined bomber jacket. "I think I'll wear my new coat."

"All of us?"

"All of us." He nodded at Muse, still asleep on her quilt, her catnip toy now tucked under her chin. "Well, nearly all."

"Very mysterious." Mercy zipped the baby into her snowsuit and slipped on her own puffer coat.

Troy ushered Mercy and Felicity through the house and onto the porch, where he stopped to put the baby in the stroller.

"A stroller for a walk in our snowy woods." She smiled. "Interesting."

Mercy tramped alongside Troy as he pushed the stroller over the snow-covered gravel path around the house, under the grackle tree, and out past the flower and vegetable beds. They passed the back garden, where the WWII memorial to a fallen bomber pilot held the place of honor. She thought about the history of this place and the people who'd lived and loved and celebrated Christmas here over the past 150 years—Civil War heroes and 1920s heiresses, poets and pilots, husbands and wives and children.

And now Mercy and Troy and Felicity.

At the end of the garden path stood the wrought iron fence that surrounded the house and its grounds, marking the beginning of the woods proper. Beyond the fence, Mercy spotted the remnants of the Christmas farm, where they'd found the Scotch pine. To the left was an old wooden gate that opened onto a plot of land framed by a high stone wall much like the one that housed the memorial. The space had once been home to a Victorian sunken garden, with flower beds and lawn surrounding an ornamental pond. Somewhere along the line the garden had been abandoned, the water had dried up, and the beds had been lost to weeds.

The dogs ran up to the gate, whining. Mercy saw lights twinkling in the garden.

"What is this?"

"Why don't we go in and see." Troy pushed open the gate and Elvis and Susie Bear disappeared inside. He pushed the stroller after them, and then turned, offering Mercy a gloved hand. "Come on in."

Mercy stepped into the sunken garden and gasped. Where once upon a time the forsaken ornamental pond had shimmered in the summer light there was now a skating rink, ice glinting in the winter sun. The space around the rink was groomed, covered with velvety drifts of snow. Stone benches flanked the edges of the rink; ice candles glimmered in the corners. Ropes of lights strung from old gas lamps crisscrossed the rink, creating a ceiling of illumination. The effect was dazzling.

"It's beautiful," she whispered.

Troy pointed to a small deck box tucked along the stone wall. "Our skates are in there."

They laced up their skates while the dogs sniffed every inch of the place and the baby slept in the stroller, snug in her snowsuit and swaddled with baby blankets.

"How did you do this?"

Troy shrugged. "Levi helped."

"How did you even think of it?"

"I remembered our Christmas Eve at the ice skating dance party and asked Levi how we might erect a rink. I figured we'd buy one of those kits, but he suggested the sunken garden." He pulled out his phone and hit play on "Perfect," by Ed Sheeran.

"It's spectacular."

They made their way to the ice, a smooth, polished surface ideal for skating. They glided into each other's arms.

And began to dance.

They sailed around the ice, laughing and kissing and twirling.

The baby cried, and Troy skated over to the stroller, pulling it out onto the ice. Together they pushed the baby around the rink, the dogs slipping and sliding beside them, Felicity giggling, crying no more.

"When she's older, we'll teach her to play hockey," said Troy.

"Of course we will," said Mercy. "The family who skates together, stays together."

And on they skated, their baby between them, round and round and round on the gleaming ice, under the twinkling lights and the winter sun.

The perfect end to a perfect Christmas.

FIVE MONTHS LATER

"It's a girl," Mercy told Troy, reading the christening invitation that arrived one day in early May. They were in the garden, watching little Felicity toddle around after the dogs. The azaleas were blooming and the flower beds were dotted with tulips and jonquils and crocus and snowdrops. "Lada Mercy Volkov-Zima. Lada is a lovely name."

"I prefer her middle name." Troy gave her a kiss.

"Lada is the Slavic goddess of spring." She kissed him back. "Olga's invited us to the First Congregational Church on the green for the ceremony, and then to her new shop on Main Street for a tea party." Olga had relocated her business to a bigger space in Northshire, to be closer to Lazlo's friends and adopted family, who were now her own.

"I still prefer her middle name," he said.

"You would." She laughed. "But Lada is perfect. Because spring is the season of hope. The promise of the winter solstice fulfilled."

"True enough."

Mercy took her husband's hand and together they followed their little daughter as she chased Elvis and Susie Bear through a sea of snowdrops. She thought about Uncle Laz, and how he'd given his life for his true love and their child. She watched as Troy lifted Felicity up into the air, sweet with the scent of spring, and their child giggled with joy.

And, just like the Snow Maiden, her heart melted.

ACKNOWLEDGMENTS

What fun to write a story set in December, a month so steeped in myth, mysticism, and miracles. A magical time! Writing a mystery is itself a kind of a magic trick, and each time I'm able to pull off this magic trick only with the help and support of so many people who are, just like Tiny Tim in *A Christmas Carol*, "as good as gold."

Making *The Snow Lies Deep* into the book you now read required a cast worthy of Dickens. Beginning with the one and only Pete Wolverton, who with the wisdom of St. Nick himself kept reminding me that "This is a Christmas mystery." A sleigh full of appreciation and admiration to Pete and all the fine folks at Minotaur Books / St. Martin's, a Santa's Village of smart elves: George Witte, Andy Martin, Kelley Ragland, Allison Ziegler and Kayla Janas, Claire Cheek, Jonathan Bennett, Rowen Davis, Chris Leonowicz, Alisa Trager, Kiffin Steurer, copyeditor Tom Cherwin, and proofreaders Tania Bissell and Ken Diamond.

December in New England is straight out of Dickens, American style. Here in my corner of the woods, a host of angels appears whenever I need them most: the swell dogs and human personnel of the Vermont Police Canine Association and Vermont Fish & Wildlife; the gurus of the University of New Hampshire's Natural Resources Steward Program, Lauren Chase-Rowell, Mary Tebo Davis, Rebecca Dube, and Jo Russavage, as well as my fellow stewards; wildlife biologist Cheryl Bentley, and the entire Conservation Commission of Salisbury, of which I am honored to be a member.

A sincere Ho-ho-ho! to my amazing Career Authors: Hank Phillippi Ryan, Dana Isaacson, Brian Andrews, and Jessica Strawser; Gina Panettieri, my agent, friend, and Mrs. Claus to me and my Talcott Notch colleagues—Amy Collins, Saba Sulaiman, and Nadia Lynch; and the carolers who make up my beloved Scribe Tribe, my fabulous roster of clients, my classes of writing students, and the unfailingly generous crime-writing community.

Most of all, a choir of ringing Alleluias to my family. Growing up in a nuclear military family, an ocean or more away from the rest of our relations, I nonetheless adored Christmas, because my parents celebrated the December holidays to the max, as Americans are wont to do. It was a sacred time in more ways than one, a way of honoring our faith, our culture, and our traditions in our home away from home. Wherever we were in the world, Christmas remained a constant source of comfort and joy and my mother's indescribably delicious fudge.

We carry on that tradition, New England style, adding the obligatory candles in the windows, trees cut from the Christmas tree farm down the road, and New England Egg Nog. Our family is bigger these days—Alleluia, indeed!—thanks to kids and grandkids and significant others. All you lovely people in our Lee/Munier/Bergman family—you are my dearest blessings: Alexis, Greg, and Mikey; Trisha and Chris; Elektra, Calypso, and Demelza; my mother and my husband, Michael. All of you enrich my holidays—and my life—year in and year out with light and love and laughter.

I wrote *The Snow Lies Deep* during one of the longest, coldest, and snowiest New England winters in recent memory. Winter isn't winter here without a dog at your feet and a cat in your lap. No one loves snow more than our own snow dogs: Bear, Bliss, Blondie, and Coco Puff (especially Coco Puff)—a love equaled by Ursula the Cat's disdain of both snow and dogs. There was no writing a Christmas mystery without them.

Finally, a very holly jolly thank-you to you, dear readers, for choosing to spend time with Mercy and Elvis and me. You are my greatest surprise, my greatest pleasure, my greatest gift. Without you, there is no spring around the corner. My Christmas wish for you, to borrow once again from Dickens: "May every day be thought of Christmastime . . . a kind, forgiving, charitable, pleasant time. . . ."

ABOUT THE AUTHOR

Paula Munier is the *USA Today* bestselling and award-winning author of the Mercy Carr Mysteries and a Senior Agent at Talcott Notch Literary. She's also written three popular books on writing, including the bestselling *Plot Perfect*. Along with her love of nature, Paula credits the hero dogs of Mission K9 Rescue, her own rescue animals, and her volunteer work as a Natural Resources Steward of New Hampshire as her series' major influences. She lives in New England with her family, four dogs, and a cat who does not think much of the dogs.

For more, check out www.paulamunier.com.